T0129481

RAISING HELL

RAISING HELL

A DROP INTO HADES

SEAN GILLIGAN

RAISING HELL
A DROP INTO HADES

iUniverse books may be ordered through booksellers or by contacting:

iUniverse
1663 Liberty Drive
Bloomington, IN 47403
www.iuniverse.com
1-800-Authors (1-800-288-4677)

ISBN: 978-1-5320-0387-5 (sc)
ISBN: 978-1-5320-0388-2 (e)

Library of Congress Control Number: 2016913185

Print information available on the last page.

iUniverse rev. date: 08/19/2016

Present Day: Force X the first Coalition Penal Regiment goes into the fight against Islamic State in the Middle East. An unconventional approach to fighting an Unconventional War against Islamic Insurgents in the Middle East. In our unstable world National leaders need to look at adapting to expanding terrorist threats at home and abroad.

CONTENTS

PROLOGUE

On the day Colonel Mann was handed the job his life changed. He was hand picked from the U.S. Special Forces to come up with a plan for a revolutionary fighting force. It was a new concept for Mann and the Western Coalition nations, who were at war with a new threat emerging in the Middle East, The Islamic State. America the leading Superpower and their Coalition Allies having suffered casualties in The Gulf War, Iraq and Afghanistan since early 2000, were reluctant to put boots on the ground in this new insurrection in Iraq and Syria. Into this uncertain scenario, the idea of using an expendable military unit emerged from the bowels of the Pentagon. Colonel Mann stood before the Generals and CIA advisors as they briefed him on his mission. "Put together a military unit, using selected convicts from our prison system. Train them in Special Forces tactics, as a Quick reaction force to be used in future operations."

It was a decade before the emergence of ISIS, when Colonel Mann got the wheels in motion. It was a tedious process for there were many obstacles to overcome. It was kept top-secret from the start, for western political leaders would never publicly sanction such a ticking time bomb. The Pentagon put it under the umbrella of the Black Ops. Having used Americans and foreign soldiers as mercenaries for years, this new unit was an extension of foreign policy. It was a new tool, in the experimental phase for dealing with sensitive modern issues the world was dealing with, war on terrorism. The concept of the new Penal Army Unit is about a rarely used, little known, controversial method in the modern history of warfare, using condemned criminals to fight in near suicidal missions. Russian and German Armies were known to have Penal army units during the Second World War. The Devil's Brigade (1st Special Service Force), was the combined Canadian/US Commando unit in WW 2, which set the standard in quick strike Special Forces in the Allied camp. The Germans had Skorzeny's Commandos while their enemy used Russian Spetznaz units on the Eastern Front.

Colonel Mann received detailed briefs on these precursors in Unconventional Commando style fighting units. After revising his plan over months he came up with a working plan. He recruited a Head quarters team, composed of American and Canadian Forces officers. He would recruit from the prison system for his new unit's cadre. The unit would be called Force X. It would be formed and begin training at selected U.S. military bases. "How long before you can have this unit operational Colonel?" Mann looked new elite regiment was then disbanded in 1995, replaced by the new JTF-2 Commandos. Colonel Mann initially skeptical, began to believe that his new unit could be useful after all. In the new unconventional war against Islamic insurgents in the Middle East, which was spreading into a global war on terrorism, allied conventional armies were becoming obsolete. Special Forces who could do the job, were too valuable however to be risked in suicidal, behind the lines operations. However, a small team of convicts, trained and properly motivated could achieve goals out of all proportion to their numbers. The seller was if these convicts perished, who would care? They were the dregs of society, a hidden card for the West to play against a shadowy enemy.

This tale is fact based fiction, in this context I believe a unique look at the present day War on Terrorism and Global Conflict. The main characters and heroes although largely fictional, are based on real life people. This tale shows the personal, close reality of warfare where opponents are so close you can see the color of their eyes. Many soldiers have come from the streets, ghettos, many having been to prison. It is a fact that some soldiers have been offered two choices by the courts: join the army or go to jail. Army units are a virtual cross-section of their society, including every class. As in *Platoon* the movie, these recycled convicts are primarily the scrapings of the barrel. They have grown up in violent, uncompromising environments were death is ever present. With relatively short basic training, they are thrown into war's hell. These men are used as pawns in war, their lives are treated as an expendable asset by governments. For a reader who has not faced death in some form it may give an insight. From the safety of one's home, or wherever, a feeling and understanding of those who risk life and limb daily might be entertaining. I have left a bit of a surprise for the ending, with a few questions to be answered. These will be addressed sometime down the road eventually in a sequel. For the fight against worldwide terrorism is ongoing. Where the tale will end only the future will decide. But unlike past conflicts, North Americans no longer have the luxury of ignorance, for the war has arrived on our shores.

CHAPTER I

BAPTISM OF FIRE

Flashback: It was his first action, dropped into the cataclysmic hell of battle. The year was 1965, Jack McGee was 19 years old. His unit B Company, 501st Regiment, 1st Air Cavalry, US Army. Born in Kentucky, he was following his family line. Ancestors had fought for the British Army during the French-Indian War (1760's), then the Revolutionary War against Britain, 1812-14 in the ill-fated attempt to wrestle Canada from the British Empire, the Spanish-American War, the Civil War on the Confederate side, WW1, WW2, Korea and now Vietnam. Now on that fateful morning the young soldier looked out the Bell Huey chopper side door in anticipation. Sitting beside and around him were eight other members of his platoon. All were heavily loaded down with combat gear for the coming battle. Draped over Jack's neck and biting into his skin was a belt of ammo for the M-60 machine-gun, 100 rounds of steel jacketed 7.62-mm bullets.

His piercing blue eyes noticed every fifth round had a red ring on the tip. Tracer rounds he remembered from his Basic training back state side at Fort Hood, Texas. Gripped in his sweating, trembling hand was his personal weapon, an M-16 semi-automatic rifle. In the rucksack before him, he had packed 200 rounds of 5.56-mm steel jacketed bullets for his rifle. In his webbing strapped to his 6' lanky frame were four magazines, each loaded with 20 rounds for his rifle. The rest were in clips of five, to be loaded as needed. Also packed in the ruck were three 60- mm mortar rounds, two 81- mm mortar rounds, 6 fragmentation grenades, two smoke grenades, two canteens of water, six days of rations, one spare radio battery and two Claymore personnel mines. Also strapped to his webbing belt was his M-16 bayonet, entrenching tool, ammo pouches with magazines, a 20-foot section of coiled rope, three feet of coiled wire, which among other things could be used to garrote (strangle enemy sentries) encountered on night patrol. All in all, young Jack would go into action with over 100 pounds of gear.

Jack squinted out the open side door at the jungle below as the Helo pilot flew low, whipping the chopper from side to side, skimming over the treetops. It was called contour flying or Nap of the earth. In the door the gunner aimed the M-60 MG hanging from the roof and sprayed a burst into the jungle ahead. Jack gasped as the chopper rose and dropped, the effect was shocking to the uninitiated, leaving a queasy feeling in the guts, as his stomach was sucked in by the G's. The ground below looked evil and foreboding to the young soldier. Sergeant Hall his platoon sergeant sat across from him, a grim look on his face. Jack could guess what the Sarge was thinking. "I'm looking at an FNG[1]... who will be FUBAR in about 10 minutes..."

B Company 501st Regiment 1st Air Cavalry hit LZ X-ray minutes later. Jack could smell the cordite now, from the US Artillery which had saturated the Landing Zone just minutes before they landed. Smoke wafted across the clearing beside the nearby mountains. Jack had been told with the rest of the Company, that they would make history here today. For it would be the first ever wartime use of American soldiers inserted into combat by helicopter[2]. They also heard during the briefing from the CO Colonel Hal Moore, to expect a few hundred NVA or Viet Cong in the vicinity. In fact, the Division Command and Intel (CIA) had no idea how many NVA were in the valley. Colonel Moore suspected privately there would be much worse awaiting them.

Mission: Close with and destroy the enemy and capture the surrounding terrain and hold till relieved. Despite his age, Jack was not a naïve idiot. He took a last drag from his Camel cigarette. Then he cocked and loaded his M-16, putting a 5.56 round into the breech. His other hand gripped the rucksack in front of him. Now he felt the hot surge of

---

[1] FNG: Army term for Fucking new Guy FUBAR: fucked up beyond all recognition

[2] Heliborne Operations used in conjunction with Airborne Drops were the fastest way to deploy troops

adrenaline course though his veins. He focussed his mind as he entered his zone.

Sweat dripped down his forehead, hot, salty and stinging his squinting eyes. It was searing hot and he smelled the particular odor, the stink of the Vietnamese jungle in his nostrils. He tilted his camouflaged helmet back on his shaved head, wiping the sweat off his forehead with a handkerchief, which he then wrapped around his neck. The Huey pilot lowered the chattering twin engine chopper through the rising smoke over the LZ feeling his way almost blinded by the dust, debris and smoke to the designated landing spot. The chopper thudded and shook as the skids crashed through the foliage of the jungle below. Bits of foliage chopped to ribbons, whirled through the air as the ground slowly rose to Jack. He and the other members of his section grimaced and held on as the Huey rocked from side to side. "Get ready boys!" The Sarge yelled.

"Holy Shit!" Jack yelled as bits of dirt and foliage blinded him. The veteran Senior NCO merely smiled at him amusedly as he finished his last cigarette. "It's OK Sonny! Just keep tight on my ass! Who are you?"

"Airborne!" Screamed eight troopers, as they psyched themselves up for the impending drop into combat or as they would soon find out, Hell. Hades as the ancients called it. Hades being the god who ran the dark place. "How Far?" Sergeant Hall yelled. "All the Way! HURRAH!"

"O.K. Troopers! Look at me! Everybody out! Go! Go! Go!" Private McGee did not hesitate. He booted his rucksack out the door, then jumped out after it. Lowering his foot to the landing skid, he balanced then pushed off hard. He grunted as he hit the ground five feet below, rolling to absorb the impact, as he had learned while on his Jump Course at Fort Brag, N.C. a mere six months ago. He had performed the required six jumps and received his coveted Jump Wings. Since then he had done three mass drops with the 501st Regiment on exercises in the U.S. The Huey roared loudly above, as the other soldiers disgorged from the chopper in rapid succession from both side doors, as they had been trained in the previous months. Jack squinted his eyes about him, as the backwash of the rotor blades, swirled dirt, grass, artillery smoke and corruption in the air about him. He could see nothing. He struggled to restore a sense of calm, while trying to orientate himself to the ground mentally. His M-16 was gripped firmly in his sweating right palm, his left hand found and hoisted up his heavy 100-pound rucksack from the grass, slinging it over his shoulder.

"Fuck! Move yer ass!" Jack roared to no one in particular, more to motivate himself. He spat before him dryly, then grunting hoisted himself to his feet, shifting the heavy rucksack on his shoulders. His muscles ached under the tension and strain, but from deep inside himself felt a growing sense of excitement. This was his time…to be initiated into combat…to lose his cherry! The Hueys turned and burned as their cargo bays cleared of Air Cavalry troopers and flew off back toward the base in the south. A few minutes later all was quiet in the Au Shau Valley. Jack slowly knelt on one knee in the tall grass, surrounded by the 32 men of his platoon. Sergeant Hall nearby was surveying the area to the front with his binoculars. Jack could hear the squawk from the radioman's 25 set, tuned in on the command frequency. It was eerily silent now. "21 Bravo this is Niner! Move out to the ridge ah…150 yards to your 12 over." "Roger that Niner! 21B out!"

"OK! 1st Platoon! Move out! 1 Section left, 2 Section Right…3 Section follow and give covering fire if we contact the enemy!" Jack a member of 1 Section, got up and followed his section I/C Sergeant Hall. Minutes later they took the low, sloping ridge, overlooking the LZ below. He watched as other platoons moved outward as well, securing the outer perimeter, facing the north, east and west, the big mountain looming to the north. It was from here Colonel Hal Moore had been informed he would find the hidden NVA.

Back in the battalion CP, Colonel Moore was calmly looking over a map, surrounded by the B Company CO, Major Ring, the Sergeant Major, a radioman and the Artillery Rep. "Listen up I expect the enemy to attack from the north, here and here. We only have about 60 men till the second lift arrives, so we hold the high ground and secure the LZ first. I want artillery support on that forward slope of the mountain. Sergeant Major get the Mortar Platoon to dig in at that copse of trees there. Have them ready to support the two lead platoons ASAP!" "Sir! Mortars stand to!" The tall RSM was a seasoned combat vet and paratrooper. He had combat jumps from WW2 and Korea under his belt. Moore nodded as he headed off, his tall lanky frame, the epitome of the unflappable warrior. Moore nodded satisfied his RSM would handle the mortars efficiently.

Ten minutes later the first NVA was found. Two Air Cav soldiers pushed him before Colonel Moore, then forced him to squat before the steely eyed Colonel. "Found him squatting over there in a hole Sir! He seemed to be watching our positions. Could be NVA Recce Scout Sir." Colonel Moore nodded to the soldiers guarding this runt. He did not look like a soldier dressed in black rags. He looked at the suspected VC scout, who returned the look with an impudent smirk. Moore looked at the tall imposing figure of the RSM beside him. Without a work the RSM kicked the feet from the prisoner, gripping his hair he yanked his face up then swatted him on the jaw. He shook the prisoner till he stopped wailing. Colonel Moore smiled and waved for him to stop softening the prisoner up. "Good Work RSM McDonald! Interpreter question this damn fellow."

The South Vietnamese soldier came forward and began yelling at the crouching prisoner, swatting him on his head. The prisoner glared back insolently, muttering in short staccato sentences. Sergeant Quan Lee stared at him, then looked grimly at the Colonel. "Colonel Sir! He claims there are over 5,000 NVA from the 390th Regiment, hard core NVA on that mountain. And there are more regiments in the area. And they all want to kill Americans!" Moore nodded then ordered his radioman to call the Artillery Support base and register the Mountain for bombardment. As the wheels were set into motion so did Col. Moore's brain.

"Gentlemen. We can expect the first attack soon. Major Ring, look to your Company Sir." Minutes later the first wave of NVA hit the B Company perimeter, as Colonel Moore had suspected. Jack watched as they broke the tree line, 200 meters to his platoon's front. The M60's opened up first, short rapid, well aimed bursts cutting into the ranks of NVA soldiers. Dozens fell to the ground from the accurate bursts. There was the dull thud of mortars behind, then white phosphorous rounds burst in front of the attacking wave. These first rounds indicated the mortars were on target.

"Mike 6. You are on! Fire for effect!" Mounds of dirt shot into the air, the high pitched wine of shrapnel hissing through the foliage, cutting into the bodies of the NVA. Huge gaps appeared in their ranks, but still they pushed on. Jack could hear the whistles and shouts from the NVA commanders, urging their men forward. Jack calmly took aim at an advancing NVA soldier, now about 100 feet before him. He calmed his breathing, watching through the sights, taking aim at his center of mass, his chest. He spread his legs a bit, eased his elbows out, forming a triangle of support for his weapon. He felt relaxed now, he was in his zone. Then the order came… "Platoon to your front! NVA in open… Rapid Fire!' Lieutenant Stamp shouted. Suddenly the air erupted as the combined firepower of 1st Platoon hit the enemy. To see the combined firepower of a single infantry platoon is one to observe. A well trained platoon of 30 odd soldiers with modern weapons can unleash a devastating amount of firepower: semi-automatic rifles, automatic small arms join medium machine guns, light mortars, anti tank, grenades and other nasty things on an approaching enemy. The noise and deafening explosions can scare the uninitiated, as Jack slowly squeezed the trigger. His M-16 barked and the empty casing ejected into the air. His right eye blinked as he watched the NVA stagger then tumble to the ground.

"Fucking right! First one buddy!" He smiled as he switched to the next target, a short, squat lad. He aimed a bit higher then squeezed his trigger again. The round hit the man in his throat. A spray of blood shot into the air as he dropped his gun. He watched as the man in agony, grasped his ruined throat, then he sunk to his knees. The last survivor who had made it 50 feet in front of Jack's position, stopped then threw up his hands in a gesture of surrender. Jack and his section took aim and riddled him, his blood soaked corpse dead before it hit the ground. Mortar and heavy artillery whined overhead, then the crump as they exploded on the mountain side left Jack with a pleased feeling. "Not bad for FNG's eh Sarge?" Jack smiled at the Sarge as he walked by. The taciturn Sergeant nodded with a faint trace of a smile on his smoke darkened face.

"That was the start Sonny! Platoon check yer Ammo! Medic take the wounded to the CP. Section Commanders

O-Group." The first attack had been defeated. But all knew the worst was yet to come….

That had been some time ago now. Jack was physically and mentally exhausted. It was near 6 p.m. as he glanced at his watch. He spat dryly as he continued to dig his slit trench further with his entrenching tool. Mounds of dirt were flung out of his trench, like he was some oversized groundhog, enlarging its underground tunnel. The dirt fell on top of bodies. Around Jack's trench were a lot of bodies. He had dragged them from the surrounding area and piled them like sandbags around the top of the trench for added protection. He had read how Spartans piled the Persian dead at Thermopylae, to strengthen their thin defences, against waves of invading Persians. A pile of dirt fell into the gaping mouth of one NVA killed in the last attack.

"Stand to! Here they come lads!" Jack popped his head up and saw them. He gripped the butt stock of the M-60 chopper. He had taken it over after the gunner was wounded in the last attack. Jack had helped carry him to the chopper down below. "Take care Jack! Hold this fucking LZ till I get back!"

"You bet Jose! Got nowhere else to be right now. Hey… you owe me a beer back at the mess!" Jack shook his buddy's hand as he lay on the deck of the Huey. He noticed the blood congealing in pools on the blood spattered floor. The chopper carried 10 wounded crammed in like sardines. Jack lifted off the last crate of ammo the chopper was delivering. He waved at the pilot and gave him the thumbs up. The pilot looking down at the young soldier, his face and body covered in the dirt and soot of battle. He smiled and saluted him, then lifted the over-laden chopper off the ground. Jack led a section of reinforcements, all laden with boxes of rations and ammo back to his platoon area. By this time the company was reinforced to over 450 men.

Lieutenant Stamp shot a Para flare into the air, highlighting the advancing wave of NVA in the sky. The platoon opened up a vicious hail of fire into their packed ranks. The noise was deafening...then the medium mortars from down in the LZ joined in. Each round of 81 mm HE hit with a roar. Everything above ground within 150 meters was cut to ribbons. Five minutes later the attack was over. Jack gasped as he surveyed the area to his front. His M-60 barrel smoked in front of him from the continuous rapid fire he had laid down.

He figured he had fired over 1000 rounds. Piles of bullet ridden NVA corpses lay before him, stretching back for 500 meters. He figured he had wiped out hundreds of the bastards. "Cease fire 1 Platoon!' It was Lieutenant Stamp from his CP down the line. Jack lifted his smoke blackened face over the lip of his trench and leaned an elbow on the chest of a dead NVA. He looked down at the young man's face. Riffling through the pockets he found a pack of cigarettes. He smiled seeing they had a French label. "Don't mind do you comrade?" He flipped one out and put it in his dry lips. Lighting it he smoked, enjoying the strange aroma. Taking stock, the Sergeant went up and down the line of the platoon. He dropped two boxes of machine gun ammo off at Jack's trench. "Good job young fellah. How you holding out son?" "Just warming up Sarge. Am I still an FNG?" Around the perimeter troopers whooped sensing victory, taking pot shots at a twitching corpse.

"Just keep that saw going Trooper. Our guys depend on you OK?" He looked down at the young soldier, his eyes gleaming white on his blackened face. Jack nodded then the Sarge walked off to the next trench. For the rest of the evening and well into the night, the NVA kept coming. They were launching brief, probing attacks, interspersed by shelling from mortars and light artillery. By now Jack's platoon was down below 50%, around 14 effectives. Most like Jack, had been wounded at least once, but the young Air Cavalry troopers hung on grim and determined. In the final attack, the NVA succeeded in reaching their lines. It was hand to hand, no holds barred combat in the trenches for over an hour.

An NVA had leapt on Jack as he fired a viscous hail into a line of NVA, wiping them out. Jack fought the screaming NVA, booting him in the pills. He felt a knife scrape his ribs, then the hot blood trickle down his stomach. In a last desperate act, as both grunted and yelled, he plunged his bayonet into the NVA's stomach and ripped upwards. The man looked into his eyes gasping out his last breath, his fingers clutching his hands as Jack twisted it cruelly into his guts. Jack looked into the dying man's eyes as he pulled his bayonet free.

The enemy sank to his knees on the bottom of the trench dead. Jack kicked the corpse, stuck his bayonet into his scabbard and opened up his M-60 again. He saw a group of NVA standing over the trench of his buddy Lou on his right. They were bayoneting him as he lay slumped over the parapet of his trench. Jack screamed in hate as he poured lead into them. He saw the tracer rounds set their uniforms afire as their bodies twisted and jerked under his murderous hail of point blank fire.

"Everybody down! Rounds coming in!" the Lieutenant had requested and received close in fire support, virtually on top of his platoon's position. It was a mix of heavy artillery (155 mm), 81 mm mortar and fast air...rocket firing choppers and Thunderbolt ground attack aircraft. These dropped 500 pound bombs, 20-mm cannon and napalm rockets. The men scrambled for their trenches as the first wave of low fighter bombers flicked their wings then dived in toward them. The ground shook around Jack and the earth heaved. The shock waves numbed his brain and deafened his eardrums. Small numbers of surviving NVA retreated back to their lines, leaving scores of dead and wounded around the Air Cavalry defensive lines.

It was first light when he came out of his concussed state. He smelt the cordite and napalm around him, that gasoline smell. He had no idea how long he had been here. He stood up slowly and peered out of his trench. All about him the ground smoked. He urinated as he smoked, not even noticing his urine was falling on the stiffened corpse below him. He took a swig from his canteen and lit up another smoke. His eyes hurt, his body ached from every joint. Jack saw his platoon area was a scene from Hades. Surrounding each position were a mound of bodies piled four feet high, burnt black and shriveled, pieces of bodies lay everywhere on the bloody grass. He remembered reading about "The Little Bighorn" catastrophe. The Greasy Grass as the Lakota Indians called it. This must have been what it was like for those early Cavalry troopers Jack thought. Most were ripped and torn to shreds ...definitely Fubared! Now the hostile Indians were replaced by a new and motivated enemy.

"OK Son. Let's get you out of there." He did not protest as the Sarge lifted him out of the trench. Two of his mates joked with him as they helped him down to the LZ, stumbling in a dazed state to freedom. At the battalion HQ a medic looked him over. He realized then for the first time the state he was in. His uniform torn in shreds was slowly peeled off. He was scorched black from the heat of artillery and napalm and soaked with dried blood, enemy as well as his own. His body was covered in welts, bruises, burn marks and scratches. His helmet was dented with blows from enemy rifles as well as shrapnel and ricochet rounds. The worst wound was to his ribs where the NVA had stabbed him. It seemed every limb and sinew were stretched and strained.

The medic cleaned and dressed his wounds. Then Jack looked up from the stretcher and gasped silently. For before him stood God! It was Colonel Hal Moore and the Sergeant Major beside him. The Colonel smiled and knelt beside him. Laying a soot blackened hand on his bare shoulder he offered him a light for his cigarette. "How we doing Sir?" Jack whispered as the medic shot morphine into his arm. "Giving them hell son. Don't worry, you're on the next chopper out." The Colonel looked sadly down at Jack, not knowing how depleted the battalion was. But when Saigon H.Q. tried to pull him out the Colonel refused bluntly. Jack also put up resistance to being medevacked. "I'm not going Sir. I want to…(gasp) go back. Have to finish it…"

"You've done enough from what I heard Trooper. I'm proud of y'all!" The grizzled Sergeant Major smiled as he bent down and patted Jack on his begrimed hair. Jack was airlifted out as the Colonel promised about an hour later. The chopper took some fire as they lifted away. Jack heard the zing as bullets ricocheted off the sides, then the door gunner opened up a vicious hail of return fire. Then he passed out as the morphine and the shock of battle overwhelmed his tired weakened body.

The rest of 1st Air Cavalry were air lifted out days later. They had won the battle, but it had cost them dearly. Over 150 killed and several hundred wounded out of 600 who fought at LZ X-Ray. The enemy NVA Regiment was decimated though, in effect wiped out. They had counted over 3500 confirmed KIA's. Also they had captured piles of enemy weapons, radio intelligence and several prisoners. Unfortunately, the senior enemy Commanding officer had escaped to fight another day. After abandoning LZ X-Ray, the NVA returned days later. They looked down on the piles of rotting corpses left by the Americans. The Air Cavalry also left their calling card…death cards stuck in their mouths. Colonel Lin Dok grimaced as he looked at his dead soldiers.

The tone was set for the remainder of the Vietnam War. The Americans judged battles by body counts. The Viet Cong came back after the Americans had left. No matter how many were killed, more took their places. Like the tide of the Pacific Ocean retreating then returning to drown the beaches at high tide. It would be a decade later when the final tide of Americans retreated, leaving Vietnam forever. Leaving behind devastation and thousands of dead and a scared landscape. For the NVA it was a pyric victory covered in the blood of a dead generation. Jack McGee, 19 years old when he had fought that bloody day in the Au Shau Valley survived his baptism of fire and his one-year tour of duty. He met an American nurse who had nursed him back to health. She was Gloria Lee Gifford, a tall dirty blonde haired beauty and she gave him regular messages as he lay in his bed. It was at an American Hospital in Saigon a week after he was medivacked from the Au Shau battle. Jack awoke one morning lying on a hospital cot. Gloria Lee an 18-year-old nurse, was attending to Jack and several other wounded members of his company. "Holy Shit! I must have died and gone to Heaven."

"No Private. You are alive, in Saigon." Gloria smiled as she bent over him. She helped Jack into a sitting position, and began to change his dressings, before breakfast was served. "I mean Miss that one of your beauty, must be an Angel!" Jack leaned against her chest, feeling her heart beating against him.

"Come now. Flattery will get you nowhere!" Then Jack burst into laughter, joined by Nurse Intern Gifford. "OK help me out of this fucking bed please nurse?" Jack smiled as she flickered her long eyelashes up close.

"I will have to have the Doctor's permission first Private." Jack muttered as she pressed him back in a prone position. She gasped as his old dressings were removed. Jack laid quietly, looking up at her blue eyes. "This shrapnel wound on your knee...we will have to watch it closely. Or it will turn gangrenous."

"Ya so what?" Jack said bored. Gloria slapped his chest smiling, "That will mean we will have to remove your leg Mister." Jack put his hand on her thigh, "I couldn't ask for a prettier surgeon...hack away at me!" Over the next week, Jack and Gloria Lee became slowly very close. When he was finally allowed to leave the hospital, going on two-week R&R, Jack invited her out on a date. They hit the beach outside Saigon, where Jack seeing her in a bikini fell in love. After he rejoined B Company 7th Cav, Jack fought in several battles against determined NVA and Viet Cong. Promoted to Sergeant and winning several medals, Jack returned to the mainland a hero. He was based at Ft. Hood with the

7th Cavalry. Gloria Lee Gifford, his nurse transferred there and that year in 1967 they were married. By the 1970's when Jack left the army, they had produced three children. One night in their small house off base Jack sat beside Gloria reminiscing about their first date. He lowered his gaze, taking in her buttocks, a very revealing scarlet thong, adorned with violet bows highlighting the delights below. She had long, graceful legs with white stockings, gleaming, red high heels, and her long hair, blonde with golden shades, tied in a long ponytail dangled down her back, swirling in the air as she opted to dance before him.... The children were in bed so Jack and Gloria partied in privacy.

Jack put on the music, Tammy Wyonette, CCR and other 60's blues and rock songs they loved. Gloria moved rhythmically as slowly she stripped down to her lingerie as Jack sat drinking, mesmerized by her hypnotic movements. He smiled as she then sat down on his lap, taking a glass of wine from him. They kissed as she lay back in his arms. "What a wanton hussy I am married to. You know what you are hon... seriously?"

"Seriously? When are you ever serious Jackie?" She purred in his ear as her tongue licked him, while her hands messaged his scarred body gently. Jack groaned as her fingernails scraped along his skin as he sank back.

"You are seriously, a real woman Gloria Lee my love. Most women can't touch you! God put you on Earth for guys like me. Most people are here to annoy real men... soldiers like me. But you...are well separate, unique."

He kissed her chin as she smiled rolling her eyes. He swilled his can of beer, chucking it in the fireplace. "Could you?" Gloria smiled, pulling his arm free and slid off his lap, got up to fetch him another drink.

"Since you are full of compliments...and you did get my favorite wine." Jack smiled as he watched her go to the fridge, drinking in her long, athletic legs, her swiveling buttocks, her long, golden hair never failing to dispel his rage against the machine. She returned with two beers, popping one handed one to him and one for herself. She sat back beside him then toasted him. "Cheers to us my love. I love you Honey!"

That night Jack carried Gloria into the bedroom, as the blonde goddess held his shoulders giggling. "Oh Jackie...you animal! Don't hurt yourself...or little me!" Jack laughed at her, then flung her onto the big four poster bed. She gasped as she bounced on the mattress rolling over on her back. Gloria crawled over to him, like a large feline predator. "Meow!" She smiled, helping him off with his clothes. Jack lay beside her, swilling down his Coors from a can, then placing a 6-pack on the bedside table, as Gloria busily tore off his pants. "Hey you! Ease up girl!" But Gloria pounced on his thighs spread-eagled, looking down at him. "Oh stop your whining soldier! Time to man up!" Gloria flashed her white teeth at him.

Jack stared at her, trying to ape the look of the stunned, shell shocked survivor he once was. "Yes Sir Mam!" Gloria flung his drawers over the floor then pounced on top of him.

Jack for once lay back as his blonde, foxy wife performed on top. When it was over some time later, they lay beside each other, gasping, drained, satiated. "Gloria Lee you never fail to surprise me." Gloria sipped on a glass of her wine, stroking his neck. "I could not ask for a greater compliment my Dearest." Jack butted out his smoke, finished his can of Coors in one go and flung it against the bedroom wall.

"OK breaks over.... fall in Private!" Gloria squealed as Jack flipped her on her stomach and spanked her butt. She laughed as she struggled to lift her torso off the bed, grinding into him. Jack who indeed could ride a horse, being in 7th Cavalry refused to be bucked off, riding on her back and slapping her sides. Gloria gasped and drained fell back on the mattress. An hour or so later, both fell exhausted back on the pillow. The hot blonde beauty curled up against him then kissed him. Jack finally fell into an exhausted slumber, with Gloria glued to his side. Gloria nursed Jack slowly back to health, after Vietnam had screwed him. He was one of the lucky ones, for many of the returning soldiers there was no recovery from their mental and physical wounds.

They went biking in the Virginia Mountains that week taking their 10 speed bikes. Jack marveled at her as she led the way. He had to put out just to keep up to her, watching as her muscular legs flexed. It was an idyllic time for the two, as they fell deeper in love with each other, before fate would intervene. But as the years turned over, Jack would not be required to go into another conflict in the 1970's, something Gloria was relieved to see. They moved from base to base during his service, but retained their Kentucky homestead. Jack Sr. took his growing son Jack Jr., on his first hunting and fishing trip in 1978. He took the time to school his young, but attentive son on developing his skills and instincts. He found him to be a quick learner, for on his second fishing trip in that year he reeled in his first fish. The two enjoyed the moment while it lasted, for all too soon they both knew Jack Sr. would be off to war again. For young Jack Jr. knew he was the future of the McGee clan. He had decided he would join the Army as soon as he turned into an adult. Soon Jack Sr. would turn over the family mantle to young Jack and he could barely wait. As he grew up in Kentucky, young Jack honed his skills in the surrounding woodlands, learning to handle a variety of weapons, to canoe, fish and trap small game. Jack Sr. was proud of his young son, passing on his own hard won survival skills.

CHAPTER II

THE FRENCH FOREIGN LEGION

Ten years later: **1986.** Jack McGee now 39-years-old moved to Canada. Separated from his wife and kids, he wanted a new start and adventure. He left the American Army after the Vietnam War, frustrated, bitter and angry. He felt his country had betrayed him and his fellow soldiers, his brothers- in- arms. He had given more than ten of his best years and his manhood to his country, the U.S.A. For what? The country had lost their first war and civilians and politicians lay the blame on the soldiers. "Fuck them! Gloria I've fucking had it! Let's get the fuck out of here!" Gloria knew that Jack was not in his happy place at that moment as he sat drinking heavily. "Where Jack? This is our home. What about our children? I can't just up and leave!"

Jack nodded then took another shot of Jack Daniels, sitting before him on the table. He lit up a cigarette, one of the French imported brands he liked. It was the same type he had looted off the dead NVA a decade ago. His mind grappled with the problem. What was he to do? What had the gods and fate planned for him? He was restless, he needed to find himself. So he finally sat down with Gloria and decided his future.

"OK Honey, I understand. I am a soldier, born and bred OK?" Gloria at 37 was still a stunner Jack thought. It was a hot day in Kentucky, where his historic family plantation was located near Louisville. The thermometer on the wall read 88 degrees. Gloria was wearing a red halter top and skin-tight bleached cut-offs. It showed off her busty figure perfectly, as well as her long, athletic legs. He smiled at her as she tossed her extra-long, thick hair teasingly. She knew it turned him on, so as she swayed past him, his hand reached out and caught a hand full of her thick mane. She squealed as she fell onto his lap. Then he kissed her long and hard. That night they made love for hours before turning in. As Gloria lay curled up beside him he had a last smoke. "Hon, I made up my mind. I'm going to Canada tomorrow. Y'all stay with the kids till I get back."

"But Jack, honey… when will that be?" Gloria whispered into his ear. Her Southern accent still sent shivers up his spine. "How the heck do I know my Lover? Maybe a while. But I will return that I know. I got some business to straighten out. But this here is my home! Our home…OK?" Gloria stared long and hard at her lifelong friend, lover and husband. It was a rare thing she knew for a military family like theirs to get along so well.

"Yes Dear darling Jack hon. Good night." Jack kissed her full, pouting lips, smelling her feminine fragrance. He memorized every feature of her cool, soft skin on him, the curve of her nose, the silky soft hair on his skin. He knew it could be his last....at least for a long time. Then slowly he drifted off to sleep, dreaming of battles fought a long time ago...the sickening smells of combat. Cordite, blood, decaying flesh and screaming...he was back again in the steamy jungles of Vietnam! He awoke refreshed and looked at the naked body lying at his side. He almost changed his mind right then. He rolled Gloria over on her back and grinned as he mounted her. Gloria moaned as he penetrated her, her body automatically kicking into gear. Later that day they rode to the airport. Gloria cried as they embraced good-bye. "Make it home to me soldier."

Jack McGee got off the plane in Montreal Airport late the next day. It was June 4, 1986. Retrieving his bag in the terminal, he sauntered off outside, blinking in the warm, bright sunshine. He hailed a cab and told the driver to take him to the Canadian embassy. He had to get the lay of the land here he thought, he knew little about Canada being from the deep South of the States. The driver stopped for a coffee at a Tim Hortons on Catherine Street. Jack got himself one, finding he liked the strong brew. He found out the Embassy was closed for the day, so he booked himself into a hotel for the night. That night in the hotel lounge, Jack met his destiny. He saw the recruiting poster and not understanding the French words he struggled to try and decipher its meaning. He took another swig from his beer bottle and belched.

"Bien Venue Mon Ami." Jack looked down on the young man standing beside him smiling. "A'm sorry Mister. Ah don't ah compri… I'm Jack from the States." He invited him to sit down for a talk though. He explained he was an experienced soldier. He had quit the US Army and looked for some adventure and a challenge.

"Ah Bon! I am Jacques! I see you are interested in perhaps joining les Legion?" Jack eyed him nonchalantly as he eyed a young woman sitting nearby. "Don't do it son. Tempting though." He smiled as the young Quebec woman saw him and smiled as she toyed with her drink. Since he was married Jack had been true to Gloria.

Jacques saw this, turning to Jack as his American friend asked. "Er…what exactly is the Legion Monsieur?"

"La Legion Entregere Mr. Jack mon Ami! Bon en Anglais, The French Foreign Legion. It is part of the French Army. They accept recruits from many different countries. You may be running from the law, they do not care. But you must swear allegiance to Les Legion and France of course. If you desert they hunt you down."

Jack listened with interest. "Really? Never did hear of it down South. I am an army vet though, so it sounds interesting." Jacques smiled. "Please Monsieur Jack! Let us have another drink, and I will tell you about this famous Army Regiment non?" Jack nodded smiling and shook the man's offered hand.

Over the next few hours and a few drinks, Jack and his new buddy Jacques got acquainted, and Jack got acquainted with the French Foreign Legion. One thing he liked was when Jacques told him he could remain anonymous. Make up an identity. The Legion did not care, as long as you performed whatever they asked. Over the next few days, with Jacques' help, he hooked up with the Recruiting Officer who was visiting Montreal. Captain Schmidt was a tough paratrooper, who had fought in several battles with the Legion, and had the scars to prove it. He had hard blue eyes, which bored into the American standing before him. Of German heritage, Herman Schmidt was the son of an SS Officer, a member of the infamous 2nd SS Das Reich Division. Convicted of war crimes, his father was sent to prison. After a few years' incarceration he was released. He joined the Legion and had fought in Indo China at Dien Bien Phu. He and a few other German Legionnaires had escaped after their Regiment was trapped. After a long trek, they had escaped the Viet jungle, having fought and killed several Viet Cong guerrilla patrols tracking them. His son Herman born years after in Germany, learned early what it took to be a soldier. Now at 39, he was tough and fearless like Jack.

He sized up Jack quickly, his hard, blue eyes like stones. One veteran soldier observing another, a time tried tradition since Roman days. "So my friend, you think you have what it takes?" Jack nodded slowly as the stranger's eyes bored into him. "Yes Sir. Ah… I am a veteran of Vietnam. Killed many a Dink there. I like the Army life. If you want a trained fighter I am your man." "Excuse me Jack. If I may...you said, A Dink?"

"Yes Sir. I mean the enemy, Slopes...Viet Cong, NVA, little yellow bastards." The two soldiers laughed together. A short time later Jack signed the agreement, binding him to a term with 5th Regiment Parachutist, Legion Entregere. He would first go on Selection training at a French Army base for six months.

Six months later 1987: A Legion base in North Africa. Having completed months of grueling Selection training, Jack was on parade with his Battalion, 3rd of the 5th Reg. Legion. His face and skin was a deep bronze color. His body was muscular and hard as the men in the ranks beside him. Captain Schmidt personally pinned his wings on his breast. The two locked eyes then a trace of a smile appeared on the Captain's face.

"Congratulations Para McGee! Now Soldier, you are ready to defend the Honor of France, and the 5th Regiment Yawohl?" Jack stood rigid before the Captain, as his unit stood proudly at his side. In the background, the regimental band payed Le Marseillaise. At that point nothing mattered, except his need for action.

"Sir! To the Death! Sir!" Jack shouted out the required response, in his accented French. That night Jack and his new buddies celebrated by getting paralytically drunk! Several fights erupted, blood flowed. Then the fighters laughed and embraced, sworn to fight beside each other. It was a month later when Jack met his Legion Initiation into battle. His Company, Première Company 3rd Battalion where parachuted into Africa, in the French Congo. They were hunting for Local Brigands and terrorist groups allied to Al Queda Moslem factions. Jack stood out time and again. His sixth sense smelled out ambushes and his eagle eyes the slightest trace as they tracked African enemy patrols. After the first week he had the highest tally of kills…45 confirmed, plus several prisoners. He also learned how the Legion treated its prisoners.

If they refused to talk, they were buried up to their chins in the jungle floor. Red army ants then got at them. After an hour or two they began to talk. One frightened Negro terrorist, on interrogation, gave them the location of their main camp, deep in the Congo jungle. The entire battalion closed in for the kill days later. After days of slow, careful reconnaissance, they attacked at night. Jack assigned to forward scout, took out several Congolese sentries, knifing them silently, slitting their throats. His face camouflaged, wearing a camouflaged sniper suit, he flitted silently through the thick foliage. The sound of the jungle crept into his brain, birds, monkeys and buzzing insects. He looked carefully at the illuminous dial of his wristwatch. "03:30. Witching hour. I love this shit." Quiet orders were passed on, then the violence began. The sharp reports of rifles, machine guns and grenades split the quiet jungle air. Screams and shouts echoed for the next 15 minutes before suddenly it was over.

At the end, Jack stood panting in the center of the enemy camp. The adrenaline pumped through his veins. He knew he had killed, at least 50, maybe more. The last one was a fat officer. He had enjoyed that one, shooting him in his fat ass as he had tried in vain to run away. Then his bayonet, on the end of his Para assault rifle sank into the fat officer's gut. He spat on him as he wriggled beneath his Para boot. Then he fired a 7.62-mm slug, which blew apart his guts and shot his spine.

As his Company Commander talked on the radio to the Battalion C.O., Jack joined some of his comrades for a smoke. "It was fucking good eh Jack comrade?" Jack looked at his fire teammate, a Spaniard nick-named Loco. "Nothing better, except Sex!" They chuckled softly, Jack taking a swig from his canteen, the cool water soothing his burning throat. Sweat trickled down his forehead under the Jungle camo hat he wore on his shaved skull. His cam fatigues were almost black with sweat as well, as he stood in the midst of the group of victorious Legionnaires. Later they learned they had 468 confirmed KIA's and 36 prisoners. Jack heard the radioman call it in, adding Jack's unit had 6 or so friendlies wounded. Jack had been hit by a ricochet, or a piece of shrapnel in the kneecap. He didn't notice it till his Sergeant asked about the rip in his fatigues.

"Ah Sarge...appears ah have a little Scratch. Anybody got a Band-Aid?" A medic handed him a bandage.

"Oui Para McGee. Get it fixed quick, prepare to move out Platoon." After rapidly cleaning and bandaging it, Jack joined his platoon, who were soon moving out at a quick pace, as they headed for the LZ to be picked up by choppers. Thirty minutes later, Jack was aboard the French Army Puma, as it flew above the jungle. It was the end of his first Legion combat mission. He spat out the open side door, sitting beside a burly Platoon mate. They smiled as the Legionnaire offered him a cigarette. Back at his base, days later and fully recovered from his battle wounds, Jack received his first Legion medal, for conspicuous gallantry. Jack McGee in his second army, having tasted the smell of battle again, felt at peace.

Later that year in 1988, Jack was transferred from the 5th Regiment of the legion to the crack Special Forces 1st Group. He received special insertion training, passing the HALO jump course. He exited from the rear ramp, at 22,000 feet off the African Coast. Jack was exhilarated as he rocketed down to Earth in a head down position at 200 mph. He felt exhilarated as he slowed down at 4000 feet, levelling off in to the standard belly down stable position. Checking his altimeter, strapped to his chest strap, he waited till he was 1100 feet above the ocean. Then he yanked on his pilot chute and tossed it, seconds later his main canopy opened, jerking him hard. He gasped aloud, always relieved as he checked his main chute, watching the elliptical square open over his head, then glancing at the dark water below.

Jack activated his life vest, pulling on the toggle, filling his vest with compressed air with a hissing sound. Jack coolly went through the drills, undoing the strap holding his rifle secured to his shoulder. The veteran jumper released his weapon and rucksack. It dropped to dangle below him on the 15- foot drag line, his foot kicking it to make it swing to the side. It hit the water with a splash seconds later. He gasped closing his mouth, forcing himself to relax, bend the knees a bit to take the impact, so he would hit the water boots first. He looked forward at the horizon, seeing the water surface through his peripheral vision. Sensing his timing was on, he yanked down on the two toggle lines, braking his chute and stalling his forward speed. He laughed as he tried to run across the surface to the shore. He had not yet mastered the new art of pond swooping yet and after a few meters he plunged into the water. Surfacing he spluttered and quickly got his bearings.

He saw the surf boiling on the beach 100 meters ahead and began to swim. His training had hardened his body over the last year, his stamina kicked in as he dragged his parachute anchor and equipment along with him. His jump instructors had told him earlier during the course, that if he lost anything it would come out of his pay. Jack dragged himself and his equipment, 120 pounds of it onto the beach 20 minutes later, completely fucked. He lowered his goggles, squinting in the moonlit night, gasping for air.

"OK let's get it on." He shouldered his load, cocked his assault rifle and jogged off the beach, heading on a compass bearing he had calculated would take him to the objective. He arrived panting two hours later. He gasped as he stood before the assembled base team of French

Paratroopers on his freefall course. His cam fatigues were soaked with sweat and steaming in the heat. "Well done Trooper. Relax, have a cigarette." "Merci mon Captain!" He smiled darkly at the Legionnaire Course Officer as he dropped his gear and accepted a light from the tall officer. He was one of 30 recruits to the Special Forces Unit and was second to complete the final course. At 05:00 A.M. the last one staggered in and they got on the lorry to return to the Legion base at El Qatari near Casablanca, Morocco.

Jack parachuted in on his first mission somewhere in Africa two months later. It was a covert long range reconnaissance mission, a four-man team jumped from 20,000 feet at night. Jack followed the blinking red light in front, located on the rear of the patrol leader's helmet. Jack knew the leader Lieutenant van Holdt was competent and had one of the newest GPS navigation devices strapped to his chest strap. His breathing came in controlled bursts inside his oxygen mask. He stretched his muscles and arched, then brought his arms back to his sides and straightened his legs. The classic tracking position increased his horizontal velocity, he felt his heart pick up as he felt the speed.

"Fucking aye! No life like it. I can't believe they pay me to do this shit!" Slowly he closed on the leader, as the others formed up beside him. In a tight V the Foreign Legion team shot through the darkness to the jungle far below. Jack glanced at the luminous dial of his altimeter, then felt his rucksack below ensuring everything was in order. He had over 100 pounds strapped to him, vital to his mission. 90

seconds earlier he had stood beside his team on the ramp of the C-117 Starlifter turbo jet transport. All four of the jumpers stood in a group checking their oxygen masks and equipment, each checking the other's pins in their chutes. Jack slapped his mate's back. "You're OK Rutger. Ready for a stroll?" In communication with his team with built in radios in their masks, the team gave each other the thumbs up and turned to the crew chief who was linked up by radio to the cockpit. Jack rocked on his heels as he felt the big transport slow to exit speed, as the pilot radioed 1 minute. The crew chief also wearing oxygen flicked the red light on and lowered the rear ramp to the horizontal. "I guess I don't have to say, it is time you Legion boys hit the silk." The Legionnaires were all experienced, their eyes glaring at the dark void ahead then whooping "Airborne! Allez! Let's go!"

Jack felt the old surge of adrenaline now…seconds to go. The green light blinked and they were off. The Lieutenant rolled off the ramp doing a 360- degree front roll, then tracked off into the night as the other three hurled after him. In seconds the ramp was empty, the crew chief smiling as he shook his head, then raised the ramp up. "Crazy fuckers." He reported to the Captain jumpers away, then the C-117's powerful twin turbo jets rocketed to full power and climbed into the clouds and banked for home base. Jack and the others broke off at 4500 feet above the dark jungle canopy, spreading out before their chutes billowed out.

Jack grunted as the harness jerked his body and slowed his fall dramatically. He blinked to clear his vision behind the fogging up mask. He wiped it with his hand, then reached up grabbed the toggles and ripped the Velcro straps off the risers. He located the others before steering hard to form up on the leader. The camouflaged main chutes were difficult to see even to the sharp eyes in Jack's head, but he was trained for it. "OK the cruise is over. Time to put on yer hard hat and go to work." Jack whispered into the mask, followed by click of static. The leader in front did a slow right turn as he searched for a landing spot.

"Ok there is a clearing. Follow me in tight men." A short 30 seconds later the four men swooped in low and landed in the thick grass. Jack rolled and was relieved to find he was uninjured. A freak accident here would not be good timing. No hot nurses or hospitals here. This was isolated Injun country. Rapidly the team gathered their chutes and raced out of the clearing. They piled them together and spread camouflage branches over them. Lt. van Holdt knelt in the center as the three others checked their equipment and weapons before loading them. A GPS locator was left with the para gear for pick-up by a recovery team. Jack and the others knelt in a tight group as the officer briefed them with his map spread out under the red light of his flashlight. Silently the four men faced out, listening for any sounds in the darkness of the jungle.

"Ok you guys march routine. You know your positions, Jack the tail end Charlie. We move at night only, so we have about four hours to find a checkpoint hide." Jack nodded then quietly they moved off like ghosts in the night. This was not the movies Jack thought. Noise discipline was tight, all signals were by hand, the only sounds were the jungle birds and animals. "Freaking eerie. Like Nam all over. A new bunch of bad guys, new fuckers to deal with." He stopped as the dark shadow before him held up his hand after an hour.

In the lead Lt. van Holdt had frozen like a statue. The others heard it and slowly dropped to a knee. Jack felt his heart race, his thumb slowly flicked the safety off his Glock 9 mm pistol held in his right hand. A minute later the enemy patrol passed by, Jack clearly heard them babble and grinned. "Fucking dummies. Amateurs." The French patrol let their counterparts go, their mission was covert at this point. They reached their first checkpoint before dawn. Half an hour later the four men huddled under the camouflaged pauncho. Van Holdt took first watch, so the others opened ration packs and ate before snatching an hour of sleep. Jack awoke later as his sniper buddy Rollon nudged his arm. "Wake up sleeping beauty, you're up." Jack glared at his joke, his head felt like a pumpkin, as he rubbed his hand over his shaved skull. So it continued for the next week, then as they neared their objective Lt. van Holdt radioed to the base camp. He got an update and orders from the Legion HQ, locate and observe the suspected terrorist training camp at the map reference grid.

Jack and Rollon went forward first. In their ghillie sniper suits, they disappeared in the dark jungle in seconds. Jack leopard crawled slowly forwards, followed by Rollon at his feet. Reaching a small rise, Jack nudged the tall grass aside with the barrel of his sniper rifle. He pressed the scope sight to his right eye, then slowly swung in an arc. Nothing to be seen. Moving slowly in an arc, he finally located it. A clearing about 100 feet down a slope, with tents set up. Rollon eased up beside him, as his spotter he had a powerful telescope which he set up on a bipod. "I see you." Rollon whispered as he looked at a group of figures strolling about the tents. The dim sound of a generator told the sniper team these ones were well equipped.

Over the next week Jack took notes, number of troops, equipment, level of expertise, and layout of the camp. Several times Legionnaires crawled right through the camp undetected, for by now they knew these were not elite soldiers. They had numbers though, Jack counted 250 by that first week. Most were young African tribesmen, recruited by the terrorist operative Al-Queda. 'The Base' as Jack was briefed, the Arabic name, were leading disruptive attacks across the African continent. Jack was not surprised to hear the group was suspected of being funded by the CIA. The intent was for the Jihadis to fight the Soviets in Afghanistan.

After weeks of watching the camp, they located and identified the leaders. Two tall bearded Arabs were training the African recruits in suicide bombing vests and small arms. Jack and Rollon were ordered to take the leaders out. Jack spent a day with Rollon choosing a good spot overlooking the camp. He lay under a cam net with Rollon spotting nearby. "OK Rollon." He had the Arab leader in his sights, as he stood speaking before a group of Africans. One of Osama Bin Laden's senior Lieutenants Moamar el Khafir. Rollon sighted his scope on the other Arab leader. He watched as the Africans grinned as Mohammed Abu Sayaf demonstrated how to use a mercury switch and attach detonator wires to a pipe bomb. "Ready Jack. You call it."

Jack bit his lip as he relaxed and gently eased his safety lever to fire. "Roger that Rollon. You got Sayaf? I got this fuck Khafir. Prepare to meet your virgins. In one...two. Three...squeeze..." Both snipers had been equipped with silencers, so the shots barely sounded in the thick jungle foliage. Jack's bullet entered his target's ear drum, while Rollon put his between his man's eyebrows. The watching African recruits watched in stunned horror as the two instructors slowly sank to their knees. Blood sprayed from their heads onto their white turbans, then toppled forward to lie twitching on the ground. Panic gripped the camp as shots rang out, then fire erupted from machine guns spraying the foliage. As the sniper team edged slowly back, leaves and pieces of tree bark flew in the air everywhere. Flocks of startled birds soared into the sky, monkeys screamed as they swung overhead through the jungle canopy. Searching patrols swept the surrounding jungle, but they had no idea where the ghosts were. Jack and Rollon crawled into the hide later that night.

Jack and Rollon whispered to the Lieutenant. "Two confirmed kills Sir. The camp seems to be in a bit of disarray it appears. So what is the plan?" Van Holdt congratulated his men before radioing back to base. They stayed there for another day, directing two French Air Force Mirage jets onto the camp. In a precision strike, the camp was flattened by several laser guided bombs. Before they pulled out, van Holdt radioed back "Camp neutralized…KIA's figure 265. Wounded 130 Over."

When he emerged from the bush after the mission ended, Jack had cemented his reputation, as one of the Legion's most feared killers. Reports were he had personally killed over two dozen of the enemy, vicious African thugs who had been attacking French, American and Allied installations. Jack and Rollon were honored for taking out their targets without being identified. The French leaders wanted no criticism from their American Allies. After returning to their base camp, Jack went on leave for two weeks in Paris. His reward for a job well done. After tasting the local nightlife Jack phoned home. He felt his heart strings tug as he listened to Gloria sobbing at the other end.

"Jackie hon! I miss you so much! When are you coming home to me?" Jack smiled thoughtfully, for on one hand he loved his new job. He was by now a crack sniper and was adding to his tally steadily. The pay could have been better though. He did however miss Liza and his young family. "I don't rightly know sweetie. How are things at home Gloria?" He listened as Gloria replied. "Tight eh? Well I am wiring you half my pay till I get back. I will call you in a few days. Then we are off on another mission. Bye lover. Kiss me."

Gloria was holding her young daughter Ashley as she blew a kiss into the phone. She sat down with Ashley bubbling noisily on her knee. "Yes baby. Daddy will be home with us soon." She kissed Ashley's soft cheek and hugged her, a tear slowly rolling down her cheek. The nurse was dressed in tank top and shorts in the hot evening as she sat on the porch, her eyes gazing off in the distance.

It would be another three years before Jack came home to her. He did pay for her European vacation once each year however. Each time Jack was stunned by Gloria's appearance. He had half expected her to turn into one of those overweight mothers, with bad hair and skin. Gloria however bucked the trend. Her trim body was accentuated by a pair of great legs. Her blonde hair uncropped belied her age. After each trip he hugged her tight, promising to return when he could. He told her The Legion treated him well, it was a first class outfit, good men and real action. It was a hard life but fulfilling for the career soldier like him. "Besides I am under a strict pact. AWOL means you betray the Legion. Police will hunt you down. If yer lucky it's prison in some shithole for ten years or more. Another three years and I can retire for life."

Gloria had nodded sadly, assuring him she could hold the fort in Kentucky till he returned. In 1990 Jack finally decided, telling the Colonel of his decision to return to Kentucky after his tour was over. By 1991, after four years' service Jack was honorably discharged, with the thanks of France, having received the Legion d'Honoure for conspicuous gallantry. Colonel Brandt shook his hand on parade that day in Southern France.

"Merci Sergeant McGee. The Legion thanks you for your gallant service and to France. If you change your mind give me a call." McGee saluted and responded affirmative before marching off the baking parade ground. That night he drank for free in the mess as his comrades got him pissed in celebration. Arriving in Toulon Airport Jack was greeted by Gloria and his young children. He grinned as Gloria ran to him, in a flowered, body hugging dress. He swept her in his arms as she planted a kiss on his cheek. Ashley, Jack Jr. who was on leave from the Middle East and his younger sister Meghan followed. The veteran ex-Legionnaire now, forgot his sadness on leaving his mates back in Morocco. As the children gripped their father by his legs, Jack whispered in Gloria's earlobe. Jack laughed as he squeezed her, then lead the way out of the airport with the children racing to beat him.

Jack celebrated on departure leave with his family, visiting the French Mediterranean coast. Before returning home, he wanted to sample the local sights and festivities. He stayed at a beach resort in Corsica. It was an idyllic retreat, with Gloria turning a few heads in her designer swim suit. As Jack lounged on a chair in an outdoor café, he was served by beautiful dark haired women with olive tinted skin and bright smiles. He picked up souvenirs on shopping trips for Gloria and the kids. He had saved up a considerable sum of money from his Legion service and put it to good use for once. La Glize on the French Riviera was his last stop. He sat at a canal bistro till the wee hours of the morning drinking vintage wine and calvados with local girls. Before leaving on a jet back to Kentucky Jack McGee had left his calling card over a wide area of the Mediterranean.

Gloria knew his wild, dark side and still loved him for it. Many of her friends were not so lucky. Most had soldier husbands at one time or another and divorces were common. Also more than one had lost their husband in combat in Vietnam or other exotic places across the globe. Then there were the horrific injuries and suicides. When they finally walked into their ancestral home in Kentucky outside of Louisville that autumn in 1991, Gloria felt very happy indeed. She had turned 41 with her family around her, her man was back and her house was in good repair. When she finally pushed Jack onto the bed later that evening, she unleashed herself on him.

Meanwhile thousands of miles away, their son Jack Jr. was back on duty. The young soldier who was now leading a platoon of American Paratroopers in the 82nd Airborne Division, was training for operations in North Africa and the Middle East. In his early twenties, Jack Jr. was like his father a natural soldier. His early days had formed his view of the world he was to live in. He knew of his family history, which extended back to the first days of the colonization of North America. It was blistering hot in the African desert as Jack marched beside his platoon of paratrooper grunts. The dust wafted up into the air from the files of marching

Chapter III

PRISON

I t was the changing of the guard for the McGee clan. Jack Sr. who was retired from his life fighting wars, was being replaced by his son Jack Jr. The whole family celebrated at their Kentucky acreage as the young McGee returned from his first overseas posting. "Well done son! You are a soldier now. Survived your first mission. So how was it?" Young Jack filled him in as Gloria and the other female family members bustled about to serve the men at the big barbeque in the back yard of the McGee estate. A week later Jack and Eliza were married in the local church. After their honeymoon Jack returned with Eliza, now officially part of the McGee clan. His father Jack Senior, or Jack 1st, set his oldest son and wife up at a house near the family acreage.

"You look like you got it made Son. That Eliza reminds me of Gloria when we were starting out. Well done, you're on your way. What is your plan for the Forces?" Jack Jr. and his Dad were walking in the luxurious rear lawn smoking cigars on the gorgeous spring day. It was 1991 in early April. They watched as the women worked on Gloria's garden, planting flowers and vegetables, working in jeans and t-shirts. "Well the talk is the next war is in the Middle East. Maybe Iraq or Syria, both are terrorist havens. President Bush is fixing to kick some ass I reckon."

Jack Sr. blew a ring of smoke as he looked up at the sky. "Maybe so. Good luck on that. The 82nd Airborne is a good outfit, but why don't you try for the Special Forces? Better training, pay and probably better action." His son nodded in agreement. "My plan exactly. I have to do another year in the 'Borne. My C.O. said he would put the papers through as I am meeting the standards." After discussing his son's future, the older McGee changed the subject. "Say son do you want to go jumping?" Jack Sr. was intent on taking up civilian skydiving, as a replacement for military parachuting. They agreed enthusiastically and when approached, the two McGee women were on board as well. That Sunday they loaded into Jack's 4x4 and went to the local drop zone.

Both the men were already licensed USPA skydivers, so they went up first. They jumped from a Twin Otter at 15,500' and did a 2-way exit. After releasing from the plane's open door, Jack held his father's arm grip on his suit. He arched hard as they fell 'down the chute.' As they approached terminal velocity, he glanced at his altimeter. "15,000…14750…good! We are stable." Jack looked in his father's eyes, nodded and released his grip on his arms. They took turns gripping each other, forming a series of had returned from his run into town for supplies that night. Eliza had taken a shower before getting ready for bed. The big, burly intruder was waiting for the young blonde as she emerged from the bathroom wrapped in a towel barefoot. Her scream ended when his huge paw clamped over her mouth. Eliza squirmed as she was dragged to the door, her feet kicking in the air, as she tried to fight the huge intruder. Her eyes bulged as he man-handled her, her towel sliding off to the floor. She looked in the dark face as he held her waist tight, her breasts openly displayed pressed to his chest. Then the door opened before the struggling pair. Jack stood there, then Eliza stopped fighting as she slumped limp in the masked man's arms. Jack looked at the pair before him, Eliza's face tilted backwards as she fainted, her long hair swaying over the big boots of the intruder, her toes dangling in the air as he held her nude body in his paws.

Jack's blue eyes slitted fiercely as he took in the sight of his gorgeous wife and this huge stranger before him. He saw the look of surprise in those dark eyes, then Eliza's naked body slid slowly from his hands to the floor, to roll sideways to lie at his feet. Jack glanced down at her momentarily as he clenched his fists. He saw Eliza's naked breasts rising up to him from her panting chest, her thighs spread open. "Too bad fucker. She would have been nice eh?" Jack side stepped the kick launched at his privates, then the knife aimed at his throat. His adrenaline and training kicked in as his mind went into auto drive, his arms and legs moved in a blur. He kicked the man's knees hard, making him grunt in pain before dropping beside Eliza's body. Jack did a spinning heel kick, breaking the man's jaw and ejecting several teeth. Blood sprayed out from the screaming intruder's open mouth, as Jack kicked him in the abdomen, sending him reeling backward on the floor. Jack strode silently forward, a fierce look of determination on his face, stepping over Liza before placing the towel over her nude body. Shortly Liza awoke, groaning as she struggled to get up. Her mouth gaped as she saw Jack before her, hammering blows into her would-be abductor's face. The man dropped to his knees, blood oozing from his face. Jack stepped back and kicked him hard in the chest, Liza heard the sickening sound of bones cracking, as Jack continued to rain blow after blow on the big man, dropping him on his back with a groan.

Eliza recognized him vaguely, an African immigrant, who worked in town near her hospital. Several times she had smiled at him as he carried her groceries to her truck after her shift at hospital. In her tight fitting nurse's uniform, the blonde, foxy woman was oblivious to his hidden desires. Jack beat him now to death with his bare hands, as Liza gathered herself and called the police. When the sirens blared outside, Jack finally regained his control. He gasped and stared at Liza who was sobbing as she stood wrapped in the towel before him. "Oh Jack!" He hugged her as she fell into his arms and embraced him. The two police officers walked in to find Jack and Liza standing beside the twitching body. His face was beaten to a bloody pulp, so even his mother would not have recognized him. His shirt was stunned as she was humiliated by Forest, while Jack sat in the prisoner's box, his anger bubbling as he watched helplessly. Jack Sr. and Gloria attended the trial and gave statements as to Jack's military service record and character.

"Is this normal for a married woman to shamelessly and provocatively strut about in front of people like poor Mr. Jenkins? He was a good citizen we have seen. Mrs. McGee tempted him and he reacted as most men would have. Certainly he did not deserve to die in such violent fashion. He did invade the McGee home. But he did not hurt anyone. Who knows what he was planning? We have no evidence he wanted anything more than to talk to Mrs. McGee. There is a precedent for women of loose morals inciting men to act out of their normal temptations." Racial tensions were peaking during that time, so Jack was made the sacrificial scape goat. The jury sat for days before announcing the guilty verdict on the reduced charge of manslaughter in the packed court house. He was sentenced to life in prison for his violent defense of his wife. Jack was led away in chains as Liza sobbed in the front bench. Beside her Jack's father tried to console Liza, while Gloria sobbed on his other side.

Jack looked at her and smiled. "I will be back Liza. Take care of the kids till I do." She held a Kleenex to her face and nodded as she watched him go. That evening Liza slept with her two young girls, crying herself to sleep. Jack spent that night in his new home. His cell mate lay in his bunk smoking as Jack sat on his, after pacing for an hour. They eyed each other silently. Like two bears in the woods.

"Tough break. Life is a bitch sometimes. Only fellah you ever killed?" Rod nodded as he read the magazine, Hot-rod, his favourite car magazine. The conversation turned to cars, which was one of Jack's favourite pastimes. He loved vintage fast cars. He was working on a Lincoln Town car before his arrest. It was an early 70's model, now sitting in the garage, beside his 1967 Ford Shelby Mustang.

Slowly Jack and Rod became friends, while Liza and Jack Sr. pursued an appeal. She visited him in the jail whenever she could. For Jack it was his lifeline to the world. Some old friends, his Dad of course with Gloria and relatives visited him regularly. But it was Liza who really kept him going. While he was locked away, Liza gave birth to twin boys. She was not allowed to bring the children on her monthly visits, which did not help Jack in his daily struggle to keep up his spirits. As the appeal bogged down in court, the days turned into weeks, then months. That December Jack spent another holiday season separated from his lover and soul mate. It was the roughest part yet. He was handed Liza's present before Christmas. "McGee your old lady sent you this."

Jack sauntered to the door and took the parcel from the head screw. He muttered his thanks and returned to his bunk. He lost himself in Eliza's letters, family photos with his young sons, named Sean and Mike. Jack read them over several times, Liza keeping him up to date on the outside world. Finally, he pinned a picture of her beside his bed. Rod looked at the beautiful smiling face and complimented Jack.

"Hang in Jack. That sweetheart of yours deserves to see you get out of this hole." Jack nodded as he stared at her smiling face in the picture. He slept well for the first time that night as he dreamed of her. He saw her running along a beach, her arms held out to him. But he could not reach her, as hard as he tried. "What does it mean?" Rod had listened as Jack told of his dream the next day. "Well it sounds like your frustration in here. You want to run to her and can't. At least you have a woman to get to. My girl left me, abandoned me after I landed in here."

Jack nodded as they chatted, before getting up and pacing the floor. Rod went back to his magazines, both lost in thought as the hours dragged by slowly. One day as he exercised in the yard, he read a paper. The headline story was about the latest crime wave. A killer was on the prowl in San Diego. After killing six women he was termed the 'San Diego Strangler" by the local media. He posed his victim's corpses in parks, sitting or lying on benches, with a letter they had been prompted to write before he strangled them. The City police pinned it on the board in the local precinct. "I am sorry for being a prostitute. I deserve to die. God forgive me." Jack felt angry and betrayed by his country, while psychopathic killers prowled the streets.

Summer 1993: It was two years later when Jack got finally received a reprieve. He had lost his appeal finally in 1992 after Eliza hired a new civilian lawyer. Jack was frustrated and sunk into depression. He learned that the U.S. Army had cut ties with him, issuing a Dishonourable

Discharge upon his final conviction. He contemplated suicide briefly before Rod talked him out of it. "Hang in there buddy. Look at that sweetheart waiting for you. That is why you have her picture buddy. Things can change quickly. Life can be funny that way." Then late that autumn Jack got a visitor. In 1993 a top-secret organization was being contemplated in the highest circles of the Pentagon and across the border in Canada.

It was a secret collaboration between the U.S. and Canada, forming the first joint military unit between the two nations since W.W. 2 (1st Special Service Force). In Canada's capital Ottawa, the Liberal cabinet struggled to pass the bill approving it. Finally, the Defence Committee allowed it to proceed, on the condition it was kept top secret. In Washington President Bush rubber stamped the request from the Pentagon. War was on the horizon and as he confided to his closest confidants, "We need all oars in the water. If this gamble does not work, we lose a few convicts. In 'Nam they were half convicts anyway. This is the new order gentlemen. Fight the enemy on their own ground by their rules, meaning there isn't any." This new unit however would be different, for its recruits were selected from top security jails, throughout North America. Most were violent offenders, murderers, serial criminals, thieves, rapists... some of worse crimes against humanity.

Jack was interviewed in his cell by an Army Colonel, one day at Missouri State Penitentiary. Jack was transferred there with Rod that year. He was getting used to his new digs when the head screw tapped the bars of his cell. "Prisoner McGee it is visitor time. And no it's not yer young lady this time." Puzzled Jack stood waiting as the cell door clanged open. "Does this visitor have a name?" The guard looked bored at Jack and shook his head before leading Jack down the long walkway to the visitor area. Jack sat in the chair as the guard (head screw as Jack called him) left him alone, till the door opened and the stranger walked in.

The tall hard faced officer looked through his file, then stared at the lean frame of Jack as he lounged on his chair casually smoking a Marlboro cigarette. It was a rare treat for him, smoking only being allowed on limited occasions. He had struggled with the enforced restrictions. But he wondered who this mystery man was and what he wanted. "Are you a lawyer?" Jack sat smoking in silence as the stranger ignored him, leafing through a file of papers studiously. Slowly he straightened up, his head still bent over his file, then raising a finger to Jack.

The tall stranger smiled as he glanced from Jack's file to the lean hard frame of the convict sitting before him. "I am Colonel Mann, U.S. Army. I can have you out of here Jack McGee. I am selecting men for a certain gig. I can't say much more right now but I think you might have what it takes. By the way, that is a nice wife you have. Now I am not saying this will be easy, but you had a record as a good, young soldier. I am forming an experimental army unit. The recruits like you, are from prisons like this one. Well, what do you say?" Jack looked at him as he inhaled on his

The naysayers, military and political, tried over and over to have the unit disbanded as a waist of money and resources. But the Pentagon persisted, as did the Force X C.O. Colonel Mann. Small units were formed to continue training in a more hostile environment. Colonel Mann set the exercise up personally. It took months getting the logistics and approvals, but finally Force X arrived in Ellesmere Island, located in Canada's Arctic Islands in January of the next year. On the march to the North Pole in howling, -50 C wind, they perished in droves. Jack was the only one of his unit to make it. Behind for hundreds of miles, convicts lay frozen to the ice. Polar bears finished off a few who had wandered off, in a desperate, faint hope they could escape.

It was like another world, a surreal forbidden planet for the escaping convicts. No one heard them scream as the giant white polar bears stood looking at the frozen stiff human snacks. One pair of convict deserters marching south, came around a block of ice, still thousands of miles away from safety. They stared fearfully into the eyes of the polar bear, then felt the bear was no threat. In fact, the polar bear had stalked these humans for several miles. It looked at the convicts with a harmless almost playful persona. Highly intelligent, the young polar bear was judging if his prey were dangerous. The two convicts were armed but had no bullets for their guns. Indeed, the firing pins had been removed by the suspicious MP's, before they were landed by the icebreaker weeks earlier at the start of the exercise.

"Hey Duke man. He is harmless. Here I'll give him a piece of jerky." Duke laughed, relieved as Manny his buddy dug in his pocket and pulled out a piece of rock hard beef jerky. The three-hundred-pound bear looked amused, sniffing as the half- frozen convict held out his hand tentatively. "Here ya go bear." Waiting till Manny was close, the polar bear made his move, lunging forward a huge paw swatted the convict. Duke grunted as he flew through the air to land feet away. Manny went for his knife finally, but the polar bear was moving at a full charge. His scream ended as the bear stood up before him, then came down in the death lunge. His teeth bit into Manny's throat, then shook him violently. His rucksack and weapons flew threw the air in an arc, as his corpse swung from the bear's jaws. As he twitched in a final death throw, blood dripped from his severed throat to the snow below.

Far off Jack thought he heard something. A distant wailing sound. "Ah the damned wind! This place is the opposite of Hell, a frozen lifeless shit hole." He checked his compass then he led the three survivors forward, their bodies bent into the hellish gale biting in their faces. As they set up their tents at the end of that day, miles behind, the polar bear was celebrating an unexpected feast. He tore open Many and Duke's guts and ripped chunks of flesh off, giant paws rested on their gaping mouths as it huddled under a block of ice. It was content, the thick fur keeping it insulated from the icy air as the bear ate. The two luckless convict escapees kept the bear's stomach filled for days, before resuming the normal routine of hunting for normal prey. When the exhausted, frozen survivors were pulled out in February of 1994 Jack and a few others remained out of an initial compliment of 200 Force X convict recruits. Colonel Mann and his officers decided to revamp Force X after the first Arctic debacle.

As the months plodded by, the Penal Army unit evolved, the faces constantly changing with the continual brutal training. Many attempted escape, ultimately failing and ended back on parade before Colonel Mann. Finally he selected a new boot camp, in the middle of New Mexico, a barren, unforgiving desert. The convicts died in droves as they marched through endless miles of baking sand. Some committed suicide, others of heat stroke, rattle snakes, tarantulas and other nasty critters. Jack had survived along with a small cadre of others, who learned to adapt to the harsh life, going from the extremes of freezing hell of the Arctic to the blistering heat of the desert. Forming a bond with a few close unit mates, Jack swore he would survive this phase and return to Liza.

Years later in a secluded, seedy Gentlemen's club on the east side of Edmonton, Alberta, a late night party was underway, that meant drugs were involved of course. The young man assigned to drop off a pound of crack heroine after seeing the front door was locked, pressed the buzzer on the front door. After a few minutes the door opened, and before the surprised young man stood an old man who could have been his grandfather.

"Merry Christmas Son!" It was Christmas Eve, as Fred "Ace" Newman realized. He finished the last of the weed he was smoking then smiled slyly at the wizened old man. "Merry Christmas Mister. I got your present." He produced the heavy bag and waited patiently, yawning for he was tired. This was his last drop off for the day and he wanted to get back home. "Come in, come in… ah, what is your name Sonny?"

"Freddie and yours Dude?" The old man took the package from Fred and waved him inside before closing and bolting the heavy oak door behind him. "I am Sidney Castillo. Come down to the cellar. Do you like young women my friend?" "Of course ah, Sid. Why do you ask? By the way that'll be $5500 for the stuff."

"Peanuts my friend. Maybe we can make a deal if you are open minded."

The old man led the way to the basement, where young Freddie got the surprise of his life. For sitting, lounging in chairs where some of the hottest babes he had ever seen. Sidney introduced six of them, Peggy, Katia, Michelle, Sherry, Jackie and Melissa. They were young, twenty-something, sexy, for their trade was sex. Sidney employed them, starting as exotic dancers, then as hookers. Sidney handed Fred an envelope first. "$5500 in cash as promised. Would you be interested in any of the ladies this evening?"

Fred looked hungrily at a tall busty blonde, dressed in cut-off painted on jeans and a black bra, that barely covered her massive breasts, which threatened to escape from the micro- bra at any second. Michelle smiled at him as she sat in a provocative pose, smoking a cigarette, and sipping on a glass of champagne.

"Hi there Freddie! I'm Michelle!" She giggled at her friend beside her, a statuesque dark brunette, both had smooth, silky olive hued tanned skin. "And I am Jackie, please to meet you." Jackie dragged on her cigarette, elegantly blowing rings of smoke before her, from her scarlet, pouting lips. She wore a black leather evening dress, with cut-out ovals, showing off her 38-26-38 figure inside. She tossed her thick pile of long hair over a bare shoulder, exposing the deepest cleavage Fred had ever seen. She batted her long fake eyelashes, her olive green eyelids mesmerizing him. Her eyes were sparkling, of a blueish hue as she gazed up at him.

After a moment's hesitation, Freddie was sold. "How much for an hour with Jackie...and Miss Michelle?" They settled on $650 with Sidney, then the young delivery guy led the two tall, gorgeous foxes by the hand to a nearby room. Jackie and Michelle worked regularly as a tandem. After stripping for him, they undid his trousers as he sat drinking by the bed and took turns. Freddie took his time, running his hands through their bobbing heads between his thighs. He gasped as Jackie moaned and inhaled powerfully. Michele the tall curvaceous blonde, tossed her wild blonde hair and looked up at him, her tongue licking her lavender painted succulent lips. Freddie was no virgin, but these two were like nothing he had ever had.

After the session was over, he pulled Michele up on his knee, bouncing her before him, her massive hooters gyrating like ripe melons. He circled her waist, then fondled her smooth, silky buttock cheeks in his palm. Jackie squirmed up and sat down on his other knee, then Fred kissed Michelle's upturned mouth. He groaned as their tongues met, caressing each other. He felt their spiked heels dig into his legs teasingly as they lounged against him. The sultry hookers whispered to each other. Then Michelle slithered up beside Freddie and whispered in his ear. "I have a proposal for you my young lover. I and Jackie here, have had a belly full of that old guy out there owning us. How would you like to be our new boss?"

Freddie smiled as he looked at the two grinning hookers before him. "I was thinking more or less along those lines myself Michelle my dear." He kissed her ear and whispered his plan to the giggling women.

An hour later Fred emerged from the room grinning ear to ear. The old man smiled as he watched him walk out, Jackie and Michelle lounging in his arms, silly smiles painted over their sultry, handsome faces. Sidney smiled as his two hookers handed him the money from Freddie, then sat down beside the others at the table. That night the sexy young hookers got high on cocaine and liquor which flowed freely. Fred and Sidney sat at another table playing poker. Finally, at around 5:00 A.M. Freddie made his move.

"I have a new proposal for you Old Man. I like these girls, and plan on taking them with me. What do y'all think about that?" Sidney looked appalled at the young man, then chortled aloud. "Sonny that is funny! These here women, these whores are my property. I don't think you have the money or expertise to..." Suddenly the old man's eyes opened wide for Freddie had just produced a pistol from his pocket, pointed directly at him.

"This Old Man gives me the option. You are no longer required." Sidney suddenly stiffened, his eyes opening wide in sudden fear. "Oh I see. Well perhaps we could arrange a deal?" Freddie grew bolder as the women watched their boss beg for his life. Freddie looked at Michelle and Jackie, who smiled and urged him on.

"Well yer see. I've heard about your methods. These girls tell me you had one of them killed for trying to leave on her own. That tells me you are a ruthless, fucking asshole. Good-bye Sidney. Thanks for giving me the opportunity to save these poor, unfortunate ladies." Sidney went for his hidden revolver under the desk, but Freddie beat him to it. The gun barked and the .45 slug fired point blank, hit the old man between his eyes. Freddie watched as the old man stared with a look of surprise at him for a second, then his head slumped backward and he sighed, his last breath. Freddie stood up and walked over to Sidney, patting him on his shoulder. Smiling he then walked over to were six of the prostitutes, Peggy, Katia, Michelle, Sherry, Jackie and Melissa sat at the table.

All were stoned drunk by now, one brunette Jackita with a cigarette dangling from her lips, her gorgeous girlish face dangling over her cleavage as she sat passed out. Michelle and Jackie sat on a love seat giggling as they shared a joint, to celebrate their newly won freedom from their hated pimp boss. Freddie put his arm around a flaming red headed beauty, Katia wearing a red halter top, short red vinyl skirt, and a gold chained tiara in her thick hair. He lifted her limp body off the chair in his arms. "Come on honey. Let's get acquainted eh?" Katia pouted her glossy lips as she hung from his arm, her clothing enhanced with a black dog collar and black polished spiked high heels. "And Mr. Sidney?" Katia whispered in his ear. "Don't worry about him darling. He won't be handling you no more. I am the new King on this throne!"

Freddie had a threesome that morning with Katia, Michelle and Jackie. After finally getting his fill of the three gorgeous foxes, he got up and poured himself a Scotch and lit up a joint. As he sat there looking down at the three sleeping beauties, stretched out on the bed before him, the police burst in. "Police hands up!" Freddie looked at the dark clad figures of the EPS Tactical Squad as they entered the bed room, their automatic rifles pointed at him. "Oh Oh. OK... I'm yours Officers. At least they are safe from that old bastard out there. I did them a favour!" He pointed at the sleeping hookers on the bed, finished his Scotch, smashing the glass at his feet, then took a last drag of his joint. Slowly the young man raised his hands over his head. One officer handcuffed him as another read him his rights. Jackie, Michelle, Katia and the other hookers after being awakened stood in a huddled group outside the club house, dressed in assorted lingerie as they watched Freddie being handcuffed and led off by the Edmonton police.

"See Ya later Ladies. Pleasure was all mine." They blew him kisses, promising to visit him inside the slammer. After a search of the house, all six of the prostitutes were taken in and booked. Meanwhile Sidney's cadaver, splattered with dried blood was dumped into a body bag and loaded onto an Ambulance gurney. Michelle and her consorts were escorted out of the crime scene, to awaiting Police cruisers for transport downtown. A year later, an American Colonel and a Canadian Major visited Freddie in his cell at the Alberta prison. His trial had ended months earlier, the verdict was guilty of manslaughter. It would be ten years with good behaviour. After the interview the army officers left a smiling Freddie, the newest recruit of Force X. It took a month to complete the paperwork before Freddie and a dozen other selected inmates were released from the cells in Edmonton, Alberta and flown down to Fort Bragg, North Carolina. Freddie was allowed one phone call after reaching his billet, a barracks on the sprawling army base. He rubbed his newly shaved head as he dialed Michelle's number she had given him.

"Hi Michelle baby!" The blonde giggled as she answered. "I have a new arrangement with the Army. I am in boot camp so I have to go away for a while Michelle. But can I see you when I return?"

"I promise if you come back baby, our first night together will pale by comparison. You will find two ladies, waiting and willing to make you very happy."

The next day started abruptly at first light. The American Colonel and a gaggle of uniformed MPs greeted the new recruits outside the large barracks building that dreary rainy day.

"Gentlemen, well you are welcome to your new temporary home, Fort Bragg. I am Colonel Mann. You are the newest recruits of Force X. You will begin training shortly after you are issued your equipment. The first rule is, if you break any rule you will be summarily tried and executed, understand me Privates?" Freddie stood in the ranks of shocked convict prisoners, momentarily wordless as they looked at Mann.

"Hey asshole! I'm hungry... when is chow?" The Colonel furled his eyebrows as he looked at the inquisitor. Barely showing his anger, Colonel Mann approached the slouching prisoner, a rough looking, older man with a bit of a gut, who stood slouching at the end of the line of convicts, a slight smirk on his whiskered face.

"Good question Private. The mess facilities eh? Do you know how to use a knife Recruit Private?" The Colonel smiled as the watching Officers and NCO's behind him grinned knowingly. They had watched this routine over and over for the past two years. Walking over to the smiling convict he stood before him. "Slim Pickens they call me Sir. Yes, I do, as a matter of fact. Hand that pig sticker over asshole!" Colonel Mann produced a wicked, six-inch blade from his belt. He had been trying out various knives as issue fighting knives for Force X. He smiled thinking this would be the first good opportunity to test it. "OK Slim, would you take this knife and try and stick me with it. I bet you would love to do that eh?" The watching convicts and Military Police gasped as they heard his words. "OK men, stand back while I teach Mr. Pickens here, a quick lesson in knife fighting etiquette." A few minutes later Colonel Mann stood in a ring with Slim Pickens, surrounded by jubilant, cheering convicts. "Stick him! Kill the bastard!" Colonel Mann eyed the crowd, who were suddenly into the impromptu fight. Mann seemingly unintimidated, nodded at the convict who advanced on him with the knife pointed threateningly at his gut. "Come to me. That's it! Come death come."

Suddenly the officer's hand shot out, punched Pickens's arm aside as he strode forward. Slim yelped in pain as Mann shot an elbow into his chest, knocking him backward into the watching convicts. Some protested as Mann sprang backward, then Slim angry now lunged at him with his knife arcing through the air. Mann side stepped him, using his off balanced attack against him. He stuck his leg out and tripped him, then using one arm, knocked him to the ground. Mann circled him, then gripped his knife hand, twisting it cruelly behind his back. Slim yelled in pain as his arm nearly broke, Mann smiling as he applied more force to the joint.

"Ahh! No stop! Please... fucker!" Slim gasped then dropped the knife to the ground as Colonel Mann finished off his helpless opponent. He had not broken a bead of sweat during this demonstration of unarmed combat to the now silent, stunned convicts. He finished by gripping the hapless Slim by his throat and putting him in a deadly choke hold. The man uttered choking gurgling sounds, as he was lifted off the ground, arms and legs flailing wildly. "This is Unarmed Combat 101 Gentlemen. In the upcoming days this will be an integral part of your training. The Sergeant Major will discuss seating arrangements OK?"

The convict's eyes bulged in fear and pain as he stared at the cold steel eyes of the Colonel towering before him, then he screamed as he was flung through the air, to land on his back. "OK shall we go to work, er Gentlemen?" As the Colonel nodded to the NCO's, big burly MP's brandishing their batons, the convicts were shoved and beaten into two long lines, then marched off in the cold, drizzling rain down the runway to the line of buildings a few miles off in the distance. The convicts uttered groans and muttered oaths of violent repercussions as they tramped off sullenly. For many who had never been on a serious run in their criminal lives, it would be a painful, torturous initiation. Barely half a mile down the road, men started to fall out. Unable to keep the pace, the out of shape convicts pleaded with the hovering Military Police. They received little mercy and were punched and kicked after the plodding formation of convicts. A mile later many started to get sick, vomiting on the men around them. The victims covered in filth yelled insults, punching the sick convicts in anger. The MP's did not intervene as the convicts ended up rolling in the mud as they fought viciously. After they were pulled apart, the men were pushed back in formation and the run continued, up a long, winding trail. Many gasped in delirium as they were driven on like cattle.

"What kind a shit is this? Wait till I get my hands on that prick! Damn screw!" A burly MP snarled a warning to shut up. "Left right left! Don't slouch you scum!" Two hours later the men returned to their barracks, staggering like dying men. The MP's smiled darkly as they escorted them inside, fingers on their pistol holsters. "Ten minutes you lot, line up by yer bunks for inspection." The Military Police were far from convinced these dangerous criminals would ever be soldier material, but it sure would be fun in the meantime! Freddie smiled silently as the men complained about him. "I can do this," he thought as he fell into a well-practiced routine. Mind in neutral, body in gear. As the daily physical training increased in intensity, so did his resolve.

In prison he had been like a fish out of water. A chained shark, a predator of the highest order in chains. Now he could release a lot of pent up energy. Slowly his body responded to the harsh discipline and training. The pounds he had put on in prison wore off, his muscles returning to his former self. Besides he consoled himself, he had two women waiting for him. After two weeks of running in PT gear the convicts were issued their first uniforms. The old style cam fatigues were devoid of any insignia and ill-fitting for the bulk of the convicts, who had little idea of looking like soldiers. Another of the new intake, Sean McGinn could have cared less, as he ran in the ranks beside these civvy fools. Still he mentally sized up the ones in his platoon.

The twenty odd convicts showed little interest in becoming friendly with their new mates. Sean was ex-Canadian Army; he was not concerned with making friends for life. What he did know was if this show led to combat, this unit had to close ranks. But before that there would have to be sacrificial lambs to the slaughter.

It was the way it was in every unit he had ever been in. The better the unit, the higher the casualty rate. In The Canadian Airborne Regiment, barely 25% of the new draft made it past the first month. When he had been indoctrinated (recruited) into the Canadian Airborne Regiment in 1983, he had survived the first month along with one other new guy. Some could not run a mile in the time limit. Some did not have the will to jump from 30- foot mock towers. Some were injured, some quit under the strain and pressure put on them by their instructors. But he had stood in the graduating parade square every time. The final test to make the 'Borne was the Airborne Indoctrination Course. It was Hell Week for the Paratrooper recruits. Little sleep, run everywhere, the penalty was 50 push-ups if you were caught walking. Then a final 3-day exercise and run 12 kilometers back to base in full kit, fighting order, helmet, rifle and rucksack. On that hot, humid day the sweating recruits stood on the baking hot parade square, awarded the coveted Airborne coin. After serving his time in the 'Borne, three years being the minimum, he was posted out to another infantry battalion. There Corporal McGinn ran afoul of his Company Sergeant Major, after posted to 1 RCR in London, Ontario. It was 1987 when McGinn lost it and killed his tormentor, CSM Gross. Convicted of 1st degree murder, subsequently he was dishonourably discharged from the Canadian Army and sent to jail for life. But like Jack Jr., he was to get his second chance after a visit by Col. Mann. McGinn walked out of Kingston Penitentiary in 2014 and never looked back.

McGinn was one of Colonel Mann's later recruits, the perfect convict for Force X. It was the newest, revamped version of Force X Penal Battalion. About half of the convict recruits by now had some military experience. Many were experienced in weapons, soon becoming proficient in basic weapons skills. Others were skilled in the latest high tech methods, vehicles, explosives and communications. As Force X training continued evolving, individuals were slotted into various training courses to hone their skills. Soon Sean McGinn would run into another veteran soldier who went by the nick name Lucky Jack, given to him by his fellow convicts. As the convicts sweated through their training, McGinn was getting used to his new brothers in arms. He knew that like it or not, he would have to trust his back to these fellow convicts. But first he would need to crack a few eggs. Of course the Army would do most of the work for him. When the shit hit the fan, McGinn knew many of these convicts would not survive. It was the day he ran into Jack McGee, he knew instantly they would become blood brothers. After a twenty-mile route march to begin the day, Jack and Sean squared off on the playground...the instructor's name for the assault course.

"So son...figure you can take an old dog like me?" McGinn laughed at the taunt from McGee. He waved him forwards, then like two rams locking horns they grappled and fought. Around them the rest of the platoon paired off and sparred, urged on by the MP's and unarmed combat instructors. Amidst the yelling, cursing and grunting convicts, the ground was churned up by their combat boots in a life or death struggle.

CHAPTER IV

FORCE X BOOT CAMP

As he lay on his bunk that night, convict recruit McGinn was thinking. He had been in boot camp for a few days now. He grinned as he recalled the sparring session with the big American. Jack had fought hard but both of the seasoned soldiers had ended up in a draw. Sean finished his last cigarette and butted it out in a can.

"I plan on being one of the few who makes it out of here and back to the world. McGee is one I can trust I think. Well I guess we will see." Outside the barracks building, alert Military police patrolled on the look-out for escaping prisoners. Occasionally the silence of the evening would be broken by gun shots and shouts and another convict met his end. At the crack of dawn the next day, the convicts were rousted from their cots, bleary eyed and groaning as they stood for roll call in the freezing, inky blackness of early morning. After all were accounted for, the long day began with PT...physical training.

Jack McGee smiled to himself as the gasping convicts struggled with the pace set by their PT instructor. Many had probably never run this far since grade school. Some of them had not even made it out of grade school. They were the bottom of the barrel, society's rejects, the sweepings of the gutter, born again lifers who were at the end of the line. Jack 1st had gone to Vietnam with similar men. Sometimes in the juggernaut of war, after enough men had been sacrificed, the unit jelled together. Now it was his son's turn to march through the fires of Hades. As he ran in the ranks, Jack could feel the flames scorch his sweating body.

He could not explain it, nobody could, but it had been that way since man went to war millennia ago. It just happened, maybe the survivors closed ranks out of necessity. Most had little in common, but after weeks or months of misery, fear and death they changed from undisciplined civilians into trained killers. Jack had seen good soldiers crack under the strain of constant death and mutilation. He had heard the saying, "Man's courage is measured in a cup. Some drink it dry in one gulp. Others savor it over a lifetime." So far Jack had sipped from his measure and had savored the taste of it...reckless courage. Jack was a rare breed like his father. Born for war he did not shirk from it, he wanted it! In his new mate McGinn, he had found a like minded Force X recruit. Over the coming weeks they formed a bond, unbreakable by the harsh training and steel discipline. Later they knew harsher tests would come, only the strongest would prevail. So now was the time to see who you could trust your life with. There was little room or error, for in the heat of battle it was crucial to be a close knit team.

October 1, 2014: "OK Ladies, breaking into double time...Double March!" The Colonel smiled as he lit up a cigar as he stood watching beside his Humvee. "One of my sister's Guatemalan cigars. I've been dying to try it out! Well Eddie what do you think of our new recruits?" Major Eddie van Zandt of the Canadian Army smiled grimly. He shook his head as he puffed on his pipe, the rain splattering his raincoat. "Scum of the Earth Sir. Most will be dead within days I expect. I'm just not sure how this unit will survive training, let alone a battle." Colonel Mann nodded as he watched the convicts running by, as sheets of rain poured down.

Over the next week, the new recruits of Force X were sworn into the ranks of the joint US-Canada experimental army unit. "Recruits Rule Number 1. If you break any rule, you will be punished harshly. Try to escape, assault on a civilian or Officer will result in an RTU and execution of your sentence for your vile crimes...meaning life or death. Release your inner inhibitions and I will watch you swing. Any questions?"

"Yah Sarge. Are yer a fucking faggot?" This came from a surly convict named Slash, for his reputation with a knife. The MP Sergeant McPhee glared at the smiling, lanky, shaven headed convict standing in the front rank. By now they were dressed in newly assigned Army Camouflage fatigues, without any insignia identifying them. The other thirty odd convicts quietly laughed at the MP's pissed off face. Many had reluctantly accepted the reality of their new life. But to a man they despised the Military Police. Just another form of screw.

"Step forward Recruit." McPhee walked up to Slash as he shuffled forward. Stroking his baton club held behind his back in his ham-like fist, the MP grimaced as he stared coldly into his eyes. "Would you like to take a swing at me Asshole?" McPhee clenched his burly arms threateningly as Slash nodded grinning. He stepped out of ranks, then went at the stocky MP as he showed off his boxing form. He jabbed at McPhee who took a glancing blow on his cheek. Slash darted forward trying to catch the MP off balance, then he was punched hard in his gut. Slash gasped and his cheek twitched convulsively, as an uncontrollable rage overtook him. Without hesitating he cocked his fist and drove it at the MP's face. McPhee for a big man moved like lightning, dodging out of the way, he swung his club. It struck Slash hard on the temple with a crack, dropping him at the MP's polished boots. McPhee looked down and casually spit a stream of tobacco juice, striking the groaning convict in the face, then he was dragged off by two smiling MP's.

"Corporal throw this Recruit into the tank for the night. I want him on Defaulter's Parade at 23:00 hours." McPhee tapped Slash on his skull with his baton as he groaned at his feet. "Yes Sarge." The tall Corporal kicked Slash to his feet and half dragged him off the parade ground, jamming his baton into his back to urge him on. "Now then anybody else? No? Good. It's time for your morning run. Corporal Rivera take them for a stroll. You have two hours. Have them back at barracks for 09:00 O.K.?"

Corporal Rivera, unknown to the slouching convicts, was a long time marathon runner, whose specialty was the Iron Man competition, a 25-mile grueling march in full gear over rolling, challenging terrain. He was transferred to the new Force X (on loan) as a training NCO from U. S. Special Forces. Today he would take the recruit platoon on a shortened version of that, but for the unseasoned convicts, it would be a good test. "Platoon! Attention! Right turn. Quick March....breaking into double time, Double Time!"

The convicts cursed as they stumbled into a jogging trot, tripping over their ungainly, brand new, unbroken combat boots as they headed for the exit to the camp, into the forested training area to the south. It was humid and the sun soon beat down on them as they chugged puffing along an endless trail through the thick woods. It was nothing like prison they thought. The most they saw of the world was the Exercise yard for a few hours a day. Their biggest worry there was how to score a joint, or a pack of cigarettes. Three meals a day and a cot, all paid by Joe Taxpayer. An hour later, they were running, breathless, stumbling blindly up a steep slope. Some cried, other swore viciously, some fell in the dirt begging for mercy which never came.

Several out of shape convicts dropped out and retched along the trail. Guards escorting them, armed to the teeth, soon 'encouraged' them back into formation, with swings of their clubs and booted feet. "C'mon you fucking Swine! Move your Ass!" Rivera stood at the top of the hill, having arrived there ten minutes before the first convict. He was not even sweating as he pulled out his smokes from his cam pocket and lit up a tube. His dark eyes narrowed as the first convict reached the summit. Jack McGee gasped as he stopped before Rivera, eying his smoke and smiling. "Good work McGee. Hit the ground and give me 50!" Convict McGee shouted "Corporal!" His body hardened from years of previous service with US Airborne didn't hesitate. He knew the consequences. He counted off each push-up loudly as Sean McGinn reached the summit next and soon joined his newest running mate. "So join the Army. See the world!" He grinned at Rivera. One by one over the next half hour the rest of the Platoon reached the summit. A few were half- conscious as they were dragged along by their platoon mates, or kicked before the baton wielding MP Instructors.

"What a sorry fucking lot y'all are! You make me want to puke! But don't y'all worry none. I am just getting started with you! And remember this. There is no quitting this place. The only way out is feet first, get it? Right ladies, left turn, Quick March...Double time!" An hour later, just before 09:00 AM as Sergeant McPhee had instructed, the recruit platoon arrived back at barracks. An ambulance was also there waiting. Three convicts were loaded into the back,

Officers decided to have an official regular burial parade every time a convict perished. As the ranks thinned in 1st Platoon Force X, new replacements kept arriving to take the place of the deceased convicts. Slowly Colonel Mann and his men whipped the fledging unit into shape. But he was losing his patience, for it was closing on a decade now since he had started this experiment. "I am going to the General tomorrow. We need to offer these guys something. Have any ideas?" The Canadian Major looked thoughtfully at his boss. "How about a bullet to end it all Sir."

The first big parade was after the first live fire Exercise on the Ranges. By now they were training with real weapons and live ammo. "These guys are dangerous, as much to themselves as the enemy, if they live that long." Colonel Mann said tersely to Major Van Zandt near the third week of Boot Camp. By now the weakest, infirm and unmotivated were gone, leaving a small group of more dedicated, hardened convict recruits.

"Yes Sir. And today is their first day on the Ranges. Live fire. Any special instructions Sir?"

"Let's see Eddie. Make sure the MP's are ready for anything. And are my two Seal Snipers ready to go?" The Major nodded smiling at the tall handsome Colonel. The SEAL snipers, were expert marksmen, told to fire on those convicts who fired on anything other than the assigned range targets, Figure 11 targets 200 meters away.

"Yes. A little extra live training can't hurt can it? Let's just keep the collateral damage down right?" That day Recruit Lukas, a psychopathic killer opened up on his training section, killing three and wounding two. Jack killed him by shooting him through the back of his steel helmet, splattering his brains over the grass. The two SEAL snipers took their fingers off their triggers as all watched Jack standing over Lukas's blood spattered body. The burial ceremony that week was the biggest, with ten bodies dumped unceremoniously into the neatly dug graves, wrapped in their GI issue ponchos. The convicts looked on silently during the burial ceremony, as they stood like statues in their ranks. After the Unit Padre had concluded the brief ceremony the convicts were dismissed. They stood in huddled groups, talking in low tones as cigarettes were passed around.

"Well fellahs, worms got to eat too eh?" Recruit Maggot chuckled happily as he shoveled dirt into the hole before him. The others watched him silently, all wondering when it would be their turn. That week Jack held a meeting with a few trusted platoon mates. Friday night, they moved to sort out a few of the worst bad apples in their barracks. One Convict recruit Freddie Berezow they found out was a pedophile from Toronto. As two burly privates pinned the man to his cot, Jack kneed him in the gut, pressing his weight down. He heard the man gasping for air as Jack squeezed his throat in one hand. Jack held the garrote in his hands as he bent over him.

"So yer like little children, eh Berezow? Well I'm doing y'all a favor. You don't have to worry about combat, or suffering through this training. It is meant for us real grunts. No my friend, your time is up. Say yer prayers if y'all know one, you dumb fucker." Jack wrapped the garrote wire around the man's thin neck, then reefed hard.

He watched emotionless as Fred's tongue shot out of his gaping mouth. "Hold tight lads, I think old Freddie isn't ready to depart our platoon yet. Stop struggling and I will allow you to die quickly Berezow." He continued to struggle however, till slowly Jack choked the life out of him. When Jack stood over the lifeless body, he kicked it viciously. "OK boys string up the son of a bitch for the meatheads to take care of."

The duty NCO found the dangling body in the washroom the next morning. Corporal MCBurnie lit up a cigarette as he surveyed the body, Berezow's eyes bulging from their sockets, his dead corpse dangling from the overhead light by a rope. McBurnie saw the belt secured around the convict's neck and a stool beside his feet.

"Good! Private Berezow. About bloody time, ya fucking pig." He aimed a roundhouse kick at the corpse, sending it spinning off to the side, bouncing off the sides of the shitter walls. Then laughing quietly, he finished his smoke and went off to the Duty office to report the unfortunate accident. Sergeant Flood smiled grimly as McBurnie reported in. "Found one in the shitter dead Sarge. Private Berezow. What do I do about it?"

"Here ya go Buddy. Fill it out and drop it off at the MP Shack." The Corporal nodded, grabbed the Incident Report form and stamped off. McBurnie scribbled on the report over a coffee in the mess, before handing it in. The US M.P.s did the required investigation, reporting weeks later that it was a confirmed suicide.

Nearing the end of the first month the Force X recruits began their first field exercise. Marching out into the training area at the crack of dawn, the Force X platoons led by their Officer and MP Sergeant separated after ten miles. "When we get there we will do a little digging. This is a defensive exercise." The MP Sergeant yelled as the convicts trudged along in the heavy rain, grumbling the whole way. After another five miles of struggling through thick brush, swatting mosquitoes and sweating profusely, the MP Sergeant called a halt. Explaining the basics of a defensive exercise, each pair of convicts was allotted a spot. "OK soldiers. A slit trench protects you while you are holding a position. You may be shelled, shot at, bombed or have tanks coming at you trying to crush you like a bug. First stage is to dig low enough, that your body is below the ground, about 1 to 2 feet. Then it is gradually lengthened and deepened to 4 to five feet deep. If time permits it becomes an L- trench. One half is covered with tin or branches to cover it. This is your overhead protection. OK shovels out, you have 30 minutes."

The convicts stared dumbly at each other, as Jack took out his entrenching tool. "Start digging fellahs. The trench is not going to dig itself." Colonel Mann and his HQ visited the training area as the platoons began to dig in. Lt. Munroe checked his watch as he supervised Jack's 1st Platoon. After half an hour he blew his whistle. The convicts gasped sweating as they stood over their holes. "Listen up. Lie inside your holes. Live rounds will be fired over your positions in one minute." Fear showed on their faces as they dived head first inside their pits. A minute later on the dot, Lt. Munroe nodded to Sergeant Foote. The MP Sergeant cocked his rifle and sent live rounds skimming over the convict's heads. Dirt flew in the air as the cowering recruits dug their fingers into the ground, desperately grinding their faces into the mud. After a few minutes the whistles blew again. "Clear! OK men start digging. In one hour an enemy tank will drive through your position. By then you should be down at least four feet, or I will be sending a telegram to your family." Jack smiled at Sean beside him in the trench. "Ha that old trick eh? Watch these fuckers dig now!" The convicts were all business now, adrenaline and fear driving their bodies, dirt flung high above their heads as they desperately dug to save their lives. It was mid morning when the whistles blew. Officers and NCO's yelled. "OK stop! Every body down! Tank attack."

The convicts leapt inside their trenches, as the sound of engines approached through the trees. Jack peered over his trench while he crouched next to McGinn. Two Stryker armoured vehicles broke the treeline ahead, followed by a huge, lumbering M-1 Abrams heavy tank. He felt the ground shake as the three vehicles approached slowly. On top of the heavy tank stood Colonel Mann, smiling down at Lt. Munroe and his convicts.

"Your boys ready Lieutenant?" Munroe nodded and waved him forward casually. Mann directed the driver as the first Stryker armoured vehicle rolled over the first trench. They heard the screams of terror as dirt and diesel fumes sprayed down on the crouching convicts. One by one the vehicles rolled over the mounds of dirt. Afterward the Officer and MP Sergeant went to inspect the position. For a minute they were not sure if any had survived. Colonel Mann jumped off the Abrams tank and strode back to the Lieutenant. "Well Lieutenant? How are your men?" Munroe looked down at a trench, with a body lying in the bottom.

"Three passed out, five shat themselves. Recruits McGinn and McGee are having a smoke sir." Mann laughed and patted the young Lieutenant's back. "Carry on Mr. Munroe. I have another platoon waiting."

One man who had carelessly tossed his cigarette beside his trench, got on the MP Sergeant's wrong side. Ordered to bury it at the bottom of his trench, he was told not to stop until the Sergeant was satisfied. Twenty- four hours later, the unlucky convict had to be hoisted out of the 20-foot hole by a rope. As his fellow convicts hauled out the sweat lathered, dirt covered recruit, the Sergeant handed him his cigarette butt. "OK Private burry it." As the others watched the private filled in the deep pit for the next hour. Then hoisting on their packs they force marched back to barracks. Colonel Mann was pleased as he watched them march back to base.

The next week, October 7, Force X went on parachute training at CFB Edmonton. After the three-week Para course, they would be flown further North for Arctic Orientation training. For almost all of the criminals, this was breaking new ground...or in this case, Ice and freezing sub-zero temperatures! At the same time as Jack McGee's platoon started its jump training, other Convict platoons were being formed and starting their crash course in Army basic "boot camp" training. Freddie "Ace," Sean, Jack, Slash and Maggot were smoking outside their barracks that evening. They watched with smirks as the new convict recruits went running by. "Ha! Look at them assholes! Pick up the pace ya fucking pile of shit!" Maggot cursed, taunting the convicts as they glared at him. The watching group of older convicts smiled silently, recalling their own initiation over the previous month.

"Ya we're through that crap boys. But this show is just about to begin. I wonder how many of us will be left when it's all over?" The five convicts looked darkly at each other, knowing that they were condemned men, about to enter the jaws of Hades. Jack whispered, "We are a band- of- brothers fellahs. We stick together, cover for each other and we will make it through hell or high water." As they walked to their barracks though he wondered if he was being overly optimistic. Jack felt a chill go up his spine, then took a last drag on his Camel before crushing it with his combat boot.

After a shower he retired early for once, for he knew the future looked bleak.

November 2, 2014: Jack's platoon was in the final jump phase of their basic parachute course. By now the platoon had been whittled down to 18 men. The Instructors, veteran paratroopers drawn from Canada and U.S. Parachute units, were relentless and uncompromising in enforcing Airborne standards. Several of the convicts had failed the PT test. Thirty sit-ups, 10 chin-ups and a timed speed run of 5 kilometers. Failures were removed and placed in new platoons to repeat their basic training. One convict, faced by repeating Hell week, committed suicide, hanging himself with his belt in the barracks washroom that night. Another was shot by MP's trying to scale the barb wire fence surrounding the barracks compound. His blood spattered body was left to hang from the wire over the next day. As each platoon was formed up for the morning run, they were marched by the dead convict's corpse, to observe what happened if they tried to escape.

Jack completed all the required jumps by Friday, November 6. Three of his platoon had been killed during the week, some had panicked after having partial malfunctions in their chutes. They had exited out of the Hercules transports at 1000 feet. As they struggled to cut away their malfunctioning main chute, the panicked recruits froze as they plummeted to Earth, which rose like an express elevator toward them. Jack had watched as the last screaming, terrified convict had pulled his reserve finally...

too late. The white reserve chute opened at 100 feet above the ground, the body bounced off the DZ turf as his chute finally inflated, then drifted down slowly to cover the dead convict's body lying on the hard turf...like a burial shroud.

Finally, later that afternoon, Jack and the rest of his platoon of fifteen men stood at attention as they were handed their Jump wings by Colonel Mann himself, "Well done Trooper McGee! Y'all done well, so far." For Jack, it was the first step, to returning to Eliza and the world.

"Thank-you Sir!" Jack smiled as he looked down at the gleaming wings pinned to his camouflage shirt. He knew he had passed the first phase, now he was a paratrooper again. It was one thing he was a natural at and once more he had regained a bit of his former pride. His fellow 'brothers in arms' beamed at each other beside him. They were mainly new to this, and soon Jack was seen as their mentor and leader. This was not lost on Colonel Mann and his officers, for they needed leaders for this new unit.

In December, Jack McGee was promoted to Acting Platoon Sergeant of his platoon. It was now designated as Pathfinder/Recce Platoon. At the time it was about half strength, above average convicts were taken from other platoons after completing their Basic Para courses to make up their strength. By now they were taking their advanced Freefall course. For they were told, as Pathfinder/ Recce Platoon they were the elite of Force X, first in, last out in combat. As such they had to be tougher and meaner than the rest of Force X.

"Combat eh? Just what does that mean Jack? The screws are kidding us right?" A young convict quizzed that night. The others in the barracks lounging on their cots listened up intent for once as Jack spoke at last.

"Don't rightly know Son. Combat to me means we are going to war though. That means real shooting, killing and dying. Why do ya think they gave us these pretty uniforms? And these past weeks are not for our personal fun. My advice son, except you are already a dead man, then you can function effectively as a soldier. As the old gladiators used to say, ultimately we are all dead men. But we can choose how we die, standing on our feet as men, instead of dangling by our necks and crying like little babies!" It was little consolation for the young recruit though. He sobbed himself to sleep, thinking of his mother who had cried when he went to jail.

Dec. 2014: The next month, Jack's platoon finished their freefall training. Like all their training, everything was rushed. Normally months long, their pathfinder course was crammed into a few weeks and led to numerous failures, accidents, injuries and fatalities. When Jack and his convict brothers finally received their Pathfinder badges, twelve smiling, hardened faces, still camouflaged from the final exercise looked at each other. Colonel Mann was pleased for finally he had his first unit, the elite Pathfinder Platoon virtually ready for its first mission overseas. His U. S. Army superiors, Pentagon General Staff Officers, Intelligence men from CIA and their political masters were already debating on when and how to use this new Force X. For a new war in the Middle East was looming against the new guy on the block, the Islamic State, ISIS or ISIL. Islamic hard-line terrorists in Iraq and Syria who had carved out chunks of territory, moving into the power vacuum as civil war erupted. Originally they evolved as a branch of Al Queda in Iraq, then split off becoming more extremist.

Col. Mann cleared his throat finally addressing his Force Staff. "OK Eddie, I think we need to throw our Pathfinder Platoon a bone, pardon the pun." Major Eddie van Zandt, his ranking Canadian officer and Exec Officer chuckled at the CO's jest. "Agreed Colonel, what do you suggest Sir?"

"C'mon Eddie, we're old soldiers. What do you get on graduation...drunk? We'll watch them closely of course, sealed in the compound. They can get stinking drunk, fights that we will not know about? And... ahem...a few ladies of the night who do not hold high moral views of our new heroes?"

Many of the HQ staff stared at the Colonel and laughed. He had to be joking, reward a bunch of scum condemned by their country? But no one dared to object when Colonel Mann asked for comments. The head shrink asked for his opinion shrugged. "You are the boss Colonel Mann sir. I suggest these ones be left out though." Mann took the list of the worst psychos from the unit psychologist, handing it to Eddie.

"Sir! I'll have the Sergeant Major organize a little grad party for our Heroes. Least they deserve before the next phase." The Colonel and his officers relaxed in the O's Mess, downing a few Scotch shooters, as they looked over the next planned phase, *Operation Ice cube*...training in Canada's high Arctic. As the Colonel outlined the basic plan over a map of the training area, the assembled group of officers peered intently over Colonel Mann's shoulder. First in would be the Pathfinders, they would freefall in at night in a HALO jump. At this point the officers raised eyebrows and gasped. They argued back and forth till Lt. Greene spoke.

"Sir, with all respect. These guys, convicts in cells a few months ago, are being asked to perform a highly dangerous, and militarily advanced mission...in a frozen wasteland?" Mann looked serious for once at the young platoon officer of the Pathfinders. He held up his hand like a school teacher with unruly kids.

"No Lieutenant. They are not, repeat not, being asked anything. They are ordered to do it. Any refusal will be dealt with harshly understand? Refusal in war means death, and mark me gentlemen we are now at war with our new enemy, these ISIS bastards. The Islamic State as they call it. Since 2014 they have carved out captured territory in Northern Iraq and Syria. Both countries have been unable to stop them. They have captured vehicles and arms from panicked Iraqi and Syrian units. In the process they have attracted recruits from both countries. It is a snowballing effect, the Middle East is unstable as usual, but now their tentacles are spreading to Europe and across the world. Recruits have joined from all over the Arab world, lately from Western nations, including the U.S. and Canada. To win we need these men, these convicts trained, and ready to die if needs be. Do I make myself clear? By the way, if you want to quit there is the door. I don't want any shrinking violets here. Does everybody get it?" The room went silent for a minute as the Officers absorbed the Colonel's lecture. The assembled officers eyed one another, then back at the steely eyed C.O. "Yes Sir!" The small group of officers finally replied together. Colonel Mann nodded satisfied as he lit his cigar.

Meanwhile in the barracks of the Pathfinder platoon, later that evening, the men were celebrating their graduation. They were supplied with tables of booze and a feast of the best food they had seen in years. A barbeque was set up on the rear deck, soon the cook had the steaks started as the convicts attacked the first liquor they had seen in months. It was unexpected and for many all the better.

"Dig in you layabouts!" Maggot roared as he opened a bottle of tequila and took a long swig of the strong liquor. The others laughed and dived in, soon singing lurid Army songs they had learned over their basic training. The convicts lined up as the cook called out. "Steaks ready guys. Help yourself to the fixings, potatoes, salad and ice cream." After the feast was over an hour later, the Military Police (or meatheads as the soldiers termed them) entered escorting a dozen women. The barracks went silent as the women and convicts stared at each other. Sean and Jack looked at each other, slapping each other on the back. It was getting better by the minute they whispered. "Three cheers for the CO lads!" Jack roared, raising his glass of Jägermeister. The convicts thought about this, then nodded and raised their glasses as one. It was a ground breaking moment for Force X. For the Colonel had gambled and won. By allowing the convicts a night of R&R, he accomplished what the previous decade had not. Force X came together that night, jelling into a unit which would go into combat soon, carving out a reputation the world would come to know.

Jack smirked as he looked over his glass of Jaeger at two of the female guests. They were both tall redheaded Irish girls, dressed in tight fitting nurse's uniforms. The two women returned his look boldly, slowly they smiled at the convict soldier. Jack thought of Liza back home, then back at the two smiling redheads.

The room was dead quiet for what seemed an eternity, as the convicts and their guests, a group of recruited local women eyed each other. The men dressed in their dusty, stained camouflage fatigues stared in drunken, undisguised lust, nudging each other and stifling giggles and dirty jokes. The dozen odd women, mostly hired prostitutes and Escorts gaped in stupefied looks bordering stunned disbelief at the lean, hard faces of their clientele. The Pathfinders were momentarily dumb struck, not having seen women for a long time. "OK you guys. The Colonel has told us you have till first light to enjoys these ah… Ladies' hospitality. We'll be outside so don't go anywhere too far. Or try anything funny. Reveille at 06:00 tomorrow. Enjoy your night, soldiers. It'll be your last for a while!" Jack moved first, rushing to the two nurses. "Hi I'm Jack!" They smiled as he looked at them. "Hi Jack! I'm Cyntia, this is my sister Cybilla."

"Greetings Cynthia and Cybilla! Welcome to Pathfinder Platoon. I will be your guide. First I think you need a drink." The sisters grinned at him then followed him to the makeshift bar arm in arm. Later Jack retired to a room with the two statuesque red headed sisters. One convict, an ex-biker nick named *The Hog* played a guitar, as slowly one by one the convicts paired off with the other women. They were handed drinks and after conversing a bit, started dancing reservedly as The Hog strummed a tune amidst shots of liquor.

Freddie strolled up to one of the women. She had her back to him as Freddie tapped her shoulder. The tall blonde turned and gaped wide eyed at Freddie. "Oh my God! Look Jackie, it's Freddie." Both of the women were wearing skin tight mini skirts, low cut sport tops, dark stockings and high heels. "Hi Michelle and Jackie! So good to see you again." The two women flashed smiles at him then rushed forward into his arms. The other convicts watched as Freddie embraced the two foxes. "So tell me girls, how did you end up here?"

"Well we started up our own business Freddie. A Private Escort Service, started with our former boss's seed money. We want to thank you for what you did. Jackie and I have escaped the Hell we were in. The others have joined us; we have six of them here tonight. "Freddie nodded as he took a swig of ale from his mug.

"Hey let's have a seat and get caught up." Michelle and Jackie were guided to a table, Freddie slipping an arm around each of their waists to protect them from the leering convicts around them. As the night wore on, Freddie got the news from the two escorts. "You might as well know Michelle and Jackie. This is a top secret army outfit, all convicts like me. Soon the flap is, we are going to fight somewhere. So tonight I want to get to know you better. That first night I was out of my head. Barely remember anything at all!" He took Michelle to the dance floor as a song by *Alice in Chains*, The Rooster began, the stereo system set up and operated by a couple of Michelle's escorts. Freddie hugged Michelle tight as he hummed along with his date.

"I love this song Michelle, Rooster! So fitting isn't it? A guy off to war somewhere. They haven't found a way to kill me yet." Michelle nodded to the younger man, tossing her thick mane of blonde hair. At 42 she was experienced with the 'rough trade'. Since Freddie had helped her to escape the seedier part of prostitution, she had cleaned up her act, helping Jackie and the others to join her. Her Escort service called M&J's Escorts was established, restricting their clients to only the most financially gifted. She was now approaching millionaire status. Hearing of the sudden offer by the Military by coincidence, she volunteered her ladies for a negotiated group price. "It will probably be my only chance to serve the country eh sweetie?"

Freddie laughed as he held her tight as they danced, then Sean joined them with Jackie in hand. Jackie the statuesque brunette who was Michelle's partner and BBF, smoothly slid into the dance as Sean embraced her. "Hi Honey. I am Jackie." Sean smiled as their eyes observed each other up close. They lost themselves in the dance as others packed the dance floor now. Sean who was recently divorced, found he was falling for this busty 41-year-old. She was good looking and obviously had taken care of herself. She looked very fit, with her tailored clothes speaking of the hidden secrets within. "Hey let's go for a walk." Jackie touched her nose to his cheek, then her tongue licked him. "My thoughts exactly Sean." Slipping out to the rear yard, Sean sat with her at a bench in the fenced off rear yard. He shared a bottle of bubbly with Jackie as they chatted for the next hour. He felt a sudden urge for her as they bonded. He whispered in her ear finally.

"Say when I get out of this mess, can I talk to you again? Or are you taken?" Jackie smiled as she sipped her bubbly. 'As a matter of fact, I am single as of today. Sure I would love to see you again Hon!" Then Sean the convict soldier and Jackie the escort embraced and kissed. It was a long one, for that brief time he was removed from his violent world, in the arms of a real woman.

As Jackie went off to check on her young escorts, Sean peered over his shoulder at the two red headed nurses, the two women smiling at them at the end of the table. He nodded and picked up his mug as he stood up and slapped

Jack on his shoulder. "Right you are Jack. I think we should socialize!" Jack that night put aside his thoughts of home and Liza. For with Cyntia and Sibylla close at hand, it was easy. That evening Jack and Sean continued to jell, establishing themselves informally as the platoon leaders, punishing the liquor and the two nurses for hours. "Hey ladies! Mind if we join you?"

"Jack of course. Sit down, and who is your friend?" Cyntia flashed a smile at Jack before turning her green eyes on Sean. "This is my comrade in arms Sean. Meet Cyntia and Sibylla." After taking her offered hand and kissing her painted fingernails the two sisters laughed. The ice broken, they chatted as more convicts got up dancing. "Would you like a dance Cyntia?" Sean stood up and escorted the red head to the floor.

After the dance he was pulled aside by Jackie. "You are not getting away from that easy Mister." Then they laughed embracing on the dance floor as the red headed nurse rejoined Jack and Sibylla. Later inside the dark bedroom, Jack smiled as the two red headed nurses lap danced before him. He cheered them on as the sisters unzipped each other's uniforms and stepped out of them. They stood before him in black leather lingerie as Jack leaned back on the bed, smiling up at them. "Nice! So would you girls like to take a knee?" Cyntia and Sibylla nodded and sat on his knees as he poured them a fresh glass of wine. "Cheers ladies!" He touched his glass to theirs, then they drained them, Jack reaching for the bottle again. "Jack would you like us to finish our dance for you?" The sisters chimed together, their lips pouting at him.

Jack looked in her big green eyes, stroking her red flaming hair. "Shit I must be dreaming. Sure but you don't have to get up sweet heart." Cyntia kissed him then, beginning to writhe and grind herself against him. Her sister did likewise on his other knee. Slowly articles of clothing dropped to the floor, studded leather bras, skimpy red thongs, till finally Jack fell back on the bed, as the two sisters climbed on top of him. He laughed as they pinned his arms, their naked breasts pressed hard into his chest. "Surrender to us Jack! We are unbeaten Cybilla!" They told him of their other claim to fame. They were the WWF women's tag team known as *The Naughty Nurses*. Jack held up two fingers, in the Gladiator plea for mercy. Cyntia and Sibylla sat up over him, bouncing on his body, then raising their arms in the air in triumph, then hugged each other.

"I have never been so fucking turned on girls!" As the two naked sisters laughed hysterically on top, he lit up a smoke and leaned back with a contented smile. "Thanks Colonel. I owe this to myself. Forgive me Liza." Soon the bedsprings squeaked as the three enjoyed the long night ahead. After midnight, Jack emerged from the bedroom elated and drained. He led the two grinning sisters, slightly disheveled in their uniforms hand in hand from the room. His mate Freddie led his girl, Michelle into the vacated bedroom. Jack and his platoon and their new friends got blind drunk over the next few hours as the convicts enjoyed a rare night off. Cyntia made the rounds before ending up with Jack again. He led her into a vacated side room for some privacy, finally emerging with her an hour later. Cyntia lounged drunkenly in his arm as they danced to a Rock ballad by Metallica, *The Unforgotten*.

"Will I be forgotten Jackie?" She giggled as she lay her face against his. Forgetting his worries, he consoled the young foxy beauty. "Baby how can I forget you?" He lied as he ran his hands down her curved spine. She leaned forward in his arms, kissing and licking his ear as they danced slowly and erotically. Jack was in the zone he thought drunkenly, as the red head raised one thigh along his leg, teasing him as her fingernails stroked his neck, then circled around his back. She had climbed up his side as Jack walked back to his table, searching for a fresh bottle as Cyntia held onto him for dear life.

Jack looked at his watch as he weaved through the crowd of inebriated convicts and ladies of the evening. He still held Cyntia in one arm, the now inebriated nurse would have dropped if he had not supported her. He sat down and finished another shot of Jaeger as Cyntia tumbled into his lap. "Soldier pour me a drink." Jack smiled as she giggled drunkenly at him, then planted a kiss on his mouth. A minute later he noticed Cyntia had passed out while they had been kissing. He got up and finding her sister Sibylla nearby, took off outside to get them some air. Many men would have taken advantage of the two young girls. But Jack still had morals. After reviving Cyntia he made it his mission to serve as their personal escort for the rest of the evening. As the dawn approached Jack was sill outside with the nursing sisters. By now both had drifted off to sleep, sitting once more in the convict's protective embrace.

It was 04:00 A.M. as Sean grabbed a bottle of Jack Daniels and sauntered outside with Jackie grabbing his hand. He sat down beside fellow convict Jack. Jackie squirmed next to Sean as he opened the bottle and poured himself and the table a glass. "How's the night going?" The convict beside him was swigging on a mug of beer, apparently unware of his presence. "Heh buddy! Are yah still breathing?"

Jack unaware of Sean, grunted as the convict dug him in the ribs. "Piss off shit head." Seconds later they were locked in a wrestling match on the floor, as the revived nursing twins and Jackie circled them hooting and cheering. It was a wickedly short fight, but brutal as they punched each other several times, ending with both men bruised and bloodied. The crowd who had joined in, returned to the festivities as Jack sat down at the table once more. He gripped the JD bottle and took a swig of the fiery liquor. The other convict sat across from him wiping blood from his mouth. "Here mate! This will fix yer yap." Sean reached out and took it, holding it to his mouth he took a long swig. "Thanks Jack! You sure are a buddy." Jack explained to the puzzled women who could not understand how the two who had just fought, could sit down and drink like nothing had happened. "Sweetheart! You thought this was the first time we ever danced? Heck we go way back." Then they explained their first fight months before. The three women laughed as the two soldiers shared their war story with them. "I just didn't care for the way he looked at me."

Jack McGee laughed. "So I said, I'm from Kentucky. You a Canuck?" Sean replied, "Ontario Yank. You know the Ottawa Valley?" Jack shook his shaved head, rubbing the new scar from his recent skirmish. "It sounds as if we have something in common. Irish grunts!" After the scrap the soldiers returned to drinking, telling the women this is how soldiers get to know each other quickly. Sean smiled slowly then clinked his glass on Jack's. They chugged down the whiskey before slamming their glasses on the table. The glasses were refilled by Jack till finally the bottle was drained, the two convicts deep in conversation.

"I served my years in the Canadian infantry. I made one mistake in my life. I killed my Company Sergeant major. And let someone see me do it." Jack nodded as he sipped on his JD, letting the fiery liquor explore his insides. "I imagine you had your reasons. We will discuss it later perhaps. Ah there they are the nursing staff here to rescue us. Hey enough shop talk for now buddy. Here Cyntia and Sibylla take a knee."

Finally, it was dawn, the barracks room went quiet. Jack lay asleep on the couch after ensuring all the JD was gone. Cyntia lay beside him, her nursing outfit long gone. Likewise, her sister lay over Sean as he slept soundly, her long stockinged legs dangling off his thighs. The next morning, which broke a few hours after the booze was drained, most of the women were dragged out half-conscious by the waiting MP's.

The convicts of Pathfinder platoon were formed up outside, still blind drunk and singing filthy X- rated army songs. They cheered wildly as Jack and Sean carried the two comatose, twin nurses in their arms to the waiting bus. The last women to climb on the bus where Michelle and Jackie. Freddie embraced the blonde escort as Sean said good-bye to his newest sweetheart Jackie. They whispered promises of seeing each other again. Then they kissed good-bye. The two convicts helped their dates on the bus, then waved a farewell. Michelle and Jackie stuck their heads out open windows blowing their lovers kisses. Badgered by the MP's, the two close friends handed up the limp bodies of the nursing sisters to waiting hands inside the bus. Slowly their half dressed bodies were hauled inside, leaving their legs poking out the window as the bus rolled off to the camp gates. "Bye-Bye ladies! Thanks for the entertainment!"

Dec. 26: Escape & Evasion Exercise: Colonel Mann was fairly satisfied with the recent progress of Force X. With a brief pause for Christmas and Boxing Day, he reviewed material he had gathered on the latest Special Forces training. He looked through his notes on *"The World's Best."* At the top of the list was the SAS.[3] U.K. 22 SAS Regiment were the elite of Special Forces, setting the standard.

---

[3] SAS: 22 SAS Regiment, U.K. Elite Special Forces from SAS; The World's Best, author Peter Darman

Selection training: At Sterling Lines camp. Four-week course includes hill walking (humping rucksack up mountains); navigation, physical training, marches and classwork. Test week: six hill exercises in Ellan Valley and Brecon Beacons, Wales, culminating in a 64 kilometer endurance march. Weight carried is 20-25 kg. plus personal weapons. Continuation training: (14 weeks): students are taught signalling, demolitions, combat medicine and survival skills. Ends with Escape & Evasion and RTI ex.

Strength: 4 Squadrons in Regiment: unknown but estimate 800.

Canada: Canadian Special Service Force: A brigade sized force based in Ontario, 3000 soldiers. Most are trained in airmobile, parachute and commando qualifications. Includes The Canadian Airborne Regiment; 1st Battalion RCR; Royal Canadian Dragoons (armoured); 2 RCHA (artillery) including E Battery attached to Airborne Battle Group; 2nd Combat Engineer Regiment; 427 Tactical Helicopter Sqn.

Airborne Indoctrination Course: 2 weeks of intensive selection training on posting to Regiment. Failures- (are RTU back to home unit). At the end of final exercise and forced march to base (10 km) the Airborne coin is awarded to the graduate students on parade in CFB Petawawa. [4] Canadian Airborne Selection: 6-12 months: basic infantry and weapons skills training; Basic Parachute course (3

---

[4] The author went through this in 1984 as a member of 3 Commando, still has Airborne coin from that day

weeks in Edmonton); failures go to other units of SSF (not the Airborne Regiment). Commando Course: Advanced training (2 -3 months): emphasis on speed and endurance with long forced marches and assault courses, followed by mountain and arctic warfare training and exercises in Northern Canada/Arctic. Advanced training: Helicopter drills, tactical parachuting, small unit tactics, patrolling, navigation, field medicine, arctic/forest survival, escape & evasion exercises. Volunteers go to elite 42- man Pathfinder Platoon: Reconnaissance Platoon is trained in HAHO/ HALO freefall parachuting, small boat, submarine insertion, Counter-terrorism operations.

3: French Foreign Legion: French Special Forces Elite: 8500 personnel: Selection: three months: Drill, inspections, marches. 1st month: 10- km. in full kit. Wk. 2: 15- km. Wk.3: 20- km. Wk. 4: 60- km.

Second month: weapons training, drill, forced marches, obstacle courses, 500- meter course in under 5 minutes. Third month: mountain and winter warfare training; Test: 200 km march in four days with full kit.

2nd REP: Pass para-commando course (parachute, close quarter battle training, endurance marches, signals, Reconnaissance/Deep navigation, demolitions, small boats, jungle, mountain training)

Reconnaissance & Deep Action Commandos: Selection classified.

4: Joint Task Force (JTF) Commando, Canada: (Replaced SSF in 1990's): Selection training: Classified

(Here Mann put red lines under the training of this Elite Regiment). Mann used these three units as the basis of Force X's continuation training and selection. He knew of US Special Forces of course, US Green Berets, US Navy Seals, US Rangers. Apart from the emphasis on underwater and small boat training, counter-terrorism, the advanced training was similar to the first three. Mann was a realist, it would be foolish of him to try and match these elite unit's skill and élan, gained by decades of experience. It had taken him a decade to put together Force X and still they were not ready for combat. So late in December, he issued orders for the first of many advanced courses.

Pathfinder Platoon was the first selected for the Escape & Evasion survival course. It was planned carefully by Major van Zandt, who had participated in this course as a SSF paratrooper. It was 1-2 weeks long and the students were broken down into small 3-4 man units. In a typical scenario, the unsuspecting soldiers were duped into thinking they were being inspected after a field winter exercise. After the CO of the unit, would tell the men they would be undergoing selection for courses coming up. Inside a side room, the men went in, then were jumped by waiting course staff. Tied up and blind folded, they were forced to wait in a room on their bellies for an hour or so. As they found out, resistance was futile, there was no escape.

Sean McGinn was the last one to be brought in. Two big MP's surprised him from behind and over powered him. Before he knew it, he was lying on the floor next to

Jack. After an unsuccessful attempt to escape, sandbags were placed over their heads. The prisoners were in shock. What the hell was happening? Some thought the unit was being disbanded and the convicts being sent back to their cells. Sean and Jack gasped under their sandbags, as the hated MP's poured water over them, almost suffocating them in the process. Finally, the Platoon Officer came to brief them.

"Pathfinder Platoon, welcome to the Escape & Evasion course. This is advanced selection training for the unit. Failure means you will be assigned other duties in the Regiment. Listen to these rules: There will be no escape prematurely so do not try. If you do and are caught, you will go straight into the slammer for the duration of this exercise, a maximum of two weeks. We will equip you for winter survival, issue you with Arctic gear, two weeks of hard rations, a compass and a pack of matches for each four-man unit. You will be transported to Wainwright Base in Alberta. You will have to basically walk about 300 kilometers to get to the final check point undetected. Everyone you see will be your enemy. If spotted do not try and run, there is no escape. You will be locked up in an MP cell for the duration of the course. You may undergo interrogation and torture, for this is what happens if your real enemy catches you. You will be watched closely as to how you behave, divulging information means you have been broken and automatic failure and rejected from the Platoon." Lieutenant Greene looked down at the convicts lying on the floor as the guards removed the sandbags.

The convicts gasped in shock as the officer went on. Forbidden was to break ay civilian laws, stay within a narrow 100- meter corridor while marching on the co-ordinates provided, testing them on navigation as well as survival skills in the dead of winter. There would be no weapons or shelters provided, no stoves or lights. In other words, they would be treated as escaped prisoners and hunted down ruthlessly. After Lieutenant Greene's briefing, they were released from their bindings and issued their winter gear. Each was frisked by MP's, ensuring they had no weapons or personal items hidden away. Then they were loaded onto 5- ton trucks and driven to Wainwright from Edmonton. It was cold as Jack and three others from his team were let out on a road deep inside the huge base. Jack watched the truck roar down the road, as the other convicts stared about them at the white wilderness about them. "OK guys, lets get off the road and we will have a talk." Off in the woods the four convicts debated how to go about this surprise training course.

"First we have a meal. I will do the navigating if there are no objections?" The others, Freddie, Maggot and Hog-Man nodded sullenly as they got their hard rations out. They built a small fire as Jack checked the map he was given and orientated to the ground with his compass. "OK boys, we should be about here. We have to get here in two weeks. So strict rationing. We use snow and ice to make water. We have to move fast, about 25 to 30 km.'s a day. Any questions?" They shook their heads as the fire heated their rations. A half hour later they began to slog through the snow along the road. It was march or croak Jack thought grimly. "Merry fucking Christmas!" The convicts cursed as they plodded along, with -40-degree C wind chill winds whipping their arctic parkas. Hours later they arrived at the first check point down the deserted road. Jack left their names pinned to a tree at the marked shelter that had been set up.

To his surprise he saw Sean McGinn run from the tree line towards him, followed by three other convicts. "Hey McGinn! Nice to see you buddy. So you were the next team after us?" Sean nodded, brushing his mustache, trying to knock off the icicles that were growing there. "Well done Captain Obvious! They don't get anything past you Yankees eh?" The eight convicts chuckled as Jack glared at the Canadian.

"OK we need a plan. How the fuck do we get to the finish line?" The convicts pondered the question as they knelt in the protection of the snow-covered treeline. It was Sean who came up with the idea first. "Listen up, this exercise has been designed to ensure we get caught right? So we have to out smart the screws. On foot we have no chance, we need to acquire some transport." Jack nodded at this sage advice, but how to do it?

In the end, Jack and Sean set up their own improvised road block, then waited for transport to arrive. It was later in the afternoon that first day, December 28. By now all eight of the convicts were half frozen and getting desperate.

"Maybe we should give up Jack?" Jack glared at the convict, young Private Wood. He cuffed the man on his head angrily. "If I ever hear you say that again, I will tie you to a tree and leave you here!" The others looked at Jack dubiously, then shut up, for they knew he was not kidding.

"Shut up! Listen…a vehicle is coming!" The convicts hit the deck as sure enough the faint sound of an engine was coming from down the hill. The old Ford Econoline van stopped as the driver peered out the windshield, seeing the tree trunk across the road. "Damn it! Where the hell is the base road crew?" He put the van in park and opened the door to inspect the obstacle. Suddenly he froze to the iced road. From the snow bank emerged a sight from Hades itself. "What the hell?" Several snow covered apparitions appeared from the white haze, then encircled him. Jack tried to smile at the old man, "Afternoon. Who are you? You are in a restricted military zone, can I see your papers?" The others watched as the old trapper fumbled in his parka.

"I have permission from the base commander Sir. I am checking my trap lines. I am Bear Eagle, I have been trapping and hunting here for decades." Jack listened as he talked outlining his resume. At 67 years old, the old Indian knew this area like the back of his hand. An Indian of Sioux ancestry, this had been his tribe's hunting grounds for centuries before white man came. "Well I am not going to kill you Bear Eagle. Maybe you can be of use to us." The old Indian's face crinkled into a grin, his weathered skin looked like raw hide to the convicts, but his pale blue eyes were as sharp as an eagle, hence his nickname given to him as a young brave half a century earlier. "Of course Mister... er Jack. I would be glad to help our brave soldiers. Many have perished out here, my ancestors called this the Sacred Hunting grounds. I think their spirits haunt it, but under my protection you will be safe...more or less." So after they agreed to work together, Jack said, "We need a lift down the road. Our snow mobiles have broken down. We are searching for some missing soldiers. We will hitch a ride in the back of yer van Eagle. If anyone asks, you have not seen anybody O-Kay?"

"No problem Jack my boy, Hop in." The grateful convicts piled in the back, squeezing in beside Bear's equipment. As he drove down the road, Jack sat beside him. "There is some jerky in the back sonny. Do you smoke?" Jack nodded rapidly as the old man held out a tin of his home made cigarettes. Jack handed some back, then lit up with Bear's lighter, one of his few modern conveniences. "Oh nice! You made these Bear Eagle?" The old man nodded as his eyes peered through the snowy haze before him. "Yes sir. I do not buy white man's trinkets. I grow my own tobacco, dry it and roll it with my cigarette machine. Cost next to nothin'."

He smiled at Sean sitting next to him, as they sampled the Indian's crude cancer sticks. "Well not bad old fellah. Even have filters, a strange aroma. But nicotine is all I need." Bear Eagle cackled as he listened to these young white men. It turned out that the old trapper was a godsend for the lost convicts. They ticked off check-point after check point, covering fifty kilometers by noon. At each one, the convicts took turns racing to the check points. They had to leave their names and time of arrival for the course staff to keep track of them. Inside the makeshift check point shelters they found some supplies, extra rations and instructions. By the time they had made the half way point Jack and Sean were getting nervous.

"How come we have not been stopped yet? We have not seen a soul all day!" If they could have known, they would have relaxed. For the staff were in the process of rounding up captured convicts all over the area. Jack and Sean's teams being the furthest out, at the extremity of the base were left to the last. Even Lt. Greene had estimated they could not cover more than 20 odd kilometers by the end of that day. So in fact they had a head start. It was later that afternoon when finally, the van approached the first road check point. Manned by MP's the van was waved over to the side of the road. Jack had prepared for this, now the convicts lay hidden under a tarpaulin, with the Indian's trapping gear spread over it in case the van was searched.

"Afternoon Sir. Military Police, can I see your papers please?" Bear Eagle nodded as he handed them over. The MP Sergeant inspected the base pass then nodded, as he had been briefed on the old trapper's presence in the area. "Very good Mr. Bear Eagle. Have you seen anybody on the road back there?"

"Well let's see. As a matter of fact, when I first got on this road, I thought I saw something. Some guys running into the woods. Three or four of the buggers. Who are they?"

"Escaped prisoners we are searching for Sir. Very dangerous killers. Do not approach them, they are desperate and might do anything. What is in the back?" Bear Eagle got out and stretched as they talked and lit up another cigarette. "Like one sonny?" The burly MP shrugged and took one, though he rarely smoked.

"Trapping and fishing gear, yer free to take a look if ya like." He grinned as the MP Sergeant coughed, as the harsh smoke irritated his lungs. Bear opened the rear door and the Sergeant poked his head inside. In the dim light he saw the pile of traps and fishing gear. He shivered as a sudden blast of icy wind went down his neck.

"Ya looks Okay Bear Eagle." The old Indian nodded, his head hunched in the wind. He slammed the rear door shut, almost taking off the MP's head. "Ok I have to finish checking my lines. Can I get out of here?"

Sergeant Collins looked at him suspiciously as he butted out the cigarette with his combat boot. "Yah OK. Let us know if these guys show up again OK?" The Indian nodded as he climbed in the cab door. Shifting into gear he waved at the half frozen MPs as they raised the barrier pole. In the back Sean, Jack and the others stifled their laughter as they lay under the tarp. "Hey, like those Greek guys in the Trojan Horse! We are getting into Troy!" A mile down the road the old Indian trapper called all clear. Back in front, Jack lit up another cigarette as the convicts chewed on beef jerky and dried, smoked fish.

"You can have our rations old Timer! Thanks for helping out." By now he suspected old Bear Eagle knew exactly what was going on. The Indian nodded to him as he drove along the wind swept road. They passed the final check point as the sun went down that day. "I have a cabin up ahead. I guess you fellahs would not mind holing up there for a while?" That evening the convicts sat around the roaring fire place. He had fed them a stew of venison and bear meat, mixed with his home grown vegetables and wild plants.

"This is Force X survival boys!" McGinn roared happily as he held his frozen hands over the fire. Bear Eagle after checking his lines, returned to find the convicts happily entrenched in his cabin. He saw they had cut wood, stacking it neatly by the fire. "You boys like to try some of my home made hooch?" Jack and the Pathfinders nodded like their very lives depended on it. That night in the warmth of Bear Eagle's cabin, Jack and the convicts sampled his home made liquor. "Its 120 proof boys. So take it easy. I do not want to have to bury you." Bear Eagle's face crinkled as he laughed at his humour.

The old trapper watched as they swilled down their glasses. They shivered as a wave of burning alcohol entered their shrunken guts. In an hour they were inebriated, laughing and roaring as they exchanged tales with the ancient Indian trapper. Finally, they passed out by the fire place, as outside, Arctic blasts shook the log cabin. The next day Jack and Sean went on a trip with the trapper, as he inspected his trap lines mentally taking notes. Over that week, as the Exercise staff hunted for them, Jack and the convicts were instructed on Arctic and woodland survival by Bear Eagle. They built shelters and Igloos in the woods, even staying in them for hours to test them out. They learned how to build simple shelters at first. They surveyed the surrounding woods, looking for caves and hollows to start with. "Choose natural bivouacs fellahs. Use the trees, bury under the drifts around them, use the branches as over head cover. If you have a shelter or tarp, anchor it with snow blocks. Once you have the inside carved out, make a small hole in the roof, so you can have a fire inside." Jack and Sean mastered the techniques quickly, then taught their teams as the hours passed.

By the end of the week, the convicts were becoming adept at building snow trenches, snow caves then snow houses (igloos). Later Jack and Sean constructed a manual on Winter survival and building shelters. The type of shelter you build will depend on: the materials available, tools available, what you are sheltering from (wind, snow, cold, rain, insects, etc.). How long do you intend to stay at that location? Snow caves, natural hollows are perfect if you are on the move and do not need a permanent structure. Size depends on the number in your party. Take your time building complex structures, do not sweat. Provide adequate ventilation to prevent carbon monoxide poisoning. In snow shelters like dug outs or igloos inspect ventilation holes regularly and repair walls as required."[5] By the second week, the convicts had built numerous shelters along Bear Eagle's trap-line route, so he could use them later if required. Finally, two weeks later, the eight convicts emerged from the bush and hit the road. Bear dropped them off at the final check point, as the MPs and Lieutenant Greene stared at them in stunned disbelief. Thinking they had perished long ago, they had almost given up searching for them. The other teams had all been captured after a few days, spending most of the exercise locked up in police cells. Reunited after being trucked off the wilderness training area, the convicts released from the MP shack, whooped as Jack and Sean emerged victorious from the back of the 5- ton truck.

Lt. Greene stood by the MP's in silence, as the convicts carried the surviving escapees on their shoulders, parading them before the hated Meat heads in a victory lap. The officer shook his head, a slight smile on his face, then retired to his office to write an after action report. Jack and Sean McGinn were praised for their ingenuity in difficult conditions. The grape vine in Force X made them a legend as the only ones who had made it, beating the screws at their own game. Colonel Mann however knew he had succeeded in the aim.

"Result: Pathfinder platoon had jelled into an elite fighting unit. I recommend these men (McGinn & McGee) are promoted to NCO level. All the convicts I recommend for future employment. Lt. Green I/c."

---

[5] The SAS Survival Handbook: John 'Lofty; Wiseman. Pg. 254-260.

Jack and Sean laughed as they watched the trucks pull away. Falling in the front rank, dressed again in their Army fatigues, they ran for miles through the training area before breakfast. The laughter died as they struggled to keep the pace as Corporal Rivera yelled insults at them. "OK you heroes! Close up! Pick up the pace!" But this time the Pathfinder Platoon finished as a group, surprising Rivera as they arrived back at the finish line. As usual the end was at the Assault course, or the Playground as Rivera called it. He gazed at the sweating, gasping convicts trying to recover their breath.

"Right then ladies! Who knows what is next?" McGinn pointed at the ropes dangling from a 30 foot A frame. Jack and Sean were first up the ropes, tapped the overhead log beam before sliding down. In pairs the convicts clambered up the ropes, then traversed the obstacle course. Rivera stood timing them with his stop watch. "Get up that net you slackers! Remember this is without equipment!"

Chapter V

OPERATION ICECUBE 1

January 2015: CFB Namao, Edmonton, Alberta. Force X was being reorganized and expanded as Colonel Mann and his officers worked on the experimental army unit. He pushed his officers to hound the new recruits, for the clock was ticking. War was looming on the horizon. That month many of the new recruits had completed their preliminary basic army training. The emphasis shifted, now Force X needed to qualify hundreds of convicts to parachute. As this would be a primary qualification, it proceeded slowly but steadily. For those qualified, now their training kicked into the next gear. Many had never seen a real winter before, being from outside of Canada. Jack's new running mate, Sean McGinn filled him in. For his extensive service, even Jack was new to dealing with freezing cold. Force X were issued that Monday morning with their new Arctic gear. Long johns, thick wool socks, wind pants, mukluks, fur lined mittens, toques, Arctic parkas, snow shoes, the list continued on and on. In 1994, Jack McGee had been one of the few survivors of Force X's first Arctic exercise. It was a disaster and Jack still remembered that hell with a shudder of uneasiness.

"Holly shit! Where the fuck are we headed? The freaking north pole?" Said half-jokingly by one laughing convict, the room of dazed convicts went silent. "That is hilarious. But not wrong by allot Private." The massively built MP Sergeant smirked at them. "You will be in the boonies men. No sign of civilization for days and days. No roads, buildings, warmth, booze or women. So I hope you enjoyed your stay in Edmonton. Many of you will never see the world again. Okay, in the lecture room double time. The next lesson is "How to avoid and treat frostbite." As the convicts staggered out of the Stores room, loaded with an armful of Arctic gear, many of the newer recruits shivered at the ominous warning.

"Frost? What is that?" One man snickered oblivious to what the word meant. He was from Mexico, never having seen snow or ice before arriving in Edmonton a month before.

During the two-hour training lecture, Pathfinder Platoon sat in horror as they watched the training film on Arctic warfare. Photos of actual frostbite stunned the convicts, many almost vomiting. "When it turns black, the limb comes off men. Fingers and toes go first, followed by ears, noses, lips, then whole limbs. But don't worry you lot. We will give you boys a bullet by then." They were told how to ward off frostbite by seasoned Arctic veterans, Inuit Rangers. How to use the buddy system.

"Take off your heavy clothes before getting in your sleeping bags. Building emergency shelters in the open. Lighting fires, changing your socks and inspecting feet regularly, drying wet clothes." For the balance of the week it continued, interspersed with long marches in Arctic gear, snow shoeing techniques, pulling toboggans with their tents, fuel, rations and ammo packed in. Several men from each platoon were then detailed to assist the Regiment's riggers to start rigging equipment for the jump the following week. Then the detailed briefings started for Jack, Sean and the platoon. They sat staring at the map of Northern Canada in quiet for once. The briefing officer pointed at the map with his map pointer. "Edmonton is here men. We take off and fly north up to the Yukon Territory. Here is Yellowknife men, the northern edge of civilization as you know it. About 100 kilometers due north, Pathfinders will jump first. Zero hour is approximately 02:00 January 15. We expect -45 Degrees C of frost, that is Centigrade."

A hush went through the room as they absorbed the officer's words. "At that temperature, I assure you any skin exposed for more than a minute will be frozen. So remember your frostbite training men. In 1994 Force X spent a few weeks on Ellesmere Island. These photos are of your predecessors. Of a total of about 200, exactly ten men made it back alive. Private McGee is the only one remaining here today!"

The next day, they boarded a big C-130 Hercules transport aircraft for the first Arctic training parachute jump. The Hercules was buffeted by wind as it climbed into the frozen skies over the bleak Alberta winter landscape below. When the side doors opened twenty minutes later, the two sticks of convict jumpers gasped as the icy Arctic air hit them like a fist. "Oh fuck! I am going to die!" Jack grimaced at Sean beside him in the starboard stick. It was his first winter jump, as it was for the bulk of the convicts. "Hey Canuck! Yer weren't kidding!" Sean grinned as he leaned on the fuselage, shifting the harness biting into his shoulders.

"Oh the best is coming Yank!" Then the green light came on beside him. "Go! Go! Go!" Sean and his new buddy Jack leapt from the open doors almost simultaneously. Even with his balaclava covering his face, Jack felt the biting ferocity of the Arctic wind. His lungs were frozen as he gulped in the -40 C air. His eyes watered under his Arctic goggles as he peered at the dial of his altimeter. "Fucker…18,500! Another minute of this shite!" His body rocked as he went through a cloud bank, straining his head up he could barely make out the line of dark figures plummeting to Earth from above him. Sean zoomed up in front and waved his arms before swooping past him. A minute later Jack read his altimeter. The dial passed 2500 feet…time to get the laundry out! He gripped the pilot chute at his hip and yanked on it, then relaxed in a stable box position.

He grunted as the main chute jerked him, then opened with a loud crack. He gasped breathing hard as he checked out his chute and equipment. One by one, a line of chutes opened in rapid succession around him. Jack and the platoon followed procedures, more or less, dropping their heavy equipment bundles before landing on the frozen turf of DZ Buxton, north of CFB Namao, the army base. Jack rolled in the snow as he hit the ground, grunting as the wind dragged him several feet, snow kicked up in a spray over his face. Sean jogged by a minute later, carrying his chute in his jump canvas bag, rucksack over his back, rifle gripped in his fur lined glove. He wiped the frozen icicles of his mustache as he gasped in the stiff Arctic breeze.

"So yank…was it good for you?" Jack spat dryly as he hoisted up his gear and trundled through the snow after his new buddy. "You Canucks deserve to live in this shit. I prefer my Liza's bed in Kentucky!" Then both erupted into laughter, as they headed to the RV point far off in the distance. Soon after the rest of the platoon struggled to catch up, several limping from the rough landing. But they had survived their first taste of winter! A week later: The convicts got their mission briefing before they boarded the aircraft, at the airhead at Edmonton International Airport, 30 kilometers south of the city. It would be a night drop at 20,000 feet in Canada's northern territories, 100 kilometers north of Yellowknife, Yukon Territory.

The training mission would last for a month, the planning staff in Colonel Mann's Headquarters estimated.

The Pathfinder Platoon would be joined by the full battalion the next day, after they had chosen and marked the Drop Zone. The companies would do a static line drop. Then they would march over 1200 kilometers across the frozen tundra and attack a small outpost and airstrip, Bathurst Inlet, on the Arctic Ocean coastline and attack and capture it. It was estimated that Force X would take a month to march, suffer hundreds of casualties, up to 70% of its strength of 1000 men.

The second phase would see the survivors march along the coast due east, to Repulse Bay, on the coast of Hudson's Bay. By the end of the exercise, Force X would march close to 3000 kilometers in all. Colonel Mann added a third and final phase for the best of the surviving convicts. They would pull their toboggans and snowshoe or ski across the frozen ice to Iqaluit, on far off Baffin Island. This would be a harrowing task he knew. The Arctic Ice pack was rarely flat, pushed and heaved up into ice ridges by the underlying currents, then frozen rock hard. For exhausted men carrying over a hundred pounds of gear on their backs, leaning in the traces pulling toboggans weighing several hundred pounds, it would be a supreme test of endurance and will. Then pulling, struggling over hillocks and ridges of ice and snow, not having any idea of how long this hellish torture would last, was the true test of a man's endurance. Colonel Mann would travel to Iqaluit in an Canadian Coastguard icebreaker with his senior officers. He would film the arrival of his Force X, if and when they arrived. Most of his staff had their doubts if any would survive the gruelling test. Colonel Mann admitted he has set the bar pretty high, but this was an unconventional unit, unbloodied in war so far.

"I want to show the Generals back home boys! It should convince them of this unit's readiness for war!"

In January, the Arctic would throw allot of obstacles in their way. Killer sub-zero temperatures, a harsh, barren landscape and little food or shelter. They also had to haul all of their supplies, (food, water, ammunition, weapons, tents) on their backs and walk/march the entire 1200 kilometers to the final objective. Anyone falling out of the ranks would be left for dead. So on that chilly January morning, the Pathfinder Platoon got their exercise briefing by Lt. Green the Platoon I/c. It would be a night drop at 20,000 feet in Canada's northern territories, 100 kilometers north of Yellowknife, North-West Territories.

Then they would march over 1200 kilometers across the frozen tundra and attack a small outpost and airstrip, Bathurst Inlet, on the Arctic Ocean coastline, a set piece attack, capture and hold it. "You will hump the 1200 kilometers carrying your gear and pulling your section toboggans, pushing hard that's about 30 K's per day. Chinooks will be on stand-by to ferry us over particularly nasty areas. Pathfinders you will recce the objective with patrols on skis. Take notes and don't be observed. Companies will get their orders for the main assault when you get there. The first thing we will learn here is that plans are flexible, so we adapt on the move, as we will in combat. Then we hold the objective and await orders. Any questions men?" The convicts sat in their chairs in silence, contemplating the uncertain future awaiting them. This time they were short of wisecracks and the usual sarcastic jokes to lighten the mood. They thought over those words. 1200 kilometers. Most had never walked more than 20 k's in their lives before assigned duty to Force X. That day they wrote their last letters home. Others knelt beside their bunks praying, the first time for many.

H Hour: the laden down Pathfinders boarded the waiting Hercules transport, idling on the tarmac outside the hanger where they had geared up. The troopers could barely walk, as they stumbled over the iced tarmac. They cursed as they hoisted themselves up the lowered rear ramp, then gasping loudly as they sat down heavily in their assigned places on both sides of the cabin. Several wiped sweat from their foreheads, as they were weighed down by over 150 pounds of attached gear. Sean and Jack, sitting by the side doors as the Number 1 in the port and starboard sticks were the only ones who were smiling now.

"Last one on the deck owes beer buddy!" Sean quipped as he reached in his Arctic parka for his smokes. Jack gave him the thumbs up. "I'm in! I drink JD though." The Crew chief radioed the pilot the OK for take-off as he raised the rear ramp with a whirring noise. The pilot radioed the control tower.

"Flight C- 130 Alpha, you are Ok for take-off on Runway X-Ray over." The co-pilot acknowledged as the big transport lumbered down the taxi runway, then headed for their assigned take-off point. "Conditions are a 40 knot wind from the north Captain. -45 C. R.H. 60%. Estimated flight time 2.5 hours."

"OK boys hold on." Captain McMahon set the flaps, before going to full power. The crew and paratroopers felt the latent power in the aircraft, as the four Pratt & Whitney engines went to full power, the four giant propellers cutting into the cold air, blowing kicked up snow behind the plane. The pilot cut the brakes allowing the power to surge the plane forward with a jolt. The Hercules picked up speed rapidly, as it cruised down the take-off runway, then pulled up into the sky. Jack smoked as he and Sean looked calmly at each other. Beside them several of the terrified new guys had shut their eyes, praying softly they would survive this.

02:00 A.M. The Hercules was nearing the drop zone in the Yukon, north of Yellowknife. The crew chief Warrant Officer Laflamme spoke to the two Jump Masters, Sean and Jack. Then the gears were kicked into motion. "Look this way! Stand up! Check your equipment!" The two JM's checked their own gear then quickly went down the two sticks of standing paratroopers, checking their gear. As they finished the red light came on beside the side doors. "One minute! Air breathing masks on." Jack repeated the order as the rear ramp lowered and felt the big C-130 slow to jump speed. It was standard procedure, for paratroopers and civilian jump aircraft. Jack and Sean fitted their masks on, ensuring the oxygen was feeding OK. After sounding off, each man shouting his jump number, (from the back to front, 1 to 12) the JM shouted Number 1, the same sequence for both sticks. They grinned through their facemasks at the Crew Chief, who gave them the thumbs up and waved them to the open ramp, now horizontal with the deck.

"Have fun out there boys!" Jack and Sean led the way to the edge of the ramp. Watching the side light, they saw the green light blink on. Feeling the familiar adrenaline rush, they looked out into the black void ahead. Then they lunged forward without hesitation. The Crew Chief watched them go, their bodies doing a front roll before disappearing, followed in rapid succession by the two sticks of a dozen masked Pathfinders. Within seconds it seemed the aircraft was empty. W/O Laflamme raised the ramp, ensured it was secure before telling the pilot over the Intercoms. "Package delivered. Ramp secure Captain." The co-pilot acknowledged as he checked dials on switches. As the 26 paratroopers fell at terminal velocity below, the C-130 went to full cruising speed, then did a slow banking turn back for Edmonton. In the darkness below, Sean checked his altimeter on his wrist. "17,500'. Whew! Airborne! I love this shit!" He peered through the darkness around him, then at the ground far below. Lights twinkled off in the distance, otherwise he could not make out anything. Then a dark figure came in on his side. Sean joined up with Jack, forming the base of the formation. One by one a dozen others came in to close up. All were in communication by hand signals, as Jack followed the GPS heading. The Platoon 2 I/C, Lt.

Green had given him the critical job of navigation in this night drop. Greene was back at the airhead, for the CO did not want to risk losing any of his Officers in this training jump. A minute later Jack gave the break off signal. They were now below 5000 feet ASL.

Sean tapped his buddy, then turned to the side and tracked off, reaching a safe distance. After slowing his speed, he felt and grasped the pilot chute handle, a small golf ball located on his right hip. He glanced for a second at his altimeter, he was just under 1500 feet. He grunted as the chute opened seconds later. Gasping in his oxygen mask, he looked up to check his chute. "Oh Oh! Fucking twists!" He reached up and gripped the risers to stop the chute from twisting the lines. "Fucker...malfunction! Emergency drill! Time to go."

The line twists had reached the top of the main canopy, causing the cells to deflate slowly. Sean knew if he had landed with the added 150 pounds strapped to him, he would fracture half his bones. He grabbed the red handle on his left riser firmly with both hands, twisted it and yanked downwards. Holding the cut away handle which dangled free in his left hand, he gripped the silver one on his right riser strap. It was the reserve handle, his last chance to live. He looked down for a brief send, something they taught you never to do. He felt his heart race, as the dark ground now visible was rising at him with increasing speed. His last thought as he looked at his altimeter was 1000. As he yanked down on the reserve handle, he knew he was below 1000 feet. Everything happened so fast he was barely cognitive of it. If his reserve failed now, they would not have to bury him. He would hit the ground at over 130 mph, and disappear into the frozen tundra, gone forever. A brief vision of the escort, lovely Jackie, flitted through his racing mind. Then he felt relief as the reserve cracked open above him, slowing him from over 130 to 35 mph in a few seconds. He gasped as the harness dug into his thighs. He checked his altimeter with relief, "Wow. 550! Ok get the laundry out." He undid his chest strap, then lowered his rifle and equipment, flicking the two quick releases below his chest. Seconds later he came in for a landing, flaring the two toggle lines.

He heard his ruck hit below, then his feet touched the snow as he swooped into the wind from the south. He ran as he touched the snow, then elated he whooped with triumph. "Stand-up! Awesome!" He stood looking up as the line of chutes came in to touch down around him. Sean unbuckled his mask, reeled in his chute and packed it loose in the canvass carry bag. He shouldered the heavy ruck and carried his C-7 rifle in one gloved hand, then headed for the RV point. It was 03:00 when the last Pathfinder reached the RV. They piled the chutes for collection later by the DZ crew, arriving in snowmobiles with the main mass drop later in the day. Jack counted them as they formed a circle around them. "Who is missing Sean?" It turned out it was one of the new guys. They never found him, Jack finally radioing back to Edmonton. "Missing one man. Should we search for him over?" Colonel Mann shook his head at the radio operator seated next to him.

"Negative over. Proceed with mission out." Jack packed up the radio and addressed the platoon.

"Ok guys, let's get this DZ marked. This is what is going to happen…" The main drop went in as planned the next morning just as the sky began to lighten. Jack and Sean watched as the two lines of C-130's approached from the south-west. Jack radioed to the lead aircraft in the van. "DZ Controller to Hercules, wind 15 knots from the north. We have green smoke on our location Over." From each corner of the drop zone, the pilots saw the rising green smoke as the Pathfinders lit up the corners. Jack fired a flare from the center to mark his precise location. On the ground the Pathfinders watched the huge planes roaring with a loud din.

The pilots acknowledged and steadied at 800 feet as the doors opened. To see your first mass airborne drop was a spectacular sight. Twenty-four Hercules lined up in two long columns approached slowly, looking like big UFO's in the dark sky, their fuselage and wingtip lights blinking, the steady rise of noise from their engines gave the Pathfinders a feeling of power here. The DZ crew of Pathfinders watched as the sky filled with hundreds of chutes. "Shit boys, I think I'm getting a hard on! Airborne! Hurrah!"

They gasped as suddenly a couple of mid- air collisions occurred. Two troopers had got tangled up going out the door, their main chutes wrapping around each other. Jack and the other Pathfinders watched the roman candles, as the injured troopers flailed all the way down screaming. The two convicts bounced off the frozen tundra to lie in a heap before the stunned DZ team. In all four were killed, with several minor injuries before they cleared the DZ, around 08:30 A.M. The convicts formed up in platoons and headed off on the long march north. Also parachuted in were several heavy all terrain tracked vehicles and snow mobiles.

Dropped with three cargo chutes, attached to pallets, the heavy equipment left off the lowered ramps, before the two sticks of paratroopers followed out the side doors. The assigned MP's and Corporal Rivera of the Instructor team took them over. The three tracked vehicles sped over the cleared DZ, picking up the dead convicts and packing them and their equipment into a towed sled. The frozen corpses were dropped off at their objective days later for burial in Force X's first commissioned graveyard. Around mid morning Force X took there first break. Dumping their gear, they stretched, went to urinate in the snow and brewed coffee. Half an hour later the shouts echoed, radios squawked over the frozen landscape and Force X continued the long trek north, followed by the tracked vehicles. The platoons, over a dozen of them in four rifle companies, strung out the Force over several miles. Heads bent the convicts leaned into the Arctic wind as they marched.

Back in Edmonton, Colonel Mann watched their progress from a military satellite feed. Major van Zandt briefed him on the latest reports. "We have five confirmed dead. Three missing and presumed dead. Force X is on their heading. All gear and bodies secured by Rivera sir. Except for the three missing of course."

"Very good Major. Better than we expected eh? Well it will be a few days now, no need to be glued to our seats. Let's go out for some fresh air and a smoke. Get the Rangers to search for the missing men Ed." Eddie nodded and the two senior Force X officers left the control room in Namao Army base. They discussed the future logistical arrangements as they looked up into the frigid air. The final part would see Colonel Mann's HQ travel by Chinooks to the icebreaker HMCS Labrador, now cruising north from St. John's Newfoundland. The CO would *rv* [6] with Force X in Aquilut, on Baffin Island[7] at the end of the month… and End-Ex, the term for end of exercise. To most soldiers it was the prized word all were waiting for! The C.O. Colonel Mann looked forward to that day, to meet the last surviving Force X convicts. He was not sure how many if any would make it that far. "I bet on a 100 or less Eddie." The Canadian nodded slowly.

"Yes Sir, that would be my guess. Maybe Pathfinder platoon and a few assorted stragglers." Mann puffed on his cigar with a smile. "Well we will see. I threw them a bone. Now let's see who grabbed it!" They laughed as Mann referred to the party a few days earlier. Secretly he

---

[6] RV: rendezvous a standard Army term for a pre-arranged rally point during peace or war operations

[7] See Map of Canadian Arctic mainland and islands (Google Maps)

was pulling for the Pathfinder Platoon. For the upcoming proposed mission in the Middle East, he would need them. His reputation was now on the line, as well as the entire Force X Penal Regiment. The haggard, half frozen survivors finally reached the airstrip, 30 days later. That icy, frigid February 16 day they were down to 500 odd effectives. Strung out on their line of march were the frozen corpses of hundreds of convicts, who had met their fate. Some were found by sentries frozen stiff, after falling asleep curled up in their foxholes. Many had been finished off by prowling Polar bears, who had tracked the dwindling lines of trudging, half dead Force X convicts.

Some falling to their knees had begged to be shot. But none of the convicts were given live rounds for their weapons. Off in the dark Arctic night, the sound of their terrified screams haunted the Force X survivors for days afterward. Only the hardest of the hard had made it, which is exactly what Colonel Mann had planned for. After the final attack on the airstrip at Bathurst Inlet, manned by Canadian Inuit Rangers, Jack's lined, frost bitten face looked over the unrelenting landscape, then back to his platoon. His boys had performed well he thought. Arriving early that morning, he personally scouted the Ranger's positions around the airstrip. He radioed back to the HQ. There were about two dozen defenders with small arms, light-skinned vehicles and snowmobiles. Pathfinders created a diversion, before A and B Companies did a flanking assault on the settlement. C and D Companies then attacked and assaulted from a 90-degree angle to the diversionary assault and took the airstrip. The convicts whooped yelling hoarsely as they waived their weapons at the grinning Eskimo Rangers. Before Jack stood eleven men, the only survivors of his platoon. He smiled at them as they lit up smokes and checked their weapons, clearing them before cleaning them. "End-Ex lads! We made it. We will be evacced in about an hour. Everybody check weapons. Brew up!"

"Seriously Jack? Yer not shitting us?" Jack nodded at Hog, the shaven headed biker. He dragged on his cigarette contentedly as he finished cleaning his C-7 rifle. A few men were gathered around an impromptu fire, brewing up rations and coffee. "Nope, just got the word from Niner on the box." He indicated the platoon radio beside him. By now Jack was the uncontested leader of his platoon, attached to A Company.

The big Chinook choppers arrived as Jack had forecast an hour later. A Company and the Pathfinders went last... first in last out. But for once Jack was wrong. The Chinooks dropped the frozen convicts off after a short fifteen-minute ride, to a small Inuit Ranger camp. They were ordered to bivouac for the night, post sentries and clean weapons before having a hot meal. The Arctic tents were set up hurriedly by the frozen chosen, as Jack called them cheerfully. Sentries patrolled the perimeter in hour long shifts, before crawling frozen into their assigned tents. Sean sat on his air mattress beside Jack, offering him a smoke from his pack. Jack smiled, his dry lips cracking from weeks of exposure to the Arctic air.

"Thanks Sean buddy. Yer did well on the march. Here Sluggo! Pour us a cup of coffee." The burly Italian from New York State nodded as he bent over the bubbling pot on the stove. He handed Sean and Jack a plastic Melmac cup of steaming brew. "Well I am not totally new to this game Jack. Infantry is the toughest job on the planet. This trip isn't over yet I bet!" Jack nodded as he blew on the hot coffee and sipped on it.

"Well let's get some shut eye. I have the sentry roster posted. Wake me if you have a serious problem." After finishing his cup of coffee and a cigarette, Jack tucked inside his sleeping bag. He was asleep in minutes, as outside the only noise was the stamping and cursing of frozen sentries and the ever present wind. Many had regretted the day they had fallen afoul of the law and the peelers, for this was like a bad dream.

At first light, so to speak, the next morning the whistles blew in the cold, darkness. "Up and at 'em boys! Hands off yer cocks! On with yer socks! We move out in one hour!" The NCO's and MP's harried the convicts, loudly cursing as they crept out of their sleeping bags, they gulped their breakfast down hurriedly. Then the tents were torn down and packed into the toboggans, and at exactly 06:00 the lead elements lead by the Pathfinder Platoon trudged off into the icy blackness. The seconds ticked by, the minutes, then hours as they plodded step by step in the snow, straining on the harnesses attached to the toboggans. After the first day, all the convicts were dead on their feet as they struggled into the night camp. "That there, I figure is the Arctic Ocean guys. Do you know how many explorers died to see that sight? In fact, the Franklin Expedition disappeared out there over a century ago." Sean waved his mits at the pile of frozen ice, showing off his knowledge of the Canadian Arctic. "They found the last survivors near Starvation Bay years after searching for them. Two ships the H.M.S. Erebus and Terror, the entire crews perished here. They found evidence of cannibalism on the bones. I heard they found the two ships about a year ago north of Franklin Island. Pretty frigging amazing eh Jack? We are walking in the steps of ghosts. Its march or croak now lads. Fall out and yer dead were you lay."

Sean slapped Jack's shoulder, chuckling as his Yank buddy smiled before he dropped his heavy rucksack on the snow and sat down on it before lighting up a smoke. Sean sat down beside him and lit up. "Been looking at the map Sean. I figure were headed to here, on Hudson Bay. Some frozen piss hole called Repulse Bay, the nearest settlement for hundreds of miles." Sean bent over to look at the map and nodded.

"Yep, sounds about right Yank." So it went for Force X, as day after day dragged by. After the third agonizing day, Pathfinder Platoon was down to ten men. They buried Private Flounder that evening. He had contacted frostbite and a bad case of the flu. With little medical remedies on hand and no end in sight he had surrendered. The shot rang out in the darkness. They found him lying in a pool of red blood. "Dead on duty Jack!" Sean handed him the man's dog tags. After rolling his body into the hole and shoveling snow over him, Jack muttered a quick prayer then whispered Amen. A week later they staggered into the small inlet where Repulse Bay stood. To the Indian residents there, they looked like ghosts...ice covering their beards and frosted Arctic gear. They fell into their tents like dead men, slowly performing their tasks like robots...with dying batteries.

The final march to Iqaluit began the next day. The force was down to 185 men, after the injured and lame were evacuated back to base camp far south. Colonel Mann ordered the walking living who were taken out sent back to prison. Later those who had been injured where given the option of going through basic training. Jack and Sean joined the remaining survivors for the final death march. As they headed across the frozen wasteland of Hudson Bay, pulling the toboggans across the frozen ice, Jack thought the moon could not look this foreboding. By the end of that week, even the hardest of the convicts were at their breaking point.

As Sean and Jack knew, they had hit the wall...and were now moving past it! That final day they spotted the far off smudge of the Baffin Island coast. "Fucker! Look Sean... boys! That's it...our objective!" Colonel Mann stood on the bridge of the icebreaker HMCS Labrador, tied up to the jetty in the port settlement of Iqaluit that afternoon. Slowly as he peered out in his binoculars the dark shapes came

All of Force X were paraded before him, the 200 hard bitten survivors of *Operation Ice cube*. With Colonel Mann stood several generals and CIA agents in civilian clothes. "Well done Colonel! We need your men in Iraq in a few weeks. We are starting the big push there in Iraq to drive ISIS into Syria. Then we finish them off there." General Steiner smiled as he shook the Colonel's hand.

"Thank-you Sir! Force X is ready as I can make them in the time limits. But they have not seen the desert yet. But I doubt it is any worse than the playground they just came from!" He watched as Force X marched off to their barracks. They looked like soldiers now he thought. But the real test of combat was about to thin their ranks even more. He was pleased to know, the next batch of recruits were just being enrolled into Force X. After a one-month crash course, they would join Force X in the Middle East deserts. The crucible of battle against ISIS and their Allies would complete their training he thought happily. That night Jack and his cohorts got blind, stinking inebriated once more. Then one by one, they passed out on their cots. The dozen hard bitten veterans of Pathfinder Platoon snored the night away, after drinking every bottle of booze dry.

For they all knew, war was on the horizon...soon Jack would be back in battle! It would be Jack's second war, for his platoon mates however, it would be their initiation into man's oldest pursuit...war! They boarded the U.S.A.F. C-117 Super Starlifter on Sunday, March 22. On the long overseas flight to Kuwait, where the Canadian base was situated, they were briefed on the upcoming mission. Lieutenant Green, their new Platoon Commander, a former member of Canada's Elite JTF-2 Commando Regiment, outlined the mission to the hard faces of the convicts. "Operation *Impact* men. Canada's role against ISIS or ISIL, the self termed Islamic State in Levant, Syria and Iraq. The world is watching us. They are hard line Islamic fanatics. They say you have to respect your enemy before you can defeat them. So we will not take them lightly. That being said, I remind you we have never lost a war in our history. Oh yes, I mean Canada of course, you American Yanks please excuse me, no offense intended." The convicts listened intently, a few snickering to each other.

"None taken...Sir." Jack responded as he puffed on his tube in the noisy cabin of the huge transport. The gaggle of soldiers laughed quietly, breaking the tension a little. "Now then, we land in Kuwait, here in about six hours." He pointed on the big tactical map spread out before him on a pile of footlockers strapped to the floor. He pointed out the area of the conflict, Iraq, Syria and stretching across the Middle East from Turkey in the north, to the Persian Gulf in the south.

"After we land I will get a more detailed briefing. I can tell you we will probably be tasked with behind the lines missions. Small units of platoon size or less. We want to hit these ISIS fuckers where it hurts the most. Hit his rear areas, supply and support bases. We want these bastards to fear us. They declared war on us, Canada, US and our Allies. They have tortured and beheaded unarmed civilians, anyone they capture. Anyone who does not convert to their extreme interpretation of the Koran, their bible, faces beheading. So any of you who are thinking of changing sides, I would not recommend it. Anyone caught trying to desert, I will personally shoot myself." The men nodded sullenly as they absorbed this veiled threat. In other words, it was becoming clear to Jack and the others, they were sent here on a virtual suicide mission.

Either they came back victorious, or not at all! After the meeting, they returned to their seats in silence. Each man retreated to his own private world, as they checked their equipment and weapons, some sharpened their knives, some scribbled last letters to folks back home. For these might be their last words they ever wrote in this lifetime. Jack lay back in the seat lighting up a Camel cigarette, then took out a picture of Liza. It was a bit old, with worn edges and from early 1992. She had been biking with him to get back in shape, having just given birth to his first son. Jack smiled as he fingered it, she wore a tight outfit, her long blonde hair flying in the wind as she rode before Jack in the Virginia mountains.

"Jack dear, are you close enough to read?" Jack laughed as he saw she had embroidered in red stitching; "*Ride This*" on her tight cut-off shorts. "Oh Baby! I wonder...do you still have those curves?" Jack fondly recalled those long bike rides years ago. In the plush forests, Hoosier National Forest, north of Louisville, Kentucky was one of his favorites as well as Liza's. Then there was Daniel Boone National Forest, south-east of Louisville., named after the famous American frontiersman. Jack's mind went back in time, recalling studying him in grade school. He was one of his early heroes, patterning himself somewhat after Boone. That evening as he lay on his cot in the canvas tent, Jack recalled more scenes from his early life in Kentucky. When he was a young ankle bitter, Jack went on hunting and fishing trips with his father and brothers, imagining Daniel Boone himself had preceded him over a century before he was born.

He was saddened when he read of his ultimate, but glorious death. He had volunteered to fight in the war between the new territory of Texas and their war of independence against Mexico and General Santa Anna. After arriving at the fort in El Paso with his Kentucky Volunteers, rough frontiersmen famed for their extraordinary shooting and fighting skills, they were a valuable addition to the Texans ready to make a stand against the huge Mexican Army advancing on The Alamo. In the fierce fighting that followed Daniel Boone reinforced his already legendary status. When the beleaguered force was nearing its end, he could have escaped on horseback, but he chose to stay and fight with the doomed Texans. Riders had been sent out begging other nearby American and Texan forces to relieve the surrounded defenders of El Paso and The Alamo.

In the end there was no relief and all the heroic defenders were killed, the prisoners shot on orders by General Santa

Anna. It was the Texan's version of the Spartan's heroic defense of the Hot gates at Thermopylae. The 300 Jack thought proudly. It had led his Dad to later volunteering for the Vietnam War. The rest was history as he thought leading to his present predicament. "I hope that is the way I go here, if I go. My name immortalized for eternity. Centuries from now, I will be remembered. Like Achilles at Troy. Alexander the Great, King Odysseus, the greatest warriors of our History." Then he shook himself out of his revelry.

"Shut up dummy. What would Liza say? Like General Patton said, "Your job is not to die for your country. It is to make the other Bastards die for theirs!" Criticized for not following orders, sacked in Italy for striking a soldier in hospital who had no wounds. But feared by the Germans as the best Allied General at modern mobile warfare. He smiled as he kissed the photo in his hands. He recalled that story of Patton visiting ancient ruins and battlefields. He claimed to his Officers to their amazement. "I remember this place. I was here when the final siege began. The Carthaginians stood on the parapets as the Roman African Legions began their advance." He felt he was an eternal warrior, passing through history like a tourist, to witness great moments in warfare. He had fought in the First World War as a young Lieutenant, getting his first taste of war and armoured tactics. It would be a quarter of a century before he went to war again. America's most feared General, and most hated by both sides. Arrogant, a glory hunting war maniac. He died in a freak traffic accident in Germany months after in the Arctic. Well another day in the Force. Hurrah!" But as Sean pointed out, you can not make an omelet without breaking a few eggs, a few convict expendables.

Now Colonel Mann felt Force X was ready for battle. He looked at it like his weapon, his war hammer to bludgeon ISIS to death with. Training was over for now, it was time Force X was blooded in action. Then the next day, the war began for Jack, Sean and their new comrade-in-arms. Were they ready was the thought in their minds. Would they see their sweethearts again? As if the gods wanted to up the ante on them, a tragic event occurred at the heart of Canada. After a series of failures, the Islamic terrorists learned from their previous mistakes. One home grown terrorist on his own, had killed a reservist at Ottawa's National Memorial. Anthony Carcillo died while on duty at the monument and another reservist narrowly escaped. They were armed but their weapons were unloaded. The Quebec based French Moslem then had commandeered a vehicle, drove onto Parliament Hill, penetrated the RCMP security and entered the sacred Parliament buildings. He died in the ensuing gun battle. On March 22, six armed Islamic sleeper terrorists entered the Parliament Buildings with concealed automatic rifles. The security guards were slow to detect them and died in a withering hail of automatic fire. The coordinated attack penetrated the House of Commons. It was filmed live by the cameras as the stunned Canadian public watched later. It was Paris all over again, as the Moslem gunners enfiladed the cowering politicians. They were also armed with grenades and explosives, all purchased in their host country.

The screaming stopped after the six gunmen finally expended their ammunition, as blood filled the political chamber. Screaming in Arabic the frenzied terrorists beat the surviving political leaders with their gun buts, then tossed the grenades into the benches. Explosions rocked the bloodied halls as the RCMP closed in outside. As they waited for orders, the terrorists detonated their explosive packs inside. When they finally entered it was far too late. Canada's government was effectively wiped out in one bold stroke. Colonel Mann and his Headquarters heard the horrific details as they flew across the world to a date with fate. "Oh my God! Over 300 fatalities! Hundreds more injured…the Parliament Buildings on fire and gutted. I am sorry Eddie."

Major van Zandt choked back tears as he sat beside Colonel Mann. "Thank-you Colonel. I only have one thing on my mind. Cold blooded revenge! When we get there, we unleash Hell on these fuckers! I will personally kill the first one of our guys who shows any mercy. We eradicate these scum once and for all!" Colonel Mann nodded and laid a hand on his Executive Officer's shoulder. "Yes Eddie, well said. I concur my friend."

CHAPTER VI

FIRST STRIKE: OPERATION IMPACT

March 23: 08:00 A.M. After an eighteen-hour flight, the two Canadian Air Force C-117 Starlifter Air Force transports with the 200 convict soldiers from Force X, the first trained cadre from the secret force, arrived at the Canadian Airbase in Kuwait. The massive four twin- turbo jet airplanes had met a tanker enroute for refueling, after crossing the Atlantic Ocean, enabling them to do the flight without touching down. Jack and the others trudged off the rear ramp after the C-117 planes had taxied to the off-loading area near a giant hangar. The heat hit the men as they exited, trudging down the ramp, carrying their rucksacks and weapons.

"OK Platoon form up. Let's go boys move it!" Jack ordered as he stood before the huge transport.

The dozen men of the Pathfinder Platoon formed up in two ranks immediately. The other platoons of A Company followed suit. The platoon officers took over and lead by Pathfinder Platoon marched off. Entering the confines of the big hangar, they were halted. Colonel Mann, the CO was there to greet them, having arrived hours earlier in a comfortable chartered Bombardier jet airliner. After the Force X men were stood at ease, they set down their equipment and the CO gave them their first briefing. "Welcome to Kuwait Force X! Today we begin our mission for which you have undergone initial training." The men shouted the required reply," Yes Sir!" He knew what the convicts were thinking. Why train in the Arctic for a desert operation?

"This is the desert men. We will take the next few days to acclimatize.[8] You've gone from −40 something, to +40 something. We will conduct some desert training, that means long marches and basic routine in this er... challenging environment. While you do this, I will be planning our first tasks. So use the time, this is your chance to show me, you deserve to go back to the world! For those who have met the standard, I will recommend that your punishment, for

---

[8] Fact: In 1985 the author was a paratrooper with the Canadian Airborne Regiment. That unit travelled from Northern Ontario on Winter Exercise (-30's) to Texas for desert Ops (+90 F). To acclimatize we marched the next day in full combat gear through the desert. The Americans advised our CO against this. Fortunately, no one perished, some suffered minor heat stroke.

whatever reason will be commuted. Any failure to meet that standard, will mean that A, you are dead, or B, you will be returned to finish your sentence. That means for many of you, the death penalty or completing your sentence." A few of the watching Force X men shuffled nervously in the ranks, for they knew from his hard face he was not kidding. He glared darkly at them before continuing.

"That's all for now. Officers dismiss the men and carry on with platoon training!" The platoon I/C's took over, saluting Colonel Mann, then turning over the convict soldiers to the Platoon Senior NCO's.

"O.K. men, ruck up, let's go for a stroll." Jack grimaced coolly as he ordered the platoon on their first desert march. "It's march or croak!" He smiled evilly, remembering the old army saying. The others groaned as they hoisted heavy rucksacks on their backs and shouldered weapons. "Platoon! Attention! Right turn, Quick March!" Exiting the hangar, the sun glared down on them, sweat already started streaming down their faces before they went 100 meters. Before long they were panting from exertion, still dealing with jet lag, lack of real sleep, the Pathfinder platoon grunted and swore viciously as they trudged along a dusty road around the air base. Eyes watched them from sentries on watchtowers and airmen attending various parked aircraft.

Jack an experienced veteran, stuffed a plug of tobacco into his mouth, his mind detaching from his body, as mile after mile of desert road passed under his dusty combat boots. An ear splitting roar erupted behind them, startling some of the convicts as they struggled to match "Lucky Jack's" blistering pace in front. Then a CF-18 Hornet fighter jet screamed down a runway and took off, rocketing just over the heads of the sweating soldiers. Sweat streaked eyes followed it, every man envious of the pilot as he glanced down at them, from his cockpit window, his face hidden beneath the dark visor and grey air mask.

"Fucker! Look at him...I saw him give me the finger!" Freddie cursed as he walked beside Jack. Hog spat as he loped along giving the departing fighter the finger. As the platoon trudged along, the dust slowly built up around them. Several convicts coughed, as the ones in the rear were enveloped in the dust cloud. "Well he's a smart fucker, stayed in school back in the day. So shut up and march." Jack retorted as he watched a second CF-18 scream overhead with a deafening roar.

"Yah get some!" Freddie shouted after them. They watched the two fighters form up, as they headed west to attack another ISIS position. Beneath each fuselage they carried two 500-pound laser guided bombs and several radar guided missiles. Two hours later, the platoon halted before the hangar. The men were drenched in sweat as Jack told them to relax. He dropped his own ruck and set his new C-7 assault rifle on top before lighting up a cigarette, then taking a swig from his canteen. The men groaned and spat dust from dry throats. Most sat drained and listless leaning on their rucksacks, fatigued and dazed looks on their sunburned faces as they sat heavily on their packs, steam rising off their soaked camouflage army fatigues.

"This is like a bad dream." Freddie hissed softly as he sipped from his canteen. Jack stood up and stretched, his eyes frowning in narrow slits in the harsh sunlight as Lieutenant Greene approached from the hangar. The platoon slowly got to their feet as their Officer stood before them. They looked at his clean, polished boots and immaculate uniform as he addressed them. "Platoon at ease. Good job Sergeant McGee. So everybody acclimatized to the desert? No issues Sergeant? Good, we have not lost anybody yet!"

The convicts looked at him in dazed silence, some biting their tongues. For they had lost many men so far. Presently at a dozen men they were at 1/3 strength, and the war had not even begun for them.

"Tonight men, we will get a briefing on our first mission. For the rest of the day relax and check your equipment. Do not stray from your platoon. Your billets are over there Sergeant. Take the men there for now. For tonight's mission you will need weapons and basic fighting order. The details you will get later." "Sir!" Jack saluted Greene, who returned it and strolled off back to the hangar.

"OK boys, rucks on let's go." The dozen men followed Jack over to the tents, lined up along one side of the hangar. Stripping off their shirts the convicts relaxed. Setting up cots under the shelter of the canvas, many slept exhausted from the first desert march and the long overseas flight. Like Jack, their bodies had grown lean and hard from the relentless rigors of their training over the past months. The shirkers and riff raff were gone now, only the hardest remained... survival of the fittest reigned here. No political correctness determined who still survived. Jack closed his eyes as he lay on his cot. His mind half conscious went back to his wife, far away. He dreamed of lying with her, his hand tracing over her smooth, silky tanned skin and her long fair, bleach blond hair. "I will return for you my Love! Soon we will be together Liza my dear!"

20:00 that evening. Jack and his platoon were in the briefing room. Joining them were Colonel Mann, his HQ officers and a small team of hand-picked, Canadian soldiers. The convicts eyed them warily as they talked.

"Joining us on this mission is a team from JTF-2 men. These men will act as our advisors and guides. They know the ground intimately and our enemy...ISIS. So listen to them closely. We will go in near Mosul at 03:00. We freefall in and should land here...about 5 Klicks from our target. It is an ISIS FOB (forward operating position). We suspect this camp will have several high ranking ISIS leaders. We will sneak inside and assault it with thunderclap surprise. Kill sentries first, silence is paramount! If possible, take prisoners men as we need intelligence. Questions?" The men said nothing, simply staring at the hulking JTF-2 Commandos standing off to the sides. They were bearded and dressed in foreign uniforms, having been here since the beginning of Operation Impact in September, six months ago. Jack noted their hard faces, noting their cool, professional air. He felt respect for them, obviously they had seen combat, death and they had killed.

At that moment, thousands of miles away, Jack's sweetheart Liza was strolling along a beach in California. The blonde nurse had aged well over the years. Now in her early 40's, Liza was a stunning beauty, her body enhanced by her skin-tight swimsuit. Her skin glowed a bronzed hue, her long blonde hair had grown longer and now tied into a long ponytail, trailed down her back to dangle below her knees. Her green eyes flicked her long, curvy eyelashes as she walked sultrily along the beach.

That evening her bedroom was dark and ominously silent, as the blonde goddess slept peacefully, the sound of her breathing the only sound. Thousands of kilometers away Jack slept in the desert awaiting battle. He dreamed blissfully of his lover, as if she was right there, in bed with him.

09:30 hours March 23: Major van Zandt walked up to Colonel Mann in his headquarters tent. He held out an envelope to his CO. "Sir. This was intercepted by our mail boys. It is addressed to Sergeant McGee." The tall Colonel opened it reading the letter. It was written by his, wife Liza and inside was a recent photo of her and daughter Ashley, in her slinky black bikini on the beach in California. He smiled as he looked at the blonde 43-year-old goddess and her equally stunning, aspiring model daughter Ashley McGee.

"A lucky man our Sergeant McGee. Was he not imprisoned for killing her would be rapist?"

"Yes sir, I guess I can sympathize with him, looking at her. What do I do with it Sir? He is about to go on a very hazardous mission...maybe his last." Mann nodded at his trusted second-in command.

"Give it to him, but after he returns. If he returns that is. He is vital to this mission, the leader of our Pathfinders. But I will review his file. I think this lovely lady Liza, and her daughter deserves to see him again yes? After all, I think by then he will have earned his freedom. If the Gods allow it, he will return to her. I will send a letter to her letting her know. Remind me tomorrow Eddie? Remember we owe ISIS a kick in the butt!"

"Very good Sir. I agree, I will talk to him after the mission. I think we can trust our boys to kick some ass Sir!"

02:00 Hours March 24. Jack boarded the camouflaged Canadian Air Force C-130 Hercules, strolling up the rear ramp carrying his parachute and fighting gear. The platoon followed him and were greeted inside by the JTF-2 team. "Welcome aboard Sarge. I am Corporal Hinde, or you can call me Lion, my code name."

"Jack is my handle, so you are along for the show?" They shook hands as Jack set his equipment down on the seat inside the big Hercules cabin before fishing out a pack of Camels and handing one to Hinde.

"I volunteered for this. Tonight we are going to have some fun." Lion flashed a smile, his white teeth outlined by a burly beard. He was tall and physically imposing to the shorter Jack, like the rest of his team allot older than Lion who was 27. They sat down on the seats as the engines of the Hercules revved up. The rear ramp whirred as it lifted up to the closed position, sealing them inside. The plane jerked as it slowly rolled forward, cruising down the taxi lane to the runway. Minutes later it roared down the runway, it's navigation lights winking as it roared off into the night, lifting off at precisely 02:20. *Exercise Pegasus Snake* was underway, as Colonel Mann and his officers watched the black silhouette of the camouflaged plane disappeared into the night. There was an air of excitement and anticipation in the air, for it was Force X's baptism of fire.

03:05 hours: The red light by the side doors blinked off and on. The Hercules Crew chief nodded to Lion who unbuckled his seat by the port door. He was the Jumpmaster for this jump. He stood up and motioned at the watching Pathfinders. Each of the dark faces were alert, each feeling the sudden rush of adrenaline.

"Look this way! We are at 20,000 feet. Winds minimal. We will do a ramp jump, just follow on my ass O.K.? Who the fuck are you?" Jack rocked on his heels as he stood up, then slammed Sean beside him.

"Hurrah Airborne!" A chorus of voices answered him. Lion grinned at his fellow JTF-2 team as they buckled on their chutes and adjusted their equipment, including oxygen masks, then dawned their camouflaged jump helmets. "Check your equipment!" Standing up the jumpers went through the familiar drills doing pin checks.

"OK guys ready...who are you?" "Airborne hurrah!" The two lines of paratroopers closed up forward as Lion gave them a thumbs up, then turned to the open ramp, his piercing blue eyes scanning the desert below. Jack's eyes were honed in on the red light beside him, his adrenaline pulsing now, as he rocked back and forth on the balls of his desert boots in nervous anticipation, hands doing a last check of his straps and feeling his ripcord. Suddenly the light turned green...it was time to jump! He took a deep breath from his mask as he ran after Lion who hurled himself into the night air. Jack gasped as he hurtled off the ramp, throwing his arms forward and arching hard as they had been taught before. He dimly heard the Herc behind him and the wind whistling around him...he felt exhilarated in the dark silence. "Relax, relax. Good nice and stable!"

He felt himself stabilize, then brought his arms back slowly and his heels together in the track position. Slowly as his forward velocity increased, he closed up on Lion before him, till he came up on his left side. Lion looked over nodding to him, then tapped his wrist altimeter. Jack brought his right wrist in briefly glancing at his altimeter, seeing the dial pass 19000 feet. Casually his right arm gripped Lion's waist strap linking the two together. A minute later they were joined by the rest of the platoon, the JTF men following at the tail in a tight bunch. Lion signaled in front, banking in a slow turn to the north. The rest banked immediately following him. Lion was following his GPS beacon as team leader, he pointed the formation at the DZ. All 16 in the team tracked forward in a tight group, till they dropped below 5000 feet. Lion signaled to break, and in a precise manner they broke off one by one, fanning out to the sides. Jack slowed his streaking body, throwing his arms forward hard, assuming the belly down position he glanced at his altimeter.

"3000 feet, time to pull! Better frigging work!" Jack was recalling that last malfunction in the Arctic...a near miss. He reached for his pilot chute behind and below his chute pack. His gloved hand gripped it tight and jerked it out, tossing it with one smooth motion off to the side. He arched relaxing then he felt the jerk above him. He glanced up and breathed a sigh of relief, there it was! A beautiful elliptical square chute spread above him, then the small slider slid down the riser lines. Then he looked around seeing the dark shapes of the other's chutes crack opening around him. He reached up and gripped the toggle lines, sliding his fingers in the grips, tearing them off the Velcro straps and punched them down.

"OK! Ah Lion, there you are son!" He spotted Lion a short distance ahead and gripping his toggle lines, steered his chute after him. The others formed up in a big V formation, looking around and below as the desert floor loomed up at them. Jack came in then as Lion turned into the wind, Jack jerked his chute right, then breathing faster, flared the chute. He landed in the desert sand perfectly and ran it out. He gathered the main chute into a ball, picked up his rifle then headed for Lion, the platoon trailing close behind him.

"Good work!" Lion hissed as he removed his helmet, then his oxygen mask. "No noise! Get everybody in and we will dump our chutes here savvy?" Two JTF-2 men from the DZ team would stay there and secure the chutes, to be picked up by chopper. It was standard practice for the Commandos. Apart from the cost, at nearly $10 G's per rig, they left no sign they were ever here.[9]

"Gotcha!" Jack hissed back as he stripped off his jump gear and grabbed his C-7 assault rifle. From an ammo pouch on his waist belt he removed a loaded magazine. Inserting it into the rifle, he cocked the action, sending a 5.56-mm round into the barrel. "One up the spout guys!" Jack whispered as his platoon likewise loaded their weapons and checked their gear. Ten minutes later the team was ready and headed off on Lion's compass bearing. He wore a radio headset, a bandanna tied over his long fair hair. "Charlie 12, this is X-Ray! Over." "Charlie 12 Roger." The voice hissed in Lion's ear. "X-Ray here, 5 K from your pos over."

"Roger X-Ray out." Lion smiled at the others and waved forward. He strode quickly through the desert night confidently leading the platoon to RV with the ground team. In the rear, the Pathfinders trotted in an Airborne shuffle to keep up with his fast pace. One carried a 60-mm mortar, while two others carried shoulder fired M-72 rocket

---

[9] One Canadian story: a soldier on exercise flung a cigarette but on the ground. His Sergeant made him dig a 15- foot deep hole to bury it, taking most of the night. The point was never leave any evidence that you were in the area.

launchers. Each man had 300 rounds for their rifles, plus grenades, explosives and a belt for the C-9 machine gun, or the 'Saw' as Jack called it. They reached the RV with the JTF=2 advanced ground team at 04:00. Quickly Lion spoke with the ground team then briefed the Pathfinder Platoon.

"OK guys. Our target is just over the ridge, about 600 meters. My guys have their outlying sentries spotted, about 12 of them. Once they are taken out, we have the camp pinned down. Then you will move in. Questions?" The convicts shook their head silently, each keyed to a razor sharp edge for the coming fight.

"Got it. OK guys, this is what we came for. Extreme violence! Let it out, controlled like the pros! And don't kill them all. We want a few prisoners OK?" The blackened faces nodded in silence, only Maggot's psycho face grinning at Jack. Sean and Freddie grinned at each other as they clasped hands in a secret handshake.

"OK RV here after and we bug out for home. Choppers will meet us back at the DZ. OK let's get in position." Slowly the dark figures crouched as they moved forward, splitting off into four man teams, to reach their specific targets. Slowly over the next hour, they crawled across the ground, closing on the enemy in front. About 200 meters away, an ISIS sentry stood guard at his post. Mohammed Abdulla had just turned 19. He was in a tense state as he tried to pierce the desert blackness before him. Several times he thought he heard noise. "Ah settle down. Allah be praised! Soon I will kill an Infidel and be awarded my 100 virgins!"

Then he turned slowly and froze, his hand gripping his AKM rifle trembling. For he was staring at a dark figure up close. Before he realized this was not his relief, the knife buried into his neck and ripped through his windpipe in a sudden flash. His body hit the sand softly, his sightless eyes staring at his killer above...already glazing over, for he was stone cold dead! The dark figure bent down and wiped his bloody knife on the twitching leg. He went through the dead ISIS sentry pockets, relieving him of his personal effects and weapons.

"Hmmm. Easy...look at the fucker twitch!" The JTF man crouched down and ripped the weapon from the ISIS man's dead, cold hand. Ten minutes later, the last sentry followed Abdulla to his final resting spot! Lion whispered in his mike, then tapped Jack who lay beside him. "OK Jackie... it's your show! Hit hard and get back quick OK?" Jack smiled nodding, then hissing at his team, lead them forward leopard crawling slowly over the sand to the winking lights of the tents before them. The Pathfinders were finally poised for their first strike. Meanwhile back in Colonel Mann's HQ tent, the tall CO (Niner as he was called, his radio call sign), was watching a big screen before him. It showed a satellite feed from a U.S. military satellite overhead, at 45,000 feet, in Earth's lower ionosphere. As the radar tech operated his computer laptop controlling the images, highlighted by infra-red, Colonel Mann watched his combined team approach the ISIS camp. He nodded as he looked over at Major van Zandt. "Well this is it eh Eddie? Four months of planning and training. This is all a crap shoot isn't it? A gamble with a dozen of our convict's lives. Still I feel my neck is on a line."

"Don't worry Colonel. I have confidence this will work out. Our men are ready for this." Colonel Mann grunted as he sipped on his coffee cup, then sat down on a chair and watched the screen. "First team approaching the camp Sir." The radar tech's calm voice outlined the Pathfinder's advance on the enemy encampment. "JTF-2 ground team have taken out the sentries. They have a clear run in Sir... and complete surprise!"

"Yes...so far so good." Colonel Mann crossed his fingers, as professional and experienced as he was, still a little superstitious. His narrowed steely gaze watched as the glowing red forms slowly entered the camp's perimeter. The tension heightened as the critical phase began, each man intently focussed.

Jack moved his team by two's, slowly moving from one tent to the next. Silently he motioned Maggot and the big Indian Chief forward. He pulled his knife from its scabbard and indicated how to deal with the enemy. Maggot grinned as he knelt by the first tent, pulling out his own wicked blade with a rasp of metal. He stroked the razor edge along his throat, feeling it's razor sharp cold metal and let out a low, menacing chuckle.

Then he disappeared inside, followed by the 6'6" Indian's hulking form. Inside the tent, Maggot looked down at the sleeping figure below him. He was a young man of

Arab descent, with a short beard and rather good looking Maggot thought. He bent over him and leaned his hand on the man's mouth. "You forgot to shave asshole! Don't worry, I'm a trained barber!" The ISIS recruit's eyes stared up at him in sudden horror, then he squirmed violently on the cot. Maggot cackled evilly as his blade cut the man's throat from ear to ear. Gouts of blood shot in the air, speckles landing on Maggot's face and camouflage jacket. Maggot laughed at the twitching, dying man. "Shhh!" Maggot whispered as he grinned at the dying man, then released his hand.

The young Arab stared sightlessly up at his killer, his mouth gaping wide, blood covering his lower lip and coagulating in his beard. Chief grunted as he shoved his knife into another Arab's chest. It cut his heart in half, killing him before he was even awake. It was over in a minute, the two silent figures left the tent and their six occupants dead on their cots. One by one the tents were taken out, as the three teams of four leap-frogged each other. Finally, they saw the big command tent, with aerials sticking out of the top. Outside several jeeps were parked and two sentries stood by the door flap. Jack motioned his men in and he whispered his plan. "OK gents, this is the tough part. No sneaking up here...we hit them with the heavy stuff. Nick I want the MG here by the sandbag parapet. When I open up you hose the tent. Chief. One rocket launcher round on that jeep OK? Freddie take your team and circle around the side. Make sure no one sneaks away OK?"

"No problem Lucky Jack!" Freddie grinned and his team slinked off quietly. Jack whispered into his radio handset. "X-Ray over." "Rover Over" Lion replied coolly. He was watching through night vision binoculars, having noted the progress so far. He was also in communication with his other teams, JTF-2, Iraqi Special Forces, including several snipers and a mortar team just as a back-up weapon system.

"Alpha 1 ready at position X for final over," Jack whispered as he watched his team's final preparatory movements. "Roger that and seen Alpha 1. Remember bring us a chicken over." Lion used the pre-arranged code word for prisoners. Jack smiled grimly and replied, "Roger that... get the pot boiling out."

The two sentries by the front of the tent were enjoying a smoke and chatting when the Para flare arced overhead and burst in a brilliant white light. Achmed a young 19-year-old university student from France, stood stupefied as he stared up at the small chute as it slowly drifted above him, hissing as the white phosphorous burned turning the night into day. "Allah be praised!" His partner grunted as he unshouldered his AKM assault rifle. Then the first short staccato burst erupted in the still desert night from the light machine gun beside Jack. Suddenly all Hell erupted in a growing, hellish roar. Achmed and his fellow sentry were the first to die, the 7.62 mm rounds tearing into their black uniforms ripping them apart and hurtling them against the canvas tent, then they sagged down to sit in the desert sand, their red blood seeping into the sand.

"Unleash Hell!" Jack screamed getting into a kneeling position. The machine gun spat a stream of lead across the front of the tent, ripping inside and causing untold mayhem inside the ISIS HQ tent. Just as a tall, heavily bearded man tossed the flap aside and exited, Chief unleashed the laser guided rocket from his Milan shoulder fired launcher. It streaked over the 50 meters in a split second, entered the big Arab's gut and flung him back inside the tent like a rag doll. Inside terrified eyes watched the torn body flung across the tent, then the rocket exploded with a thumping roar. The sides of the big tent were ripped asunder, the camouflage nets tossed high in the air, followed by body parts and allot of blood spray.

"Let's go!" Jack roared as he leapt to his feet. The other teams covered the four convicts as they charged the tent, screaming as they went. Inside the tent was a smoking ruin, blood spattered corpses everywhere. Jack went across the tent, kicking bodies for movement. Finally, he found his target...a live chicken cowering under a pile of dead ISIS men. Jack reached down and yanked the skinny bearded man up by his neck. Dressed in a white, flowing garment he wore a white turban...obviously different from the rest, who were dressed in black or mixed cam army fatigues.

"Check the others boys! OK Fuckers, let's go!" He butted the panic stricken, stunned Arab, pushing him before him out of the smoking carnage of the tent. "Booby trap those vehicles Freddie!" His young Pathfinder subordinate nodded and knelt by the first jeep and pulled an IED from his fighting gear pouch. Others from his team fixed improvised magnetic bombs to the other vehicles, then quickly followed Sean's lead back to the RV. The last one, Hog the ex-biker, took the time to empty a gas can over the tent and the smoking contents. It erupted immediately in flames. He grinned as he trotted off. When their buddies found them the next day they would be cooked...reduced to the size of black pigmies. The convict laughed with glee, as he looked back one more time. "Force X says hello assholes! Lame assed amateurs!"

Around the camp the other teams were in action. A relief convoy was seen approaching from a desert track leading out of the rear of the camp. The 60-mm mortars coughed several times, sending the mortar rounds arcing high into the night, slowly descending silent and deadly, then detonated around the convoy. The lead vehicle, a Toyota 4x4 truck mounting a heavy machine gun, burst into flame and careened off the track, torn bodies ejected out of all sides, as it rolled to a stop. Five minutes it had taken from the first round fired, when Lion watched with satisfaction as the last of the Pathfinders exited the burning, destroyed ISIS camp. Then he heard the metallic sound of tracks approaching. Two Russian made T-72 tanks loomed into view, followed by some BTM armored carriers (belonging to former Syrian Army) about a kilometer to the East. He switched the frequency on his radio. He had been expecting some type of armoured response in the vicinity. "Rabbit this X-Ray, we have some trade for you over." Circling 5000 feet above, the lead CF-18 pilot responded. "Roger X-Ray, have the Tango on screen. Can you paint it for me over?"

"Roger that! One minute over!" He focused his laser sight on the lead tank as it roared toward him, the long barrel of the 115mm main gun slowly traversing on the camp. The CF-18 banked over and dove toward the desert as it came in hard on its missile run. The pilot armed his laser guided missile, flicked the toggle switch and it detached and streaked toward the Earth. Lion looked over the laser sight and closed one eye, as seconds later the missile hit the lead tank. There was a muffled crump, then the turret flew and arced over the still moving tank chassis. The shock wave hit him seconds later...like a woman's warm caress in the night he thought with pleasure. He put the laser on the second tank as it swerved to avoid the lead tank and tore off on an angle, trying to avert its partner's fate. Lion followed it as it desperately swerved form side to side.

Lion grinned to himself, "Forget it mate, you're already dead." The following CF-18 spat a stream of 30mm cannon shells at the convoy, shredding it. One vehicle after another caught fire and blew up, running figures were ripped to shreds by the 30mm cannon rounds, leaving sprays of red mist in the air. Another missile hit the T-72 square in its side, lifting it in the air, the right track ripped off and flung with fragments hundreds of feet in the air. The tank came down hard on the side with a loud thump, the commander flying out of the turret hatch. Then the ammunition racks inside exploded, in a rapid chain reaction. As the CF-18's arced upwards, the convoy was destroyed utterly. "Rabbit Target neutralized. Have a good night over."

"Roger X-ray. Your taxi is on its way, Out." Lion radioed the signal for the planned withdrawal to the LZ. Twenty minutes later the last "taxi", a big twin rotor Chinook medium lift helicopter took off from the LZ and Jack and his men were on the way back to base...with one chicken in hand! Jack grinned at the stunned Arab ISIS prisoner sitting handcuffed and blindfolded at his feet. The lone survivor of the ill-fated ISIL camp! Freddie passed him a cigarette, as the other jubilant Pathfinders lit up smokes inside the big chopper's cargo bay. Sean exhaled smoke pleasurably and looking down kicked the glaring prisoner.

"Fuck you Asshole! Yer not dealing with helpless civilians! We are your worst fucking nightmare...a bunch of Godamn killers!" Maggot roared with laughter and spat on the kneeling prisoner with contempt. "C'mon Lucky Jack, can I play with him? I want to carve him a new asshole." The others laughed at Maggot.

"Sorry Maggot. This chicken here...is for the CO...and our ticket home." The JTF men snickered as they stood nearby, the convicts looking darkly at them, but remained in a good mood, for they had survived for another day. Slowly a mood was building amongst the convicts. They could do this, kick some butt and live.

"Check your weapons boys, make safe. No rounds up the spout!" As they casually sat checking their weapons and unloading them, Jack finished his cigarette. He was calm and cool headed as he leaned back in his seat. Then he closed his eyes, and pictured Liza's face again...as he had last seen here years ago. "Shit! How long has it been now? A decade?" He fantasized making love to her again, trying to picture how she would have changed. His last picture of her in his wallet was several years old. But he knew her, she would still be hot...even over 40, for she knew how to take care of herself. He had trained her himself, getting her to work out regularly. She was an avid swimmer and diver. Shit...she had even done some Civvy skydives!

Her last letter to him in prison last year, she said she was doing weight lifting and a little running. "I am a nice, svelte 138 pounds Honey! I think you will like my new look! Besides I will kick your ass if you don't!" Liza had written, then had ended it with her love mark...the impression of her lips on the bottom of the letter.

"Oh Baby...you lovely tart!" Jack breathed aloud and emitted a circle of tobacco smoke from his mouth. "When I get back, y'all take a good look at the floor..." He chuckled to himself.

"Because you'll be staring at the ceiling for the next two days!" Lion finished as he stood towering above him. Jack opened his heavy eyelids, then a grin split his face. "Read my thoughts eh Lion?"

"No Lucky Jack," Lion used his familiar nickname by now. "I heard them. Hey...good work back there. My boys will take the chicken off your hands." Jack nodded in agreement as Lion reached down and dragged the Arab across the floor by the scruff of his robe, booting him hard in his ass. "Thanks Lion, maybe you can guarantee his safety, my boys are still in the mood! In the mood for a little payback in blood!"

Lion sat the Arab before his group of JTF-2 men. The stunned Arab looked up at the masked men towering above him. But he remained silent, as he saw their dark eyes peering down at him, fingers resting on their weapons. The Chinook chopper swayed back and forth as it followed a nap of the Earth approach back to the airbase, the CF-18 patrol escorting them from high above.

Back at the base, Colonel Mann stood outside the tent with Major van Zandt having a smoke. "A good start Eddie. Successful...amazing really. No friendly casualties to speak of eh?" Eddie nodded with a smile. "Yes Sir. And at least one chicken in the bag! Now maybe we can get some good Intel for our next move."

"Amen to that. A CIA team has been notified. They will want a crack at him I expect as well. But they will have to ask me nicely first. So after ten years our political masters back home will see our value now."

"Just like a game of chess. We move one pawn at a time. What next? A knight? A rook? Or a Queen move!"

The officers chatted quietly, scanning the night sky, awaiting the arrival of the Chinooks, which came into view an hour later. By now the desert sky was lightening as the sun broke the horizon. Jack's Chinook touched down on the tarmac gently, the last of three. As the rear ramp whirred down, Lion led his team off, two hulking JTF-2 men holding the captured ISIS leader jerking him roughly as they followed Lion. Jack followed shouldering his assault rifle, followed by his Pathfinder platoon.

He formed them up in two ranks outside as they watched Colonel Mann, Lieutenant Greene and Major van Zandt and a MP team approach. "Good work Sarge. I will brief the men back in our lines. Move out." Jack saluted the platoon commander and marched the platoon off to the tent lines. Colonel Mann stood before the JTF-2 team and the prisoner. He stared at the shabbily dressed Arab, seeing the once white robe smeared with dirt and blood and ripped in places. "Take him to my HQ tent. The MP's will take care of him there." "Yes Sir." Lion replied coolly. "And us Sir?" Lion indicated his Commando team idling nearby.

"We will debrief you after you have had you lunch. Good work." Colonel Mann nodded dismissing him.

"Thank you Sir. OK lads let's go" Lion replied, then they marched the prisoner off to the HQ tent, followed by the MP squad at a respectful distance.

March 25, 2015: Meanwhile back in the world, in America in particular, Mrs. Liza McGee was in Arizona settling into her new home with Ashley. She had sold her home to her elder son Mike. Her son now 26, had made money working in the off shore oilfield as a driller. "I am making big money now Mom." Mike assured Liza as she stood outside of her Kentucky property. Mike's employer, *Panther Deep Sea Drilling* was heavily engaged in the

Designed for those younger, fitter women who pushed the envelope as her Mom Liza had termed it. "Yes Mother!" Ashley had giggled. "Just like you eh Mommy?" Ever since she knew her mother, Ashley looked at her like a mentor, a model for herself. She had no weak points that she could see. But born and raised in a Kentucky backwater from a poor farming family, she had limited job opportunities. She had gone into nursing as the best career available. It was not great money, but it was fairly secure. Then she had shipped overseas in the Gulf War. It changed her life forever, for after meeting Jack she was married and started a family. Liza may have been old to Ashley, but as she sat on the lawn chair in a bikini, Liza impressed even her daughter. Ashley like many young women relied on her beauty to get ahead in the world. So she spent most of her time preparing herself mentally and physically to making it in the modelling world. What where the latest fashions? What make-up and scent to use at an interview? How should I get my hair done today?

But as the guys on the beach, Imperial beach, south of San Diego, California had seen first-hand, age mattered little as far as Liza was concerned. Liza was one of those rare women whose beauty increased as she aged. She looked no more than her early thirties, or given enough preparation in her late twenties. She was in better health and condition than many women a fraction of her age. And she was a mother of three grown young adults. To encourage Ashley and her other children, she had always been very active. Biking, jogging, swimming, diving amongst other activities and had even done a few parachute jumps. "When Jack gets back I'm going parachuting again. Do you want to join us darling?" Ashley nodded smiling.

"I guess you mean in the air?" Liza feigned astonishment slapping her daughter playfully. As they lounged in their back yard after getting back from the Model camp in the desert, dressed in their bathing suits Liza sipped on a margarita. "Ash my darling I have been lucky...and blessed. I'm not rich by any account, but I have you, Mike and Meghan. All I need is my dear Jackie back!" She sobbed wiping a tear from her cheek, as Ashley hugged her sympathetically. Later that night inside the villa, Liza went through her photo albums, taking out a favorite. She sipped on her drink as she listened to the stereo, a mixed CD played old time favorites. Tammy Wyonette sang her big hit, "Stand by your man and he will always love you..."

Liza closed her eyes, seeing him before her as she gripped the old photo. Jack had been photographed in the desert while on maneuvers with the 82nd Airborne Division. Ashley with her headphones on was listening to more modern tunes. She smiled as she gazed at her sexy Mom, stretched out on the couch as if she was asleep, a dreamy smile on her lovely face. She wore her bikini outfit like a second skin, her long painted nails stroking the smooth curve of her belly, fingering her pierced belly button, then tracing along her purple bikini thong. "Oh Mom!" She nodded her head as she listened to *Biff Naked* scream out, "I love myself today!

Not like yesterday! I'm cool, I'm calm, I'm gonna be OK Uh Huh! I love myself today! I love myself today..."

Liza's eyelashes flickered open as she looked at Jack's picture again and sipped her iced drink, then watched as Ashley sprang to her feet and danced in her strap on sandal heels, tossing her long hair madly. "Woooow! I was walking in a dead man's shoes and was hanging in a dead man's noose...." Ashley sang at full volume. "Ashley! What are you...like what are you doing?" Liza laughed waving her hand dismissively at her young baby girl. "Kids are so silly today! Ashley that's not how you dance to this! Oh yes. I know you can dance by the way." Ashley looked down critically at her mother as the two faced off. Music was one of their biggest barriers, both coming from totally different eras. "What Mom?" Ashley said taking off her headphones to hear her mother sing to her. "Hold him and kiss him and love him and kiss him. And after you do, you will be his. Show him that you care oh yah...!" Then Liza got up and started a slow dance with Ashley.

Liza held her daughter's hands as they danced. Again Ashley had acquired her Mom's natural ability to dance to just about any kind of music. It was like it was engrained in her DNA. Which did not mean she liked dancing to slow, country love ballads written by, in this case Tammy Wyonette, someone she had never heard of. She rested her head on Liza's shoulder and grinned and bared it though, to please her Mom.

"OK Mom I know you miss him, so do I. And I love you." Liza whispered back in her ear as she closed her eyes. "Thanks Hon! I love you too. Soon he will be here, and Jackie will take your spot I'm sure. He loves dancing with me!" Ashley giggled, "Yes I am sure Mom. Funny, I have a problem seeing his face right now, it has been so long!" It was a good time for Ashley as her modelling career began to take off. It also took some pressure off of Liza to pay the bills. That week, Ashley handed her Mom her first big paycheck. It was $20 G's which Liza used to for the down payment on her new desert villa. Ashley was more than willing to donate it, for Liza had written her in as co-owner and named her as the executor of her estate in her will. "If something happens to me Ash Hon, I want you to be taken care of." Ashley gasped as her mother laid it all out.

"Mom shut-up! Nothing is going to happen to you. You are in the prime of your life! My friends all say that. You should do something, maybe someone wants a…more mature model?" Liza laughed, not in the least bit offended by her daughter's slightly insensitive remark. "No way José! The first thing they would do is change me, cut all my hair off. That like isn't happening to me! Jack would kill them!"

Chapter VII

OPERATION MONTE CASINO

March 27, 2015: *In faraway Iraq:* "Gentlemen be seated if you please!" Colonel Mann's voice boomed in the big hangar. By now there were over a hundred men present. The noise died down to a low murmuring as they took their seats for the mission debriefing. Also present beside Force X Officers, JTF-2 Commando, Special Operations Regiment, were senior US and NATO theater Commanders, Iraqi military Liaison officers, CIA and assorted others. "OK Operation Pegasus Snake. The first mission for Force X, is over and I claim a major success. We hit the ISIS hard gentlemen. His FOB near Mosul is gone, estimated at least 500 confirmed KIA and one important prisoner. He has been ID'd as their local Chief Mohammed al Karim. We are in the process of interrogating him. Afterward CIA will have a crack at him. Our friendly forces suffered only a few light wounds, zero

KIA. So to those who have doubted the success of Force X, read it and weep!"

Laughter erupted from the crowded hangar. Colonel Mann allowed himself a hint of a grin. He cleared his throat as the cheers died down to a low rumble. "So where do we go from here? This mission has left Mosul still in ISIS hands. This war is far from over. To those of us who are career officers, this should be good news. We still have a job and work to do. Now to sum up the year so far. We have pushed ISIS back in Iraq. Our air strikes along with our Allies have hit the enemy hard throughout the Middle East and North Africa as well. My good friend Colonel Mark Cheadle, who you may know is our U.S. African Command O.C., has sent us this brief." Colonel Mann paused as an aide handed him the teletype sheet. "We are assessing the results on the target in Sabratha, Libya. The target on February 19, hit an ISIS training camp 50 miles west of Tripoli. Noureddine Choucane mostly likely killed. Choucane was the ISIS leader who masterminded two attacks in Tunisia in 2015. The Bardo National Museum in Tunis killed 22; Souse: 38 KIA. *The Times* has reported at least 30 ISIS recruits (many Tunisian) were confirmed killed on site in Sabratha. The *Libya Herald* reported the town hospital received 41 bodies. Hussein Dawadi, the Sabratha mayor gave similar numbers."

He also said most of the killed were recent arrivals recruited throughout the country. The air strikes were carried out by our USAF F-15E fighter jets with laser guided bombs. Reconnaissance was monitored by our Special Forces, imbedded Navy Seals, recce drones, satellite imagery and other surveillance equipment. Colonel Cheadle states the militants were in the process of planning: "a major attack outside of Libya, either in the region or possibly Europe once more." Mann paused for effect as the news sunk in. He saw the pleased looks as the good news reverberated amongst the buzzing crowd in the room.

Mann smiled pleased he now had their full attention. "This is a continuation of a theme gentlemen. This was not our only victory in Libya. In 2015 we terminated Abu Nabil, a high ranking Iraqi militant, when we hit Sirte and Derma, Eastern Libya. These ISIS bases were effectively levelled. Our Seal teams surveyed the damage with drones the following day, listing the dead in the hundreds. The Command and Communications Systems were destroyed, along with weapons plants, including IED manufacturing facilities, personal explosive packs, fake passport document processing offices, vehicles, small arms, ammo dumps, the lot were atomized. If that occurred in our forces, we would be set back months, if not for years."

Again grins and polite laughter erupted from Colonel Mann's audience. Mann held up his hand for silence. "However, let's not order the medals and cheering band yet OK? This is a real shooting war. Men will die, good and bad. The Gods of War are fair in that respect. On the negative side, in Yemen on February 22, we have heard of Canadian weapons falling into the hands of the Houthi rebels. Several of the weapons are state-of-the art sniper rifles. They were sold by *PGW Defense Technology* based in Winnipeg, Manitoba. The client was Saudi Arabia who were ambushed in Yemen, losing several of these .50 caliber Timberwolf and Coyote sniper weapons. If these get into ISIS hands it may cause us some damage."

"Or may be used in terrorist attacks anywhere ISIS can operate. So apart from defeating ISIS in the field, we seek to limit or prevent the number of these weapons and technologies from being used by ISIS. Already they are imbedded in our home countries as France, England and Europe in general had found out last year. And in California recently, through their use of Internet recruiting to create home grown radical elements. Islamic Extremism is a worldwide plague and our Western values are frequently used to aid and abet our enemies. We have to follow the rule of war and the Geneva Convention in our approach. ISIS, Al Qaida and other terrorist groups have no such restraints. They see everyone as a target, and have no qualms using defenseless human shields to hide behind. The latest bloody attack in Ottawa, Canada highlights the gravity of the situation gentlemen." This stirred up angry comments as Colonel Mann had desired. He took a drink of water to compose his finale. The fact Force X was now bloodied only slaked his thirst for more!

"After the dust settles in the next little while, I will look at our next move, in co-ordination with our Coalition units there. I would suggest liberating Fallujah and Mosul from the enemy. That would open up Tikrit. Once we have these northern cities, we sweep northwest. Here we have the Syrian border gentlemen. The Syrian districts of Al Malikyah, Al Hasakah in N.E. Syria, bordering Western Iraq are firmly in the grip of ISIS. We take these next, then move on Abu Kamal in central East Syria, establishing a foothold into Syria were ISIS will make a stand I believe. First though we consolidate in Northern Iraq, advancing on the northern towns of Erbil near Mosul, Jogahl, Malla Ulya, Tall Kayf, Khorsabad, Ali Rashsh, Bakhdida, Bartylla, and Qura Tapa. In central Iraq in Al Quaim District we face the Syrian district of Abu Kamal. ISIS is already pulling their heavy forces (armor, artillery) across the border into Syria after our latest push."

Mann paused and took a sip from his glass. His dark eyes glared intently at the large campaign map beside him. As he continued he poked his metal map pointer, outlining the future campaign. "Of course this is my own humble view. This is a rapidly changing world here. Russia has entered the conflict, primarily to keep their interests in their ally Syria in place. They are also at odds with Turkey, after they had one of their jets shot down a few weeks back. Now we have this tentative truce in place. If it works it will possibly assist us in concentrating on our principle foe ISIS. However, it will complicate things, in an already complicated scenario. Who will be our allies going into Syria? We have to operate in collusion with a former enemy Russia. I intend to get clarification on Rules of Engagement before Force X goes in to that muddle. They have no idea what collateral damage is, nor the Geneva Convention for that matter. It is a club, like Thor's Hammer, Mjolnir to the Norsemen, crushing everything in its path. Our goal is send ISIS and their followers to Helheim, the Norse version of Hell! I do not think the Vikings allowed virgins in Hell." Cheers erupted from the enthused crowd.

"Who knows what will happen days from now. Force X in summary then, has been bloodied as we soldiers say. We are the largest combined Allied unit on the ground in the Middle East. By the end of this week I will have a force of 900 men ready for action. Last night we sent a dozen in. Remember your history gentlemen? At the Battle of Thermopylae, the Spartans sent in a token force of 300 against nearly a million Persians. At the battle of Cannae, the following year, 30,000 free Greek soldiers defeated 10X their number! History is a lesson not to be forgotten gentlemen. Last night's Hot Gates bought us some time...to plan our master stroke, our Cannae! That's all for now gentlemen." The Colonel stepped off the podium to applause. The first mission had gone better than he had suspected. By this time tomorrow, the closed world of the Allied military would here of Force X! Sooner or later the politicians would, although a few select Canadian and Americans knew, but the public masses would not, if Colonel Mann and his team did their homework. When he finished here the Force X unit would probably remain in the clouds of war, obscured by other, prominent Allied units. He did not want public fame or notoriety, leave that to the prima donnas back home.

Meanwhile half way across the world, Ashley sat beside her mother on the leather couch on the big verandah of their log cabin. The two lovely blondes embraced, tears streaming down Liza's cheeks. Ashley sniffed as she cried softly beside her, resting her chin on Liza's bare shoulder. Then they prayed for Jack's speedy return. That night as Liza slept in her big four poster bed, the cell phone buzzed beside her on the night table. She awoke in a dazed state after being in a deep sleep. "Hello? Who is it?" Liza sat up on her elbow, turning on the night light on the bedside table beside her bed. Yawning she rubbed her eyes as she listened.

"Lizzy honey is that you darling?" Liza sat up suddenly in bed startled to alertness. Her hand lifted the long hair from her face, tossing the loose strands of blonde hair over one shoulder as she lay semi- nude in the big bed. "Jack? Jackie my Love is that you?" Liza bit her lower lip, to stop it from trembling.

"Yah baby! How are ya?" Jack sitting in the big tent, winked at the radioman as he sat drinking a can of cold Canuck beer. The radioman gave the thumbs up before leaving for a smoke outside to give him some privacy.

"Oh Jack! I am alive and so are you! When (Liza gasped breathless) ...oh Honey! When...when will you come back to me?" Liza climbed out of bed, throwing on her silk nightgown before racing to find Ashley in the next room.

Ashley moaned sleepily as Liza shook her excitedly. "Ash Hon! It's your father on the phone!"

"I have to make this quick Liza! I'm out of the crap can as I called it. Kentucky State Detention Center. I spent the last year in Lexington Fayette Jail in Kentucky. I've been on the move since then. I can't tell you where I am... its a secret. I'll tell you all about it later OK? I love you darling, just recently it came to me how much. I got your last letter and it hit me. These is no woman like you!" He smiled as he remembered his last fling with a woman, the red headed Cyntia! "Well I still need a nurse after I get out of this shit!" Jack thought happily to himself. He would hire her as his personal assistant after this show was over he promised himself. "Ya owe it to yourself," Jack remembered the old 'Nam saying from his father Jack Senior.

"Thank-you honey. I've been working out with Ashley... Oh you should see your daughter! A knockout, did you get the pictures I sent?" Jack stared at them as Major van Zandt handed over Liza's recent letter. Jack stuffed it in his pocket after sniffing her fragrance on it, and the impression of her lips on the paper.

"Mother of...Liza! You are so freaking lovely! And Ashley! She was a babe the last I saw of her! Now she's a bigger babe eh?" The radio op snickered as he listened from the doorway and Jack laughed as he heard Liza laughing. Then the video screen blinked on as the cell's video image of Liza appeared. The radio op coughed excusing himself, as he choked on the tobacco smoke, turning to leave Jack alone in the tent.

"Ten minutes and I have to cut you off Sergeant." Eddie van Zandt said poking his head inside the tent, catching a glimpse of Mrs. McGee, sitting partially topless in her bed, after Ashley had slid down her nightgown. Her busty cleavage stunned him momentarily, Liza's flashing smile greeting her now attentive audience. "Wow, got yer video on line here babe! Better cover up a bit. Never know who else is watching." Liza slipped into her nightgown, as she got out of bed. For the next 10 minutes she speed talked, Jack barely getting in a word. By the end he was updated on all her news, including her new desert digs. "OK got to go Liza my darling. I will buzz you as soon as I get back. Give the children a big hug for me. Can't wait to see the new spread! A cabin...Spanish villa in Arizona! You are as smart as you are gorgeous! Love you babe!"

"Bye Lover, see you soon!" Liza smiled and blew a kiss at him, batting her green eyes. Jack returned her kiss, then the cable feed went dead. Outside the tent, he relaxed smoking as the CO walked up. "Thank-you Sir!" Jack saluted the tube clamped in his teeth. "Well you deserved it Son. I can tell y'all, I'm putting you in for a release, and sentence pardoned...as soon as we are done here. Do your job son and stay safe...for her not me." Jack nodded, "Will do Sir. How long y'all reckon before we finish this war?"

"Hard to say right now. But I hope by the summer. If any luck you will see your wife for Christmas! But don't y'all hold me to that." Colonel Mann smiled at the irony of it. He was talking to a man who he had found rotting in a jail cell with no future. Now they were chatting like old comrades…the Army saw all kinds he mused. "Roger that Colonel." He finished his can of beer and dragged on his Camel cigarette with gusto.

"Truth be told Sir, I'm kind of enjoying it. Better than rotting in that damned cell. I want to see her, Liz and the kids Sir. But I am a soldier to the bone! After seeing my father experience 'Nam and the Foreign Legion, I want a solid victory, before I retire. My family reputation is on the line." Colonel Mann nodded smiling.

"Ditto Sergeant. Now keep this our secret, don't want yer boys getting over their heads or distracted eh? Right then, off you go Lad!" Jack butted out his fag, then saluted the CO and left for Force X lines. That evening he enjoyed a night with his boys, drinking themselves into oblivion in true Force X fashion, as Colonel Mann threw them another bone, opening up the drinking mess so they could live for the moment.

April 2015: The next phase of the war on ISIS, kicked into second gear over the next week. A combined Army of Iraqi and Kurdish forces laid siege to their stronghold in Mosul. Intense heavy artillery bombarded the dug in Islam fighters, followed by precision jet fighter strikes, controlled by JTF-2 and Canadian Special Operating Regiment teams, working with a cadre of Iraqi and Kurdish Special Force teams. As ISIS was degraded inside Mosul, Colonel Mann was ordered to hold Force X in Reserve. So he kept his convicts training hard in the meantime. His far sightedness brought them to a new level of readiness. Like their forbearers, the 1st Special Service Force he had the whole Regiment train in mountain warfare and close quarter urban warfare.

It was tough, brutal training for most of them had yet to experience the hell of real combat. Injuries were many including fatalities. Scaling mountain cliffs, several had fallen to their deaths. Again the Pathfinder Platoon, the incumbent Elite unit of Force X led the way. Jack first and foremost lacking fear and being a veteran soldier, had previous mountain courses during his time in the American Marines and 82nd Airborne Division. It was hot and arid as usual as he climbed the sheer rock face on Mount Sidon in Northern Iraq.

He reached up carefully, feeling blind with his fingers, and then he felt the crevice. Controlling his breathing he stretched his lean body, his boot soles resting on another crack in the rock below. He pulled himself up slowly, using his legs for strength, till his eyes squinting fiercely, came level with the crevice.

"OK. Now put a piton in," he hissed, unhooking the metal piton from his belt, he jammed it into the crack. He hooked a screw clamp onto the ring of the piton, securing his lead rope through the gate, then twirling the gate clamp to secure it. He leaned back testing his weight on it...it held. Whistling softly, he took a hammer from his belt and pounded the piton hard into the rock face. "OK dude, just like old Bear Gryllis would have done, (he leaned over his shoulder to peer at the man below), Going up." The man below peered up, looking beneath his mountain helmet. "Gotcha Sarge," Al a 22-year-old new recruit replied, then relayed the message down below. He peered up as he waited for Sergeant McGee to lever himself up to another anchor.

Thirty minutes later Jack slowly hoisted himself over the last rock precipice. He lay on his side gasping from the effort. He chuckled as he regained his breath, then looking around the summit stood up slowly.

"Nice view up here," then he chose a large rock as a support and looped a clove hitch knot and secured the rope tight. "OK Al, bring 'em up." One by one, his Pathfinder team mounted the precipice to the top. Jack took a swig from his canteen, set his radio and rifle down before him and lit up a cigarette. The others looked at his cool, tanned face as they joined him. More than one shook his head in wonder. Some were still shaking from climbing the 270-foot sheer rock face...from the exertion it took (carrying about 80 pounds of gear) and terror.

"Shit Jack! I survived!" Freddie gasped as he lay down panting. Jack nodded, "Good for you. That was the easy part though." The others sneered at his arrogant self-confidence. Then Jack picked up the radio handset, "Niner this is Alpha 1. At summit, send the rest up over." Colonel Mann far below nodded to the radio op who acknowledged. "Major! Up they go. A Company first. Then B, C and D."

Over the next three hours the entire Force X mounted the cliff, following the ropes dangling from high above. Only two refused to go. These were new guys, FNG's to Jack and his boys. They were quickly hustled off the mountain by MP's. Colonel Mann ordered them back to base, locked in cells, for transport back to prison. The rest took the hint and struggled up the mountain. They had greater fear of going back to that hell, than dying on this damned rock. Colonel Mann and his HQ went last. Finally, early that morning, all were on the top. Colonel Mann wiped his brow with a handkerchief. He then issued orders and a simulated assault began on a mock ISIS position on the mountain. He watched critically as his Companies launched into the assault.

Yells followed the explosions of pyrotechnics, blank rounds erupted in a growing, deafening crescendo. He finally called END EX as the last position was overrun. Force X had done well, mission accomplished. He felt the actual attack would probably be easier. For he designed his training to be twice as hard as combat. The Pathfinder Platoon repelled over the cliff on their ropes, while the Rifle Companies took the easier but longer route down a trail on the far side. Jack supervised the retrieval of the ropes and other gear, loaded his men into trucks, and left for base camp. They took showers and after cleaning their gear, were sipping on beers when the rest of Force X finally arrived. Jack felt good, he was growing more confident in his team. Even the new men in the Companies had surprised him.

Colonel Mann was also pleased as he smoked a cigar in the O Mess that evening. Soon he felt Force X would be ready for its biggest trial to date...Operation Monte Casino!

April 1: At that moment in time, Elizabeth McGee, or Liza to her close friends, was thousands of miles away back in the world. That night she was invited to one of her best friend's private parties. She was a Supermodel, Anastasia Cortina, something like Liza, she was a mature woman in her late 40's. She looked barely 30, Liza thought as she was greeted at the door by her friend. Liza had drove from Arizona to Los Angeles for the exclusive party after Anastasia begged her to come. "I have some exciting things to discuss my dear Liza."

"OH Elizabeta! Love your outfit! Come in my Dear!" Liza smiled flashing her brilliant smile as they hugged, before Liza walked into the luxury villa. Anastasia had told her it was a fashion costume party. "Wear anything you like Honey." Liza was tired from the two-day trip, but hid it well as she entered the front door.

Liza came dressed in one of her own pseudo-fashion designs. Her friend had hinted it was an exclusive, all female party, so don't be shy and Liza was not. She knew she was still a hottie, worked out hard, for she hoped Jack was waiting for her eventually. She slipped the long cape from her shoulders, standing before Anastasia. Her friend laughed. "Oh my! Wickedly delicious Love!" Liza almost blushed as several women stood nearby, sipping on champagne glasses. "Oh you...cheater! I thought I would be the only one with a mask!"

Anastasia's husky, sultry voice purred with a slight accent. Liza wore a Cat mask, covering the upper part of her face, much like Anastasia. Her long flowing mane of golden hair was tied up with purple ribbon to dangle five feet down her back to her lovely ankles, wisps of the braided ends trailing behind her. "Thanks Anastasia! You look lovely." Liza took a wineglass from her good friend and sipped the expensive Italian wine. She was introduced around the crowd, many models like her, ranging from 20-something to her age.

Like Anastasia, her olive tinted, bronzed skin was liberally displayed, as were her tattoos, one on her lower back, one on her biceps and another on her ankles. Ashley who had a few herself, finally convinced her mother a week earlier to go ahead with it. The tattooing session at a local tattoo parlor back home, had gone better than she had expected. The artist was a professional, as she had lain stretched out on the couch, she had experienced little pain as he etched her back, then her ankles. "You have perfect skin Liza. How old are you anyway?" "Oh just turned 30." Liza had lied as she lay on her belly, as Juan had laid a gloved hand on her naked buttocks. She closed her eyes as the pen buzzed, her mind wandering as the hours went by. She dreamed of Jack, his hands running over her as Juan looked down on the gorgeous, exposed body lying before him. He saw the ring on her finger, licking his lips as his fingers traced over her lower back as he finished the tattoo session. Afterward Liza slipped on her clothes to stand before the mirror. "Oh yes Juan! I love it!" She scheduled another appointment to finish it after her visit to a friend in L.A. the next week. "I can finish it then; on the weekend you return Miss Liza." Liza smiled at the bearded Juan, allowing him to kiss her cheek. She cut him a check for $200 then strode out, her high heels echoing on the floor as Juan's dark eyes followed her. Anastasia Cortina was a statuesque, busty brunette who also had a very risqué outfit.

"Oh look at my little horse tail Liza darling! It was all the rage in Naples!" She turned about and shook her hips, the long tassels of glinting green, purple and gold swaying tantalizingly over her long legs, with the newly designed leg straps, twisting from her ankles to her upper thighs. Her long brunette hair, devoid of a trace of grey, was like Liza's hair, twisted and braided into several long ponytails, dangling over her shoulders to near her feet. She flicked her long, curvy eyelashes beneath her Cat mask, then passing Liza a cigarette took one herself and lit up. She had invited Liza to get to know her better. Learning Liza was recently retired from nursing, she steered her towards a new career better suited to her obvious talent. "I think Liza you should look at acting. Have you ever thought of it?" Liza shook her head smiling at her gorgeous friend, as they strolled among the guests. Anastasia exuded an air of cool superiority while remaining humble before Liza.

"Come Liza! Let's take a walk about. I'll show you the new patio out back." Liza smoking elegantly, walked arm in arm with her friend. Many nodding to her and smiling, some of the younger crowd faintly jealous of her superior physique. Liza was not vain or dumb, though many thought she was just another dumb bimbo. She knew she was hot and regularly turned men down...who wanted her for their trophy case. "Anastasia, have you heard of the Trojan War? The heroes Greek and Trojan, immortalized in Homer's Illiad?"

Her friend nodded, for being from the Mediterranean Sea region, the history of past civilizations had gained her interest as a young student. It was so romantic she thought, the women were especially intriguing to her. She followed the theory that the reason for the Trojan War was Hellen of Sparta, taken by Paris while on an embassy to Sparta, back to his home city of Troy. Anastasia laughed looking wide eyed at her friend, stroking her arm, the soft jingle of gold armlets as Liza slapped her arm playfully.

"The point is Anastasia, that is why I am loyal to my lover...Jack. We swore then...a decade ago now, we would remain loyal to each other!" Anastasia nodded smiling at her new friend. Such passion and loyalty were a rare thing these days. She raised a hand and a server passed by to refill their glasses as they talked.

"Bravo Liza! I sympathize. It explains why you have turned that pretty nose up at some many of my, er suitors!" Liza nodded inhaling from the joint, as several models sat around enthralled by the tale. "One man wanted me for himself...years ago. Jack went insane when I told him, (the room went silent, leaning forward with ears listening). He stopped him from raping me. Now he is paying for it! And another in prison died for the same crime. No man will ever replace him...for he is my Lucky Jack!"

Anastasia's carefree look vanished, then she embraced Liza tightly. A tear rolled down her cheek, as the two hugged each other. "Liza you are blessed indeed! No woman could have a better lover. To Odysseus and his descendants!" Liza and the others toasted each other, one by one they stroked Liza's elegant shoulder. The party continued well into the evening, all the foxy models ending up high, and stone drunk. Before the party ended, Anastasia convinced Liza to try auditioning for some upcoming films. She assured Liza that her name and connections would get her a part. Reluctant at first, Liza finally submitted. Anastasia gave her advice on taking a few acting lessons to get her foot in the door. In the meantime, keep up her fitness training.

April 2, 02:00: Jack led a patrol to scout the area around the objective. Mosul had fallen to the Iraqi and Kurds. The remnants of ISIS, had retreated after the smoking city was conquered. Jack was ordered to take a patrol and pursue the retreating ISIS force. He moved stealthily with a dozen Pathfinders, following the trail north-west. Coming upon a village, his scouts surveyed the small town. Jack had the buildings searched over the next hour, finally satisfied the enemy was not nearby. He radioed back to base and his team was joined by a JTF-2 team. Mounted in jeeps, the bearded commandos arrived, they walked up to Jack's position in the center of the village. Lion his familiar contact, smiled as he walked up. "Jack, so what is the situation?"

"All Clear Lion. We have an informant we would like you to interrogate. He's the local Village Elder. Let's go and see him." Lion agreed and Jack led him to a nearby ramshackle hut. Jack walked through the old hut made of stone and cement. Ducking under the archway, Lion followed inside the low archway of the front door. Inside an ancient man squatted by the wall, his sandals resting on the dirt floor. Lion sat down beside him, setting his C-7 in his lap. "Greetings I am Lion." The old man did not stir, chewing something in his mouth. He was dressed in an old brown cloak, a white turban wrapped over his head, from which a long white beard flowed over his chest. The soldiers sat down next to the old elder, who as yet had not acknowledged their presence. Jack sat on his helmet, opening a pack of cigarettes and taking a swig from his canteen.

Lion spoke in the local dialect smoothly. He noted the poverty of the village, suspecting the old man had not had a decent meal in a while. He assured the old man that if he co-operated, they would help his village, deliver vital supplies, health care if required. "When we finish with the invaders... ISIS, the village will be safe and the government will help you." The ancient village elder nodded then stroked his long white beard.

"They were here yesterday," the old man whispered. "They were bad men, threatened to shoot me if I did not give them help. They took some of our young men to fight with them." He spat in the dust before him.

"Allah be praised, their fight is not mine. It is not the fight of my village. I have something for you." Jack sat nearby. Taking out his pack of cigarettes he offered one to the old man, then one to Lion. The old man smiled showing off his yellow teeth, taking the gift and bowing. Lion smiled too, as Jack lit their cigarettes. They followed the old man as he shuffled into another room slowly, puffing with pleasure on the Camel cigarette. "The ISIS leader stayed here for a few days. When you showed up they took off in a hurry... perhaps you frightened him." He cackled at his own humor and spat in the dust again in contempt. Back in his younger days he was a soldier, noted for his bravery. He had fought with distinction in the long war against Iran. He admired the Canadians who he saw were like him, brave, dedicated and professional.

He opened a thick door on the far side of the wall and flicking on a light, slowly went down a stairway. Jack raised an eyebrow at Lion, who shrugged and followed the old man down. Down in the cellar it was dark and smelled of unknown odors. Lion turned on his flashlight. "Ah here she is. The ISIS leader brought her here. He warned me to keep his secret, for he would be back for her. But you may take her my friend."

Jack and Lion stopped dead in their tracks beside the old village elder. For in the flashlight beam leaning against a wall, was a woman! She was young, Jack saw and very good looking. She was naked, tied up and gagged with a piece of tape over her mouth. A leather strap was bound around her throat tight and secured to a hook over her head. Her eyes were closed as the two soldiers looked down at her in surprise. Then suddenly her eyelashes flickered open. She stared up at them, then brightened. She was tense as Lion leaned down to her and said reassuringly, "We are Canadians, we are here to help. You are safe now." The woman's dark blue eyes flashed as Lion removed the gag from her mouth. The woman licked her dry lips, gasping for air. Then Jack pulled out his knife, bent over her and cut her loose from her rope bindings.

"Thank-you!" The woman whispered in accented English. She tugged on the leash around her throat and ripped it off and tossed it away. Lion and Jack helped her unsteadily to her feet, as the old man watched in silence and smoked on his Camel. Sitting her on a bench nearby, Jack sat beside her, supporting her shoulders. He could see she was weakened and had suffered abuse at the hands of her hated ISIS captors. Now she had the look in her eyes Jack and Lion saw. Silently she sat staring at them, her face said it all.

"Israel...I am Israeli. Special Agent 009...Mossad," the woman croaked dryly as Lion offered her his canteen. She attempted a smile and graciously took a long drink. Lion left returning soon after with some spare clothes, camouflage fatigues from his pack. He passed them to the young woman, who nodded smiling. Already he could see she was feeling much better. "Please take these. We will let you get dressed, then we can talk?"

"Yes, of course, thank-you." "My name is Anna. I work for Israeli Intelligence." She slid her feet into the cam trousers and squirmed into them, zipping up the flies. She flashed her big eyes at Jack as she pulled on the shirt and buttoned it. "You are lucky we got to you Anna. If ISIS got to you first....it might not be a happy ending." The Mossad agent nodded at the soldiers as she finished buttoning the camouflage shirt.

"I know. That pig! He knew, or suspected I was a Jew. But he got nothing from me. I was betrayed, by another agent I believe. I've been here for...two days I think." She took another swig from the canteen, then mopped her face with a cloth Jack gave her. Again Jack was surprised and impressed by her anger, like a physical force.

"His name is Mohammed Abu Sayaf. The ISIS leader, he took me here, had his ruffians strip me, then dangle by my heels for a day. I was whipped and beaten and starved the whole time. Then you came...thank-you again!" She stood up and hugged Jack, then Lion. "I can help you. There is much I have learned."

"Good, we will have diner, you may join us then we will chat OK?" Jack smiled as Lion winked at him, both soldiers pleased they had rescued this valuable asset. It was a bonus she was lovely and young.

"Sounds lovely, I'm starved. May I have one mister?" She gazed at Jack as he fumbled in pocket for a pack of smokes. He flipped her one as they strode toward the eating mess. Anna licked the tip with her tongue.

"Jack McGee at your service Miss Anna or 009." He returned her smile lighting her cigarette, then they tramped up the stairs. The old man followed, watching the young Israeli woman, still attractive even in army clothes.

"She would look good in a potato sack!" But the others did not hear his low chuckle. After a quick brew up, the Pathfinders relaxed smoking and chatting with their new buddies, the JTF Commandos. Lion spread the map on the hood of the Humvee as Jack and Anna stood nearby. Anna was still munching on some food prepared for her. Lion's team medic had given her a physical, treating her wounds which covered her body but were not life threatening. The medic finished giving her injections for infection and a bottle of pills for general aches and pains. "OK here we are. Boka Rotum. From what you say Anna, the ISIS boogiemen are here. The heights at Mount Sidon. There is an old fort on top, so this is the best defensive position to stop us before Tikrit. We take that fort first, then Tikrit, then the final push to the Syrian border." Jack nodded "Sounds like a plan." Anna stood leaning against Jack as she studied the map, Jack aroused by her body pressed to his side.

"Who will attack the mountain?" She whispered in Jack's ear. He looked at her, feeling her breast touch his arm gently. "I suspect we will. Force X...my boys." She looked puzzled at him. "Force X? Never heard of it."

Jack gave her the quick low down on the mysterious new player in the Middle Eastern conflict. "I want to be there. I have a score to settle." Anna's eyes flashed inches from Jack's, her gaze boring into his eyes.

"Not my call, but if y'all think you can keep up your end." In those brief moments alone, Jack knew his life was entering a new and possibly life changing phase. Anna smiled as she responded to him.

"Yes I know Jack. I'm one of the weaker sex. But in this case, hate will motivate me!" Anna took the dagger from her sheath, stroking his arm with it. "Ever done any mountain climbing?" Jack said off handedly. "Yes a little, my last was a glacier in Antarctica last year. It was fascinating, ever been there?" Anna smiled.

"Er no. Not yet anyway. Well this isn't quite the same, it is hazardous, if we are seen before we get on top, it will be ugly. I recommend that you go to the rear. You are too valuable to us." At that moment Force X was moving up in convoys. Colonel Mann had got the go ahead and arrived in the village at 10 p.m. that evening.

"Mount up!" Major van Zandt yelled jumping off the lead jeep. Jack relayed the order to his Pathfinders, as Lion mobilized his team. Jack finally accepted the new team member as his Pathfinder team boarded a big 5-ton truck. As the convoy pushed out of the village, overhead several drones buzzed past, to spy on the enemy up ahead. Force

X in a convoy of trucks, circled around to the north of the looming mountain. Another convoy carrying Iraqi and Kurds split off, to get in position to the south. By 11:30 p.m. Force X arrived near its jump off point. As they dismounted they heard the distant sound of gunfire and explosions as their Allies bumped and probed the ISIS on the mountain to get their attention. The skyline lit up as a barrage of 155- mm howitzer shells exploded. Shortly after midnight Colonel Mann sent the Pathfinders up the mountain. "Good luck Sergeant. Remember noise discipline and radio me when you reach the summit."

"Yes Sir, piece of cake." Then shouldering his ruck and rifle over his back started up the cliff. Anna followed on his heels, followed one by one by the Pathfinder team. An hour later Jack stood on the summit, surveying the plateau in front with his night vision goggles. Anna crawled over the last precipice next. Silently she squirmed in beside Jack. "Whew! I must be out of shape." She whispered sexily in his ear, then took out her canteen. The cool water soothed her parched throat. Then Jack saw the sentry approach. Anna saw him a second later, quickly stowing her canteen she slipped away into the dark night silently as she drew her knife.

"No noise!" Jack whispered then crawled away. The young Arab was bored as he patrolled along the cliff edge, shivering in the night's suddenly cool air. He dreamed of being with his promised virgins, after his glorious death promised by the head Mullah. He stopped by a big rock

weapons. Para flares soared overhead lighting up the area. Then several CF-18's screamed low overhead, followed seconds later by thunderous explosions. Another unseen jet fired it's 30- mm nose cannon, raking the ISIS positions mercilessly. Jack watched as everything above ground was cut to pieces. Then he heaved himself over the wall, followed by the rest of his team. Their weapons barked and the bodies of the wall sentries thumped to the compound below. All hell broke loose as Jack leapt to the ground below. He pulled a grenade pin, heaving it towards a nearby bunker. Ducking down it thumped inside killing or dazing the crouched ISIS men. Freddie ran forward and sprayed the stunned figures, then jumped down and kicked the bodies to be sure they were not playing chicken. Force X streamed over the wall, fanning out in all directions.

Moving in teams to give cover fire, heavy weapons sprang into action. Mortars thumped, machine guns chattered above the rising crescendo of massed small weapons as they came into action. The weight of the assault overran position after position. A sniper opened up from a high tower, picking off a Force X man. Their first casualty, the convict Private Brown shot through the head, hit the ground. He muttered a few words staring with a surprised look before dying. The sniper killed another before Hog, the ex-biker spotted him. Shouldering his Karl Gustav anti-tank rocket launcher, he zeroed the sights on the tower and pressed the trigger. The rocket hit the dark window as the sniper fired again, narrowly missing Hog, then the rocket exploded inside the sniper's lair. He screamed as his body was blown outward in a cascade of rock and stone fragments. The body flew high in the air with piles of rock and mortar, his dead, eviscerated corpse thumping on the rock floor seconds later. Jack cursed as he felt a bullet zing by, just grazing his helmet. His ears rang from the near miss as he rolled on the ground, scrambling for cover. Maggot saw the shooter first and hosed him with his automatic C-7 rifle. The dead ISIS man flopped out of the window of the castle wall ahead, his arms dangling, dropping his sniper rifle. "Oh jeez this is fun." Maggot laughed as he loaded in a fresh magazine.

An hour later the convicts were mopping up, searching for the last fanatical ISIS hold-outs. Occasional rounds barked in the night, as Force X rooted out and dispatched the last holdouts. Anna found her man toward the end... her tormentor over the last few days. In the lower level, the ISIS had established their head-quarters. Jack kicked the locked door and burst inside spraying the room. Two ISIS guards screamed, their arms fanning the air as the bullets tore into their bodies, hurling them aside. As Anna entered behind Jack, who stood braced with his smoking automatic rifle, a tall bearded Arab looked up startled as he bent over his radio. Mohammed Abu Sayaf froze as Anna leveled the barrel of her pistol at him.

"You! How... Allah Akbar! What are you...?" Anna smiled as she walked toward him. "On your knees Sayyaf. Quickly you swine, we have some unfinished business you and I." The ISIS leader sneered at the beautiful Israeli agent. "Kneel? To a fucking Jew woman?" Anna didn't bat an eye as her pistol fired, knee capping her former tormentor. Mohammed Abu screamed in pain as he fell, clutching his ruined knee. As he squirmed on the floor, Anna aimed a kick at his ribs. The ISIS man screamed as he clutched his fractured ribs in one hand. Jack covering Anna from the doorway smiled. He lowered his barrel seeing that she had the situation under control. "Stop whining Abu Sayyaf. I've only begun to have fun. Now then you can begin with telling me of your plans." She unbuckled her camouflaged helmet, shaking her long, dark hair loose. She smiled down on the Arab, who looked up at her with undisguised hate. He spat at her with venom in his dark eyes.

"You fucking Jew bitch! I'll cut you fucking tits off! Should have done it days ago when you were at my mercy!" Jack stood behind lighting up a smoke as he watched her. Her cam fatigues hugged her body tight, as if tailored for her. It showed off her curves and long legs to his hungry eyes. He had not had a taste of a female now for months. That day with the nurses, when his Pathfinders had graduated basic training. He was reminiscing the memory of the two red headed nurses as Anna interrogated the prisoner.

"Yes well you had your chance Abu Sayyaf. Now then...start talking." After the third bullet took out both of his knees Abu started screaming in agony. Blood pulsed through his hands as he tried vainly to stop the flow of his blood. Finally, he started talking, Anna sat on his chair taking down notes. When Abu had temporarily ceased to answer her questions she fired another bullet into his shoulder, running an elegant hand through her long hair. Abu spouted hate and threats, then he spilled his guts, ISIS plans, positions, units, strengths and so on. Finally, Anna was satisfied and stood up stretching she looked at Jack.

"Do you want this one? I am finished with him my friend Jack." Abu Sayyaf groaned in agony as he stared up at the tall Israeli woman. "Nope I'm good. I need to see how my boys are doing." Jack said as he inhaled on his cigarette, then turned and walked out of the room. Anna smiled and looked down with pleasure, as her prisoner writhed in pain lying in the dirt at her boots. She kicked his injured shoulder hard, then slowly raised her hand with the pistol aimed at his horrified face. She took her time, relishing the moment, letting it sink in to the suddenly fearful Abu Sayyaf. He pleaded pitifully, begging her now for mercy.

"Good bye my Dear Mohammed! I am sending you to Hell. I hear you ISIS swine have no fear of death. No? Do you see the 100 virgins yet?" The Arab's body jerked at her feet as the bullet penetrated between his eyes point blank. Sayyaf's bloody body jerked on the floor spasmodically, then twitched a few times before lying still. Anna turned and left the room and stopped before Jack, twisting her hair into a ponytail nonchalantly, before slipping her helmet back on. "Thank-you Jack. Perhaps we can have a drink later?"

"Obliged Mamselle!" Jack laughed as he slapped her shoulder, then led her out of the dark confines of the fort. Force X was pulled out just after first light. A convoy of 5-ton transports roared down the dirt road heading south to their base camp. Colonel Mann was ecstatic as he read the reports coming in, as he sat in his lead Humvee command vehicle. He looked at Major van Zandt sitting at his side.

"It went well I think. Better than I could have dreamed Eddie. Five killed, thirty wounded who should recover shortly. Estimated 260 KIA's, 23 ISIS prisoners! Not bad for an icebreaker op!" Major van Zandt nodded.

"They did well our boys. McGee I hear stood out again, got a scratch from a near miss but survived to see another day. And this Israeli, we will need to see her back at camp." The jubilant convicts cheered as the convoy rolled through the desert, many relieved they had survived their first combat mission. For the majority, it was their first time hearing shots fired in anger at them. For Jack however, it was just the latest episode in a life of violent battle. He climbed in beside Anna in a 5- ton cab, then offered his hand. Anna took it, squeezing in beside him. As they rolled along with the convoy back to their base camp Jack offered her his pack of cigarettes. Colonel Mann continued his debrief with his Second in Command. "I wanted to keep pushing on point, but the general has recalled us. C'est la guerre! Tell them we will return to base damn it!" Eddie nodded at the radioman beside him. "I would think it is a good idea Sir. Regroup and lick our wounds for a few days. I think we need to tweak

Force X a bit. I saw some potential leaders Sir. Pathfinder Platoon stood out the most."

Colonel Mann nodded as he lit his cigar. "You handle it Major. Let me know your recommendations in your after action report." Later back at their forward camp, Pathfinder platoon was dismissed by their Lieutenant after cleaning and turning in weapons and ammunition. "Read the sentry duty list men. For the remainder, you are off till reveille tomorrow. Oh I hear your drinking mess is now open." The convicts saluted the officer as he left for the Headquarters tent. They whooped slapping each other's backs as they headed for the distant tent housing their desert drinking mess. Jack accompanied by his Pathfinder team and Anna entered the mess and fought to get to the bar first. "To us boys! Who's like us?"

"Damn few...and they're all fucking dead!" The reply erupted from a dozen parched throats, then they toasted with beer as the taps in the mess went into full action. The mess staff watched, some a bit nervously at the dirty, combat stained warriors as they commenced to party. Anna accompanied by Jack, laughed and danced before the celebrating men as they roared and sung dirty songs in the victory celebration.

"You Bitch! Whoa!" Hog roared as he swilled a bottle of Scotch. Anna sat down as Jack handed her wine glass, taking a sip as she eyed him smiling. He felt a shiver go up his spine as she gave him a glowering look. Finally, as the song ended, she leapt bodily in Jack's arms. "My Hero Jackie!" Before he could respond, as his buddies shouted, "Lucky fucker! Jack! Jack! Jack!" Anna planted her lips on his with a firm kiss. He smiled as her tongue tickled his lips playfully, her eyelashes tickling his cheeks, as Anna rubbed her nose along his sensually. As she released her mouth from his, Anna squirmed in his arms to face him, kicking her legs in the air.

"So Jack? Are you ready for bed? Take me away from this madness." Jack finished his beer as he set her on his feet before him. Anna leaned in his arms, as she took another mug from the bar and swilled it down greedily. As the drunken convicts pounded the table, a photographer yelled "OK guys! A picture for the Force X scrapbook! Hold still Jack! Say cheese!" Jack held Anna to him, the two smiling as they were surrounded by Jack's platoon mates. The cameraman took several pictures as Jack hugged Anna to him, her cheek resting on his and they toasted, Jack's beer can with Anna's wine glass.

Anna smiled as she kissed his cheek tenderly. "Thank-you Jack." Then Jack swept her off her feet and strode out of the tent, the lovely agent in his arms. In his tent nearby, Jack stood before Anna as they stripped off their clothes in frantic haste. Jack gasped as he looked at her naked body, as Anna stood nude in his arms. She leaned her toes on his feet, slowly she rocked her torso, her firm, shapely breasts pressed into his chest. "Oops, sorry Liza. A man has to do what a man has to do!" He consoled himself with the thought that he could be dead in the near future. His hands gripped Anna by her hips, fondling her as they kissed. Then he sat down on his cot and Anna climbed onto his lap. Jack held her tight as she squatted on him. "Just like an American cowgirl eh Jack?" He nodded with a grin as he felt her soft skin on his.

"You're married?" Anna breathed hotly into his ear, sending shudders up his spine, her fingers stroking his muscular back. "Yes. I have not seen her for a decade though. I'm weak... Who knows, we could be dead in a few days." She nodded at that happy thought as they made out on his cot.

Jack slid his hands over her lower back, swinging Anna bodily onto the cot on her back. Mounting her easily, Jack spread her thighs wide before him as he looked down at her. Anna licked her lips sultrily with her tongue as she squirmed under Jack, her arms stretching over her head, to pull her long hair from her eyes. Jack felt her muscles tense, her soft skin pressed to his hard body. He relished the feeling, this Israeli beauty who was giving herself to him eagerly. He ran his fingers down Anna's spine, then over her naked, firm buttocks. Anna arched her back as he squeezed her, the canvas cot groaning under their writhing bodies. She kissed him closing her eyes, her long eyelashes tickling his cheeks.

"Oh Jack! You animal! Take me!" Anna breathed feeling her body tingle as she felt him grow hard and erect. Raising her feet high, she curled her painted toenails as she rested her legs on his broad shoulders, her toes tickling his skin, as if the convict needed any further stimulation! He grunted as he penetrated her, Anna's tight, fit body leaning forward and thrusting hard. His hands pinned her by her wrists as he leaned heavily on her and thrust madly away with all his will. "OH...Jackie! My lover. I need you!" Anna gasped as her body began to rock madly to Jack's thrusts, moving in rhythm with him. Her spine arched up, her breasts swaying on her panting, busty chest, slapping hard into his chest. The cot shook and groaned under their combined weight as the two made love. It was Jack's first real sex since his time with the naughty nurses and he made the most of it. Soon after he lay on his back on the cot, gasping as waves of ecstasy enveloped him. Anna lay beside him, equally spent, she licked her lips with her tongue, then kissed his broad shoulder while running her palms over his chest.

"Thank-you Jack. I needed that after a good fight!" Jack smiled nodding in agreement. "Ditto baby. Lying with you takes away some of the shit I've had to take with this lot." He hugged her naked body to him, then kissed the Israeli secret agent, closing his eyes as he explored her hot lips. Jack temporarily escaped from the hellish world he had been dropped into, as the two lovers lay intertwined on the camp cot. An hour later, after cleaning up in the shower, they rejoined the boys in the drinking mess tent. Jack and Anna were greeted by cheers from the now drunk convicts. Anna held Jack's hand as he led her inside the raucous wet canteen, leaning into his protective embrace.

Anna sat down at a table with the familiar Pathfinder convicts. Freddie, Hog and Maggot roared with laughter, slamming the table with their beer cans as Jack went for more beer. "Thank-you Freddie?" Anna said as she was guided to a seat, while Maggot offered her a cigarette. "Saw ya up there today. Not bad...for a woman." The convict was trying to be nice to Jack's new flame. Anna smiled at the heavily whiskered, shaven headed convict. Not in the least bit intimidated, she smiled as she sat down, her tight fitting cam fatigues setting her apart from the filthy sweat soaked convicts. Anna sat between the hulking forms of Maggot and Hog.

"Well thanks Sir... Maggot? Did yer parents hate you?" She flashed the shaven headed convict a smile.

Maggot sneered laughingly, "It's a prison nickname darling. I don't think it does me justice though." Anna laughed showing her brilliant smile as Jack set a mug of beer before her. Later beside a roaring bonfire Jack, Anna and the convicts partied into the late afternoon. Finally, the bar drained, reluctantly the party broke up. Then one by one they sauntered off, struggling and weaving unsteadily to their cots. Jack retired to his cot to find Anna had beat him to his bunk, lying naked under the olive drab blanket.

She moaned softly, whispering in his ear as he climbed in beside her. He embraced her tight to him, Anna's chin resting on his chest. "Sleep my hero Jack." Anna whispered as finally, days of sleep deprivation overcame her, then she drifted off to sleep. Jack nestled against her warm body, then gently kissed her parted lips. Minutes later he slept in her arms, dreaming she was his Liza. "Forgive me my darling.... soon...I will have you back!" He dreamed of Liza his girl, as he lay in his cot, his mind returned to the time long ago when they used to go biking in the Virginia mountains. She had looked back at him from her mountain bike, wearing a sweat suit she had designed herself from one of her nursing uniforms. Liza looked at him with her smoking gaze, he felt her presence like it was the present.

"Well Jack honey...if you are going to ride my ass, you might as well grab my hair!" She had laughed and flashed a smile that made Jack writhe in bed in torture, then she turned and sped off. Jack followed as Liza tore down a bike trail, her long blonde hair flowing behind her in the breeze. "Liza slow down! Yer going to kill yourself...or me!" Jack bounced in the seat as they tore down the 60 degree down slope, shifting gears as he desperately tried to keep up. Finally, Liza reached the bottom of the mountain, braking to a stop in a shower of dust, expertly swinging in a 180-degree arc to face him. Jack gasped as he pulled up braking beside her, grinning at the blonde beauty. Jack admired his lovely wife, as she tossed her long hair in the breeze.

"Liza you are a crazy woman! But I love ya all the same!" He stroked her glistening hair then reached over and kissed her. Liza flicked her wild hair from her face, her eyes flashing as she looked deep into his. "Jackie darling, I want to go jumping with you O.K?" Jack hesitated then nodded "O.K. honey. You know the risks?" She smiled nodding then kissed him. "I think so. I want to experience your world a bit. I have lived such a pampered life compared to you. I feel the need for some speed like those *Top Gun* guys!" She released her lips from his then mounted her bike and led the way back to their truck.

That weekend Liza did her first skydive jump. The year was 1993, she had turned 21 years old. Liza climbed into the open door of the roaring Cessna 206 as it waited on the tarmac followed by Jack and the other jumpers. On the way up Liza had talked excitedly to Jack, going over her training. "Relax and have fun baby. This is a piece of cake. You climb out first, grip the wing strut with your right hand firmly. Then your right foot on the wheel step. Lean out and place your other foot on the step and grab the wing strut with your left hand. Stretch your right hand out and grip the strut nice and firm, like you will do with me tonight." Liza shrugged pouting her smiling lips. "Not so fast Mister. Keep your dirty mind focused on the job."

"Sorry!" Jack laughed as he checked over Liza's parachute rig. He gave her a last pin check, then held the rip cord and small pilot chute in his hand. Jack as her instructor would deploy her main chute after she had released her hold, her body falling from the plane in the practiced arch. Jack knelt by the door as the pilot beside him nodded. "5500 feet. Should be over the DZ." Jack smiled and opened the door and secured it to the wing. He leaned his head out and did the spot for the exit, as the DZ slowly approached below. Satisfied he turned to Liza kneeling at his side. "OK Liza your turn. Climb out and grab that strut like it is me." Liza smiled then climbed out onto the wing. In position Jack watched as he climbed out close beside her. Liza let her feet slide off the step, hanging by her hands and craned her face up to him. Jack blew her a kiss then Liza let go. Jack held out his arm, till the ripcord ripped it from his hand. He waved at her as she fell away to the Earth far below, then leapt out after her. He watched as her big student main chute billowed open before he pulled his own chute. On the ground minutes later he whooped as he embraced her. "Well done Hon! You were perfect! Already for the next hump…I mean jump?"

As he slept blissfully, Jack heard her laughter ring in his ears. It seemed like he had just drifted off when the whistles blew outside his tent early the next morning. Jack groaned rubbing his shaved head, blinking his eyes as he struggled to sit up. He flung back the blanket and struggled from his cot. "Got to be kidding me! Where the hell are my boots?" Then he saw Anna was already up and dressed before him.

"Beside the bed Jack love. Thanks for putting up with me last night." She bent down and kissed his cheek as he struggled to get his desert boots on. Then she dashed out of the tent, leaving Jack to finish dressing. Pathfinder Platoon assembled outside as Jack burst from the tent. "OK boys, Roll call." Sergeant McGee called off the names, assuring himself all were present. Then he took them off for a morning run to shake off the effects of their celebration. After a few miles Jack settled into the rhythm of the morning run. Four miles later the Pathfinders hit the dirt. "Give me 50 guys, you know the drill!" A few complained but most performed the exercise with amusement. They were hardened warriors now, blooded in action against their sworn enemy ISIS. As they returned to their desert base the REMF's watched as they ran by, singing their Penal Regiment marching songs. "Who the Hell is that?" The two Air Force ground crew stood by the fuel depot watching the departing convicts. "I don't know Johnnie. They have no insignia on their uniforms. Top secret outfit. The MP's told me not to ask." The other soldier shrugged and turned back to monitor to fuelling of a Chinook helicopter parked on the taxi strip.

Sean Gilligan (Author) c 1970's on Winter Warfare training in Northern Ontario near CFB Petawawa.

top: 1984 on home leave from Canadian Airborne Regiment;
2000: Gimli Manitoba: 1st skydive in a decade I give the thumbs up

A CF-18 fighter jet waits on the tarmac, backlit by a mushrooming cloud of flames

Alcatraz prison Hell for Convicts, on an island off San Francisco where hard core convicts were kept in isolation for decades. It was shut down after the famous escape by three prisoners in the 1960's

Eliza and Ashley McGee lie on a beach on the California coast as they await Jack's return from Hell in the Middle East war

Eliza McGee poses for the camera for her first movie, The Mutants: California Invasion

Israeli Mossad Agent 009, Anna aka Matta Hari. After her harrowing rescue from the clutches of ISIS, Anna and Jack quickly create a bond, as they fight the threat of ISIS together

A convict killer being transferred from a U.S. prison by SWAT
police to the new Force X Penal Army unit)

Jack McGee's prison in the Eastern U.S. somewhere. After his conviction for murder, he would remain behind bars until drafted into Force X Penal Regiment a year later

A CF-18 fighter jet on a strike mission over the Middle East desert

Immortalized by Johnny Cash in one of his songs, Folsom Prison would prove to be a ready supply of convict recruits for Force X Penal Regiment

French Foreign Legion: Legionnaires on parade in full uniform on graduating their advanced paratrooper course. Jack McGee Sr. received his second set of jump wings.

Chapter VIII

THE ACTRESS

April 5, 2015: That evening was another hot one as Liza prepared for bed. She sat before her bedroom wooden desk looking at her refection in the mirror. She smiled for she did not see a forty- something woman. She unhooked her bra and slipped it off, tossing it on the desk top. In the background, the stereo played the sounds of one of her favorite new bands *Sonic*. She smiled as she hummed along. The lead singer, a blonde woman half her age had a beautiful, lilting voice she thought. She unloosened her long, thick mane of hair tossing it wildly with her head. "I look ah, what? Twenty-eight? OK maybe 29."

As the last song of her tape ended, she crawled onto the big four poster bed, curling up on the pillow and turned off the light. Her mind went over the events of the last month. In early March, as the bills piled up from her house construction, she realized she needed some extra cash. Looking in the local want ads, she saw a film company shooting in the area was looking for extras. "*Needed: Extras, stand-ins for upcoming film. If interested apply to Phoenix Enterprises. Call or fax to...*"

Liza sat on her verandah as she had read the paper. "Wow...should I? Well if it will make ends meet why not?" Liza after phoning to enquire later that day, was interviewed that Friday. The film director and an assistant smiled as she walked in. "Hi I am Liza McGee. I am interested in applying as a stand-in for your film." Liza smiled as she loomed over the Director Mr. Al Sikorsky's desk.

"Mrs. Eliza McGee, Yes! I remember! A pleasure. Please have a seat." Liza shook hands with Al Sikorsky and his assistant Tina Flores, who also chose cast members. Liza smiled as they interviewed her and explained the movie script. "The story is a modern version of *The Hills Have Eyes*. Are you familiar with it?" Liza replied "I've heard of it, but never saw it. That was a while ago?" Al nodded, "Yes. Its my new horror film. A story of mutants, nasty people, who are deformed from radiation exposure in the desert, from nuclear tests. They abduct, torture and kill people who blunder into their deserted town." Liza nodded as Al studied her.

"Liza I have one request. Can you model for us...in a swimsuit?" Al smiled at her. Liza nodded, "Yes, I don't have one with me." Tina Flores interrupting spoke up, "No problem Liza. Could you come with me?"

Liza smiled as she stood up and followed Tina out of the office. She returned from the change room ten minutes later, wearing a lime green bathing suit and her own high heels. Al smiled as she modeled it for him, walking back and forth in front of his desk. "Very good Liza, please have a seat." Liza sat down in the chair, her cleavage openly displayed, wearing a top 3 sizes too small. Tina whispered in Al's ear then beamed at Liza. "Well Liza I think we can use you. We offer $500 a day all expenses paid. We need a stand-in for one of our actresses. You are quite similar to her in appearance. Miss Greenham requires at least two doubles, for the more ah...difficult scenes. Well what do you say?" Liza smiled, "When do I start?"

Liza McGee showed up at 06:00 A.M. the next morning. Tina greeted her and ushered her into a nearby trailer. There she was introduced to Miss Greenham and another blonde, stand-in Jackie McVie. Tina clapped her hands as they sat at a table and drank coffee. "Look at you guys! Slightly different, but wow...I would swear you are sisters!" Liza and the other woman laughed, but it was true. "Now then, Liza and Jackie. Some of these shots you may find a bit difficult, but your work should be done in a few weeks, so remember keep your eyes on the prize. Over $3000 per week, for three weeks. Also I may ask you to perform other duties. And if things go well I will throw in a bonus. I will also keep your names for future films, sound OK?"

Liza and Jackie signed on, then as they left the star actress Chrissy Greenham talked to her doubles. "I really want to thank you Liza and Jackie. You know what you will be asked to do?" Shaking their heads Chrissy lowered her voice, "I am to be abducted by these...freaks. You guys have to do the more revolting parts. The freaks are made to look revolting, mostly make-up. You will have to do the nudity, rape scenes and physically demanding scenes." Liza and Jackie did their first scene that day. Dressed up in cheerleader outfits, the mutant freak abducted them. Liza and Jackie were filmed after the deformed old man wrestled them into his truck, while they were hitchhiking in the desert. They lay on the floor as he drove the truck across the desert to his secluded acreage. The stakes were raised, progressing over that week steadily. The directors kept up a frantic pace, as they were on a strict budget. Like his buddy Rob Zombie, Al wanted a low budget horror film, a mirror of the old style horror flicks, with graphic no holds barred violence and bone chilling horror.

Liza, Jackie and Chrissy trained together, finding they had similar training regimes. They did body building regularly in the gym for two hours a day. They also jogged 5 miles every second day and swam at the local beach on off days. They were all statuesque blondes, standing 5'11" in their bare feet. With a pair of high heels, it added inches to their height, so they towered over most of the other film actors. Liza who was approaching 42, was the oldest by far. Jackie was 32 and Chrissy the star actress was barely 29.

Liza felt a bit out of her element here, as it was her first real foray into films. Several times she had almost backed out. As a professional nurse, she was used to long hours and hard work. She had been exposed to trying duties over her twenty odd years in nursing. She had seen some nasty things in her role as a trauma nurse. Jack had been one of the rare bright spots. His wounds were relatively easy to deal with. If he had been an amputee or a raving shell shocked lunatic, it would have been far different. Both being young and unattached, the two had met at the perfect time. As if fate had intervened for Liza, the young, beautiful, aspiring trauma nurse destined to shape her future life. Now here she was a decade later, a mother of three fully grown adults. She was being put to the test by the Director, challenged like she never had before.

"OK, Liza baby. Eyes on the prize. I can do this." Part of her training regime included riding her ten speed mountain bike. In the months leading up to this challenge, Liza had ridden the bike paths in her native Kentucky or wherever she went. She included some photos of her biking training regime in her c.v. when she first applied for the job. When it arrived on Director Bob's desk that week, he had his assistant schedule her for an audition. Liza he found to his surprise, was not your average woman. Her looks and physique belied her age, as he looked over the photo montage and attached resume. "Hmmm. A decade of nursing. Likes to work out. Married, three kids. Husband is ex-army. Well Tina I think she may do nicely. This job requires women of strength as well as beauty. We will see if she handles the mental side of it as well."

Tina nodded knowing what he meant. It was not for the squeamish, or the reserved. "Well Al, this Liza McGee is no spring chicken. Her predecessor who is much younger, could not handle it. Anyway if she fails I have several women waiting in the side lines." Al chuckled and dismissed her. "Good, I want to start filming her scenes tomorrow." Tina closed the door as she left, relieved that she did not have to do what Liza would soon be required to endure for the next month or so. Then again she admitted humbly, she was rather plain compared to the blonde bimbos. "And I make a lot more money as the Director's Assistant!" Tina invited Liza in to the interview room soon after, along with Jackie and Miss Greenham.

"OK girls, we are set to start filming tomorrow. Here are your scripts, study them tonight. Miss Greenham has highlighted the parts when you will step in. Liza glanced over the typed script with the hen scratching indicating the lead actress's input. Her eyes widened as she scanned the script. She touched her palm to her beating chest. She thought of Ashley back home. What would she say? Or Jack when he returned?

"Oh my God!" Liza whispered to herself. Jackie did the same as she read over the script. Tina smiled as she winked at Miss Greenham. "Any questions girls? Remember keep your eyes on the prize. This is your first shot at this Liza, make it a good one. I want your best effort OK?" Liza jerked her head up, then smiled.

"Yes no problem. Who is the guy shooting this scene with us?" Tina filled her in quickly, then let them go for the day. "Get your rest Jackie and Liza. It will be a long day tomorrow. Remember the first day is usually the most trying one to get through. Have a good night." Liza and Jackie waved and walked out of the trailer to the parking lot. Liza gripped the folder in her long, purple polished nails as she walked beside Jackie.

"Well Jackie, what do you think? Ever done this kind of thing before?" Jackie striding beside Liza in high heels and a tight short skirt shook her head. "I was an exotic dancer for a few years. I am used to old rubbies trying to paw at me. I am hoping this is the beginning of a whole new life. And how about you?"

"Totally new to me. Just retired from nursing. I once had a psychiatric patient, a senile old man, try to pull me into the bath tub with him. I tell you it's not easy giving a 70- something man a bath. Yuck! I hope I never get that old!" She laughed with Jackie before they wished each other a good night. Liza climbed into her old truck and started it up. As she drove to her rental apartment she thought of Jack. "Where are you hon? When will I ever see you again?" A tear streamed down her cheek as she drove down the dusty desert track. She cried herself to sleep that night, as thousands of miles away Jack slept with Anna.

Liza and Jackie showed up at 07:00 A.M. the next morning. Tina greeted them and ushered them into the female change room. Soon after the two stand-ins watched as Miss Greenham was being filmed in the lead off scene. Playing the part of university cheerleader, she falls into the hands of the man playing an evil mutant, who abducts her and her cheerleading team in a secluded wayside inn. Liza tried to focus on her part coming up, as the horrible mutant carried off the limp body of the actress to his underground lair.

Later in one scene Bob Rothman, the actor playing the mutant abductor, stood between Liza and Jackie. He looked up at the two hot, blonde beauties who towered over him by a foot. "OK girls. I have to ah, make out with you here." Liza furrowed her thick eyebrows, as the old actor showed his yellow horse teeth at her, chortling wickedly at his lame joke. "Like whatever it takes, eh Jackie?" Jackie smiled as they scurried off to the change room and away from his prying eyes. After a brief smoke break, the two stand-ins were called in for the next scene. Liza felt herself shiver as she steeled herself for her first foray into the film world.

The camera crew chuckled as the gaffer yelled, "Scene 2, take one." The cameras rolled as Bob entered and lunged at the two blondes. "Hello my pretties! Come to Daddy!" Liza gasped as the old man grabbed her roughly, gripping her buttocks and pinching her skin in his palms. Scene after scene was shot as old Bob made out with the two abducted women. The actress doubles leaned on him as he kissed and fondled them, then stripped them naked. "Let yourself go Liza!" Al the director shouted. Liza who was naked and supposedly unconscious as Bob carried her, let herself go limp, her face dangling back off his arms.

Then Bob dumped her on the cot, her body bouncing before lying on her side. The camera lens zoomed in as she lay still, her arms and legs tossed in abandon as Bob bent over her undressing. Bob who had never been in a film before, was recruited for his natural rough appearance and low position in society. A small town criminal, spending half his life in jail, he was deemed a natural for the part. After a break, the next scene began. Liza moaned as Bob carried her body, over his shoulder inside his secluded, dilapidated rundown shack. She was gagged and bound then tossed bodily inside a locker. For this scene she had to spend an hour or so locked in the foot locker. Liza soon found her physical training was paying off, as she was pushed to new limits of endurance. It was hot that day, nearly 100 degrees as Liza lay inside the wooden locker. She panted feeling claustrophobic, as she struggled to breathe. "Keep your eye on the prize!" Liza thought as she panted, against the rag stuffed into her mouth. She closed her eyes, trying to picture herself lying in Jack's comforting arms back home. Liza was finally released an hour later, she and Jackie helped out by film crew. They wrapped towels around their naked bodies, sweat dribbling down their tanned skin.

"Awesome ladies!" Al beamed, as they toweled off before the Director. Bob adding, "I never would have thought you girls were not trained actors!" Liza looked at Jackie, the two shaking their heads as they walked by the short, rotund actor and retrieved their clothing. Liza did not complain, for she had heard her predecessor had been fired for that. "That is why you were hired, so if you do not like it there is the door." Al Sikorski had dismissed her without hesitation. "Time is money. Find me a replacement Tina!"

By the second week, Jackie went to talk to Tina. She cried as she told her she had enough. The last scene she had to lie in a bed for hours, tied spread-eagled as old Bob abused, tortured and raped her. Her piercing screams were still being reviewed by Al and his crew. "I know it's tough Jackie. Remember it's just another week. Liza has come to me also, but she is hanging in. Stay strong, you are doing awesome! Everyone says so. If you quit, you will regret it later. Now what do you need?" After talking with Al, Tina offered both stand-ins a hefty bonus after the final scene and a few perks...and future offers. In the final scene, Jackie was hung in the cellar, then her strangled body put on a slab for dissection by the insane freak.

Liza shot graphic scenes with the old man, both naked in a tub, then she was in bed with Bob and a few of his nasty friends. For in this scene Bob's family, his father and brothers decided they wanted this one to give them children. Liza slept with them for the final three days. For twelve hours a day, she lay in that bed, with four very freakish, very frightening looking old men. In the last scenes, after he strangled them, Bob hung Liza and Jackie by their heels in the slaughterhouse. The film would undergo digital enhancement later, but for these bloody scenes, Liza and Jackie were sprayed with buckets of pig blood.

Her athletic body was put to the limit, she had to maintain graphically explicit poses for long durations as the cameras rolled. In the final shot of that first week, Liza lay backwards over the foot of the bed. Her chest panted as her head dangled backwards, her eyes staring past the whirring cameras, at Jackie and Chrissy who watched her. "Eyes on the prize!" Liza thought over and over, feeling the furry skin on her legs. She swallowed hard, biting back the desire to hurl. "Cut! Wrap it up. Well done people! That is a cut! Liza...beautiful darling!" Al helped her off the bed, hugging her. Liza in her bare feet was taller than Al, as he held her arms, a tear streamed down her cheek. "Well done, a towel here please! I will talk to you and Jackie later. Thank you again! Can you do more shots if we need you? I will be editing and deleting some scenes. It is an ongoing project, so I will count on you two for the next week or so."

Jackie and Liza hugged as they wrapped the towels around their waists. "I guess so Al. Another week or so?" He nodded "Yes, and pay is in this week." The next week saw them re-shoot some of the graphic scenes. For Bob and his fellow actor's delight and Liza and Jackie's disappointment, Al had wanted to raise the stakes.

At the beginning of May, Liza was finished and was handed a final check by Al. "Thanks a lot Liza. You were fantastic. I will give you a call down the road for sure!" Liza shook his hand and left with Jackie in her F-150 pick-up truck that Saturday afternoon. The movie debuted months later. Liza had not seen *The Mutants* as she had moved on from that first movie of her career. As it was, she had nightmares for days after her part had finished. That evening back in her home, Liza entertained her new friend Jackie. They had found that indeed they were virtually twin sisters. Liza got a call from Ashley, as she and Jackie sat on the front porch drinking and chatting about their first experience with film. "Mom Hi! I'm in Barbados...a swimsuit shoot. It's awesome...how was your film debut?" Liza smiled at Jackie, enjoying the peaceful desert evening.

"It was...an eye opener darling. But I got the prize!" After a short talk, Ashley assured her she would be back in a week. An hour later, Liza showed Jackie to her bedroom saying good night. "Sweet dreams Jackie." Liza was fatigued as she soon went to sleep, her near naked form curled up on the sheets, her glistening high heels dangling over the edge of the bed. "God was he a freak!" Liza shook her head, trying to make light of it, thinking of the old actor Bob. He certainly got into his part she thought, spurred on by the Director, manhandling her and Jackie with gusto. Now finally home, she could take pride in having stuck it through to the end.

"Oh Jackie Hon! Come back to me!" Then slowly Liza drifted off, lying on the bed stripped to her thong, for it was hot that evening. A week after getting back from filming *The Mutants*, as Liza slept a strange dream visited her. Suddenly she was back in ancient times, amongst the fabled Amazon warriors. She dreamed she was an Amazon Princess, daughter of an Amazon Queen Scylla. After a big, bloody battle against a tribe of dark, mysterious half human/ half- winged vultures called Sloths, sent by Hades himself to subdue these barbaric warrior women, the Amazons are victorious. Piles of dead Sloths lie at the feet of Scylla and her warriors.

The Amazon women took no prisoners, cutting the heads off their dead enemies, and spiking them on poles about the battlefield as a warning. Do not mess with the Amazons was the warning to all. After a victory party, a Sloth herald arrived at the Amazon camp seeking Queen Scylla. "My Queen Scylla! My Lord Baktur begs a truce with Ye. He seeks peace with the Amazons, and is pulling his army back to our lands. He seeks your agreement in a truce and commends your warriors for their valor in battle!"

"Indeed! He concedes? Finally seen the light the fool. Amazons are invincible! Very well then. Tomorrow at the River of Tears, I will meet him for terms." The Sloth herald bowed humbly, as guards lowered their spears.

"Agreed Queen Scylla!" The herald bowed before the blonde Queen's throne, as the Amazon guards and her daughters snickered from the sidelines. The shortest of them was nearly six feet tall, all towering over the short, grotesque, Sloth. His scaly skin and fangs were sending shivers of disgust up the spines. The Queen sitting on her gold decorated throne, held a hand to her lips silencing them till the Sloth left. "That one is one of the handsomer Sloths I have seen Amazons, the others would make a fat sow run for safety!" Liza laughed as she sat beside her lovely, golden haired mother. All of the Amazons were stunners, but the Royalty were goddesses. The next day, Liza accompanied the Queen's party to the appointed spot on the River of Tears.

Liza writhed in bed as the dream tormented her brain. Her eyes rolled in their sockets as her body went limp... she was his! The Sloth flapped its huge wings and lifted her bodily into the air, her long hair flying in the breeze, her arms and legs dangling as she lay helpless in its fanged claws. Then Liza morphed back in her own body, fell into the arms of another hideous Sloth, picked up bodily as it ran off with her. Liza groaned feeling it's claws grip her soft naked skin. Tossing on her bed she screamed in utter bone chilling horror.

"You Amazon...are mine now!" Liza looked up into it's deep, dark, eye sockets, it's blood shot eyes, like black pits from Hades staring into hers as she shivered in horror. "No... No... the tongue!" The Sloth's jaw opened wide, exposing its hideous fangs to her as it hissed like a reptilian monster, then it's huge forked tongue shot at her gaping mouth as she screamed in terror! "Please...Stop!" Liza screamed as she felt its tongue, overpower her own tongue and penetrate into her gaping mouth, cutting off her scream suddenly. She sat bolt upright in the bed then stared into...the blue eyes of her friend Jackie.

"Liza! Are you O.K.?" Jackie had woken up as Liza had let out her ear piercing scream. Liza stared wide-eyed in her dimly lit bedroom, her head darting from side to side... searching, then into her friend's concerned eyes. "Oh! Yes,

Honey...just a bad dream! Wow! What a vivid nightmare! Oh and you were in it with me!" Jackie dressed in a nightgown sat beside her friend, stroking her bare shoulder soothingly. Liza's chest panted hard, her heart still going like a trip hammer. Her bare breasts rose and fell, her fingers trembling as she covered them. She shivered still feeling the claws pawing at her. "My God! It was the worst dream! These half human monsters were carrying us off to their lair...Amazons! I was an Amazon!" Her trembling fingers stroked her heaving chest as she fought to slow her beating heart. "Hon! It's O.K. A silly dream as you said."

Jackie smiled reassuringly as she stroked her friend's chin in her hand. Liza smiled as she hugged her friend tight. "Thank-you Jackie. If my husband can not be here, I am glad you are! I need a smoke!" She got up out of bed, smiling as her friend helped her. "Liza you are like so hot! No wonder they wanted you in their lair!" She laughed as Liza furrowed her brow, as she took a cigarette from her pack, offering one to her friend. "Thanks Liza. My thoughts on your dream, probably you are stressed out a bit from the film scenes."

"Yes, I should not be doing this, but...what the Hell eh?" They laughed as Liza lit their cigarettes, blowing a stream of smoke in the air as she sat down by her night table, then crossed her legs as she gazed out the window. "So O.K....are you good now?" Liza smiled sheepishly, "I think so. Jeez it was so real, so vivid! I can feel my skin crawling with their scaly fangs on me! You know, thinking of it. That film we did, maybe that brought this on. That old freak, like his cold, bony fingers were like claws. His bad teeth like fangs. It feels like Hell!"

Jackie nodded as she inhaled on the cigarette, then coughed. "Like gag me! I like so do not want to hear about that creep!" Liza smiled then giggled at her young friend, who was a virtual mirror image of herself.

"I was just thinking...how is your hubby doing?" Jackie changed the subject, puffing on her cigarette nervously. Liza took a drag from her cigarette as she leaned beside her. "I know he is fine, a tough warrior as I have said." Liza smiled as she continued. "He scares me though sometimes. It is his second war you know, he thinks he is invincible. I hope he is right. My Jack will be home...soon." Jackie nodded sadly. "I need a guy like that."

"Don't worry Liza darling. He will be so glad to see you! You look awesome! I am so proud to have you as my friend! My friends thought you were like my older sister at first. A couple of my guy friends even wanted to date you." Liza smiled at this, as she finished her cigarette then took a gulp of water. She laughed as Jackie took her long ponytail, looping it around her own neck playfully. "I don't doubt it Dear, but I prefer older men who can handle me...like Jack. But not too old either!" Jackie nodded as she finished her cigarette. "I agree, nothing over 25." Liza laughed at this, joined by Jackie as they embraced and hugged each other. "OK Hon, off to bed. Good-night. Let's talk again tomorrow morning Jackie hon."

After chatting, and feeling better, Liza went back to bed. It was 03:50 A.M. when Liza drifted off back to sleep. The strange dream did not return, now she dreamed of Jack. They were on a deserted beach alone, her bronzed tanned body wearing a bathing suit. Jack raced her to the surf as they laughed, the boiling surf tossing them about. Liza finally emerged from the warm water, her skin glistening in the hot sun. Her smoking gaze on Jack, she swept her long hair back behind her neck, stretching her muscles as she posed for him. Jack was lying on the sand, in his bathing suit, his muscular, tanned body as she had last remembered him. "Come to me Liza my darling!" Liza flashed a smile as she lay in bed, her last memory was of them lying together, on a deserted beach somewhere in the Pacific. As she lay in bed she whispered to him far away.

The next week she loaded the F-150 truck and accompanied by Ashley, headed for the Pacific coast. "I want to find a secluded beach I have never heard of Ash Hon. When Jack comes home, we will go there. Maybe do a little yachting?" As the wind blew her hair wildly through the open truck window, the blonde woman smiled. She fingered her designer sun glasses, as the hot sun beat down on the desert Interstate highway. Unknown to Liza, Jack was fighting for his survival in the Middle East inferno. Ashley did the navigating as she drove to the Pacific coast. "Oh here is one Mom. Newport Beach south of Los Angeles. Or Laguna Beach?"

Liza glanced at her daughter, smiling as she sat behind the wheel. "Pick one Hon. I am your chauffeur for the day. How far to the coast?" Ashley flicked the screen of her notepad, checking the nearest highway signs.

"Well it depends which way we head. We are on I-8 now, just inside the border from Arizona. If we go due west to San Diego we can be there in about six hours or so. Imperial Beach on the coast. Step on it Mother!"

"At your command Ashley." Liza jammed the accelerator to the floor, watching as the speedometer needle passed 115 m.p.h. The F-150 vibrated as it shot down the highway, headed on a collision course with the Pacific coast ahead. As Ashley had predicted, they arrived south of San Diego at just past 6 p.m. It was idyllic that day, as they parked and sprinted for the beach, tearing off their clothes before racing to the water.

Sea gulls took off from the surf, as the two blondes screamed running and diving into the water. Liza felt refreshed after handling half a day driving. "Whew! That was freaking worth it!" She lunged breaking the surface, spouting water as Ashley broke beside her. Like a pair of dolphins, naturally gifted in the water, they swam out to the deep water. They raced each other as spectators watched from the beach. When they finally walked back to their clothes an hour later, the setting sun glinted off their bodies.

Liza had chosen a new lime green, sparkling string bikini while shopping with her daughter. It accentuated her new tattoos nicely she said to Ashley, as they lay on their towels, soaking in the last of the day's sun. "Oh yes Mom! You look super awesome. Like I can't believe you are my Mom!" Liza flashed a bright smile as Ashley rubbed sun tan lotion on her back, then down her long legs. She closed her eyes as she rested her cheek on her bicep, day dreaming as she lay on the palm tree lined beach.

She had no idea that Jack was undergoing a different sort of existence. For across the world, his unit was being put through its paces. There were few breaks between the endless runs, pack marches and weapon drills. For Jack it was a routine thing, sort of like being at a sports' team training camp. That day Force X lost several men during training. Colonel Mann ordered the bodies to be quietly buried. He had assigned a grave yard for Force X, much like the existing one in Canada's Nunavut Arctic. By the end of training a few weeks later, the cemetery in the desert was christened with two dozen crosses. Jack had found one the last morning, hung inside his tent. A new man to the platoon, Jack suspected he would not last. "I just got a feeling about him." Sitting in the canteen beside George Mann, one of the original Pathfinders smiled. "Yes but we are not all Lucky Jacks here yer know." The others laughed at his joke and jided Jack till he joined in. His thoughts were far away as he lay on his bunk that night.

It was the same all that week for Liza. She had stopped worrying about seeing Jack. Her thoughts had to be on holding the fort till he returned. The next day she watched as contractors worked on her new villa. She discussed the design with the engineers from the contractors. "I want it to look like a Roman villa. My husband is away for a while. When he returns, I want it completed for a surprise." The building engineer nodded.

The building crew worked flat out, encouraged as Liza and Ashley strode by in their summer beach ware. Liza caught more than one stealing glances at her, as she exercised in the yard with Ashley. Once every week Liza and Ashley went swimming at local lakes. Liza felt this was the best work-out and she was a natural long distance swimmer and diver. By early that spring of 2016, the villa was nearing its completion, already her first film was paying off. Shortly after the McCann villa was complete, Liza got her second film offer from Hollywood. "Oh my God!" Ashley gaped wide eyed as Liza told her. They hugged giggling excitedly, as Liza read the script e-mailed to her. It was mind blowing to the 40 year-old retired nurse. But for Ashley, she saw her mother's obvious beauty and talent. Her mental discipline and hard work were beginning to pay off. Liza's body looked stunning in her skirt and sport top. Almost no body fat, muscles rippling from her limbs and torso. "I do not take steroids Ashley. I've seen what they do to people. I don't want to look like a man. I am a feminine woman first." Ashley accepted this sage advice from her mother.

"I know Mom, some models are being pushed to take them. Then they are discarded a year later."

Liza sat on the new porch reading her movie script later that evening. She scribbled notes here and there, for the Director had asked for her critical ideas within a week. Also this time, Liza was to be given a more prominent role. Although not the lead actress, she had a significant part and dialogue. "Just another stepping block Ashley." Her daughter smiled as she handed her an iced tea and sat down.

"I should look at acting don't you thing Mom?" Liza thought over the question. "I would not be in a rush hon. I am just a beginner at this acting thing. You know what we need? An agent, I will talk to my friend Anastasia, she can probably set me up with someone." The next day Liza connected with Anastasia in L.A.

"Congrats darling! I knew you would get another offer. Yes, I can get my agent to call you. If he can't handle you, he will know someone who can." Liza said good-bye, her mind at ease as this issue was settled. Now the only thing missing in her life was her husband Jack. She felt in her heart he was OK and soon he would return to her. "My Odysseus! I am waiting for you!"

Jack and Force X at that moment were getting ready for their riskiest mission to date. It was a small unit action, behind-the lines to rescue several hostages. It was a battle for Liza to concentrate on her own life and this new film. Liza put even more effort into it as she struggled to keep focussed on the present goal. To be as ready as she could for this key role. So she spent considerable time on the Internet. Knowing little about the true story of the San Diego Strangler, she went on line to get background research. She found several articles about it. Ashley sitting at her side on the verandah, was appalled as Liza recounted the grim account of the serial slayings of half a dozen women.

"So my character is the last of his victims. This killer abducts me, keeps me prisoner for a month. Here the director has to get inside this animal's head. No one knows what really happened then, for he was never caught. He wants me to become this woman. What was she thinking? How did she try and get through the hell of that time in captivity?" Ashley squirmed nervously in her chair as she listened to her mother.

"Mom this is like, really freaking me out. Maybe you should not do this. It' s like playing with the devil!" Liza smiled and patted her daughter's arm to reassure her. "Hon! It's a movie, I will be fine, besides Hollywood wants me, I just can't quit because I am having second thoughts. All the great ones do movies where they are at risk. I am doing all my own stunts too, although there is a stunt double I hear. The final scene will be the most challenging I think. My character is hung by the neck in Central Park." Ashley shivered at this revelation, then she reached over and hugged her mother. "Promise me Mom, take care of yourself, I need you." Liza laughed at Ashley, patting her back. "I will be fine Hon, I promise."

Chapter IX

RESCUE OPERATION

April 5, 2015: Iraq Force X Forward Op Base Cirillo: The Intelligence Officer of the Force, Captain Langois stood before the assembled Officers of the Force X O-Group. "Gentlemen, your Attention please, we have ISIS on the defensive. With the successful attack on Mosul, they are on the retreat towards Syria. If we retain the momentum, they should be pushed out of Iraq by the end of the year certainly. This week we will have liberated Tikrit. The Kurdish Peshmerga can mop up the North of Iraq by themselves, with a few of our JTF-2 teams to advise them, along with our air support as required. General Constable is already planning on striking ISIS bases in Syria. The next phase of Operation Impact is under way; our Aurora surveillance planes are mapping the ISIS positions for our CF-18 strikes coming. Meanwhile the enemy is getting desperate. Their fear tactics are trying to scare us. We have a report they have kidnapped at least two Western hostages recently. If true they are two Canadian women, some other Western models. Colonel Mann will now take over. Sir."

Colonel Mann got up and returned the salute before taking over the podium. "Force X has been tasked with a rescue mission Gentlemen. Our Convict Penal Regiment are being tasked to rescue Western hostages by our gentlemen politicians, using that term loosely if I may." The assembled soldiers smiled, a few chuckling at their C.O.'s accustomed dry sense of humor and lack of political correctness. "This will be risky for Force X. We are at present locating where exactly ISIS are holding the hostages, but we believe it is near this town of El Harish, located in Syria about ten miles from the border with Iraq. The stakes could not be higher in this operation, we foul up and everything we have accomplished to date will have been in vain. I have asked for Special Forces to be sent in our stead. But the generals have promised me, if we are successful Force X will be expanded. So we will go ahead with it. I like the SAS motto, Who Dares Wins. So Force X will dare and win. Here is a recent photo released by ISIS of the hostages. Believed to be several Western females."

He nodded to an aide who put the picture up on the big overhead screen. The crowded tent hushed as the picture loomed before them. As the room went silent they stared at the two women, in bathing suits...gorgeous models apparently, staring into the camera as a hooded ISIS man stood behind them. "ISIS has stated that unless Canada backs off they will be executed.... beheaded and burned, like the others they have captured."[10] Mann now had a grim look on his face as the tension started building around him. "I can tell you men, we will not back down to these...fucking cowards. This one is behind the lines work Gentlemen and the world is watching! This will make Force X's name... good or bad. The stakes are high, but I expect...no demand success! I do not lose nor I assume do you. I am planning the mission right now, we can expect to go in at any time, these women are counting on us and the clock is ticking. ISIS has threatened to behead these two ladies! As soon as our surveillance pinpoints them I am sending our boys in force. No one sits this one out, I am using the entire Force X! Including you and me! Either we come back with them or not at all. As the Spartans said before Thermopylae "Come back with your shield or on it!"

"Sir every one of our boys is all in." Major van Zandt stood up. "Sergeant Major says we have 950 effectives, including lightly wounded....no one wants to sit this one out Sir." Mann felt a bit giddy with the excitement, choking a bit, trying to control his pride in his hardened convict Regiment.

He nodded "Thank-you Eddie, O.K. this is a 24-7 Operation. Platoon Commanders get your men ready to rock. Company Commanders in my tent in 10 minutes. O.K. to your stations let's roll!" The Israeli agent Anna Zollmann was escorted into Colonel Mann's HQ tent just

---

[10] In addition to the numerous grizzly beheadings of captured western civilians they burned alive a captured Jordanian pilot.

after midnight. The Colonel sat before a map with Eddie and the Company Commanders working out the assault details. "Colonel Sir, this is Israeli Mossad Agent Zollmann. She would like to speak with you Sir." Mann looked up at the young woman. He smiled as beat as he was, "Yes I am he. I am glad my boys got to you in time. Now as I am a bit busy what vital information do you have to tell me Miss Zollmann?"

Anna looked determined as the tall American stared hard at her. "Colonel my code name is 009. I heard through the grapevine about your Operation, I think I can help. I owe your boys for getting me out of Mosul. I have asked my employer for permission to work with your unit in this operation. I believe it might help turn the tide against these monsters."

"Yes I agree on that latter point, I was glad to hear of your assistance in our last attack. How can you help us?" Anna collected herself before responding. "I know this area, the people and the customs. I was in El Harish a month ago. I could infiltrate the camp disguised. If you want these women out alive, you need to know which specific building they are in, or tent or hole in the ground. I think they are good soldiers your men but not as you say silent." Colonel Mann nodded as he stared at the map on the table. He had to concur on her criticism, for apart from the Pathfinder Platoon, most of the convict soldiers were as a subtle as a fart in church. To succeed in getting the hostages freed, this had to be a surgical, subtle operation. How to get to them before the alarm was given, was the ultimate question.

"Point taken Miss ...Anna. I am waiting for the latest Intel from our *flyboys*, and we need the O.K. from Ottawa and Washington. When and if we get the go, I believe this will be the start of the big push into Syria. I hope you know of the risk you take? If they caught you...a Jew and a woman...This time you may not be as fortunate." Anna nodded trying to smile "My work is never simple. I will call my boss to OK it."

"Tell the Mossad to hurry if you please. If you are to be of any use, you will have to be in there today or tomorrow. The hostages have been given 48 hours and I don't think they're joking." His words sent a shiver through her, for he was brutally matter of fact. If something went wrong and she fell into their hands, it was too scary to contemplate. But she steeled herself to go ahead with her plan. It would make her name in Israel, if she died, she would be immortalized in a glorious sacrifice. Anna whispered a silent prayer. "If I die I commend my spirit to you God. Give me the strength to see this through and get those women out alive. Amen."

"I know them Colonel. ISIS are evil, if they succeed in killing these women, it will send a shock wave through the West. It will be my pleasure to throw a wrench in their plans." The officers were impressed by the young Israeli agent. Her slight accented English only added to her physical beauty. But underlying that was a mercuric latent energy and a quick thinking mind. Obviously she had backbone and her subtle edge added to the Force's brutal killing power, making for a deadly and winning combination.

Colonel Mann smiled at her and van Zandt. The Colonel nodded then said to van Zandt, "Eddie your team will co-ordinate with Agent 009 here, set up the details: logistics, transport, comms, code words and the like. Tom (Intel officer), co-ordinate with General Constable. I want all the fast air he can give me. Take out every road bridge, armour units at these map reference points. When we know where exactly the hostages are, we move in... the Pathfinders will secure the DZ here. The main drop goes in 60 minutes after. JTF-2 will support by chopper landing at key points. As this goes down, the Kurds will launch attacks across the border to pin down their heavy units. The fast air will fly CAP[11] till JTF-2 or we call them in as required...we have to be flexible guys. This Operation Medusa will unleash Hell on ISIS in 24 hours. It will be like the Greek Goddess, with snake like tentacles taking bites out of our enemy. OK men let us get it done!"

Then Colonel Mann dismissed the officers to execute his orders. Outside he peered into the desert darkness, his mind working like a machine as he mentally went over his plan, covering every possible contingency. Eddie tried to convince him to stay behind, it was too great a risk. "No Eddie. I'm not hiding in Coward's corner. I lead from the front like Patton." He smiled coolly at ease as Eddie nodded.

---

[11] Cap: Combat Air patrol: Jets maintain position in an oval racetrack holding position till assigned mission on ground or air.

This would be the big one, it had to succeed! "No sir Eddie. Mrs. Mann's son is not in the business of sitting behind the lines! This is the tipping point and as CO I need to be up front at the tip of the spear."

OPERATION MEDUSA: April 5, 2015: Iraq Force X Forward Op Base Cirillo:

Colonel Mann finished his orders for Operation Medusa to the assembled Officers "We have to be flexible guys. And hit like Thor himself!" Then Colonel Mann dismissed the men, nodding to his Company OC's. He had played his cards. The wheels of the machine were in motion, so he could sit back and watch it work. He would be the engine mechanic now, only stepping in when something went down or sprung a leak. Eddie had made a final attempt to persuade him to run the operation from Camp Cirillo, it was too great a risk to lose the CO of the entire force. "No Eddie. But thanks for you concern. No one sits this thing out."

He also knew that before it was over allot of good and bad people would die. So he turned to Major van Zandt. "Eddie I want you to go through every man's record. The worst of them I want detailed to suicide squads. Each one will carry armed explosives in their packs. I want them hooked up to timers, so we can remotely detonate them. This will be one of the cards up my sleeve. You might say we will kill two birds with one stone." For while Mann was bent on destroying his enemy, one thing he had was an ulterior motive.

"Yes Colonel. Amongst the newer recruits we have some rather nasty individuals. Pedophiles, serial sex killers...and about two dozen Moslem terrorists. Six planned to take over Parliament Hill in Ottawa, behead Prime Minister Harper, then blow up the works with explosives on their bodies. It failed when CSIS caught on and tried to sell them explosives." Colonel Mann smiled, "Well now they will get their chance with our help. I want these guys under close guard. When the time is right I will unleash them on our foe." Eddie smiled then left to get his aides going through the records.

Anna met Jack in the drinking mess that evening of April 5. That night a big steak dinner was being served. The Pathfinders were all there, digging into the feast with gusto. The mess was loud as the convicts unwound from the hectic day's training. As yet, many were oblivious to the upcoming mission and the chance this would be their last dinner on Earth. Jack however knew and like the veteran soldier he was hid his feelings. His closet buddy Sean suspected something big was coming, the army didn't lay on this dinner for nothing. Anna sat down between the two veterans, the only female amongst the convicts that night.

"Jack darling, do you know what is coming up?" Jack looked at her as he tore into his steak and fixings, then slugged back a pint of ale. "I suspect something special. Save the world, rescue the girl or die in the attempt."

Anna flashed a smile as she ate. "More or less on the mark. It is a hostage rescue, two Canadian women, the

ISIS bastards are going to publicly behead...amongst other nasty things. Probably hump them silly first. I am going to infiltrate their camp, so I am leaving after tonight." Jack stared in her eyes across the table, a quiet look as they connected. He would have stopped her if he could, but knew she was determined.

"I don't suppose anything I could say would stop you?" Anna shook her head "I have to get in there or these women have no chance. I will be undercover, with a Burka, find their hiding place and just before you unleash Hell kill the guards. They are probably under orders to execute them if they sense a rescue attempt. I will contact you by radio and give you directions. Then it is up to you and these men," she waved a hand at the drunken convicts roaring with drunken laughter, "to arrive and save us in the nick of time!" Jack smiled as he finished a jug of beer. "The cavalry to the rescue! Sounds like a plan. Don't worry Anna, I will get y'all out. I have to do what it takes, to get back to my woman back home."

Anna nodded knowing what he meant. "I am happy for you, you deserve it. I have a lover back in Israel. If I live, I will eventually retire to a lovely villa somewhere in the Mediterranean and raise a flock of children. After this thing is done, maybe someday we can meet again?" Jack tipped her glass with his, as they enjoyed possibly their last moment together. Jack felt her fingers lock inside of his and squeeze tightly.

"I would like that Anna. I want you to meet my love Liza. Married her years ago when I was a kid. She could be your Mother, yet I saw her on the Internet cam the other day...I swear you would think she is in her twenties!" Anna nodded as she looked at him, as they embraced tightly. "Just my luck" she thought sadly.

"I do not doubt it Jackie. Here is to our lovers!" When they retired later both needed some rack time, so they hugged each other, then a final kiss good night. Anna walked to her tent, lying on her cot she tossed and turned for hours as her mind reeled. She kept hearing her final words to him. "I will see you soon Jackie?" Anna smiled under his kiss. "Lay your money on it Honey!" Jack said assuredly, Anna had laughed then spun on her heels and trooped off to her tent, Jack following the sway of her hips and the long hair flowing in the night breeze. He sighed then turned for his own tent. It was 02:00 A.M. when Jack hit his bunk, his mind dreaming of nicer surroundings. As he slept inside his tent, the army base bustled with activity as Force X readied for battle. On the runways, lines of transports lined up nose to tail, with fuel tanker trucks filling the big fuel tanks.

ISIS Camp, El Harish: Inside the tent the two Canadian hostages eyed their captors. Both were models who had come to Lebanon to shoot a Swimsuit International Special edition. Shot on a beach outside Beirut, a dozen models from the big Western nations put on a great show. They were watched by Lebanese locals allied with ISIS the whole time. The day before they left, their hotel was raided and six were abducted. Now all six were held by ISIS in the camp. Only the two Canadians, 25-year-old blonde Laurie Black and 27-year-old brunette Jackie Olds had been identified in Al Jazeera as slated for execution.

Of the four others, one a German named Terra Holzer, two British and one Italian, all were elite models...budding Supermodels in the fashion industry. Now they squatted before the four guards, hands handcuffed behind their backs. Laurie looked at the hooded guards standing before them nervously. She turned to see Jackie beside her. "What are they going to do with us Jackie?" Her friend shook her head, "Don't you read the news Laurie? I can see it in their eyes...rape us. Then after they've had their fun kill us." They looked at the guards fearfully as they whispered.

"Shut up Infidel whore. No talking, you will see the will of Allah soon enough!" The leader a tall bearded man named Karim, smirked as he looked down on the squatting beauties in the dirt at his feet. His hooded eyes went along the line at their bowed heads, taking in their beauty. Then Karim decided. "I will have the blonde Canadian first! She will be one of my virgins in Paradise! Then the German with the big tits tomorrow night!" For the next day he would get orders to start the beheadings. It would be so much more exciting to spill the blood of these decadent Western whores, rather than the few scrawny reporters, Red Cross workers and Infidels stupid enough to fall in their hands so far. Then he rubbed his crotch and spat at the blonde busty Italian. "Allegra! Come with me, you look like you need to go to the heads." Allegra nodded struggling to her feet "Gracia Senor." As Karim left with her the other guards smirked. For Allegra would be in for more than a quick squirt. Karim they knew had no qualms about having close relationships with these Infidel women. For the rest of the night, the German and the two Brits took their turns, alternating between the four guards. By first light all six models lay sleeping on their sides in the sand, stripped nude, hair tossed wildly about them. The Arab guards played cards, betting looted jewelry and swimsuit apparel confiscated from the stripped Infidel models. They would not need this bobbles, the guards joked as they wiled away the night.

April 6: Monday, Force X Camp: Reveille was at 06:30 A.M. The platoons grumbling as they assembled, many sporting a massive hangover, they cursed as they donned rucksacks and weapons. Breakfast was served as they lined up along a dirt road, a cup of coffee and a BLT. Then they marched for an hour in the blazing morning sun, the heavy stomp of combat boots and jingle of combat gear their morning music. The veterans amongst them who had tasted combat, cuffed the helmets off the FNG's who whined. It was already widely known through the rumor mill. "Fuckers are sending us in tonight! Sure hope you guys played with yer dinks last night...it might be er last. If the fuckin' ragheads get yer, you won't have one left!"

09:00: Pathfinder Platoon Mission Briefing: Lieutenant Greene took over from Sergeant McGee after he called them to attention, saluting each other. "Thank-you Sergeant. At ease. Operation Medusa begins tonight. We will be in first, a hostage rescue mission. It will be similar to the last jump... HALO at about 03:00. Just inside the Syrian border. We liaise with our friendlies, JTF-2 and some Arab guides as before. Some will secure and mark the DZ while patrols will recce the objective. The objective is an ISIS camp here."

As the lines of dirty soldiers looked on, he pointed at the map with a stick. He rattled off compass headings, way points, radio procedures, code words and the like for the next hour. "Once the main party lands, they will form up along the attack lines. Pathfinders we will be in position, taking out the outlying sentries. If the alarm is given prematurely, JTF-2 will call in fast air and heavy guns. They will rake the camp and the surrounding ISIS positions with strafing runs and missile attacks. Sergeant McGee, position the AT teams along the access roads. Take your main group in once the green light is given. Our infiltrator agent will contact you when the time is ripe to spring the trap. You make a beeline for the hostages. Once they are secure, call me with the success signal Demarcation understood?" Jack nodded as he smoked a cigarette, jotting in his NCO message book. "And keep yer hands off them whores Lucky Jack!" Maggot jeered, the convicts sniggering, knowing Jack's reputation with the women. "I trust the Sergeant will have enough on his mind Trooper Maggot." The convicts relaxed as they laughed, the joke easing their tension.

Lieutenant Greene smiled nevertheless, not to be outdone by the convict Maggot's cunning brain. "Thank-you

Maggot, now then. After link up, we extract the hostages to the DZ, which will become the LZ for our choppers. All companies will remain in place to secure the LZ perimeter and beat back any counter-attacks by ISIS. Once we are out of the camp, JTF-2 will call in the fast air and level the place. All units when the order is given, code word *Maple Leaf,* pull back 500 meters by platoon and dig in. Anything within that area will become diced mincemeat." The grizzled convicts eyed one another grinning. "Men, we have two objectives on this mission. One is to get the hostages out alive. Two is to hit ISIS hard, no one is to escape that camp alive, the CO's orders. No prisoners, no quarter given or taken! Anyone attempting to surrender will be executed on the spot as usual. Any questions?" Silence followed as the men eyed each other and the Officer. "Sir just one." Maggot smiled crookedly at the young Officer before him.

"What is it Private?" Lieutenant Greene eyed Maggot. "Sir I picked this up in Mosul the other day. It is the KORAN, now since we don't have proper toilet paper, any objection if I wipe my ass with it?" Silence followed, even the hardest of the convicts staring at Maggot in wonder. "Stow it Maggot!" Jack said tersely.

"No Sergeant, I will answer that. Private do as you think fit. Since for most of us, the chance we will make it back are slim, I don't see it as a big problem." The platoon broke out in a fit of laughter, several slapping Maggot, the shaven headed convict as he grinned at the young Lieutenant. After the platoon was dismissed, Maggot sat in the toilet and tore out a page. He grinned as he wiped his ass with the Koran, then tore out another. "I got to kill me some more Arabs, don't want to run out."

April 7, 03:00 A.M. D-Day for Force X. The C-130 Herc revved its engines up as it sat on the desert makeshift runway. In the darkness two long lines of paratroopers walked to the lowered rear ramp. Jack led the way, his rucksack on his back, carrying his parachute over one shoulder and his rifle over the other. Once more Lion stood inside the cargo bay. "Evening Jack, you boys up for this?" Lion greeted the Pathfinders.

"I guess so, I had nothing else planned for the evening." One by one the heavily loaded paratroopers took their seats heavily. Most of the convicts had done several jumps by now, including at least one combat jump. There was some new meat however, replacements for their casualties over the past month. Freddie sat beside Jack, eying the new guy across from him. "Ten bucks says he pukes before we go."

"C'mon Freddie, they always do. We might as well bet I'll be asleep in ten minutes." They chuckled as the big plane lurched forward. The crew chief raised the rear ramp to the closed position, leaving it partly open to get the nice night breeze and a view of the surrounding terrain. "And the show begins eh?" Lion nodded smiling beside him "Why don't you come with us? It'll be so much fun!" "Thanks for the invite, but my wife would kill me." Warrant Officer Redmond laughed. The forty odd soldiers buckled down as the four powerful engines went to full power at the end of the runway, the pilot slowly turning the wheels and lining up for take-off. "C-195 ready for take-off." "Roger C-195. You are cleared hot!" The tower gave the pilot the clearance to take-off.

Seconds later the big camouflaged transport roared into the night, leaving a trail off dust, bright flames from its booster engines lighting the darkness. Behind, dozens of C-130's completed their final checks, as the rest of Force X lined up in long dark lines checked their equipment. Operation Medusa was under way. Inside the radar control room, the operators watched the lighted screens, seeing the green blip of the C-130 headed west. On converging tracks, the CF-18 fighter jets were moving at Mach 1.5 in pairs, headed for the Syrian border for the first pre-emptive strikes. 90% of the Canadian Air Force's heavy transport was involved, along with 50% of the CF-18 Squadron's strikers. Also in support were dozens of American coalition squadrons, U.S.A.F., British, French, Iraqi, Jordanian and others. In the lead CF-18, the pilot Captain Ian Broadhurst, Call Sign Red Eye monitored the HUD (head's up display) as he cruised at 15,000 feet while the Weapons Officer in the rear checked the status of the jet's weapons (500-pound laser guided bombs, air to ground missiles, 30- mm chain guns). "All systems check OK, Red Eye." Ian acknowledged as his eyes surveyed around the jet, and the ground below. In the distance he saw the border...in a few minutes he knew they would be over enemy controlled territory. On his dark helmet visor, the latest in state-of-the art helmet accessories, an array of electronic data was displayed allowing him to concentrate on flying the aircraft.

He saw his wingman Call Sign Rat catcher maintaining position on his left quarter. He was Lieutenant George Collier, a young 25-year-old from Toronto. Stationed at Cold Lake Alberta, Ian had worked helping to train Collier for the past six months. Now they would be tested to the full in this high pressure mission. Ian called over the jet's radio "Rat catcher first checkpoint in 20. Alter to new course 0125." Rat catcher responded immediately, "Roger that. Altering to 0125." The pilots punched the data into the on board computer. Both jets banked right onto the new heading. Ten minutes later they were in their CAP position. The radar station in the HQ back at base had them on screen. Several radar techs monitored the screens, talking to numerous aircraft, all headed to the zone in Syria. One by one the CF-18's arrived in position. On the ground several teams of observers were also in position. Newer high tech drones controlled by the radar site, gave close-up views of the objective area. The spotters on the ground having infiltrated the ISIS positions over the past few days now talked to the fast air assets circling above. Meanwhile the lead C-130 with Jack's Pathfinders neared the Syrian border. Lion got the signal from the Crew Chief.

"Jumpers! Look this way! Ten minutes. Seatbelts off, stand up...check your equipment." Jack struggled to his feet as the plane rocked in the turbulence, as it roared through the dark skies. They were at 12,000 feet traveling at 240 knots. Jack looked at the two sticks of pathfinders lined up behind him. Each with one hand on the man in front, faces camouflaged, eyes fiercely staring at him. Jack grinned giving them the thumbs up.

"OK steady boys! GO on the Green! Do not wait till the man in front clears the ramp! You may leave together, keep nice and tight. We want a close group in this freefall!" The jumpers relayed the orders quickly down the line. "OK Port stick first. 10 seconds.... Go!" Jack tapped Lion on the shoulder as he surged to the ramp. "Once more into the fray!" Jack moved into the routine practiced body exit position, jabbing off the end of the ramp. As he hit the air, he arched hard, arms up and forward, head back, chest and hips out.

One by one his platoon followed him, forming up on Jack at the point. Lion stood by the Loadmaster as the port stick exited, then he tapped the starboard number 1. It was over less than a minute, the plane was near empty while only Lion remained. Coolly the tall JTF-2 Commando checked his facemask and nodded to the Loadmaster "Make sure they order more beer for us. Don't want you flyboys drinking it all." The C-130 Crew Chief laughed giving him the thumbs up, then the big paratrooper ran for the ramp and hurled himself into the dark night air. His eyes squinted behind the helmet visor as he peered ahead to find the nearest trooper. He gasped as he inhaled the oxygen from his mask then relaxed. "OK boys, close it up nice and tight. Let the fun begin!"

The jump went like clockwork. Linking up in the air, with grips on their mate's harness, they formed a big V formation, the Pathfinders followed Jack on his GPS setting to the Drop Zone slightly north-east. Jack glanced at the GPS dial then at his altimeter. "15,000' bang on heading. Ok boys keep it tight." The wind buffeted his body and equipment, hearing the whizzing sound of wind through his face mask. Below he saw the ground slowly moving toward him, then the tiny lights blinking. "Our friendlies I assume." Under a minute later he gave the break signal, waving his arms. Jack watched as the Pathfinders broke off and fanned out in star, then pulled their main ripcords. Jack relaxed in his box position as he dropped lower, then seeing 2200' on his altimeter reached to his right hip and tossed his pilot chute. He grunted as the main opened, his harness whipping his body to a feet down position. He looked up with relief to see a perfectly opening parachute.

"Nice one. Ok let's get er done." He grabbed his toggles and yanked down to his hips smartly, then raised them up. The chute steadied, all cells inflated. He turned a sharp 360 pivot, taking in the sight of the chutes around him. He spiralled down to the ground, then swooped in on the Drop Zone. He flared hard 10 feet up, his feet hit and he ran forward. Gasping he took off the oxygen mask, then quickly slipped out of the harness. He gripped his rifle and loaded it, checking it was on safe. As he gathered up his chute, he watched as the other 26 jumpers landed close by, Lion swooping in to land beside him. Jack picked up his rig and packed it with his mask and oxygen bottle into the carry bag. Lion waved from nearby as he struggled out of his rig.

Jack and Sean joined him a minute later. "Good jump eh lads? Do you believe civvies pay to do this?" Lion grinned as he walked beside them as they headed to the Platoon Rv, marked by a blinking red light a mere 100 meters away. They were greeted by a JTF-2 team and a few Peshmerga fighters. Dumping their rig nylon bags in a pile, they gathered in a group to discuss the route of march to the objective. It took the Pathfinders less than 30 minutes to organize on the Drop Zone. Teams were dispatched to four corners to mark it for the follow up main drop. Patrols were dispatched to recce and secure the surrounding terrain. Jack organized the DZ crew, while Lieutenant Greene took a three-man team forward to recce the ISIS Main camp, joined by Lion and several Kurdish Peshmerga who had been on the ground for several days and acted as guides. In position near the camp perimeter, the advanced Pathfinder patrol and Lion watched the camp, marking sentry positions, targets, the night vision goggles seeing every detail clearly.

"I will control the assault from here Lion." Lt. Greene whispered, as he lay on his belly, his map laid out before him on the ground. The next phase was the main landing in 20 minutes. So far so good...the enemy was asleep, unaware of the approaching storm about to break! And in the skies circling high above was THOR...the fast air arm component of MEDUSA. Like the mythical Greek Goddess with snakes for hair, the ISIS fighters were about to be bitten by Thor's Hammer and a thousand deadly snake bites! The first to die that night was an ISIS sentry. Agent 009 or *Matt Hari* had arrived in the camp quietly. The Israeli agent wearing a long black burka, slowly, carefully made her way to the perimeter. Her eyes pierced the night from the eye slits in the dark robe as she flitted from one building to the next. She crept up behind the sentry as he stood half dozing outside a big building. Anna silently approached him from behind, then her razor sharp 6-inch dagger struck, slicing open his throat from ear to ear. She lowered the body to the ground, then dragged him behind a pile of boxes and dumped the corpse silently.

It took her a few more minutes of careful surveillance before she found her target. It was a small stone hut, identified with a black flag with a single guard outside. Anna walked up to the guard and spoke to him in fluent Arabic. The guard fingered his AKM automatic as he glared at the woman. "OK woman go inside, tell them why you are here woman." Anna nodded her head bowing, her eyes on his pointed AKM.

"Allah be praised, thank-you." Then she stepped inside the doorway. Her eyes quickly surveyed the scene in the dimly lit room. The four ISIS guards stood before the forms of the six female hostages, who lay before them on the floor. The women slept stretched on blankets, completely naked as the guards played cards, piles of jewelry and the model's clothing grouped before each guard as they laid bets. Karim the leader looked bored at the robed woman. "Who are you?" Anna flashed her eyes looking down and bowing to him. "I am a trained nurse Sir. I am here to check the prisoners, before they meet their just end."

Karim nodded darkly as he played a card, "Very well woman. Make it quick, they will meet their end in a few hours." Anna bowed as she bent before the sleeping hostages. As she began to examine the two Canadians, 25-year-old blonde Laurie Black and 27-year-old brunette Jackie Olds, the guards resumed their poker game talking excitedly. Laurie and Jackie awoke to stare into the eyes of the burka clad woman as she slowly examined them, talking in low whispers. They were frightened, for the guards had already raped the other four models, the German Terra Holzer, two British and Allegra the Italian. Anna rummaged in her carry bag, removing a stethoscope. She placed a hand on Laurie, motioning her to sit up while she examined her.

"Relax, I am Anna a nurse. I need to check your health." Laurie and Jackie lay on their backs as the burka clad Arab woman checked their heart rate and pulse. One by one Anna checked the rest of the models. As she finished she checked her watch under her robe. Under the robe her body was wired, every word transmitted back to Force X HQ. She peered up casually at the guards who were entranced in their poker game.

"Karim my Lord! The six Infidels are in good condition. Would you like me to check the four of you? Perhaps I may remain here until the time for the execution?" Karim looked down at the nurse and shrugged his shoulders. He yawned, a smile spreading on his face. "Suit yourself woman. Do you have anything to keep us awake? We have another four hours till we get the go ahead to remove these Infidel's pretty heads." Anna nodded bowing again as she rummaged inside her medical bag, selected some pills and handed them to the guards. Anna bowed her head to them submissively before turning back to the hostages.

Back at Force X, the radioman handed a signal to the shift NCO. He read it and tapped another radio op. "Transmit this to Niner ASAP. Matta Hari is in position. There are six confirmed female hostages. Held inside a stone hut with a large black flag inside the ISIS camp. Four guards inside, one outside." Colonel Mann got the message a few minutes later. He had parachuted into the drop zone a short while before, with his HQ group. They were on the march to the camp a kilometer away.

"Very good, Six friendlies eh? Relay that to Lt. Greene at once, and the hut's location. Now as soon as the Regiment is on the ground get your Companies in position. Noise and strict light discipline. When we have the Force in position, the camp will be isolated, then we spring the trap!" The Company Commanders stood beside Niner as they received their final orders, open fire orders and cease fire. The four companies, 900 odd men would be placed around the camp, covering all access and egress points. At 03:00 April 8, the low C-130 formation arrived over the DZ... the Hercules emitting a booming roar and the mass drop began. The sky filled with hundreds of chutes, as the convicts jumped at 600 feet. The paratroopers hit the ground less than 30 seconds later. To everyone's surprise there were very few casualties. As they ran to their RV points, the Officers and NCO's organized them into their units and began to march to their objectives.

Silent and grimly determined, they marched like *The 300* at Thermopylae. Jack finished organizing the DZ crew, leaving a few men to gather chutes and gear into a central location. The jump had gone well, with only a few minor casualties. A half dozen men with broken bones were left at the DZ control RV, along with a few medics and a radioman. These would contact the Chinooks that would Heli-lift out the wounded and piled parachute gear. Jack then force marched at double time to the ISIS camp with the Pathfinders...he hissed at the laggards, forcing them to close ranks. Medusa was uncoiling her snake-like hair...the snake heads were baring their sharp fangs! And so far the unsuspecting ISIS inside the camp were blissfully unaware. Most were asleep, except for guards on the perimeter. Down the road near the Syrian border sat two tank battalions and numerous heavy artillery positions. Watching them silently and in radio contact, were teams of Peshmerga, Iraqi Special Forces and Canadian Special Service Regiment liaison teams. Slowly, silently teams of snipers and assault squads moved up the line.

Force X troopers meanwhile, were on the march to battle against ISIS. Hardened by years in prison, the convicts have been through a hellish 6 months of grueling selection training and several bloody battles, now they wanted blood... ISIS blood! The JTF-2 Commandos were given the task of directing the fighter jets and drones onto the targets. They had already spotted and given target coordinates to the jet fighters circling like eagles overhead. When they heard the code word *THOR*, the attack would commence.

At 04:00 Colonel Mann, Call sign Zulu Niner got the word, all four Force X infantry companies were in their final positions. A Company would support the Pathfinder assault directly on the ISIS camp. B, C and D Companies were in blocking positions to the West, East and South respectively. In Colonel Mann's position to the North and egress to the DZ/LZ were the Heavy Weapons Company (Heavy Machine Guns: 12 of the older but well-tried M2 .50 Caliber, ATP: 12 heavy anti-tank teams with 2-man crew served shoulder launched Milan rocket launchers and 3 Mortar platoons with 12 medium 81-mm mortars.

"All call signs this is Zulu Niner, THOR! I repeat THOR in figures 5 over." The radios crackled over the 5 kilometer perimeter of the battle zone. The order was relayed 5 kilometers into the skies to the CF-18's... all the way back to Force X HQ...to NATO HQ and eventually to Prime Minister Harper's Command Center in Parliament Hill in Ottawa, capital of Canada. "Well this is it Eddie!

Years of planning, last year's selection training. All come down to this...in the next hour we will know the result!"

Major van Zandt nodded smiling "Colonel it's been a pleasure!" The Canadian Senior ranking officer shook the tall Americans hand. The Pathfinder Platoon as leading assault unit, the tip of the spear, were at that moment inside the perimeter of the camp. Silently sentries were taken out by stalking, silent Force X men, knifed in the back, garroted, or in the case of Maggot by slow strangulation with his hands. All units were told to hold their fire until the Pathfinders were spotted or opened up. Jack positioned the light machine gun to cover his assault teams. He looked through his night vision binoculars. Now the target, the stone hut with the black flag was under 100 meters away. Outside he could see the sentry standing at the entrance. Parked beside him was an armored jeep. He looked at his men lying in a ragged V line around him. He nodded to the sniper team. Freddie had the heavy .50 caliber rifle with zoom lens. Made by PGW, a Canadian firm based in Winnipeg. He focused it, termed the Timberwolf on the Arab, zooming in on high power, he looked at the man closely. His fingers made small adjustments as the cross hairs centered on the turbaned head.

"I'll see this fucker in my dreams for the rest of my life." Beside him his spotter Larry "Roachman" bit back laughter. "Clear Freddie...the bastard...he's yours, send him to Hell." Freddie slowed his breathing, shifting his body. Slowly he eased the safety off, then looking through the sight, aimed on his chest.

He squeezed his trigger finger, paused held his breath, then squeezed. Suddenly the rifle cracked, the sound muffled by the foot-long silencer at the end of the thick barrel. The bullet hit the sentry in the collarbone, deflecting up slightly after hitting the bone and shattering it in a thousand fragments in a spray into his body. The man died in a split second, but the bullet kept going at 1800 feet per second, it slashed through his wind pipe, then spinal cord before blowing out the back of his head. The man's brains and blood sprayed over the wall of the concrete hut behind him, then his lifeless corpse toppled slowly backward to thump off the wall. Inside the four sentries heard the noise and sprang to their feet, snatching at their weapons.

Karim barked out orders and two ISIS guards went out to investigate. His first thought was the idiot had fallen asleep and dropped his gun. He shook his head in anger then slowly turned his head. He looked in stunned disbelief at the nurse, into Anna's eyes. He could not believe it, for her Burka was discarded, now she stood facing him in camouflage uniform. Anna's favorite weapon a 9-mm Berretta pistol, fixed with a silencer pointed at him, her two hands griping it, her body braced with her long legs spread wide. "God is Great!" Anna hissed then she fired two shots, the first hitting him dead in the heart, the second in his throat. Karim started to crumple, his nerveless fingers dropping his AKM assault rifle as Anna switched to the second man as he started to turn. One shot hit his temple as his face turned sideways.

As the six hostages stared wide eyed, Anna hit the third man in the gap between his eyes. Her last shot struck the last ISIS man as he brought up his rifle and squeezed the trigger. His shot missed whizzing over Laurie Black's blonde head as she ducked on the ground. Anna "Matta Hari" took her time and pumped two rounds into the man's glaring eyes. Sightless he gaped around the hut, dropping his rifle he groped around stumbling for a few seconds. Anna booted him in the pills dropping him to the ground at her feet. Then she took out a knife and cut his throat slowly from ear to ear. She went from one body to the next, kicking them, shooting Karim once more in his pelvic region. The Executioner, who had already beheaded a score of hostages twitched convulsively, his dark, brooding bearded face staring up at Anna's lovely face. "Allah...killed by...a Jew bitch!" Anna smiled down at him, then spat on his face as he died.

Anna turned to face the hostages, holstering her pistol, then picking up Karim's AKM from his dead cold hand, his open fingers still clenching it. "Get dressed Ladies...I'm taking you home." Laurie stumbled to her feet with the others, as they sorted out their bathing suits from the pile on the guard's table.

"Who...who are you?" Laurie asked as she slipped on her bikini bottom. Agent 009 had her game face on, her mind whirling as she checked over the ISIS bodies ensuring they were neutralized. Then Anna pointed her rifle at the door ready for an unexpected arrival. She had the prisoners safe, the job was to extract them.

"Call me Matta Hari. Now listen. We don't move yet. Niner this is 009, Demarcation!" A few seconds later Jack got the word "Alpha 1 this is X-Ray Niner. Chickens are in the bag, move in over." Jack tapped the machine gunner on the helmet. Suddenly the Saw opened up, then all around them, hundreds of weapons opened up. The crescendo built to a deafening roar, as rifle platoons opened up, raking the tent lines, bivouac areas, vehicle parks and the odd man who happened to be outside having a late night smoke or sauntering to the lavatory. Anyone in their sights died immediately, the bullet shredded bodies thrown aside like yesterday's laundry. Seconds later mortars thumped into action, followed by ATP's rockets.

The heavy crump of exploding mortars and detonating rockets turned the quiet camp into an exploding, ear splitting inferno. Medusa's legendary snake-like hair, curled about the prey, the ISIS force in the camp was ripped to shreds, turned stone dead as the aptly named Medusa did with her victims! Those that survived the initial onslaught, burst from their tents screaming and firing haphazardly. The Saw fired in 3-4 second bursts, cutting into their ranks, bowling them over by the dozen, like so many bowling pins. Jack worked his way to the stone hut, four teams of three leap-frogging each other giving covering fire. He tossed a frag grenade at a machine gun position. Hitting the dirt, he heard the Arabs yell in panic before it exploded. Pieces of human flesh spattered around him, along with dirt and rocks.

As Jack neared the hut a Soviet era PT-76 light tank[12] burst out of cover and fired its 73 mm gun. It screeched over Jack's head and blew up 100 meters behind him. Two Force X men died as they tried to run away, the first casualties among the convicts. Jack's anti-tank crew hit the armored vehicle as they tried to reload. Penetrating the turret, it killed the commander and loader immediately. The wounded driver spun the vehicle sharply, locking one track it turned sharply right and ran over several wounded ISIS men. Bullets rattled off the sloped armour as it tore off, crushing through ISIS tents killing or maiming dozens more. The anti-tank team reloaded with another 82-mm rocket and the gunner aimed for the rear of the tank. He fired and the rocket screeched through the air, hitting it in the rear, penetrating inside the engine compartment. The wrecked tank caught fire and blew up. The petrol tanks exploded with a crump, frying the driver inside. A ball of flame shot into the air, setting men and tents afire before the tracks finally squealed to a stop. Flames shot into the air from the crippled tank. Seconds later the shells started to cook off, sending billowing clouds of flames and smoke

---

[12] PT-76 Soviet designed and built in USSR and Eastern Block allied Communist states in 1960's-1980's. Supplied to Communist Armies and satellite Allies. ISIS captured a number of them from the Syrians and Iraq when they overran parts of both countries in 2013-14.

into the night air. The camp was a bedlam of exploding ordnance, lines of red tracer arcing across it from a dozen machine guns of various calibres.

Jack reached the stone hut first, then he yelled at his men, positioning them to cover in a 360-degree arc to defend the hut area. Then he strode into the hut, his smoking C-7 rifle cocked and pointed before him. Freddie the sniper took out man after man as they charged toward the hut, coolly reloading the Timberwolf. Inside the hut Jack stopped eyeing Anna. He nodded at her in relief she was fine. "Anna, the cavalry arrived in time I take it?" Anna smiled as she stood before the six female hostages, crouched by her side, holding their ears as deafening blasts and the heavy staccato roar of the battle echoed around them.

"Yes it seems so. However, we are still in Indian country Jack. How is it out there?" Jack shook his head at her question. OK Captain Obvious he thought. They ducked low as the odd round sang through the tent, stray rounds mostly but extremely lethal all the same Jack thought. He crouched beside Anna and stroked her hair gently with a gloved hand. "Be silly to die now wouldn't it?" Anna said.

"Indeed my dear. Still a bit of mopping up to do Matta Hari. Love talking to y'all but it's time to go, there seems a bit of a lull. We'll try and get you out in the jeep outside." Jack headed back out, stuck his head out the door and yelled, "Cover me boys!" Around him his team faced out in arcs of fire covering Lucky Jack.

Anna emerged finally, followed by the six hostages in their bathing suits. "Quick! In the jeep." Jack yelled above the metallic whiz and crack of small arms fire. A series of close quarter skirmishes started, hand to hand as the Pathfinders steadfastly held off determined ISIS fighters trying to penetrate their defensive ring. Anna ushered the frightened models into the jeep as Jack took the wheel. He started the engine and it roared loudly as he gunned the accelerator. Anna jumped in beside him as the last model Allegra eased her body into the back. "Keep low and hang on! Go Jack!" Anna yelled into his ear.

"OK Anna! Heads up!" Anna saw the two ISIS men charging at them firing. They ducked as bullets whizzed off the armored sides, a few shattering the windscreen. Anna fired the AKM she had taken off Karim's dead hand. One ISIS man fell dead, his arms fanning the air madly as Jack shifted into gear and let out the clutch. The jeep roared forward with a lurch, the charging Arab survivor stopped in his tracks and tried to avoid it...too late. He screamed as the jeep struck him, then ran him over. Jack spun the wheel, the jeep dragging the screaming ISIS man under the chassis. Jack felt the bump under the jeep as it bounced over the corpse. He peered over the side door as he sped away, the body twitching in a gruesome death throe under the jeep. After a few seconds, Jack shifted into third. Under the jeep chassis the now dead body was dragged over the desert ground for a hundred meters before it finally rolled clear. As the jeep roared full speed out of the flaming ISIS camp, the Pathfinder teams disengaged and followed it. Freddie and the machine gun covered them, picking off any Arabs who tried to intercept it. Jack screeched to halt and picked up Freddie and the machine gunner. "OK boys...all aboard! Time to get out of Dodge!"

Freddie jumped up and climbed into the back, Hog the shaven headed biker picked up his MG and dropped in beside him. The blackened faced, camouflaged soldiers grinned at the crouching women below, "Hello Ladies! Having fun?" Laurie, Jackie, Terra and the others looked up at the terrifying convicts. "No but thank-you anyway," they yelled shaking with fear and emotion. Jack gunned the engine, "Cover them guys back there boys!" Freddie and Hog nodded as they saw their Pathfinder buddies fighting off the advancing ISIL terrorists, while moving in teams as they withdrew.

Meanwhile, A, B and C Company saw what was happening. The camp was clear of friendlies, so all units were ordered to rapid fire on the village. The air split apart as the massed guns of 500 plus convict soldiers opened up. Rifles, machine guns of various calibers, rocket launchers, mortars and light artillery tore into the ISIS remnants in the village, just as they charged in the first organized, large scale counter-attack. The weight of metal that hit their lines would have stopped General Picket's Division at Gettysburg in a few minutes.

The convicts laughed with glee as they mercilessly mowed down the ISIS terrorists. They didn't just shoot them a few times, they riddled the bodies, till they were unrecognizable piles of meat, blood sprays extended for meters in every direction. Heads and headless corpses were seen flying 100 meters into the air. Dead bodies on the ground, jerked and lifted a few feet at a time as they were repeatedly hit by a torrent of fire from the Force X strike force. The ISIS counter-attack lurched to a halt as their ranks were shredded.

As the jeep lurched forward toward the LZ, Hog sent tracers arcing over the Pathfinder's heads, tearing into the Arab's ranks, adding to the onslaught. Freddie aimed at single targets, taking out their leaders. Finally, they ceased fire as they got out of range. Jack kept his foot on the accelerator as the jeep tore away from the shattered, burning ISIS held village. He watched as tracers arced by to add to the bedlam of destruction.

"Fucking beautiful!" Jack laughed as Anna sat beside him scanning the flanks for any threat. Anna looked at him, "Yes I know I am Jackie! Keep going, we are almost clear!" Near the end, Freddie sagged down to lie against one of the rescued models. "Lucky Jack...I am hit!" Jack looked back to see Freddie lying on his back, Jackie the model holding his body in her arms. "Where Freddie? Anna look after him."

"I bet you enjoyed taking out those guys in the hut eh love?" Anna smiled over at him, "I did what I had to," she remarked humbly. "You know what those monsters were planning to do in a couple of hours?" Jack nodded, "I am just happy you are OK Anna." Anna checked Freddie's wound, a stray round piercing his hip, her bloody fingers clamping a field dressing on it. "You will be fine soldier, a little nick in you."

"And you Jack. You and your men were awesome." As the jeep bounced across the desert, Jack gripped her hand tightly and squeezed. Around the speeding jeep, they saw groups of smiling Force X men waving at them. The jeep was greeted at the LZ by Colonel Mann himself. Hog rested his machine-gun, slapping Freddie's shoulder reassuringly. "Hey buddy. Your OK. A ticket home from this shit maybe?"

As Jack braked the jeep and shut off the engine, he dismounted and looked up at his CO. "Sir! Beg to report, six hostages and one Matta Hari safely extracted Sir!" Mann's smile showed even in the darkness. "Well done Sergeant. See them on the Chinook safely. Then report back to me. Casualties?" Jack peered at the luminous dial of his watch. He watched as Hog helped the hostages out of the jeep. Freddie followed, Anna having stopped the bleeding, she finished wrapping a field dressing tight around his waist.

It was 04:45: "Still coming in Sir. At least two friendly KIA and a few wounded, I will know the rest in five minutes." As he escorted Anna and the six models to the LZ, Jack felt himself relax. It had been an intense 30 minutes. From the time he had led his team forward, it had been half an hour! He quickly calculated his platoon had killed over 300 confirmed. Ten minutes later, the giant Chinook helicopters arrived and touched down on the LZ, sand whirling around as the twin blades whipped the air. The ramp was already lowered and as the wheels touched the ground the Loadmaster ran out shouting, "OK bring them on board! Let's go! Hostages and wounded first! Any hostages Sergeant?" Jack shook his head as he lit up a cigarette, watching as the six models sprinted up the ramp to safety. He smiled as Anna stood next to him, shouldering her rifle, "You should come with us Jack. I will take care of your man Freddie." Jack's eyes thanked her silently.

"Can't go yet Anna. My boys are still out there. A little mopping up then I will see you back home." She nodded and smiled as she hugged him, then climbed up the ramp waving good-bye to the veteran soldier. Jack smoked wiping his sweat streaked face, then as the chopper lifted off he turned back to the battle.

As he strolled back to the jeep a cigarette in his mouth, a weight lifted off him. He knew that this thing could have gone badly. But he was pleased, he had wanted his new girlfriend Anna out safe, no matter what happened to him or Force X. He saw the Chinooks head east, with the hostages, their wounded and Anna safely tucked inside. Anna got off the ramp a half hour later, holding an IV bottle as two men carried Freddie off on a stretcher. The wounded convict smiled up at the Israeli agent 009, who had injected morphine into his arm during the flight. Anna saw him loaded into a waiting ambulance along with a half dozen seriously wounded Force X men. Back at her tent she sat down on the cot. Then her emotions unleashed a torrent of tears and pent up emotion. She took a drink of cool water from a canteen and lit up a smoke from Jack's Marlboros he had given her. "Thank-you my Lord! For getting out alive. Please...take care of Jack!"

As Matta Hari preyed inside her tent, Jack was still in the thick of the battle. "Won't be long now Liza!" Jack thought. An hour later, he had regrouped the survivors from the Pathfinder Platoon around the jeep, parked on the edge of the LZ. "OK boys, take ten, I'm off to see Niner. The old man probably has a new mission for us. Section commanders check your men. Be ready to go in a moments notice."

Meanwhile Lion was watching the camp. He saw a large convoy approaching from the Iraqi border. Another was approaching from the West, heavy tanks, armored carriers and allot of lighter, soft skinned vehicles. He got on the horn and above the circling jets peeled off from their racetrack orbits. "Red Eye, this is JTF-2! We have some trade for you. Tango at Coordinates Bingo 136 over."

Above Call Sign Red-Eye in his CF-18 fighter acknowledged. "Roger that. Rat-Catcher follow me in, bank 270." His wingman acknowledged and the two CF-18's dived toward the camp. The lead jet pickled off his 500-pound smart bombs at 5000 feet, then headed toward the approaching convoy from the east. The twin jet engines roared as the fighter levelled on the low level attack run, the jets emitting a sonic boom as it streaked over the desert. The bombs erupted in the center of the flaming camp, the shock wave killing everything for hundreds of meters and setting alight everything that could burn...that had not caught fire already.

Lion watched through night vision goggles as the jet screamed toward the convoy leveling out below 1000 feet... the hard deck. Lights flashed along the jet's wings, missiles detached and sped toward the approaching convoy, then the 30 mm chain gun kicked in firing rapid bursts. Explosions erupted along the convoy, as vehicle after vehicle exploded, veering off the road. A Syrian Army T-64 tank turret spun upward into the air, to land a hundred feet away. Cannon slugs shredded the lighter skinned vehicles, (BMP/BTR APC's) and the crews inside. The devastation was stunning as Lion watched in awe, the shock waves hitting him a few seconds later. Then Rat-Catcher the second CF-18, dropped its entire load on the western convoy. It was a massacre, the 500-pound laser guided bombs landing in the center of the convoy. When they went off, vehicles were thrown up in the air like toys, bodies were flung everywhere. It was as if Thor himself had struck them with his hammer. Then 30-mm cannon shells raked the flaming debris, anything left was chopped into ribbons.

Jack saluted Colonel Mann as the tall CO listened to the radio chatter. He had just ordered a full assault on the camp area. In the big picture, the combined Allied Air Forces were in action, hundreds of planes from US, Canada, Britain, Germany, France, Iraq, Jordan and Russia bombed ISIS front and rear areas. Anything moving on the roads was attacked, convoy after convoy was wiped out...it was Desert

Storm all over again...a massacre! The bulk of the ISIS main force army died that day. Never again could it operate as an effective force. It was later estimated over 15000 KIA's and thousands of wounded, and hundreds missing or captured. The surviving elements were left in scattered bands who fled deeper inside Syria or to neighboring Lebanon or tried to escape over the Turkish border. In the space of hours, ISIS ceased to be a coordinated force.

Jack's Pathfinder group was ordered to escort the Colonel in captured ISIS vehicles as he reconnoitered the front line...if you could call it that. The battle sounds slowly subsided, as fewer and fewer ISIS targets appeared before the trigger happy convicts. Cease fire was ordered as the platoon officers and NCO's tried to control the convicts as they unleashed years of pent up hatred and frustration. Small patrols (execution squads), were sent forward to ensure that no ISIS had survived. Occasional shots echoed in the distance as the convicts dispatched any wounded survivors. Maggot led one patrol, bending over ISIS bodies and looting them. He pulled out a combat knife, cutting off fingers to get rings. Others followed his lead, one cutting off ears, stuffing them in his bag. Maggot shivered as a gangly Southerner pulled out a pair of pliers and twisted a tooth out of a dead Arab. "Ya...look at this Maggot! Pure fuckin' gold I'll wager."

"OK Rolly. Remind me not to fall asleep in yer foxhole." As the patrol slowly advanced they chuckled at Maggot's dark humor. At the perimeter of the camp Maggot called a halt. Wearily the half dozen convicts lay down. "Take ten guys. Radio, call the platoon, all clear." Maggot pulled out a cigarette and lit up, his dark eyes peering below his helmet at the shattered, smoking ruins of the camp fifty yards away. Then a smile spread over his sweat stained, hard features. The others lying stretched out heard his maniacal laugh, as piles of dead ISIS fighters lay strewn around them. Maggot swilled water greedily as he tried to estimate the body count.

Before Maggot left with his patrol, he had the convicts pile the dead bodies into a great mound. Then Maggot tossed a phosphorous grenade on top, creating a great bonfire. "Who brought the wieners? I brought the marshmallows!" Their hoarse laughter echoed into the blackness, leaving the blackened corpses to roast for hours. For days, desert birds and animals fed on the remnants of the mounds of cadavers. The battle rolled on into Syria, leaving behind destroyed villages, burning convoys and death. The sweet smell of decaying flesh permeated the air for miles. Force X now accustomed to the smell, rolled along with the surging battle. Convicts fell from the ranks as the battle continued, corpses marked and left for the following rear echelon units to recover. Lines of wounded shuffled back from the front lines, replaced by fresh reinforcements.

April 8, 05:45 A.M. Operation *Medusa* was winding to a close. After Force X paused for breath, reorganizing, re-supplied and casualties removed, they brewed up breakfast and coffee. Colonel Mann called his Headquarters group together to review the operation. "Not bad Eddie. Lighter casualty bill than I expected. Forty killed and 70 wounded?" Major van Zandt nodded smiling grimly as he lit the Colonel's fresh Cuban cigar. "Yes sir, the casualties are being evacked in the two Chinooks as we speak. 119 total casualties. So far."

"Good, now as soon as the Companies are resupplied, I want to advance past the former ISIS camp, police the area and dig in. We can expect Allied Forces to reach us from the border this morning some time I reckon. It seems the main attack caught the enemy napping. Also it doesn't hurt that we have complete air superiority. ISIS expect to beat us, yet have no Air Force to speak of. No navy being a land locked pseudo nation. It reminds me a bit of Vietnam. But North Vietnam had some planes and ships, as well as their Communist Allies China and USSR. In Vietnam we had superiority for the most part, but difficult terrain. The Gooks could hide in the jungle, but here on flat desert where do these Insurgents hide?" Jack listened nearby as the Officers conversed while he attended to weapons cleaning for Pathfinder Platoon.

"The villages and towns Sir. They mix in with the population, no uniforms. And the civvies are too scared to finger them, expecting retaliation...like in the Afghan war... or so I heard Sir." Colonel Mann listened to his impromptu advice, as Jack smoked and sipped a cup of coffee. Sergeant McGee chatted with his platoon as they knelt in a group around him, talking to their beloved 'Lucky Jack' as he listened to their requests for ammo resupply. Colonel Mann nodded in agreement finally. He had learned in his career to listen to the experienced NCO's. He had seen the result of young greenhorns who had ignored this sage advice in Nam.

"Well said Sergeant McGee. These insurgents can be expected to attack us anywhere disguised as civvies. That is the future, winning the peace, hearts and minds as the Brits say. If we create collateral damage, as has happened time and time again in this Middle East war, the press blames us. Shit, I hope we are gone by then, this is not our bag." Colonel Mann wanted to use Force X as a relentless battering ram. Once ISIS were defeated, he would pull them off the line. The more delicate work of cleaning up he would leave to others.

Eddie eavesdropping on the conversation added, "That will probably involve us Canadians. We are good at diplomacy with the UN. Or so the politicos would have us believe. Personally I believe in real soldiering, like we are doing here Sir." The Canadian Major stood before Colonel Mann, tapping his holster hanging off his combat belt for added emphasis. Colonel Mann smiled and slapped his shoulder as the meeting wrapped up. "OK any questions men? OK, let us push ahead and finish this thing."

Chapter X

THOR'S HAMMER

Colonel Mann looked at his Exec Officer and his Senior Officers. "Moving on...in one hour or so we move out Major. 'A' Company will sweep through the village to mop up. See if you can get any Intel, maps, computer shit, if any survived...one prisoner would be nice. I don't care what he looks like." He went on detailing 'B', 'C' and Support echelon to do a pincer move around the camp, and occupy Hill 370, a height about 2 kilometers to the north-east. All the officers in Mann's O-Group nodded in agreement, the key was get the high ground. It would dominate the area for miles in all directions. There they would dig in and await relief. Get the high ground was Colonel Mann's order of the day. It had been beaten into most of the Officers heads during their Officer Cadet days. Study the battle map, move your units from high ground to high ground. Off in the distance, loomed the next strategic spot on the map spread out before them...Hill 370. Before the battle was over the grunts would call it Dead Man's Knoll. Force X moved off soon after the O-Group, it's forward elements like pincers, biting into ISIS territory, moving into the burning remnants of the destroyed camp.

April 8, late afternoon: Colonel Mann, in his small convoy of half a dozen looted ISIS vehicles led from the front. Jack drove the armored jeep, with two Pathfinders serving as armed escort. Colonel Mann sat in the front, holding a map and a radio set. He had Jack pull over and watched the other Companies as they advanced past the smoking camp. An occasional shot echoed across the desert as the convicts rooted out the last holdouts. Jack saw a few desperate survivors run for it. They didn't get very far, as shots bracketed them, enfilading fire from the pincers, 'B' Company sweeping around the camp to the west, 'C' Company from the east. The last one dropped dead only a 100 or so feet away. Jack watched it through binoculars, the black clad ISIS man dodged desperately with bullets stitching the ground at his heels.

"Fuck! Lead the target asshole!" Then a man on the saw, the light 7.62-mm machine-gun, as if he heard Jack, let go a well-aimed burst. Jack roared triumphantly as he watched the ISIS man run into the burst. Jack saw the puffs of dirt, then blood spray as the bullets ripped into his back. "Gotcha fucker!" Jack roared pumping his fist. The ISIS fighter screamed and rolled in the dirt, his hands clawing at his gut. A dull crack echoed, the shot from far off. It zinged across the sand, missing the wounded Arab by inches. "One of our snipers," Colonel Mann said. Before he could elicit a reply, a second shot rang out. Everyone watched as the wounded ISIS man jerked, the well placed shot corrected for wind, hit the unlucky man in his forehead, blood spray shooting in the air. Then a few convict soldiers walked toward the bodies, firing shots indiscriminately into the bodies to dispatch them to Hell. Jack watched as each body was kicked and relieved of personal items.

"OK Sergeant. Enough of the sideshow, Head for that little village, ah... Baka Haram. We will see what is going on and wait for the others to catch up." Mann informed them the next phase of the operation, THOR'S HAMMER had begun. Jack nodded as he chain-smoked another cigarette. The jeep roared off, slamming into first gear and punching the accelerator as Colonel Mann chatted on the radio with the Company Commanders. Reaching the village Jack pulled up in the main square. They dismounted, cocking and loading their weapons. Lion met them soon after with his JTF-2 team. The soldiers chatted swigging on their canteens in the heat. "Colonel Mann. Good job on the camp Sir... Congrats. I hear the hostages are O.K.?"

"Yes Lion. Good job with the fast air. Those convoys could have given us some grief. Keep sharp as I expect to see more of the bastards before this Operation is completed."

Lion nodded to Jack, "Yes Sir. We have more fighters on stand-by...just in case." Lion and Jack stood beside the jeep as Mann talked on the radio. Then it happened, after the village was cleared by the patrol, Jack set his rifle down on the jeep seat. A woman slowly walked up to him, dressed in a black burka. The shot rang out, stunning the soldiers for a few seconds. It was Lion who responded first. He cut the woman down with several aimed rounds from his C-7 rifle. The black clad woman screamed as the 5.56mm rounds tore into her chest. Her concealed pistol dropped to the dirt and she toppled backward to twitch spasmodically in the dirt. Lion walked over to the body and kicked the body with his boot.

"Clear!" Lion stepped over the dead Arab woman to see Jack stagger backward. Colonel Mann leaned over to Jack as he slumped onto the seat, cursing in pain. He saw blood drip from his abdomen, Jack clutching his hand tight to the wound. He looked at the CO, his eyes showing his pain, his cigarette still clamped in his barred teeth. He let out a stream of curses as he saw blood trickling from his fingers. He felt a dull throbbing in his gut, as he looked at the concerned soldiers grouped around him.

"How is it Son?" Colonel Mann asked, his hand resting on his shoulder. "Ahh...just a flesh wound Sir. Do you believe it? A fucking civvy!" The big JTF-2 man stood next to Mann his eye looking at the wound. "Better let me take a look at that. I know advanced first aid." Jack nodded and lay back on the seat groaning. Lion and the Colonel helped to remove his combat gear and unbutton his cam shirt.

The bullet had entered just below the ribs, a neat hole in and one out his back. "Hmm. Missed your spine that's good. Missed the main arteries, the Doc's will need to check your organs back at hospital. I'll give you morphine, bandage this and wrap it up." Lion checked his vital signs, taking his pulse then went to work. He opened a medical kit, injected Jack with a syringe of morphine, then bandaged him, looping the field dressing around his ribs and body before tying it. Lion finished his field dressing then slapped Jack's shoulder.

"There you go, good as new." Jack smiled at Lion. "I need a drink. Shit! First wound since the Gulf War." Mats Lungren the Swedish sniper listening blurted out: "Seriously? I was in Sweden then! Barely out of school!" Jack laughed coughing up blood, then spat dryly, hitting the dead Arab woman's corpse lying in the dust. "That's right young fellah! I don't think you would want to be there...we lost allot of good men that day. Hell almost did me then and there." Colonel Mann called in an urgent Dust Off, a medical chopper with medics to get Jack out fast. It arrived ten minutes later, Jack was put on a stretcher and slid onto the deck of the Huey chopper. The crew tossed out some ammo boxes and a few Jerry cans of water. The pilot saluted Colonel Mann and with a noisy whir of blades lifted off and swung for Iraq and the home base.

Jack lay on his back strapped to the stretcher, watching as the Huey lifted above the village. He groaned as the morphine hit him, his mind swirling. He waved an arm at Lion and the others as they peered up at him. Then he lay back and smiled as the door gunner looked down at the grizzled, combat veteran, his dirt begrimed face and stubble

serial killers, along with the Arab terrorists), their remote controlled packs of Semtex explosives stuffed in packs on their backs their only weapons. The Force X officers gasped as the convicts threw their bodies at the armored vehicles... and a tremendous explosion erupted, then another...and another. The attacking column stopped dead in its tracks, as they watched the suicidal mad men attack them. Smoking tanks and vehicles littered the front of Force X's positions. In all two dozen convicts, their packs loaded with explosives died...to save their fellow convicts. The Vikings had a term for them...Berserkers. Most were nasty criminals and knew they would never be let back into society...convicted terrorists from the U.S. and Canada, serial killers of women, child molesters. They were correct. Colonel Mann had a list of convicts he didn't care to see back at base, passing that on to his officers before *Medusa* began. They died gloriously in their last act on Earth, most oblivious to their final fate.

Each man was loaded with several sticks of high explosives, hollow charges designed to punch through several inches of hardened armour or stone huts. As the convicts climbed onto the tracked vehicles, an NCO pressed the remote control detonator, timing it for maximum effect. Convicts and vehicles disappeared in a sudden flash, pieces of body and metal flew high in the air. The last vehicle slewed to a halt just meters in front of the Force X lines, then the T-72 blackened and trackless, belched smoke from the open hatch. A blackened hand emerged clawing at the air. The convict soldiers grinned then ducked below their sandbag parapets, seconds later an ear-ripping explosion rent the baking desert. Colonel Mann watched through his binoculars as a body arched high into the air, followed by the 10-ton turret.

"Impressive shit!" He smiled grimly as the turret lifted a 100 feet into the sky, then landed heavily, it's long 125 mm main gun still pointed at the Force X line. Seconds later the smoking, torn body of the ISIS crew commander landed feet in front of the forward MG position. The two-man crew slowly raised their heads over the parapet, then looked at each other. "That fucker had a very bad day eh Sidney?" The loader checked his belt as the gunner cocked the C-8 light machine gun.

"Fuck 'em Lanny! I don't hold with fuckers who cut off heads. Just not Christian." He wiped his smoke and dirt begrimed face with a handkerchief before taking a swig from his canteen. "Stand to mates! Here they come again!" The 32-year old ex-Brit, who had got life for several hits as part of the Hell's Angels, trained his sights on a line of dark figures outlined against the skyline. He had served five years in the British Para Regiment, so found the combat an extra adrenaline rush. "Son-of-a-Bitch," Sidney whispered to himself, timing his burst to lead the line of yelling figures sprinting over the desert sand right toward his position.

Still the ISIS attacked on foot, supported by heavy machine guns mounted on Toyota trucks. Several reached 'C' Company lines. A few convicts fell as rounds flew everywhere in the chaotic fighting. Then enraged several convicts picked up their entrenching tools, bayonets or used their rifles as clubs, charging head on into the ISIS terrorists. In the hand to hand combat, no quarter was given. Maggot roared as he led the final charge, running after the ISIS fighters as they finally had enough, the survivors broke and ran.

When the attack was finally beaten back an hour later, no one from the foe was left alive. In all Force X lost 220 killed by the end of the day, 330 wounds of various types, 35 were fatal. ISIS on the other hand had received its death knell...*Thor's Hammer* had seemingly crushed it like an egg. The war continued, but ISIS never again would challenge the strength of the NATO led ground forces head on. Some die-hards escaped to other countries...and to the welcoming hands of the West...their targets. In the north the Peshmerga had them on the run, mercilessly wiping out entire units of ISIL. The Islam fighters would regroup and plan their next terrorist attack. But their plan to create a new extremist Islamic State was over. Like during the Iraq war, a new phase began. Insurgents attacked in pin prick raids or mined the roads with IED's in the familiar ways.

Colonel Mann walked down from the summit with Major van Zandt around noon that day. They slowly did an inspection of the Company lines talking to men here and there. Force X regrouped as the battle was officially over. All of the ISIS force were dead or routed. They had taken a few prisoners, all beaten to a pulp, the deceased and wounded formed up in lines before armed MP's. The surviving ISIS prisoners were searched, blind-folded and the Intel officer began a rudimentary interrogation as they were brought to a tent in Baka Harem in the rear. Colonel Mann ordered his officers to take stalk of the situation, waiting the arrival of their relief forces pushing closer to their captured foothold in Syria.

An hour later, an Allied Force had broken through the lines of the enemy along the Iraqi border and linked up with patrols of Force X. Colonel Mann was on the horn to NATO HQ back in Iraq. "General we have just linked up with advance elements of NATO and Allied Coalition Forces." General Mandel, the U.S. Commander told Mann he was relieved, congratulating him on a mission accomplished. Whistles blew as Force X formed up in their units. Officers supervised them as they unloaded weapons and were relieved of ordnance, unexpended bullets, explosives, and grenades. Then they marched down the road to the LZ to await transport back to base. 450 men had made it to the finish line. Back at their desert base in Iraq, the choppers landed, disgorged their load of Force X warriors and took off for another ferry run.

Details of Base personnel or REMF's, lined up bodies, medics tagged the dead and evacuated the wounded to hospital. Jack was one of the last to arrive at the Field Hospital, soon joined by more Force X men, his buddy Sean McGinn one of the last. Jack leaned on his elbow as he lay on his stretcher to see the newly arrived casualties. It did not shock him, he had seen it all before. In fact, prison had been worse for him.

"Sean what happened mate?" Jack asked concerned. "Nothing big Lucky Jack. A ricochet I think, or shrapnel. It was hairy for the last hour, hand to hand combat! I got this one fucker good though. Buried by shovel blade into his face! Cut the dink in half." Jack grinned at his buddy "Good work Sean. Wish I was there at the end!" Lieutenant Greene arrived to visit them in the recovery ward hours later, after the Doctors had operated. "How is it going men?" Jack and the others of Pathfinder Platoon were lined up in their beds side by side. "OK Sir. How did the platoon do?" By now he was feeling the effect of his wounds, dulled slightly by the morphine. Jack looked at the patient in the hospital cot beside him. The Force X man had hit a buried land mine during the final action. He was riddled with shrapnel, one leg amputated and one arm. Jack shivered as he gazed at the poor sod, his body in a cast from head to foot. McGinn saw the look and shrugged in silence.

"I have 12 men left unwounded and still able to fight." Lieutenant Greene answered quietly. Jack nodded, his own wound bandaged and stitched up. "What's the plan now Lieutenant?"

"That is up to the CO Sergeant," Greene answered. "It is like the old points system. When you get enough you go home. Privately Sergeant McGee you have enough. I would say half of Pathfinder Platoon should be back home soon. I am putting your papers in. Go home to your family Sergeant…good work."

"Fucking aye!" Jack whooped and high fived Freddie beside him, then gripped the young Officer's hand.

"When can I get out of this bone rack Sir…I need a drink." Lt. Greene smiled, "I'll talk to the medics. Perhaps they can release you for a little while at least." The Doctor, a young civilian from Edmonton checked Jack, Sean and Freddie's wounds later that afternoon and allowed them to leave, on the condition they report the next morning to get checked again. They met the survivors of Pathfinder Platoon in the drinking mess early that evening. Jack grinned as the hardened convicts smiled and slapped his back, relieved 'Lucky Jack' had avoided the Grim Reaper. Relieved he was still alive, Maggot and the others bought rounds of beer.

"I love you too Maggot! Hey don't hug me…my ribs are cracked!" Hog the ex-biker slammed a bottle of Rum down on the table. "Hair of the Dog Jack!" Jack grinned at the big biker and took his share, gulping a quarter of the bottle, then passed it to the next man. The party continued well into the next morning, as the convicts started a camp fire outside the mess tent. Watching it were the RSM, Colonel Mann and his Officers.

The MP Lieutenant stood beside the CO, his eyes watching the boisterous celebration.

"Sir…what do we do?" Mann looked to the RSM, "What do you think Sergeant Major?" RSM MacDonald a 25-year Army vet, leveled his icy blue eyes on the fire, as the convicts sang and danced around it. "Sir, let them blow off some steam. I think they deserve to be thrown a bone after today." He smoked his pipe as he glanced at the Meathead Lieutenant, then at Niner. Mann nodded to the massive bulk of the Sergeant Major then smiled at the MP and the other Officers. "Stand your boys down Lieutenant for now. I am tossing these men a bone. Whose round is it anyway? I think Force X deserves a little R & R?"

Around 9 p.m. Anna the Israeli agent finally found Jack. The statuesque female agent smiled as she looked at Jack leaning on a crutch, standing on a wooden table as he chugged a glass boot of beer as the convicts hooted and cheered. Finally, he tilted the glass boot over his shaved head, gasping for air, belched then grinned down at Anna. Anna smiled as the grimy soldier danced a jig as the convicts roared around the shaking table. Anna looked totally changed, her hair washed and blown over her bare shoulders. She wore a flowered dress, dark fishnet stockings and black high heels, her skin glowing beneath her jewelry.

"Well done Jack! Now please get down before you succeed in killing yourself." Anna laughed as he staggered off the bench, Anna catching him in her arms as he stumbled, then hugging the wounded convict.

"Ah! Matta Hari! Welcome to the Victory Celebration!" He embraced her tight then kissed her cheek. "Bartender! Service you… Rear Echelon stallion asshole! More beer for our conquering heroes…tab is on me! Anna what will you have my Dear?" Jack embraced Anna as he staggered toward the bar.

Anna elegant in her tight fitting, tailored flowery dress and high heels, in stark contrast to the convicts in the mess, stood out like a sore thumb. They still wore their camouflage uniforms, though many had washed and showered before the night's festivities. "I will have the house wine Jack." The bartender set down a tray of beer mugs and a bottle of red wine and glasses. Jack placed a $50-dollar bill in the bartender's hand and belched. "Keep the change my good man." The bartender smiled as the table of celebrating convicts cheered.

"So it went well? Apart from your little scratch?" Anna smiled as she poured some wine. "Yes, a toast! To health and our return to the world!" Glasses were raised and drained, then refilled hastily. "Pathfinders Lads! We fight hard, and party harder! Here's to us! Who's like us?" All the drunk convict soldiers, joined now by a few regular soldiers, including Lion and his JTF-2 buddies responded, "Damn few! And their all fucking dead!" That night there were no FNG's, for even the new guys, the cherries had counted coup[13] that day...they had all tasted death. These were the survivors who lived to tell about it. It was past midnight,

---

[13] Indian term for defeating an enemy, establishing them as Braves. Mohawks would scalp the dead foe and eat their heart if they were especially respected. It gave the warrior enhanced fighting ability or so they thought.

when they had moved outside to the roaring bonfire. The time honored tradition of celebration for soldiers.

"I suppose you will be going home soon Jack?" Anna looked at Jack, as she sat near him, the flames dancing over her face, her piercing eyes on his. Jack nodded as he swilled his beer mug. "Yes Anna. My war is over, maybe for good. I will return to my Love Liza and my daughter and son! I have not seen them for many years." Jack's mind already was picturing them, on his return to the world.

"You are a modern Odysseus my brave soldier. Let's celebrate this night then. Perhaps our last night together?" Jack nodded as he took her offered hand in his and kissed it. He looked deep in her dark eyes, memorizing every detail. "Perhaps in this life time. But as the saying goes, never say never." Anna's eyelids flickered as she laughed. "Well then Jack lead the way, the night is still young." Jack and Anna stole away into the night, the lovely Israeli agent supporting his staggering body. Slowly as the fire died the others staggered off to their tents, or passed out on the way. No one observed as the veteran convict soldier disappeared into his tent late that night, accompanied by the beautiful Israeli secret agent. Jack stood inside as Anna leaned into his arms. Her fingers stroked his neck as they engaged in a passionate kiss.

Anna showed her athletic prowess, raising a knee along his side, her toes digging into his leg for support. Jack was getting worked up as his hand supported her, as her other knee climbed up his side. "Jack I am missing you already."

Her lips moved on his as she leaned back, sitting in his hands. For a tall woman Jack felt she was almost weightless. Anna flashed a smile as she laughed, her fingers running over his shoulders as he carried her to the cot. Setting her down he unbuttoned her dress and peeled it off. Anna returned the favour by ripping off his shirt, buttons flying inside the canvass tent. His adrenaline and hormones overcame his last reserve of restraint as he unclipped her bra and slipped it off. He embraced her to him, Anna tossing her long hair free over her back, allowing Jack to lick along her throat. Her tongue licked her lower lip as her dark eyes flashed. She pulled him forward as she fell onto the cot. Jack kicked off his desert boots hurriedly, then lying beside her, she helped him off with his other clothes.

"Oh Jackie! Take me now." Annie gripped his back, her nails digging into his flesh as she arched her body upwards, spreading her thighs to him. Then he bent over her as he flexed his muscles.

When Jack awoke the next morning he was alone in the tent. He yawned as he climbed out of bed, listening to the sounds of the stirring camp outside. He was tired but refreshed, Anna had given him a sweet send-off the night before. As he dressed he stretched his aching muscles. "Good bye Anna. May the gods protect you. Maybe we will see each other again." Rummaging in his footlocker he found Anna's parting gift to him. Her sleek black panties and a note. "To my love Jackie. I had to leave early please forgive. I hope you find you lovely wife soon. But sooner or later, I feel our paths will cross again. I will never forget you, so please forgive me for my seduction of you. It must be a spy thing? You know James Bond, 007? I saw *Goldfinger* when I was young in Tel Aviv. My brother recruited me into Mossad when I was 18. It is dangerous work, but I see it as a challenge God has put before me. Much like you I think? Well bye for now. Kisses Annie!" Jack sat for a few minutes as he read the letter, before stowing it in his locker. Then he shrugged off the temporary melancholy feeling and flinging back the tent flap, strode outside as the sun came up on the horizon. He stood in his green army issue underwear as he faced the rising sun on the horizon. Jack groaned as his wound still caused him some discomfort. He held a hand to the bandage, a red stain showing his recent brush with death.

"Good morning Lucky Jack!" Jack waved to his platoon as they formed up for inspection. His buddy Sean McGinn was told that day he would relieve Jack as Platoon Leader. Sean came up to Jack smiling and clapping his shoulder roughly. "Hey buddy! Sleep well? Where is Anna?" Jack smiled wryly as he took a smoke from Sean. After getting a light, they watched the Pathfinder Platoon as Lt. Greene addressed them. They had come along way he thought since the early training days. There were allot of new faces in the ranks now. Jack only recognized a face here and there, the rest being new reinforcements fresh from prison.

Lt. Greene told Jack to head the sick, lame and lazy over to their MIR for their daily exams. Jack threw on his cam uniform and boots and olive drab cam field hat. "OK boys, let's go see the bone menders." He threw Lt. Greene a casual salute as they headed to the Red cross marked tent at the far end of the camp. Jack's mind was on women at that moment. Anna, then the twin nurses back in the world, then finally his Liza. He thanked God, for without them, he would probably not be here. After the Doctors changed his bandage and inspected his wound, Jack joined Sean outside the tent for a smoke. "So congrats Sean. I hear you are relieving me." His comrade in arms who had received a minor wound in the last battle, was still short of the points required for official pardon and repatriation to Canada.

"Yes sir. The Lieutenant tells me I have to serve a few more months here before they repatriate me with a full pardon. Colonel Mann does not want to lose all his trained NCOs. A smart fellow." Jack nodded puffing on his cancer stick. "Amen to that. I am a little reluctant to go actually. This war is not done yet." They finally parted ways a few days later as Jack got his papers for home. He hugged Sean slapping his back.

"Get some buddy! Give me a buzz when you get back. You will be fine." Sean laughed and headed off, back to the Pathfinder Platoon. Jack watched him go, then sadly he began to pack up his gear. He stuffed the picture of Liza inside her shirt pocket after kissing it. He smiled as he pictured the blonde beauty, in his arms as they saw each other for the first time in a decade. He felt himself getting healthier by the minute as he looked forward eagerly to seeing his wife. That day Anna arrived in Tel Aviv Airport,

CHAPTER XI

AFTERMATH

April 11, 2015: Two days later Jack was officially given his pardon and release from Force X. Joining him were Freddie, Maggot and several other veteran survivors of Pathfinder Platoon. For Jack McGee, it was the end of a long journey and a cross-roads. He had been skeptical deep down that this moment would ever arrive. On that morning, he was on parade when Colonel Mann called his name. Jack snapped to attention in the rear of Pathfinder Platoon in the Platoon 2 I/C's spot, "Sir!" As hundreds of eyes watched, he marched out of the Force X ranks to where the Colonel stood. He halted before Colonel Mann and saluted.

"Sergeant McGee, congratulations." He pinned the medals on his chest, then shook hands with him. "The paperwork for your release is in the works. I remember the day I saw you in Lexington Fayette Jail. Never thought you would make it this far. Thank-you for your service. You are an inspiration to the Force."

"Thank-you Colonel. I had no doubt. I have a wife and family to return to." Colonel Mann also recommended Jack and a few others for medals for their heroics in rescuing the hostages and helping Force X to hand a stinging defeat to ISIS, the Western Allies nastiest enemy since the Hitler's Nazis. They had threatened to execute any Canadians or American soldiers caught alive. To date they had failed, losing the bulk of their forces in the attempt. Frustrated on the battlefield, the Moslem fanatics resorted to their more successful terrorist attacks against civilians. In the next year following their route from the Middle east, France was attacked repeatedly, with hundreds of casualties. It was a long term problem that would not disappear, for France had the largest Moslem population in Europe.

But for Jack and his fellow Pathfinders home was occupying their thoughts now. As a bonus gift, Jack was given his first cell phone. Being old school, and doing time in the can, he had still to catch up with the ever changing technology of the new century. Cell time had locked him in a virtual time capsule, so when he emerged that day after Colonel Mann sprang him, he was out- of- date. Jack thought back of one of his favorite movies during his prison days. It was a Clint Eastwood flick, Heartbreak Ridge. His favorite actor Clint played a US Marine Gunnery Sergeant nearing the end of his career. The new Commanding Officer had termed him obsolete, "Break glass only in time of war."

It summed up Jack perfectly, for Colonel Mann had broken that glass, now his war over, the CO honoured his promise, freeing Jack and other selected convicts.

The company clerk Corporal 'Blackeye' Woodall gave him instructions on how to operate the Blackberry cell. "Thanks Blackeye, see you back in the world someday." Woodall one of Force X's newer convicts smiled at Jack. "Thanks buddy. I hope I don't have to match yer record. Have a good trip. Here are yer papers Sarge, you will fly out on a Globemaster tomorrow at 07:00 hours sharp."

Jack called Liza that night. "Liza? Hi it's Jack. Remember me?" Then he sat back enjoying the sound of her excited squealing. "Jack! Oh my God! Where the hell are you?" Jack was sitting on his bunk as he finished packing for the trip the next morning. "I am in the Middle East somewhere honey. I'll fill you in on the details when I get in a day or so. Can you meet me at the Toronto airport?" Liza gasped wide eyed as she listened to his voice. She almost pinched herself, thinking she was dreaming. "Jackie are you serious? So you are free of prison sweetie?" Jack chuckled as he listened to her excited yet disbelieving voice. "You bet sweetheart. Look it is too long a story to explain right now. I'm beat and need to rest a bit. I will call you tomorrow when I know when we will arrive OK?" Liza nodded as she bounced excitedly on the sofa in her Arizona desert villa. "Of course Jack. I will get Ashley and we will drive there tomorrow morning. I love you."

Jack walked to the R.C.A.F. C-17 Globemaster giant transport plane sitting on the tarmac in Kuwait with the others that hot day. It was April 20 when the plane lifted off and headed for North America and freedom at last. It touched down at Toronto International Airport early the next day. Jack read a newspaper on the flight. He and Force X had been overseas since last October, eight long months ago, and he felt out of touch with society...or the world to army vets. The paper outlined in one story the War on Terror in the Middle East. *"ISIS is on the defensive, retreating to its last strongholds in Northern Syria and Iraq. The cease fire between the other combatants in Syria seems to be holding. NATO forces, Kurdish Peshmerga and their Arab Allies continue to pursue elements of ISIS forces, Allied planes flying dozens of sorties every day..."*

Nothing was ever mentioned publicly of Force X and its role. Jack smiled at this, not caring in the slightest. He had never been in the news before, despite being in two wars. Jack settled into his seat as the plane filled, then at 10 A.M. screamed down the runway and lifted off into the desert sky. He looked down at the endless desert, wandering where she was at that moment. Then he closed his eyes and pictured Liza. He slept most of that day as the jet flew across the world toward his homeland. The next morning Jack and his buddies stepped off the plane after landing at Toronto's Pearson International Airport. 'We are back in the world guys!" Freddie whooped, then bent down and kissed the tarmac. Jack limped along smiling, leaning on his cane with his eyes darting about. Then he saw finally her...Liza stood in a crowd of people a hundred feet away. She stood smiling at the end of a long line of civilians, Ashley beside her. Ashley ran to him first, then they hugged, Jack embraced his daughter for the first time in years.

"Ashley! Just like your Mother! I am so happy to see you finally!" Ashley cried, her eyes locked on her long lost father. "Dad I love you! We are so happy, Mom and I! We've waited so long!"

Liza then hugged Jack and they kissed. All three of them embraced as people milled about. Jack said good-bye to Freddie and the others, then picked up his bags. Freddie was embraced by his own woman, the former blonde escort Michelle. Her friend Jackie was also present to greet them, both hugging and kissing Jack. "Good to see you ladies again. Freddie take good care of these gorgeous women." Freddie high fived him, then said, "Lucky Jack my man. If you ever need something, give ole Freddie a call." After the ex-convicts exchanged cell phone numbers they finally parted ways, each headed back to their former lives.

"Well boys I'm off with these two ladies. Good luck! Stay out of trouble or I will be back to club your heads." They laughed and waved as they parted ways, Jack hugging Ashley and Liza as they left the terminal.

"Good-bye Lucky Jack!" came the roar of a dozen throats. Jack left with Liza and Ashley, feeling clashing emotions. They had been a close knit team, now they were leaving each other forever. It left a feeling of sadness in him somehow. Other faces flashed through his mind as Liza drove the big F-350 truck across the border to Buffalo, New York an hour later. Once across the US border, the McGee family headed for Arizona. "OK Dad. Tell us your news? How did you get hurt?" Ashley squealed in the rear seat as the truck sped down the highway. "Later Ash hon. I need to catch my breath first. I tell you, it's a long tale to tell." Liza smiled glancing at her husband. "Yes we can wait a bit Jackie. You rest and I will wake you at the next stop. We should stop around Chicago for a spell." Jack slept the first few hours, then he spelled Liza, despite her protests she was OK. "I can handle it Liza. Take a break."

"Jack honey! You are wounded!" Liza said. "Yes a scratch, something to remember my last battle! I'm good, this is my way of recovering!" He leaned over and kissed the gorgeous blonde. She smiled as she kissed him back. Then Jack floored the accelerator, "I can't wait to see what y'all done with the new place." Ashley sitting in the back showed him pictures stored on her new laptop. "Wow nice!" Jack said as he looked at the new desert digs. "It is like a Spanish villa Jackie" Liza said. "You will love it. Or else!" Jack nodded as the truck roared through New York state, finally two days later they arrived at their new Arizona acreage. Jack sprang out and knelt on the ground, then planted a kiss on it.

"Hallelujah! I'm fucking home!" Liza laughed as he kissed the ground, then they danced before the exotic villa Liza had built the year before. "Jackie! Carry me inside...like our honeymoon!" Jack nodded picking up the tall blonde in his arms. He winced feeling the pain in his abdomen, but grinned and bared it. Ashley filmed it with a videocam as Jack carried Liza onto the front verandah, her long legs dangling over his burly tanned arms then set her down on her high heels.

"Liza honey! I admit it...I'm friggin' beat!" After a lavish dinner served by Liza and Ashley, Jack relaxed by the fireplace. Liza sat beside him, messaging his shoulders and back. "Back in the world Liza...like I said I would, how many years ago? And how did you stay loyal to me? No other woman would have, how could I blame you?" Liza smiled as he lit up a smoke watching her. She shrugged, "You are the only man in the world for me Jack! Many wanted me...I was tempted I admit. But a little voice in my head said no. And right now I know I did the right thing!" Jack smiled at her, then hugged her again. That night, the first time in twenty years he slept in bed with his wife. The isolated desert villa grew quiet as Jack settled in with his lover.

For Liza in her husband's arms once more, her demons had finally been expelled and she spent her most relaxing night since he had left long years ago. Like Odysseus of the Trojan War, he was at long last home in his kingdom, with his Queen Penelope! Like King Odysseus of Ithaca, he had beaten the odds. Even the Gods' will, had not stopped him from returning to his one and only true love.

While Jack and the repatriated Force X men recuperated in Stateside or Canada, the war went on across the ocean. Force X downsized to 50% battalion strength, continued to receive fresh convicts after their rudimentary army refresher course. The final Selection Phase as ordered by Colonel Mann was a month in the high Arctic. Parachuted in like their predecessors, they learned to march or croak.[14] The Selection was designed as in Elite Regiments the world over to weed out the chaff, the weak, the rejects who did not fit in. Many perished before they saw their first action. By now the base Force X had established, near Frobisher Bay, had a growing cemetery. Rows of crosses sprouted up, with the convict's prisoner ID number and date of death. A revolving team of Force X men were based there, mounting guard and performing ceremonial duties for visiting VIP's. Meanwhile at Force X camp in Iraq, the convict regiment welcomed its new recruits. Colonel Mann inspected the reformed platoons along with their Company Commanders.

"At ease men. Welcome to Iraq and the war. Soon you will follow in the footsteps of some of the best soldiers I have ever led. Some....many have paid the ultimate price for their crimes. The challenge for you will be to match the success of our best. Several have been rewarded with freedom and a pardon. They have begun their lives back in the world, a fresh start. If you distinguish yourself and survive you will have the same chance. If you fail in any respect, are deemed wanting in any task, or try to desert you will be returned to prison for execution of sentence. Questions men?"

---

[14] Term used by the French Foreign legion: France's Elite Regiment known for its long, brutal desert marches.

The tall, hard bitten Colonel looked at the faces before him, some stunned, in a state of near paralysis, other downcast, while a few had crazy grins spread over their convict faces. "Sir?" The Officers standing before the platoon looked at the Private in the ranks. "Yes Private Smith?" The man looked at the Colonel smiling. "So we are allowed to kill people, awesome. I have ached to kill again. I want to volunteer for the most hazardous mission you can devise. If I survive Sir, you guarantee my sentence will be pardoned?" Colonel Mann nodded, "Our job here men, is to win this war. In the process I will assist you in becoming useful members of society, some for the first time in your useless lives. How many of you have ever been employed in a non-criminal job? Yes, I thought so. C'mon then, don't be shy. We are all men here."

Colonel Mann looked pleased as a few hands tentatively were raised, while most just stood glaring darkly at them. "Most of you I see are career criminals. Use your time here well, look at it as a one-time reprieve. Personally I would sooner line up half of you and execute your sentences for your crimes. On the other hand, I believe every man deserves a second chance. Good luck.... RSM, takeover if you please."

In turn the Regimental Sergeant Major handed off the Force X Company to the newly appointed Company Senior NCO Sergeant Gallagher and his 2IC Sergeant Sean McGinn. McGinn had just returned from the hospital, having been wounded in Force X's numerous skirmishes. He had seen his buddy Jack off days before, promising to stay in touch. "So had enough eh Jack? Of course I need to top your body count. What are you at?" Jack had laughed slapping his trusted friend and battle partner on the back. "I stopped counting a while ago, but I think around 500 plus change." Sean laughed joking. "Wow. Do these ragheads count for one kill?"

Under the Sergeant's instruction the platoon would immediately begin the rigorous daily training to acclimatize them to the desert. After their training in Canada's Arctic, it would be easier to some, hardest for those not familiar with desert ops. Sean McGinn as their chief instructor showed them no mercy or respite.

"Platoon Attention! Left turn! Quick march!" As the 30-odd men marched off, Colonel Mann and his Officers went to the command tent. Force X continued training, working the new men especially hard in the stifling heat of the desert, to acclimatize them to their new environment. Several died of heart ailments, heat stroke and in one case firing squad for trying to kill his NCO. Colonel Mann was in touch with the NATO HQ. In late May, 2015 ISIS had lost a top leader, killed by American Special Forces. Then in a surprising rebound had attacked and captured Mosul and other towns deep inside Iraq. Colonel Mann accepted a mission planned by HQ. Force X would lead the attack to retake Mosul. For the next week the training stepped up, no mercy was shown to convicts not meeting the standard.

By the time Force X was ready for the attack a week later, dozens of convicts had perished, been executed or

RTU'd to prison. As the brutal war rolled on though, Lucky Jack was far removed, once more in Liza's loving arms. He felt like he had died and was reborn, as he spent that idyllic time with her in the new villa.

That day in early May, another hot one in the Arizona desert, Jack relaxed as he recovered slowly from his wounds. It was Liza who decided they needed to retire to the beach. He lay on the sand, watching as Liza and Ashley frolicked in the surf before him, on the Southern California coast. He sipped on his drink, his eyes slitted against the glare of the sun as he looked at them. "Mother of God!" Jack thought smiling. The two blondes were stunning in matching flowered bathing suits. They laughed light heartedly as they wrestled in the surf, then fell into the boiling surf waves. Both being accomplished swimmers, the two women seemed like mermaids to Jack. Jack laughed as their long legs broke the surface, kicking high in the air. A minute later Liza and Ashley broke the surface, some ways off. He never failed to be surprised at Liza's ability to do that, he struggled to match her ability to hold her breath underwater and travel such long distances.

Back in the day, one of his toughest tests in the Airborne Forces was the Ranger swim test. He had to jump into a pool from the diving tower, dressed in full combat gear, including fighting order, weapon, boots and steel helmet. He sunk to the bottom of the pool before stripping off his web gear then surfacing. Still holding his rifle, he then had to swim a lap around the pool. He was gassed as he had climbed out of the pool, then lay on his back gasping like a dying man. Another soldier had almost drowned when he had panicked at the bottom of the pool removing his equipment. A safety diver had pulled him out and revived him with CPR.

Jack waved to Liza as they waved back to him, he could see the sun turn their hair a shining golden hue. Then they swam powerfully back to the beach. As they slowly emerged, several men stood watching them. Liza and her daughter looked like Goddesses as they strode out of the water, curvaceous, tanned, every muscle honed to perfection. Liza heard the hoots of some of the younger men, ignoring them she smiled as she knelt down beside Jack, Ashley rolling onto her back beside her. Ashley shook her long hair spraying water over her father. "Lovely my Dear. Let me towel you off. Here's your drink." Liza smiled brightly then raised her mouth for a kiss. Jack returned her kiss then kissed Ashley, patting her shoulder. The nearby watching men, some jealous, watched as Lucky Jack bent over Liza, towelling off her body, with her latest string bikini accentuating her curves. One young man came over finally, standing next to Ashley.

"Hey darling, my name is Louie. What's yours?" Jack smiled as Ashley looked at him shaking her face, tossing her long golden hair sultrily. "Beat it Sonny. She's not interested." The young man looked at Jack annoyed. "What's it to you, old man? Come on Darling, I can show you a really good time! C'mon, I know where a good party is going down!"

He reached down and ran his hand through Ashley's long hair, then raised it to smell its fragrance. "Hey! Did you not hear Daddy? Look but don't touch, now beat it!"

Liza raised her head between Ashley and Jack. She narrowed her eyebrows as she looked up at the young man. "That's right. Beat it before you get hurt." Jack stood up and walked slowly toward the young man who stood to face him. He coolly looked over his opponent, observing him warily. Was he a threat?

"I have killed many men son. With weapons, bare handed. How many have you?" Louie looked at the hard face of Jack who stood before him. He saw the scars of past battles all over him, but his cold eyes are what froze him. Like any other animal it was fight or flight time as Jack tensed his muscles, waiting for Louie to react. As a crowd gathered to see what would happen, Louie held up his hands finally.

"Ah...sorry Sir. Just remembered I got shit to do." Liza and Ashley relaxed as Jack watched him run off, before sitting once more beside Liza, slowly messaging her back, then kissing her shoulder.

"Sorry Jack, it's our fault! Maybe we should cover up eh Ashley hon?" Her daughter nodded, as she sat up to pull on a shirt. Then Jack exploded into a fit of laughter at the two blonde women before him.

"Nonsense girls. I've got it...I am not going back to prison! Look where we are? Paradise! So let's enjoy ourselves. Relax and do whatever is in your heart's desire." Jack swigged from his rum and coke, as Liza leaned over him, her breasts caressing his chest, her long silky hair dangling on his skin. Silently she rubbed her nose on his, then her lips caressed his. Jack felt like he was floating in air, as Liza crawled slowly on top of him. Ashley smiled closing her eyes as her parents engaged in a long, intimate kiss. The hot summer sun shone down on them. Jack the decorated war vet and ex-con was back with his family having survived Hell itself.

Across the world, after Operation Thor's Hammer concluded in the volatile Middle East, the casualty count mounted. The Western politicians had seen and heard of the stunning success of this top secret army unit. Although the vast part of their countrymen had not. Even though ISIS was decimated, endless recruits flocked to their ranks, ensuring the war continued. As there were no standard rules of war, and they were not a country, how could the Western Powers conclude it? Then the new secret weapon was unveiled…Force X.

As fall approached, Force X was challenged to fight many risky missions and many convict soldiers perished. The political leaders were happy, as no casualties had to be published. The press were kept ignorant of their existence. Force X was transforming as the war dragged on into the next year. France enraged by the Paris terrorist attacks, in November the previous year joined the fray wholeheartedly. Secretly a new battalion was formed within the French Foreign Legion. A cadre of officers and NCO's, hand-picked from the regular units were given the task of forming and training the new recruits. The French government contacted their close allies, the U.S., asking for advice. The new recruits were drawn from the toughest prisons in France and North Africa. Like their American counterparts they were offered the choice: the rope or a suicidal mission.

In December of that year, 2015, Colonel Mann and his H.Q. arrived as military advisors. Colonel Mann stood before the French officers at the Foreign Legion base located in Morocco. "I want or suggest Mon Amis, you select the hardest criminals in your prisons. We train them in the art of war. As you no doubt are aware, this is how the Foreign Legion began. The training is to be harsh, brutal and without modern day restrictions. In effect, we need to break a few eggs to make the omelet. At the end of the day, as my unit has shown, you have a world class outfit. The convicts have little to say in the matter. Perform your assigned duties or die in the attempt." The French officers smiled as his words were translated. The meeting ended with the Force X officers invited into the Foreign Legion drinking mess. The Officer's Club resounded well into the night with loud, boisterous celebrations. Colonel Mann toasted his French counterpart, Colonel Siegfried.

"These Moslems have handed us a rare opportunity to display French resolve my friend. I have suffered under peacetime restraints Non? You will see my American friend, this attack on my homeland. I will unleash Hell on these swine. Blood will flow in torrents before we have satiated our need for revenge."

Colonel Mann clinked his glass with the French Colonel. "I am glad to hear it Colonel Siegfried. I and my team are here to help you achieve this noble end." The result was two months later, Force X's newly formed Regiment, the 3rd Regiment de la France marched across the Iraqi desert to join the expanded Force X Brigade. The existing 1st and 2nd Regiments were a mixed bag of Canadian and American convicts. They came from all races and creeds, from ghettos, street gangs, small time thugs and serial killers. For those who refused to fall in line, Colonel Mann dropped the axe. Like Thor himself, these mortals were crushed under his war hammer.

The hardened survivors soon met their enemy in battle. The Middle East reverberated to the titanic echoes of total war. The criminal soldiers died in droves, but ISIS and their amateur recruits perished in much larger numbers. Meanwhile Jack continued his recovery, nursed back to health by his lovely wife and former nurse Liza. Jack enjoying his newly found freedom, followed his daughter's meteoric rise in the fashion world. He went to her fashion model shoots with Liza. Liza joined them, hugging her old man and her scintillating daughter. "Yes Jack, I think we can both be proud of her. Now come on, we have things to do." Jack kissed Liza, hugging his two favorite women. Later that year, Jack got a message from his old friend Anna. He kept in touch with the Mossad secret agent on the Internet. He read the message relieved that Liza was off on a trip into town. How could he ever tell her about his time with the exotic Israeli secret agent?

"Dear Jack. Getting married in Malta. Will you come?" In October, 2015 Jack showed up, with Liza and Ashley accompanying him. Beside a historic castle on the island of Malta, Jack introduced his wife and daughter to the beautiful Israeli woman. "Liza, this is Anna, one of my comrades in Iraq. Anna my daughter Ashley." Anna Maria in a form fitting white gown, smiled at them, then hugging and kissing Jack. "Good to see you are doing better Jack. I can see you were not joking! Your wife and daughter are truly lovely!" Liza flashed a smile as she embraced Anna Maria, "I can see my husband's war was not as bad as he made it out to be after all." Annie as Jack called her, laughed lightly then kissed Ashley, who was dressed in a flowered skirt, with flowers in her long blonde hair. "Hello Ashley, your father must be so proud of you."

"Thank-you Darling. My Daddy has spoken rather highly of you. I thank you for helping him beat those bad guys. But who was taking care of who?" Annie invited them to the gala wedding reception, at one of Malta's fashionable public centers. Jack and Liza mingled with the huge crowd, meeting many Israeli and Allied soldiers, while Jack traded war stories with fellow soldiers and catching up on the action.

Ashley was busy talking to her many suitors, dancing in the ballroom well into the evening. When they finally retired to their motel room, Jack and his ladies were pleased how the evening went. It was the first time Liza and Ashley had got a glimpse of Jack's world. Liza had used the occasion to quiz Anna when they were alone in the ladies' room. The Israeli woman tried to not sound dismissive while steering away from her time with Jack. She complimented Liza on her time in nursing and still raising a fine family. Liza hugged Annie at the end, before Jack embraced and kissed his secret agent girlfriend a good night, wishing her a great honeymoon. As they lay in bed, Liza rolled over on him, gently messaging his neck, in her smooth fingers, as her chest leaned on him panting. "Jack love, I am so happy you invited us. Annie, you like her don't you?"

Jack closed his eyes, feeling her gaze on him, her eyelashes so close they tickled his cheeks. "Yes Liza, she is a good spy. We called her Matta Hari. She puts up a fight as well, but she pales to you!" Liza giggled, snuggling up in his arms, then kissing him, the light turned off as the long, sultry Malta night continued.

Jack spent that long, sultry evening in Malta with his lovely wife, catching up on what he missed over the last decade. The blonde beauty who had adopted the female fitness craze, put Jack to the test. Her own agility and stamina in bed, met his elite soldierly standards. She lay in Jack's arms, a dreamy smile on her sultry face. Finally, Jack felt he had moved on from Annie, his mistress of the desert. Still her memory failed to go away entirely. He remembered how she had looked that last night. If he had not been happily married, he thought and a few years younger.

"Oh Jack Hon did I tell you? I was in my first movie. A supporting role, but I got my feet wet as they say. It helps to move on from a career in nursing. Now you are the only one I have to look after day and night!" Jack raised an eyebrow at this. "Really Liza? Tell me about it. You in a movie? I must see it. What's it called?" Liza flashed him a smile as she curled up on his chest. "So many questions. I need to sleep."

Jack allowed her to drift off, as his mind went over her latest news. My wife an actress! Her body tattooed! What the hell is next? Later that morning over coffee Liza gave him a brief of her role in *The Mutants, California Invasion*. He gaped at her in surprise. "A Horror flick eh? OK I have to see this Hon. You were treated well I hope?" Liza touched his leg with her bare foot, stroking his shin. Jack sat back and lit a cigarette. "Don't sidetrack me hon. The movie, fill me in." Liza sipped on her coffee before outlining her role.

Jack smiled as she implied there were a few X-rated scenes she was part of. "OH no...you in an X rated flick?" Liza nodded with a slight smile. "That is why they hired me babey. You've seen me in a bathing suit. I feel honoured to still have it you know. I feel rejuvenated, emotionally, physically and spiritually. Friends of mine lost it after their first child." Jack nodded again in full agreement. He was still trying to get his mind re-adjusted, since being repatriated that first few days. Seeing the new Liza before him, he marveled at her energized look and the gleam in her captivating eyes. When he looked in the mirror, he saw a different man from when he had gone to prison. Now over

In the dark bedroom, a smile spread over his face as Liza lay pressed up to his side. Half way across the world in Tel Aviv, it was a similar scene in Anna's bedroom as she slept with her new husband. As the beautiful secret agent slept, she was dreaming of Jack. She awoke early the next morning, arising to sit on the balcony of their seaside house. She looked across the beach far off into the Mediterranean Sea. She wiped a tear from her cheek as she recalled the dream. "Jack my love. God keep you safe…till we meet again."

CHAPTER XII

SNIPER HUNT

March 1, 2016: Sean_McGinn, Jack's replacement as 2 I/C of Pathfinder Platoon in the newly formed 1st Regiment, Force X, soon to be retitled 1st Special Combat Brigade, was in camp back in Iraq's FOB Cirillo. He stood before Platoon I/c Greene in his tent. "Sergeant McGinn we have a new task. You are sniper trained in the Canadian Forces I hear?" McGinn nodded in confirmation, having completed the elite Sniper's course before his incarceration. "Good I have a mission for you. Can you pick three others from the Platoon?"

"I will look after it Sir. Sergeant McGee would be my first choice. But he is gone back stateside. The others I am getting to know, but none are sniper trained." The young Lieutenant did not go into the details. He was asked by Mann to get a team ready for a mission into Syria. He handed the news briefing to Sean, his trusted Senior NCO.

"Please at ease, have a seat and read this. By the way, your jail time. Tell me about it."

McGinn pulled up a chair before the Lieutenant. He read the clipping as he formed his response carefully. The clipping read *"Jan. 26, 2016: by Daniela Raineri: Sirte, Libya. The three places in Sirte, Libya where a sniper has allegedly shot three leaders of ISIS in the last ten days…This sniper hunting ISIS leaders, kills one on one putting the fear of God into Jihadis. Successfully killing three high level leaders in ten days as Daesh extremists gain ground in war torn Libya, North Africa, again a lone sharpshooter is said to be systematically picking off ISIS commanders in the city of Sirte one-by-one."* Lt. Greene saw the pleased look on his Sergeant's lean face. "I take it you approve?" Sean eyed the 1st Lieutenant carefully, as he finished reading the article. He smiled as he relaxed on the chair, already guessing where this was leading.

"Yes sir. A good job. Professional if I may. I suspect Seals or possibly SAS. Only a few elite units could do the job in a hostile area and not leave a sign or a trace." He asked the Lieutenant if he could smoke. Greene nodded with a frown, never having lit up in his young life. "My prison term Sir? You may know, I was charged with murdering my CSM in the field. I did and that pig deserved it. He picked the fight with me, that was his first mistake. I would not have killed him except he was a damned coward, his second error. I don't hold with lily-laced faggots leading an infantry company in His Majesty's Forces. So I took a Leopard 2 from the tank boys, drove it over his tent. The only shame is I didn't hear his screams for mercy, as others told me later. I sort of went a little crazy as I recounted later. Did a couple of 360's over his tent, reversed and switched to the MG. I hosed the tent, even though he was long gone. A bit of over kill I'll give you. I did see the remnants of him, his leg hanging from the tracks when I climbed out. His turnip was squashed into the ground. Sixty odd tons of armored death, Sir. I recommend it for your worst enemy." The veteran Sergeant finished his cigarette and butted it with his combat boot. Greene shuddered as the image of the crazed Sergeant coming at him with a Leopard 2 main battle tank at night flitted through his mind.

"Yes I will try and remember that Sergeant. So killing this man who bothered you, was it all worth it?" McGinn lit another tube, blowing a ring in the air to waft over the officer's head.

"Oh yes. Yes, it was, like a weightlifted off me. Every moment he walked on the same planet as me defiled me sir. I am a born soldier, a death tech! That thing, was put here by the Devil to torment me. The Gods put him there and said to me *Deal with it! Stop your mortal whining.* My only regret Sir, it cost me a good relationship back home." Greene's face had gone a paler shade of white by now.

"Very good Sergeant. Pick your team and report to me in two days. This will be a real mission, very risky business, that is all for now." Sean McGinn stood up and saluted casually, "Done Sir!" Then he spun on his heel and shot out of the tent at a dead run. In the Company wet canteen that evening after the day's routine training, he sat with a few trusted mates. "So then he asked me about that faggot Cross!" The table pounded as the four men roared with mirth. One almost fell off the bench he was laughing so hard.

"He looked like he was going to puke I swear. Went white as a sheet." Larry the youngest convict took a swill of his whiskey and wiped his mouth belching. "Did you really do it? Run over your CSM with a tank? What did he do to you?" He got an elbow in his ribs by a burly convict beside him. He was told to zip it, while Sean continued with his tale. "But seriously, I need volunteers for this sniper job. Who is a good shot?"

Rod Shelly held his hand up. "I been shooting since I was an ankle biter. I love it…killed a dozen back in the States. The feeling is…so fucking good." Sean nodded and took his name. By the time he left, his survey had got him a dozen names. That week he ran the dozen, his 'dirty dozen' through a rushed version of the Sniper's Course. His had been six months long back in Canada, but the Lieutenant had given him a week or so. At first light they were on parade before Sergeant McGinn. Any thought they had been handed a break from the harsh regular training was erased when McGinn took them on a 'little jog." Part of sniper training was to ensure the recruits were of the highest standard in physical endurance. Three hours later, Sean had returned with three of the dozen still with him. In full combat gear, their cam fatigues steamed in the desert heat as they gasped broken winded, hunched over before the taciturn Sergeant.

"Sir I have my first team ready." Lieutenant Greene smiled as the NCO reported at the end of the week. He had been on the ranges for the last few days. The top marksmen had consistently put four rounds in the narrow 4- inch circle on a Figure 11 at 1000 yards in any weather, day or night. One was 19- year old Roger Floody. He was a master war gamer in school, who had got into a fight with a thief who had stolen his X-Box game. He had been playing Sniper on it for a month, the thief had lost all his saved games. Roger tracked him down at school and beaten him to death. He spent six months in Kingston Pen for that, before Force X heard of him and sprang him from the hated Screws, as the Prison guards were called.

Sean McGinn had been skeptical when he heard this kid had no actual military experience. But Greene and others held that he would be the perfect recruit. No previous bad habits, starting with a clean slate. McGinn taught him how to hold and fire the new Sniper rifles, The Timberwolf and L115A3.

After a ten mile run, the sniper recruits had their morning lesson. "The L115A3 here has an effective range of 1500 meters with a competent sniper behind it. It weighs in at 12 pounds and typically you will carry 60 rounds, plus spotter optics, pistol, radio and personal gear." The recruits listened eagerly as the instructor ticked off the rifle's specs like he was discussing the weather. "This weapon is an extension of you. So I will be watching you on range. The best of you will be going on a little mission in a few days. The rest will continue to train, in the hope that someday you will be useful to the Force." His eyes narrowed as he studied the attentive recruits sitting before him, his face betraying his doubts to them.

"OK ladies, time to spread them legs a bit. It's two miles to the ranges. Ruck up." He formed up the 'dirty dozen' and they force marched to the ranges off in the arid desert strung out before them. Several looked at the merciless sun as they jogged down the desert track, the buzzards circling nearby squawking as they looked hungrily at the walking meat far below. Unfortunately for the buzzards that day, as the temperature soared over 100, none of the sniper recruits fell out. As McGinn coached them, their accuracy increased, to the point on the last day even he was pleased. Again the Sergeant ran the Sniper section back to base.

Next morning, they practiced urban warfare with emphasis on picking targets and locating the best vantage point. "So Private Sloan if the target is here in this building, where would you go?" The skinny lad with the look of a hayseed, locked at the map closely, as the group stood around the map table inside the training tent. He rubbed his stubble on his chin as he considered the hypothetical problem.

"If it was me Sarge I'd be up here on this roof across the street." McGinn nodded with a smirk. "If you manage to tag him where do you go if they spot you?" Sloan shrugged

"I'd have an egress route out the back alley. Repel down maybe to a get away car." Sean raised his eyebrows at this suggestion.

"Not bad Sloan. By the way for those of you going, don't fuck it up. You will be wired with TNT. If you get caught, or worse surrender, I flip the switch. We come back with this fucker's ears or your Mommy or sweetie will never see you again." He glared at the sniper recruits, letting them know he was serious.

March 12: Lt. Greene briefed the Sniper section on the mission. Sergeant McGinn lined them up before the Lieutenant. During their training, the snipers were not allowed to wash or shave. McGinn had the longest beard, while each one was covered in grime and streaks of cam paint over their faces. Their cam fatigues were covered in dust and grime, the dirty dozen sure looked the part to the Lieutenant in his ironed fatigues and polished jump boots. "Mission is here men. The town of Al Shiraz in the northern Syrian province of EL Bashah. We are after several top ISIS leaders who control their forces in this area. You go in covertly by jeep tomorrow night. You will be dropped off and picked up after you call in the success code word Thor 2. Sergeant you will have four men, in two sniper teams. One will locate on the main exit to the town here. The other will be up to you. Pick a second-in-command. Just in case something happens to you." Sean nodded "Corporal Rivera Sir."

Greene nodded to the blonde haired convict. He returned the nod with a smile. "There are at least two targets of note. We do not know their names but are high ranking ISIS leaders. The Colonel wants this to go well men. As you may have heard, he is tough to handle when things do not go as expected. So do well and he will see you reap the rewards." After question period ended, Sergeant McGinn watched as the men shuffled out of the tent for a smoke break. "Sir if we do this and come back, what's in it for me?" Lt. Greene looked at the convict NCO. "No promises but we will review your case. Good luck Sarge." McGinn stood at attention and saluted casually before departing. Outside he lit up and stared up at the starlit sky. "We could all be staring up at the potatoes tomorrow night fellahs." The others looked at him then laughed darkly. "Who's like us?" The snipers shouted out the traditional answer as they walked back to their tents. There was no drinking that night, as the selected men crashed out early. All thoughts were focussed on this deadly mission.

01:30 A.M. March 13: The Humvee slowed to a stop, pulling off the desert road. Four men climbed out and unloaded their equipment and weapons. Quietly the Humvee pulled back on the track and returned the way it had come. Sergeant McGinn inspected the snipers, after they had slipped on their fighting vests and packs. He had them check their rifles, personal side arms, grenades, radios and then load for bear. Corporal Rivera would lead one team with Sloan as his spotter and alternate sniper. Sean would take Private Beck. "OK move out. March routine, no talking and no noise." The others nodded, their faces partly hidden beneath their camouflaged helmets. Their cam fatigues were hidden beneath their ghillie suits, from a few meters in the dark desert they were virtually invisible. They moved out after McGinn checked his map, set his compass with Rivera and synchronized their watches. Then like ghosts they vanished into the night.

Al Shiraz was dead quiet as the four men skirted the outer houses. Sean looked through his binoculars as the others knelt beside him, each facing out to cover part of the 360-degree arc centered on McGinn. Sean bit his tongue as he tried not to grin. "Fucking shit heads. One sentry there. Ah… one on the roof there. Oh and one across the street. Now where is my ticket home?" After surveying the village he stowed his binoculars and turned to the crouching men and signaled to move out into the desert. Skirting the town, the snipers did a reconnaissance of the nearby area. Over the next hour they observed Al Shiraz and took notes.

03:30: The patrol split into their teams, then holed up for the night. McGinn had Beck take the first sentry watch. He pulled out his shovel and started to dig a slit trench. An hour later he wiped the sweat off his dark cammed face. Beck took over and draped cam netting over the five-foot deep slit trench and piled their gear inside. After the two were hidden under the camouflaged trench, the Sergeant leaned his elbows on the edge of the trench, spreading the tripod for the binoculars on the parapet. He zoomed the lens on the village and began a slow careful study of the area. Mentally taking notes, he sat down on his pack and looked at Beck beside him. The young Private was looking out of the trench, silent and still. Sean took his canteen out and took his first sip of the night. Then he took out a cigarette and lit up. He cupped his hands leaning down to the bottom of the trench. Beck looked back as the dull glow died. As he smoked Sean listened to the faint sounds in the distance. He heard the familiar sound of a religious mullah singing from the Koran.

A cock crowing, an engine whining, someone banging on a door. "It's going to be a long day. Get some rest sonny. And not a sound Okay?" Beck nodded silently, sunk down beside him, cradling his sniper rifle between his knees. He took a swig of water and chewed on a piece of dried meat. Then he curled up and went to sleep. An hour later Sean nudged the young private and handed him the binoculars. "Yer up Beck. Stay sharp, if you catch any shut eye you might wake up dead." As the Syrian desert baked the hidden snipers in their camouflaged hides, they observed a convoy approach from 'The Anvil of Allah' as it was called.

The Bedouin tribes, native to this fabled region, knew this huge, inhospitable desert, made famous in Lawrence of Arabia, like the back of their hand, having given it the name centuries ago. Lawrence of Arabia had crossed it on camel with his Bedouin Allies to launch a surprise attack against the Turks.

The convoy of mixed soft skin and armored vehicles crossed the desert and slipped quietly into the village. Al Shiraz stirred awake as the snipers observed the frenzy of activity. Sean watched through the powerful scope on the tripod set before him. He tensed as he saw the tall figure dressed in a white turban and cam smock emerge from the lead Toyota 4x4. He saw him wave to another Arab emerging from a nearby house. His binoculars swiveled and zoomed in on the building. Then he saw the antennae sticking out of the open windows. His slitted eyes widened a bit, for it was evidence this was where their targets would appear.

"Rivera you got this?" The radio emitted static as Sean's heart picked up a beat. "Got it Sarge. Do we shoot? Obviously high ranking sods." Sean agreed, this might be their only crack at these ISIS leaders. Already he noticed the posted guards at full alert, looking for possible threats. "OK, I got the tall guy by the Toyota. You target the man by the building on the left. One shot only, then go to ground. Fix your silencer first acknowledge." Rivera responded with a click, as both checked out their sniper rifles. They were the latest in high tech sniper weapons. The Timberwolf, Canadian made in Winnipeg, chambered .50 caliber rounds.

The bullet hitting the target at 2 kilometer range was designed to penetrate armour. Hitting human flesh was almost unfair. It did not have to hit a vital organ or head. The shock of the supersonic round killed the person instantly. If it hit a limb it took it off, the target bleeding out in seconds.

It would disintegrate a man's head, or virtually cut him in half. Sean loved this rifle, since firing his first .50 caliber M2 heavy machine gun, as a recruit in the Canadian Army reserve at 17 years old a decade earlier. His new toy was the 30-mm chain gun on the new LAV armored vehicles. In Afghanistan his first overseas tour, Sean heard the Afghan insurgents termed it the 'magic gun'. Their men simply disappeared when hit by the deadly cannon rounds.

The two spotters beside the snipers relayed distance and wind direction and speed as Sean eased into his firing position. His thumb flicked the safety to fire. His right eye pressed on the scope, seeing the green dot on the HUD display. He felt a thrill of adrenaline, like being a fighter jockey he thought. He focused the cross hairs on the tall ISIS man. He recalled the movie Enemy at the Gates. The Russian sniper Vasyli Zaitsev explained how a sniper felt at this moment. "The faces stay with you. You remember how he looked, if he had a shave that day. His wedding ring told you if he was married and had kids. Then you took his dog tags as a souvenir. This is not shooting at a faceless target from a distance. You are so close to him, he is like a brother."

Sean saw the man flash a smile as he smoked a cigar. "Fucker! A Cuban, I have not had one in years!" He whispered in his headset, "OK ready guys? In 5…4…3…2…1" He held his breath as the cross hairs centered on the tall ISIS man's temple. His trigger finger curled slowly, till he heard the click then the firing pin shot forward. It came as a surprise, as he had planned. The shot sound muted by the foot-long silencer, emitted a slight noise of metal striking. The .50 calibre round shot from the muzzle and streaked down range. Sean felt the recoil in his shoulder, and he breathed again and inhaled slowly as he refocused. Beside him Beck crouched over the parapet, gasped and jerked his head to Sean. The Sarge saw what had caused his shocked response. His bullet had hit the ISIS man dead on, his head exploding into a spray of blood and bone fragments. The effect on the crowd of onlookers was as he designed it…shocking, brutal and horrific. The headless body hovered for seconds, then staggered forward flailing its arms in comical fashion before toppling to the ground. The killing shot had covered over 800 meters. Rivera's round had hit his man also.

He had aimed for center of mass, the bullet exploding through his back, then blowing out his chest. The blood spray splattered over the nearby onlookers. Several toppled over in stunned shock, hit by lethal fragments of metal and bone. Others rolled on the ground screaming, while some villagers lost their minds and ran about screaming. Sean whispered to Rivera. "If you have another target one more, on your own time. Then buckle down and wait for the response." Rivera whispered affirmative. The village was in chaos as guards and sentries began shooting everything that moved. The hidden snipers fired again, confident they were undetected and taking advantage of the chaotic scene before them. Sean focused on an ISIS leader who stood in the doorway of the radio building. Relaxing in his firing position, he tracked the target slowly and coolly.

"OH yes. Has to be a fucking General!" He saw the glint of insignia on his uniform and turban, approximately 40 years old. His long beard made him look similar to Bin Laden, the late Saudi mastermind of Al Queda. The thoughts flashed through his mind as he whispered to Beck. "OK Beck, round out in 5. Watch the effect." Beck nodded as he looked through his spotting scope. The Timberwolf discharged the next .50 round with a muted puff. Beck watched the man in the doorway stagger as the bullet hit his groin. He saw his face contort and his eyes bulge out. He heard the faint scream, then he shot backward into the radio hut.

"It's a hit Sarge." Sean flicked the safety on, then eased the Timberwolf inside the trench. "How did you do Rivera?" Sean pulled out his binoculars and focused them on the village calmly. "Two hits. Two KIA." Sean nodded and replied. "Good that makes four. Phone in the code word Beck." Beck nodded and bent over the radio as the sniper lookouts watched for a response from the confused ISIS held village. Back at base a radio operator turned to the hulking figure of Colonel Mann standing nearby as the headquarters staff tracked the sniper battle. "Sir I have Thor 2. Four KIA confirmed."

"Force X has slammed ISIS again. Losing these high ranking assets will disrupt that region. What do you say Eddie?" Colonel Mann beamed at his trusted Exec Officer beside him. "Sounds good Colonel. So what next Sir?" Colonel Mann told the waiting radio operator to contact the Sniper team leader. Niner wanted a talk with Sergeant McGinn. "Thor 2 this is X-Ray Niner. Sit rep over."

Sean McGinn was still watching the village. Several patrols were now out searching for them. They were confused and had no idea where the shots had come from. "Thor 2. Four enemy KIA. No friendly casualties. Enemy in disarray, presently searching for us. Estimate 200 plus with light skin vehicles and two dozen armored cars in town. Small arms, a few rockets. Over." Colonel Mann thought over the sit rep from the sniper team, his eyes on the ground in ISIS territory. "Roger that. I am calling in the fly boys. Can you do a laser target of the ISIS facilities? HQ, vehicle concentrations, heavy weapons. Over." McGinn confirmed the order before signing off. He radioed Corporal Rivera to advise him of the plan and his team's part.

Under an hour later the Air Force arrived. The CF-18 jets streaked in from the east first. "Thor 2 this is Thunder Leader. Do you have some trade for me over?" McGinn responded as he focused the laser finder on the ISIS HQ building with all the antennae. Outside the ISIS defenders had parked several armored vehicles. Dozens of armed guards patrolled the perimeter and rooftop. "I have a high priority target for you Thunder Leader. Fire when ready." The CF-18 pilot picked it up on his HUD and keyed in the co-ordinates while his Weapons Officer in the rear selected and armed the two 500-pound laser guided smart bombs.

"Thunder Leader to wingman. Cover me I'm going in." He tipped his wing and the CF-18 rocketed down from its cruising height of 15,000 feet. Sean heard the approaching scream of its engines, but the ISIS men never heard it until it was too late. The pilot pickled off his bombs then jerked the control stick up and right. His wingman following photographed the subsequent strike. The camera in the laser guided bombs followed the two missiles, as they locked on the building, growing larger and larger. The cam lens showed it enter a window. Then a sudden bright light followed by shooting flame and smoke from the windows.

An ear splitting roar and concussion wave spread out from the target as Sean watched. He opened his ears as did Beck beside him. Suddenly the building disappeared as the walls collapsed in a cloud of smoke and debris. Seconds later debris and shattered bodies crashed down in the surrounding area. Then the second bomb hit amidst the vehicles packed on the main street. McGinn and his sniper team gasped as the vehicles were lifted into the air like toys. They cart-wheeled into the air before exploding into fragments and deposited helter-skelter about the shattered village. "Thunder Leader dead on. Target eliminated. Have some secondary targets for you over." Thunder two banked down and unleashed its payload into the burning village.

Buildings disintegrated and flames erupted as a fire storm took over in the super-heated air. Surviving ISIS and villagers ran in panic, before their clothes burst into flame. A few got out of the village alive, then the following helicopter gun ships arrived. Super Cobra and Black Hawk gunships opened up with their 30 mm chain guns like up when you get here. Liza has a few friends who might get yer attention." After finalizing arrangements Sean signed off, adding he was on leave and wanted to experience a bit of the local nightlife before leaving the desert. Jack hit the off button on his cell as he thought of Liza's numerous female guests who dropped by for a visit to the new villa. Her L.A. friends in particular who he had just met stood out for example. The Corsican Super Model Anastasia Cortina arrived one hot day. She strode toward Liza from her Porsche, a bright smile on her face. Then her sister Leanna got out and Jack stood rooted to the ground beside Liza as she greeted her friend. It was Jack's first brush with the modeling world's royalty. Both women were pretty hot he thought as he was introduced. "Liza has told me all about you Jack. So pleased you are back OK!" She kissed him European style on both cheeks as they hugged. "Forgive me my Lady. I have been overseas. It's been a long time since I've seen the world."

Anastasia smiled as he held her, then she introduced her younger sister Leanna. The elegant SpanishLatino model smiled as he kissed her cheek. "Gracia Senor." Jack was impressed by her Spanish, as he studied the statuesque dark haired beauty up close. "My sister is following in my footsteps. She is a model, though not quite Supermodel status yet. Am I right sister?" Leanna's brown eyes sparkled in the sun, her long hair whipping in the warm breeze. "Yes Anna. But I am also starring in a new European film in Cannes next week."

Liza ushered them to the verandah to serve them drinks. The talk centered on Jack's war first. He gave them the polished, censored version of course, playing down his role and injury. "Well the boys call me Lucky Jack for a good reason. Shot point blank I was. It missed all the vital stuff, got me back home to Liza so it worked out. We met in Kentucky after I returned from the Gulf War, when I got my first taste of action and first wound. She did the job then as she is doing now, so I was never worried." Anastasia and Leanna clapped laughing as Liza stroked his arm, closing in protectively. Liza had told them of his prison term. "It was so unfair to Jack! He was protecting me from that ape! But C'est la vie! He has been pardoned and back in my loving arms again!" Anastasia clapped as Liza hugged Jack tightly in her arms.

Soon after the conversation turned to Liza's first film. Anastasia commented: "I have not seen it, but by all accounts a success Liza. The talk is you are becoming an item in Hollywood." Liza was amazed when her friend told her she had talked to a few prominent Directors at a recent Director's cut gala in L.A.

"Why not come with me to Los Angeles you two? I can arrange a meeting with a few movie people to discuss Liza's next film?" Jack talked it over with Liza, who was a bit reluctant at first. Finally, she gave in, but added, "This time I want more of a dialogue. Not just play another expendable bimbo!"

"We have a deal my dear Liza!" Anastasia kissed and hugged Liza. After they departed, Jack congratulating her. "It sure seems you have a new career going baby. So while you are off to L.A., I will hold the fort this time." By this time the European villa, the new home of the McCann's, was nearing completion. Jack was adding his own influence to the spreading estate. He started to do the landscaping, renting a small backhoe and bulldozer. He put a berm around the perimeter of their lot. Later he planted palm trees and rows of shrubs around the rear lawn, discussing with Liza on where to put in a big pool.

"After that beach scene Liza, I would prefer to keep you safely tucked in my private pool. I am a bit protective of my sweetheart." Liza flashed a smile as she sat beside him, wearing a daring tight mini-skirt and tank top. She kissed him, tenderly whispering her agreement in his ear knowing he was acting in her best interest.

"Of course my Lord and Master!" Jack stroked her hair, assuring her he would not stand in the way of her burgeoning acting career. This was a new lease on life, Jack's return to her, as well as Ashley's own modelling accomplishments. With more time to pursue her movie career, it had spurred Liza on to improve herself. She had always been fairly athletic since he had known her. She now added Yoga and body building to her busy training regimen. Like many women of her age, Liza had entered a new zone. She had followed Elle Macpherson, the Australian Supermodel's career. She had been a leading model since the 1990's. Now passing

50, she was still a force to be seen in the fashion world. Liza frequently watched the Supermodel's TV show, Britain's Next Model. "Look Jack, look at Elle! She is the hottest woman on the show. Those young models are half her age, yet she is clearly superior in the way she takes care of herself. Also no one suggests that she cut her beautiful hair." Jack had to agree with Liza, although he was no fashion guru, he could appreciate a good looking woman when he saw one. "I'll give you that Liza. If I was to have the pick of the lot for a date, I'd take Elle any day of the week." Liza looked at him, then pushed his chest with her hand.

"Oh Jack! You would never get near her. She would have to go through me first anyway." Jack laughed at her, pointing out she had put her on the pedestal for him to admire. They argued over the models as the show went on. Jack was bored with the contesting models at the end. "What is with this show? The first thing they do is chop their hair off! Anyone doing that to you or baby I'd chop them." Liza laughed agreeing with him, for she valued her own long, carefully tailored blonde hair. "Do not worry Jack my love. No one is touching this!" She swirled her hair around her face, the long ends whipping his face and body teasingly.

That week Jack joined in, as she worked out in her gym she had built-up in the basement. He pushed her, urging her to increase weights and repetitions using barbell curls, crunches and presses, her muscles straining to lift the added weights. She soon added more muscle particularly her back, stomach and legs. Jack took turns pumping weights with his wife. By now his war wound was healing nicely, Jack reporting he only felt an occasional twinge now. "Well I can bench press 180 pounds no problem Liz." After the two- hour work-out was over, Jack stretched his throbbing muscles. "Oh one more exercise Liza." His blonde wife turned surprised as Jack picked her up in his arms and carried her upstairs. She protested half heartedly, for she had missed this time with him for way to long. Jack strode up the stairs easily, reaching the main bedroom he turned and booted the door shut. An hour later, Jack took a shower with Liza before she dressed and started dinner. Jack retired to the rear deck, downing one of his homemade brews.

Liza served him dinner an hour later, his favourite, roast beef and potatoes. She however had to follow a strict regimented diet, advised by her physical trainer. Over that time Liza was showing off her enhanced physique to friends she invited over. Ashley arrived that week, back from her latest model shoot. Jack delighted to see his daughter, was in the spotlight as well. "Oh Girls this is my Dad Jack! He just got back from the Middle East fighting ISIS." Jack smiled humbly as the crowd of young models smiled crowding around him, peppering him with questions. He thought of his Force X mates back there in the middle of that shit. What they would give to be with him now. "Well Sean my lad. At least you will make it out of that Hell."

That night in their bed, Jack received his own pay-off, for their sex life had never been this good. Liza's added strength

AUTHOR'S NOTES
HISTORICAL FACTS & ACKNOWLEDGEMENTS

Author Background: Where do I come from? It all began when I discovered in a local grave yard near where I lived, when I was young, that an early ancestor buried there, had a historical plaque outlining his history. It says it was compiled by his daughter, to honor her father, my Great-great grand-ancestor. He was Irish, born in Ireland and had served in the Napoleonic War in the early 19th century. He served first in the Portugal Campaign, under Lord Wellington, a fellow Irishman by the way, when the British Army was relatively small compared to the huge Napoleonic Army.

My ancestor from my mother's side, the Brownriggs and Muldoons, fought at the final battle at Waterloo, Belgium. Apparently he fought with distinction and more importantly survived that wicked, bloody day in 1815. Rewarded with a land grant in the new territory of Upper Canada, (present day Ontario) he was an early settler and one of the first Canadians. As a distinguished Officer in the British Army my ancestor already carried the mantle of a proven leader with a reputation for competence and fearlessness in battle. He formed his own Army Militia unit to fend off attacks by Americans after the 1812-14 war during the Irish Finnian Raids in the 1860's where he served again with distinction.

I feel this is pertinent to mention, having visited graveyards in many countries. I have seen ones dating back to the Revolutionary War in Boston. I have seen Civil War graveyards, WW1 and 2 memorials in Europe. I had other ancestors serve in the Canadian Forces, two great- uncles enlist during WW1, the brothers of my Grand-Mother McCauley, although neither saw action. One reputedly lost his leg in Newfoundland, when an explosion blew him into a tree. I was three years old when I met them, Great Uncle Joe and Gerald. Another uncle served in Korea with PPCLI, receiving wounds from a Chinese mortar round while he was a forward scout. He told me he was lucky, only getting shrapnel wounds, while his partner was killed. He never quite recovered from it, today it would be called Post Traumatic Stress Disorder. The point is, our history results in who we are in the present, or am I in error?

I served as a soldier in the Canadian Forces, following my ancestors, first as a Reservist infantryman. As a soldier in The Cameron Highlanders of Ottawa (MG), I enlisted at the age of 16. I served my first major assignment in Montreal, Quebec (believe it or not) during the 1976

Olympic Games. It was important for one reason, it was the beginning of my training in an anti-terrorist role. Four years after the 1972 Olympic Games in Germany, where the Black September Palestinian Terrorists captured and killed a dozen Israeli athletes in Munich, Canadian Forces were involved in thwarting any terrorists trying to launch an attack in Montreal, Quebec. It was also the first exposure for me to the Canadian Airborne Regiment who were also involved in Olympic Security. Fortunately, the terrorists never launched an attack.

I went to West Germany in 1979, my first overseas (Flyover) deployment, training to fight against the USSR during this Cold War phase. I was posted to 3rd Battalion, RCR based at Baden Soellingen, West Germany, part of the 3rd Mechanized Brigade, Canadian Forces. I had my first 'war wound' there, hit by shrapnel on the knee. It was an eye opener, during a live fire exercise at a former Nazi Waffen SS training camp called Sennelagger. During the assault as my company assaulted the mock-up urban town, adrenaline pumped through my body as I charged. It felt as close as you could get to real combat, live artillery and mortar rounds exploded around us. I could see smoke billowing from the village buildings, grenades and anti-tank rounds exploded. The noise and shouting was stunning to me, till cease fire was called. After clearing our weapons, we stood in a group for the debrief. It was then another soldier noticed my torn combat pants. On closer inspection I saw something had cut open my knee cap. I was amazed I had felt nothing during the attack, despite having my knee sliced open, likely by shrapnel from exploding ordnance. Later in a British hospital I personally cut off the patch of flesh after the British nursing staff declined. As they warned, it scarred me for life, the scar is still there on my knee. Also I had to have three checkups a day, to prevent infection. One medic told me bluntly this could result in having my leg amputated. Infection could have set in if my bandages were not changed three times a day. I found this out after missing the daily trip to the Medics and was threatened with jail by my CSM.

During this "Flyover" posting to Germany, I learned our Battalion was tasked with being the lead elements facing any invasion from the Warsaw Pact. I took it seriously when we were told to expect not to survive this suicidal mission. If we (NATO) went to war, our task similar to the first contingent of soldiers in WW1, was to slow the advance till massive reinforcements arrived from home. History tells us, if you are one of that first contingent the chances of surviving are slim. The Warsaw Pact enemy never attacked Western Europe. The closest I came to combat, was when an irate German farmer came at me with a pitch fork. It was in a village known to support Red Brigade terrorists. I was guarding my section track, an M-113 parked inside the farmer's shed. My buddies arrived to find me pointing my rifle with fixed bayonet at the shouting German, who waved his pitchfork shouting Raus! Raus! It became a cause to celebrate later in the local Gasthof in town when I was off duty!

In my twelve years' service I joined several Infantry units, including two summers of Changing of the Guard on Parliament Hill, CH of O, both Reserve Infantry units based in Ottawa. Then in 1983, transferring to the Canadian Forces Regular Component, 1st Battalion, RCR in London, Ontario and 3 Commando, Canadian Airborne Regiment in CFB Petawawa, Ontario for three years as a paratrooper. I accumulated 50 jumps during my 3-year posting to the Airborne, part of the Special Service Force, most being full equipment tactical jumps, mostly in the early morning hours.

One mission stands out amongst those military jumps. They were static line jumps (not freefall), mostly in C-130's and using big round chutes called CT-1s. We exited from the side doors at something below 1000 feet. Landings were unpredictable and you hit the ground hard, or in this case a frozen lake. It was a winter night jump, my first with the Canadian Airborne in January 1984. I was part of a mass drop, on Round Lake in Northern Ontario. It was fortunately frozen and I landed on the ice OK. Several hundred paratroopers were injured out of close to 750 paratroopers parachuting in the 20 odd Hercules C-130 transport aircraft. In all over the next few days, the entire Airborne Battle Group parachuted into Round Lake. That was the easy part, for we then trekked across the isolated Northern Ontario forests in deep snow for weeks, on snowshoes pulling heavy toboggans and personal gear (80-120 pounds).

A few refused to jump that first night I heard, (no names, no pack drill as the grunts say) and were sent to jail and had their wings removed from their uniforms. This was a disgrace of course, my view being I would rather die than have that happen to me. Tarnished for life, how could I face my friends, family or my girl friend in particular? After a month long exercise in the frozen northern Ontario wilderness we returned to camp. I bought a maroon t-shirt with the words *Round Lake Massacre* as a memento. In 1985 I did another tactical, full equipment night jump in CFB Wainwright Alberta. On landing that pitch black night, I landed on my FN rifle. The barrel penetrated under my knee and skewered my leg. I was medivacked out and underwent surgery. Again Lady Luck was on my side. I could have bled to death or lost my leg. My parents sent me a newspaper photo of me recovering in a field hospital. Airborne training was the toughest I experienced, including: Mountain warfare, Desert, Arctic warfare, jungle training, Escape & Evasion, Survival training, Commando, anti-terrorist ops., and personal hand to hand combat (with/without weapons), combat field first aid, mines and explosives courses and numerous weapons and vehicle training. Every Canadian soldier is cross-trained in a variety of skills, making Canadians among the best trained in the world. After that injury, I took about a month and a half before I was returned to full duty, a drop onto DZ Anzio, Petawawa in July 1985.

3 Commando my unit, flew to Cyprus in the fall of 1985. There we patrolled the Green Line in Nicosia for 6 months as part of the U.N. contingent. Notably I began freefall skydiving with the British Freefall team. I did my first jump from a Cessna 206 at Pergamos Airfield, Cyprus that fall. I was blown on the roof of the DZ shack, wrapping my main chute around the wind vein. After landing on the roof, I ran across it and my momentum forced me to jump off the edge, about 15 feet to the ground. I still remember one Brit jumper who was packing his chute, look up at me as I leapt over his head. I still have the picture as I stand before the stunned Brits without a scratch, one of the "crazy Canucks".

There are many tales I could tell, but I will reserve these for the future. I could write a book on one of these: Airborne Escape & Evade Exercise in Northern Ontario's Algonquin Park in the middle of winter. My platoon, 10 Platoon of 3 Commando was selected. At the end, my team and one other (6 troopers), successfully avoided capture for several days and made it back to base in Petawawa, after getting through the roadblocks hiding in the back of an old couple's mobile camper. After escaping the Algonquin Park "enemy zone" my group of escaped 'convicts' holed up in a church for the first night. The priest even fed us and gave us a few cigarettes. The next day we decided to evacuate the town where we were, believing our pursuers were on our tails. We eventually made it back to CFB Petawawa Army Base, hitching rides and avoiding capture (including Provincial Police). Back in the comfort of our barracks, we showered up, had dinner and went to our drinking mess to celebrate! When the Platoon Lieutenant, who was in a state of panic thinking we had perished in the woods, found out a week later he was so mad he ordered us arrested. The Meatheads (MP's), threw us in the base jail until our Lieutenant arrived the next day with the rest of the Platoon (all captured) from Algonquin Park. It was the first time I heard the word 'screws' as we called the MP's, amongst other things. In the subsequent trial, our 3 Commando OC Major Leavy, listened to the charges as we (6 paratroopers) stood at attention before his desk. After a short trial, the OC dismissed the charges of Disobeying orders. Major Leavy concluded, "That is what I want in my unit. Troopers who can think, alone against heavy odds, do whatever it takes to win!" As the world Famous SAS regimental logo stated, "*Who Dares Wins.*"

After my release from the Canadian Forces in the late 1980's I went back to school. This resulted in receiving my B.Sc. Degree, ultimately confidence in my ability to research and write on selected topics. Since then, after moving out west to the Prairies, I have worked mainly in the Oil & Gas Industry for the past decade.

I am a present day skydiver, after beginning in Cyprus on UN Duty (1985) with the Canadian Forces. That year was epic for me, playing my first rugby game vs The Welsh

Guards of the British Army. I played rugby for the next twelve years or so. I have parachuted for some 23 years or so, including military and civilian skydiving. Why jump out of a perfectly serviceable airplane one may ask? As one of about 2500 Canadians who do it regularly, I have difficulty rationalizing that to the other billions of people who do not. In Canada that is approximately 0.000077 % of the country. Partly it is seeking one's place in life, pushing the envelope or challenging mortality. I have long believed in my luck or immortality, especially when I was young. I have had many brushes with death, in the army and as a civilian.

I have had six skydiving jumps were I had to pull my reserve or die. I know others who had more, one female skydiver Kelsey, just passed me in 2015. Last year I won the coveted title of 'Swoop-and-chug' champion at Edmonton Skydive center in Westlock, Alberta. To explain this feat, it is a competitive thing that is a Westlock specific specialty competition. At the end of a day's skydiving, volunteers sign up for this last jump of the day. A plane load of experienced skydivers goes up to about 4000 feet. Jumping this low is called a hop-and-pop, after exiting the jumper immediately deploys his main chute. Then the skydiver steers to a selected target on the drop zone. This part is accuracy, the deal is to land as close as possible to a spot where several ground staff await you. As soon as you touch the ground the timer starts. Then one has to chug a beer as fast as possible to stop the clock!

This story: This book is one of the few modern tales by a former Canadian soldier. While a work of fiction, it is based on the actual fight against ISIS. It is a tale, based on historical facts, and a few of my own personal military experiences. Criminals incarcerated in prisons today are an untapped resource to some. For instead of being a huge financial burden on society, not to mention tying up immense resources, they could help solve a political dilemma. The story coincides with the Middle East conflict fighting ISIS/ISIL, Taliban, El Queda and other hardline Moslem Extremist Groups dating back to 2000. This is primarily a front line soldier's story, complete with real life dirt, hardship, fighting and the women who live in our soldier's lives. In all cases the main characters while fictitious, are based on real life characters and events. Also it is a look at the world of parachuting, including civilian and military.

I apologize in advance if I unintentionally offend anyone by the sometimes graphic content in this tale. More stories will follow, as I have barely scratched the surface of decades of acquired experiences. I have left a few ends untied at the end, perhaps to be solved in a future tale. Like many a mystery I have read, the author leaves more questions than answers. As in any good suspense mystery tale, I left a few bread crumbs for amateur sleuths to follow. As far as this story goes, I see no ending as yet in my mind. The war against ISIS goes on as this tale ends, as do their terrorist attacks on the west and crime in Western society.

The dark side continues in reality back in the world, in every continent. Crime continues to evolve, getting more violent. One of the latest International incidents involved the beheading of a Canadian in the Philippines by Abu Sayaf Group. Canada's Government refused to pay the ransom on his head.

The Paris and California terrorist attacks also come to mind. But back to the issue at hand this tale. To conclude the Penal Regiment will march on in the next novel. ISIS also continues to figure prominently as the Western democracy's main foe. But the longer the war goes on, I suggest an increasingly more violent approach will result. Which leads to the present question: Is there a possibility that these Criminal Army units will resurface? Only the future will answer that, but I think I have shown they have a potential place, right or wrong, in future conflicts. What better way to fight crime and the war on terror, and decrease an overloaded prison system?

In conclusion, I have to thank my friends (ex-military, serving soldiers, skydivers), my family, especially my three brothers who also served in Canadian Forces, my sister Anne Marie, who I consulted while writing/ publishing this story. Special mention goes to those military units and a legion of soldiers I have served with. Canadian, Australian, European, American, British (especially Airborne and Special Forces, including British Parachute Regiment, SAS, Marines, US Green Berets, US Rangers). Of course I have to thank my

BIBLIOGRAPHY/
REFERENCES

THE SAS SURVIVAL HANDBOOK: John "Lofty" Wiseman; Harper Collins Publishers London, U.K. 1986; Pg. 255-60

SAS THE WORLD'S BEST: Peter Darman; Sidgwick & Jackson; London, G.B. 1994

CANADA IN AFGHANISTAN: the war so far: Peter Pigott; Dundern Press, Toronto, Canada 2007

TROY: FALL OF KINGS: David & Stella Gemmell; Corgi Books/Bantam Press; Great Britain 2007

Google Maps (Canadian Arctic, Icebreaker routes in Canadian Arctic, Middle East)

COUNTER TERRORIST: Sam Hall; DIF Donald I. Fine Inc., New York, U.S.A. 1987

<u>Photos</u>: Interested readers may like to look at Wikipedia.org; Wikimedia commons:

Special mention to photographers Mr. Davric (Public Domain granted rights to use his personal works); specialized in FFI (French Foreign Legion)

<u>Photos</u>: Pixabay.com: Released to the Public Domain

<u>Note:</u> Sean Gilligan (author) from personal collection (several were not large enough for high quality therefore removed during editing)

Coalition soldiers in the Middle East war against the ISIS insurrection. Two Force X soldiers scout a tree line during the advance on ISIS positions during Operation Medussa

Night ramp jump from a C-130 Hercules. Force X paratroopers perform a freefall HALO jump in the Canadian Arctic during Operation Icecube. It is the final preparation for combat in the Middle East, where the Penal Regiment will be blooded in combat

The Devil Strikes Back: (Eliza McGee undergoes a strict weight training routine to prepare for her blooming movie career. For her part in The San Diego Strangler, she was given a personal trainer Natalie Fromm. In a few weeks after rigorous weight training, daily runs and adhering to a strict diet and prescribed pills, Eliza McGee transformed herself into a muscular fitness model, encouraged by Jack and Natalie

Mass parachute drop from a large C-117 transport. In the background behind the Drop Zone is a chain of snow covered mountains, possibly the Rocky Mountains. It would become Force X Penal Regiment's regular method in training exercises in the Arctic and insertion into the fight against their enemy ISIS. Below the descending paratroopers their heavy equipment and weapons dangle from nylon cords, while troopers on the DZ watch after landing safely

(Ashley McGee poses on rocks somewhere in the Caribbean on
one of her first model shoots. Under the close advice of her new
SuperModel colleagues the youngest of the McGee clan soon
became the newest star in the model world).

Parachuting-817630: (A Rare view of an Elite Special Forces team on route to a high level parachute jump, sit in the cabin of a large transport (probably a C-130 Hercules). They are equipped with HALO oxygen masks, helmets, freefall parachutes, altimeters and cam uniforms. This represents Force X Pathfinder Platoon inside their office. The elite of the Coalition Special Forces and Force X Pathfinders preferred method of going into action. The look of cool confidence on these soldier's faces belies the growing excitement as adrenaline builds while they approach their target. Fear of the unknown awaits these Elite warriors, but their unique, advanced skills and training allow them to do the impossible and live to tell about it

Basic parachute training 101. These paratrooper recruits are doing a low level (1000 ft) static line jump from a C-130 ramp. They have big round chutes that will open (hopefully) about 500-600 feet above the ground. After 2 weeks of rigorous ground training, they should be able to handle hitting the ground at over 20 mph without breaking bones. They then run off the DZ to begin the remaining 7 jumps or so to qualify for their prized jump wings. The elite chosen few will go on to advanced freefall training. Normally this would take several years, but for Force X on their short schedule, driven relentlessly by Colonel Mann, Pathfinder Platoon was assembled and trained in several months

A team of Paratroopers leaps from the rear ramp of a large transport (C-130 or C-117). This is a classic HALO freefall jump between 20000-30000 feet. After freefalling for nearly 2 minutes the troopers deploy their chutes to glide down silently to their chosen landing site, then begin their mission, usually behind the lines to attack their enemy ISIS. This type of mission is assigned only to small teams of Elite Special Forces and Airborne Pathfinder Platoons. Jack McGee would lead the Force X Pathfinders on several of these hazardous sorties usually lasting days or weeks.

Force X Pathfinder Platoon hurls into space off the rear ramp of a C-130 Hercules transport. For the former convict prisoners, it will be a leap into the fires of Hades itself, from which few would emerge unscathed. After their bloody baptism of fire the men of Force X would build a legend of invincibility and immortality

Anna "Mata Hari" performs a late night strip tease in Jack Jr.'s desert tent

Model posing naked during Eliza's first film, The Mutants:
California Invasion

A Mass Drop of Paratroopers by Static line, typically below 800
feet in combat. In the lowest recorded drop in modern war, US
Rangers dropped into Northern Iraq at 300 feet at night to secure
Iraqi Oilfields

Printed in the United States
By Bookmasters